1914

Thinks . . .

Thinks . . .

A NOVEL BY

DAVID LODGE

David Lodge

VIKING

VIKING
Published by the Penguin Group
Penguin Putnam Inc., 375 Hudson Street,
New York, New York 10014, U.S.A.
Penguin Books Ltd, 27 Wrights Lane,
London W8 5TZ, England
Penguin Books Australia Ltd, Ringwood,
Victoria, Australia Ltd, Ringwood,
Victoria, Australia
Penguin Books Canada Ltd, 10 Alcorn Avenue,
Toronto, Ontario, Canada M4V 3B2
Penguin Books (N.Z.) Ltd, 182–190 Wairau Road,
Auckland 10, New Zealand

First American edition
Published in 2001 by Viking Penguin,
a member of Penguin Putnam Inc.

1 3 5 7 9 10 8 6 4 2

PUBLISHER'S NOTE
This is a work of fiction. Names, characters, places, and incidents either
are the product of the author's imagination or are used fictitiously, and
any resemblance to actual persons, living or dead, business establishments,
events, or locales is entirely coincidental.

LIBRARY OF CONGRESS CATALOGING IN PUBLICATION DATA
Lodge, David, 1935–
Thinks—: a novel / by David Lodge.
p. cm.
ISBN 0-670-89984-4
1. College teachers—Fiction. 2. England—Fiction. I. Title.

PR6062.O36 T5 2001
823'.914—dc21 2001017555

This book is printed on acid-free paper.♾

Printed in the United States of America
Set in Bembo

To Julia and Stephen with love

1

ONE, two, three, testing, testing . . . recorder working OK . . . Olympus Pearlcorder, bought it at Heathrow in the dutyfree on my way to . . . where? Can't remember, doesn't matter . . . The object of the exercise being to record as accurately as possible the thoughts that are passing through my head at this moment in time, which is, let's see . . . 10.13 a.m. on Sunday the 23rd of Febru – San Diego! I bought it on my way to that conference in . . . Isabel Hotchkiss. Of course, San Diego, 'Vision and the Brain'. Late eighties. Isabel Hotchkiss. I tested the range of the condenser mike . . . yes . . . Where was I? But that's the point, I'm not anywhere, I haven't made a decision to think about anything specific, the object of the exercise being simply to record the random thoughts, if anything can be random, the random thoughts passing through a man's head, all right my head, at a randomly chosen time and place . . . well not truly random, I came in here this morning on purpose knowing it would be deserted on a Sunday, I wouldn't be interrupted distracted overheard, nobody else around, the telephones and fax machines silent, the computers and printers in the offices and workrooms in sleep mode. The only machine humming to itself, apart from those in the Brain, is our state-of-the-art coffee machine in the common room where I got myself this cappuccino with cinnamon no sugar before beginning the experiment, if that's not too grand a word for it . . . The object of the exercise being to try and describe the structure of, or rather to produce a specimen, that is to say raw data, on the basis of which one might begin to try to describe the structure of, or from which one might infer the structure of . . . thought. Is it a stream as William James said or as he also rather beautifully said like a bird flying through the air and then perching for a moment then taking wing again, flight punctuated by moments of . . . incidentally how is the audiotypist going to punctuate *this*? I'll have to give instructions, say put dots for a short pause, and a full stop for a longer pause, new para for a really long pause . . . This thing is voice-activated, stops if you don't say anything for about three seconds, but there will be perceptible pauses in the flow of words under that threshold . . . Nifty little gadget . . . Isabel Hotchkiss . . . I recorded us in bed to test the range of the condenser mike, left it running on the chair with my clothes without her knowing . . . she made a lot of noise when she came I like that in a woman . . . Carrie won't unless we're alone in the house, which doesn't happen very . . . Jesus Christ I can't have this stuff transcribed . . . impossible . . . even if I sent it to an agency under a pseudonym, from a box number GPO Cheltenham, it would be too risky . . . even if I pretended it was a piece of avant-garde fiction the names . . . there's always a risk somebody would recognize the names and send it to *Private Eye* or even try to blackmail me, fuck, and I can't change the names as I go along, too difficult, too distracting, I'll have to transcribe the bloody thing myself fuck what a bind. But perhaps it's just as well, otherwise I might subconsciously censor my thoughts for the typist . . . In fact perhaps I already did, when Isabel Hotchkiss first came into my head . . . after all the essential feature of thought is that it's private, secret, so knowing that somebody else, even some anonymous typist, was going to listen to this would completely distort the experiment, I should have thought of that . . . But then I only got the idea this morning in bed, lying awake in the dark too early to get up, I didn't sleep well, a touch of indigestion, I didn't really like that starter Marianne served, crab mousse or whatever it was . . . What I need is one of those software packages with speech recognition so you can dictate to your PC . . . only I believe you have to speak very slowly and distinctly, which might be inhibiting, spoil the spontaneity, if you had to pause . . . like . . . this . . . between . . . every . . . word . . . Still, it might be worth looking into if I do much more of this sort of thing, no doubt they're improving the software all the time . . . Where was I? You don't have to be anywhere, remember. But it was something interesting . . . Isabel Hotchkiss, no not her . . . not that she was uninteresting . . . What a lot of pubic hair she had, black and springy and densely woven, like a birdsnest, you wouldn't have been surprised to find a little white egg warm inside her labia . . . James, yes, William James and the stream of consciousness or the bird of consciousness, that was it . . . I wonder where that tape is, did I ever erase it? Wouldn't want Carrie to find it . . . pissed off with me last night because of the way I bullied, she said bullied, I would have said argued, remonstrated, at the dinner party last night with Laetitia, Jesus imagine being called Laetitia, Letty not much better, Laetitia Glover her crap about the Indians and the earth and Chief Seattle . . . That was a delicious steak last Wednesday . . . completely illogical of course to eat steak in restaurants, though it was the Savoy Grill, they must get their meat from the finest herds . . . even so it's daft to renounce beef at home and eat it out I have to admit . . . but then you don't have a menu at home so there's no temptation . . . I do love a juicy steak, medium rare, branded with the lines of the grill on the outside, pink and slightly bloody on the inside . . . [sighs] . . . BSE has deprived me, BSE and AIDS between them have made two of the greatest pleasures in life, prime beef and wild pussy, possible causes of a horrible death . . . sad. Even domestic pussy isn't the same since we . . . I wonder did she really come off the pill for health reasons or was it to make me use condoms? Trouble is, I can't tell her I've stopped screwing other women without admitting . . . of course she must have guessed that I haven't been a hundred per cent faithful all these years, but we've had a tacit agreement she wouldn't kick up a fuss as long as she never knew about it . . . When she asked me what I had for lunch with the publisher I said chicken she said 'What kind of chicken?' I said Chicken Kiev off the top of my head, a bit naff for the Savoy Grill, Carrie obviously thought so too, and my breath didn't smell of garlic, she probably thought I'd been having it off with somebody in London and the publisher's lunch was a story, ironic that . . . Perhaps in the vegetarian future people will use adultery as an alibi for eating meat . . . fuck in public and slink off afterwards to seedy beef hotels that rent private dining rooms by the hour . . . How come I'm thinking about beef? I was thinking about . . . about William James and consciousness as a stream or consciousness as a bird, flying and perching . . . the interesting question is, are those

3

perchings of the bird completions of a thought or pauses in thought, blanks, white space or white noise would be better because there is brain activity still going on all the time or you would be dead . . . *I think therefore I am* true enough in that sense . . . Must be the best-known sentence in the history of philosophy. What's the second best I wonder? But is thought continuous, inescapable, or is it as somebody said against Descartes, sometimes I think and sometimes I just am . . . Can I just am without thinking? The verb to am . . . I am you am he am she am they am, meaning to merely be without thinking . . . but is thinking the same as being conscious, no . . . There's a distinction between passive consciousness, receiving, identifying, organizing signals from the senses, aware of being alive, of being awake, and reacting to the stimuli . . . so not exactly passive then . . . but not formulating coherent thoughts either . . . So say there is a, not a distinction, but a continuum, a continuum between an almost vegetative state, no scrub that, plants aren't conscious even if Prince Charles likes an occasional chat with his geraniums . . . Say there's a continuum between a mere processing of sense data, I am hot I am cold I itch, at one pole, and abstract philosophical thinking at the other, with an infinitely graduated series of stages in between . . . Yes but it's possible to do both at once, for example driving, it's possible to drive a car without being conscious of what one is doing, changing gear, braking, accelerating, *etcetera*, quite efficiently and safely, while thinking about something entirely different, about consciousness for instance. So where does that get us?

Ah, a blank, a definite blank, for an instant, not more than a second or two, I didn't have a reportable thought or sense impression, my mind as they say went blank, I thought of nothing, I just ammed . . . So when a train of thought suddenly gives out collapses you just am, you go into a kind of standby mode ready for thought but not thinking . . . like the hard disk spinning in a PC that's switched on but not being used, like the coffee machine humming to itself ready to make coffee but not making any . . . Of course this experiment is hopelessly artificial because the decision to record one's thoughts inevitably determines or at least affects the thoughts one has . . . For instance I feel a little stiffness in my neck at this moment, I move my head, I stretch . . . I swivel round in my chair . . . I get up . . . I walk from my desk to the window . . . all these things I would normally do without thinking, I would do them 'unconsciously' as we say, but this morning I'm conscious of them because I hold a taperecorder in my hand, Olympus Pearlcorder, specifically for the purpose of . . . That was a good paper Isabel gave at San Diego . . . on modelling three-dimensional objects, she sent me a copy afterwards, there's a true scientist for you, you shag her senseless in her hotel bedroom and she sends you an offprint of her conference paper afterwards by way of a memento . . . Dead now poor Isabel Hotchkiss, breast cancer somebody told me, fucking shame who'd be a woman, one in twelve chance your tits will kill you, or try to . . . She had nice ones too, nice three-dimensional objects I remember telling her as I eased off her bra and cradled them in my hands . . . must look for that tape if I haven't erased it, I'd like to listen to it again and masturbate to it in memory of Isabel Hotchkiss.

Another full stop . . . well death is a full stop . . . enough of that enough of that . . . the campus is deserted not surpr . . . now that's interesting, I've been gazing out of the window for some time but not thinking about what I'm seeing, thinking instead about Isabel Hotchkiss, as if the mind were like a movie camera you can't have a close-up and depth of field at the same time . . . and as I stopped thinking about her the campus came into focus, or as much as it can this morning with raindrops dribbling down the window panes streaking the dirt, that's the trouble with an all-glass building they badly need cleaning, I must write a memo to Estates and Buildings waste of time their maintenance budget has been cut to the bone . . . there's another change of topic . . . It's a matter of attention, you can't attend to more than one thing at a time, like the duck rabbit picture you can't actually see them both in the same instant though you can flip back and forth between them . . . Not many people about, hardly surprising, a wet Sunday morning, staff all at home sifting through the Sunday newspapers over a late breakfast students sleeping off the booze and drugs and bopping and bonking of last night there goes a jogger though, splashing through the puddles . . . I ought to do more exercise take up squash again, not jogging can't stand running just for the sake of it . . . mind you they say sex is good exercise, one fuck the equivalent of running a mile and a bloody sight more enjoyable . . . There's somebody, who is it, a woman in a raincoat with an umbrella, not a student they don't wear raincoats they wear anoraks and cagoules or just get wet . . . a smart raincoat too with a kind of cape and a long full skirt who is it and high boots . . . Carrie had a pair like that with high heels, she used to strut about the bedroom with nothing else on to indulge me . . . not any more, wouldn't have even a quickie last night . . . I was still feeling aroused by the snog with Marianne but no luck . . . pissed off with me for throwing my weight about at the dinner table but why do people have to talk such crap . . . Who *is* that wandering about the campus on a wet Sunday morning, she doesn't look as if she's going anywhere just going for a walk, but who'd go for a walk in this ah good she's collapsing her umbrella the rain must have stopped she . . . it's that woman, the writer, at the dinner party last night, Russell Marsden's stand-in Helen whatshername . . . Helen Reed yes of course, she's living on campus in one of those little maisonettes over on the west perimeter between Severn Hall and the squash courts, she told me before dinner she's let her own house for the semester. So you won't be nipping back to London from Thursday evening to Tuesday morning like most of our visiting writers, I said, 'No,' she said, 'I've burned my boats, or is it bridges?' and smiled but there was a trapped hunted look in her eyes as she said it, nice eyes very dark brown pupils, pretty face, perfectly formed bow lips with a faint very faint down on the upper lip a long delicate neck hard to say what her figure is like, or her legs, she was wearing a long skirt and a loose-fitting top, but not skinny not fat . . . how old would you say, must be at least forty she has a kid at university another just left school, but doesn't look it . . . And what about your husband, I said, noticing her ring but foolishly forgetting she'd said my house not our house. 'He's dead,' she said, 'he died about a year ago,' just as Marianne clapped her hands and summoned us to sit down and I never had another chance to speak to her because we were at opposite ends of the table . . . Marianne arranged the seating, didn't want me to get too chummy with this attractive new woman, a widow too, he died of a brain haemorrhage Marianne whispered to me later, *'Very sudden very tragic only forty-four he was a radio producer for the BBC . . .'* There she goes, round the corner of Metallurgy, wonder where she's going what she's doing at half-past ten on a wet Sunday morning, must be lonely as hell living here on her own, *'You must come over for lunch one Sunday,'* Carrie said to her last night as we were leaving, and she said that would be lovely, they seemed to take to each other, Marianne remarked on it . . . that was a nice snog we had in the kitchen between the main course and the dessert, I had my tongue right inside her mouth and she was kneading my bum with her fingers I have an erection now thinking about it . . . It's very exciting this wordless snogging we do at parties, ever since that pre-Christmas party at the Glovers' when we were both drunk and now we do it every time we meet though we never talk about it, it's understood between us that we have to find an opportunity to do it, it's a kind of game . . . a dangerous one but that's what makes it exciting . . . Marianne managed it very deftly last night asking me to help her take out the dirty dishes as if to get me off Laetitia Glover's back but I saw Carrie looking a little surprised at how readily I obeyed and someone, Annabelle Riverdale, said jokingly to her, *'I see you have him well-trained . . .'* I wonder if Marianne is really up for it? No, I think not, I think she just likes to fantasize that we're lovers, Jasper is a dry stick she probably needs something to fantasize about when he's poking her, and if I ever said anything when we snogged, even just 'Darling,' alarm bells would ring, she would shrink back and put a stop to it because it would become serious, not just a game . . . just as well, too close to home.

Another pause another blank . . . the Olympus Pearlcorder – wonder why it's called that? Surely not because it's to record your pearls of wisdom, too corny to be true, but what else could it mean? I go back to my desk sit down in my swivel chair look at the window filled with blank grey sky how I hate the fucking English climate, imagine what it would be like in Boston now crisp cold clear air brilliant blue sky snow on the ground dazzling in the sunshine, or better still Pasadena, oranges and lemons on the bough in the back garden or rather yard as they call it even if it's several acres like Daddy

Thurlow's spread at Palm Springs . . . Shall I check my Email? No, the idea was not to do any work, not to do any task which would impose its own structure on the stream of consciousness, if a stream is what it is, more like a sewer in your case Carrie said once . . . Because it's easy to simulate human thought when it's task-oriented, directed towards a goal, like winning a chess game or solving a mathematical problem, but how to build the randomness the unpredictability of ordinary non-specialized thought, idle thought, how to build that into the architecture is a real problem for AI, which this exercise might conceivably help to solve . . .

I could go after her now pretend to bump into her or say *I just happened to see you from my office window, I thought you looked lonely* . . . No, don't say that, people don't like to be told they . . . *Just saw you passing,* then, *thought perhaps you might like a cup of coffee, we didn't really have much chance to talk last night* . . . why not? [*recording stops*]

It's 11.03. I went out intending to catch her up but she'd disappeared into thin air, I wandered round the campus for half an hour nearly, not a sign of her anywhere, not in the shop not by the lake, the Library isn't open till this afternoon, she might have gone into one of the halls I suppose to have coffee with one of her students but it doesn't seem very likely, she probably went back to her house but I didn't feel like knocking on her door, even supposing I could find out which house it is, to ask her back here for coffee, it was supposed to be a spontaneous or accidental thing, and I was beginning to feel rather silly especially as it started to rain again so I came back here just in time to take a call from Carrie asking me to pick up some milk from a garage on my way to Horseshoes. She said don't be late for lunch I said what is it, she said roast pork with apple rings, I said will there be crackling, she said of course, I said in that case I certainly won't be late . . . Carrie does the best crackling I've ever tasted, crisp and succulent, I feel the saliva sluicing round my mouth at the very thought of it. And after lunch, she said, Polo and Sock want you to take them out on their mountain bikes. I said I was hoping the kids might amuse themselves this afternoon and you and I

8

might retire for a little nap. *'No chance'* she said, and put the phone down, but she sounded amused rather than pissed off. Should be OK for tonight then . . . It's because she said no last night that I want her . . . it's the only thing that really makes me, when she says no . . . otherwise I don't think much about fucking her, I mean in advance, but if it comes into my head to suggest it and she says no for some reason then I can't rest till I've had her . . . Sad really, but that's life. Or men. Or me.

2

MONDAY 17TH FEBRUARY. Well, here I am, settled in, more or less. I've been allocated a little house or 'maisonette', as it's called (a twee, fake-French word I've always disliked) on the campus, at the end of a terrace of five reserved for long-term visitors or newly appointed members of staff. An open-plan living-room with 'kitchen-ette' downstairs, and a bedroomette and bathroomette upstairs, connected by an open staircase. It's quite big enough for me, but I miss the spacious rooms and high corniced ceilings of Bloomfield Crescent. It's designed and furnished in a vaguely Scandinavian style – exposed brick and whitewashed walls, pine modular furniture, synthetic cord carpeting – that makes me think of a Novotel, functional but cheerless. The fact that it's just been redecorated in my honour somehow makes it seem all the bleaker. I must buy some posters to brighten up the walls. I wish I'd thought of bringing a favourite picture from home – the Vanessa Bell lithograph for instance. Home. I must stop thinking about 'home'. *This* is my home for the next sixteen weeks, the spring semester.

'Semester.' 'Campus.' How Americanized universities have become since I was a student – or perhaps it just seems so to me because I went to a traditional one myself. After all, this place was already in existence when I went up to Oxford. It's what I believe is called a 'greenfields' university – very green in fact, where the Severn valley meets the Cotswolds. The University of Gloucester – though it's actually closer to Cheltenham. Perhaps the founders thought the name of a cathedral city would lend the institution more dignity. 'The University of Cheltenham' wouldn't carry the same conviction, somehow. Anyway, here it is, like a gigantic concrete raft floating on the green fields of Gloucestershire – or rather two rafts loosely roped together, for most of the buildings are arranged in two clusters separated by landscaped grounds and an artificial lake. A courtesy bus chugs round the service roads all day, dropping and picking up people as in an airport car-park. Jasper Richmond, the Head of English and Dean of Humanities, explained to me that the original plan, conceived in the utopian sixties, envisaged a huge campus like an American state university, accommodating thirty thousand students. They started building at each end of the site, Arts at one end and Sciences at the other, confident that they would soon fill up the intervening acres. But costs rose, the money supply dwindled, and in the nineteen-eighties the Government realized that it would be much cheaper to convert all the polytechnics into universities with a stroke of the pen than to enlarge the existing ones. So Gloucester University is unlikely ever to have many more than its present population of eight thousand students, and the open spaces between the Arts and Science buildings will probably never be filled in. 'We're an architectural allegory of the Two Cultures, I'm afraid,' Jasper Richmond said, with a wry smile, as we looked out over the campus from his tenth-floor office in the Humanities Tower towards the distant Science buildings. It wasn't the first time, I suspected, that he'd made this observation to visitors. In fact almost everything he says has a faintly used feel to it, like paper that has lost its crispness by being handled too frequently. Perhaps that's inevitable if you're a teacher, even a university teacher, having to repeat the same things over and over again.

At which thought I feel a cold qualm of apprehension. I can't afford to be condescending about university teachers, now that I'm one myself. Jasper Richmond showed me the entry in the Faculty course handbook: '*M.A. in Creative Writing. Prose Narrative. Tues. & Thurs., 2–4 p.m. Tutor: Helen Reed (Dr. R.P. Marsden is on study leave.)*' Russell Marsden, critic, anthologist, and author in his precocious youth of two Mervyn Peakeish novels, one good, the other not so good, who has run the course since its inception, and has retreated to his rustic cottage in the Dordogne to finish, or possibly (as Jasper Richmond rather cattily speculated) to start, an impatiently awaited third novel. I was not a little dismayed to discover on my arrival that Russell Marsden had already departed to the South of

France, as I was hoping to get some tips from him about how to run the course. The only experience I've had in this line, the evening class at Morley College for a motley collection of housewives, unemployed and retired people, accepted on a first-come-first-served basis, some of them with no formal qualifications at all, is hardly an adequate preparation for taking over one of the most prestigious creative writing courses in the country. The students, carefully winnowed from a mass of eager applicants, will have razor-sharp minds and know all about things like postmodernism and poststructuralism which were just vague rumours from across the sea when I was at Oxford, a distant rattle of tumbrils over the intellectual cobblestones of Paris, a faint babble of impenetrable jargon rising from thick American quarterlies. When I mentioned my misgivings to Jasper Richmond he said, 'Oh well, I always think good students educate each other.' I suppose he meant to be reassuring.

I asked him how long he had been at Gloucester. He sighed and said, 'Longer than I like to think about. I was one of the pioneers. When all this *(gesturing at the view)* was one huge building site. We used to attend Faculty Board meetings in green wellies.' His tone was wistfully nostalgic.

It seems to get dark earlier here than it does at home (there I go again), though of course that's just an illusion. It never really gets dark in London. All those millions of streetlamps and illuminated signs and lighted shop windows throw a diffused glow up into the sky, so that it never looks black, more like a pastel yellowy grey. Here the streetlamps planted at intervals along the service roads, and the safety lights studding the pedestrian walkways and staircases, seem rather puny attempts to dissipate the dense darkness of the winter night. Beyond the perimeter fence there are only dark fields and darker clumps of trees, and scattered farmhouses whose lights gleam like distant ships at sea.

It's eerily quiet, too. At about five o'clock there was a kind of mini rush-hour as the academic staff collected their cars from the multi-storey car-parks (which look incongruous and particularly ugly in this pastoral setting) and drove off to their cottages in Cotswold villages or their townhouses in Cheltenham, and the humbler employees of the University and the students who don't live on campus boarded buses to return to their homes and digs in the locality; but soon after six a deep rural hush descended on the campus. I can actually distinguish the noise made by individual vehicles as they approach, pass and retreat on the service road outside my front door, unlike the promiscuous unceasing background hum of traffic in London.

God I feel wretched.

Coming here was a terrible mistake, I want to run away, I want to scuttle back home to London – home, yes, that's my home, not this tatty little box. Do I dare? Why not? I haven't really started yet. I haven't met any students, or taken any of the University's money. They'll easily find someone else to do the job – there are lots of excellent writers around who would jump at it. Why not just leave, tomorrow morning, early? I see myself creeping out of the house before it's light, like a thief, loading my things into the car, shutting the boot lid softly, softly, so as not to alert anybody, leaving a note for Jasper Richmond on the table in the living-room with the house keys, *'Sorry, it was a terrible mistake, all my fault, I should never have applied for the post, please forgive me.'* And then pulling the door shut on this Scandinavian rabbit hutch and driving away along the empty service road, scarves of mist round the throats of the streetlamps, slowing down at the exit barrier to give a wave to the security man yawning in his brightly-lit glazed sentry box. He nods back, suspects nothing, raises the barrier to let me out, like Checkpoint Charlie in a Cold War spy film, and I am free! Down the avenue, on to the main road, on to the M5, the M42, the M40, London, Bloomfield Crescent, home.

Except that 58 Bloomfield Crescent has been rented for the next three months to an American art historian on sabbatical and his wife, who arrive next Friday. Never mind, send them a fax, *'Sorry, all off, change of plan, house not available after all.'* Could they sue me? There's no legal contract, but perhaps our correspondence would count as one . . . Oh, what's the point of pursuing this futile line of speculation when we all know (by 'we' I mean my neurotic self and my more rational observing, recording self) we know, don't we, that this is just a fantasy? And that the real reason I won't run away tomorrow morning is not because of possible litigation by my American tenants (or for that matter by the University of Gloucester, who could undoubtedly sue me for breach of contract, though I very much doubt if they would bother) but because I haven't got the courage to do it. Because I couldn't bear the guilt, the shame, the ignominy, of knowing that everybody I know knew that I had funked it, panicked, run away. Imagine having to ring up Paul and Lucy to tell them, and hearing the disappointment in their voices even as they tried to be supportive of their mad mother. Imagine seeing the ill-concealed smirks and smiles of people at literary parties, as they whispered to each other over their glasses of white wine. *'That's Helen Reed, did you know she went to be Writer in Residence at Gloucester University and ran away on the first day of the semester because she couldn't face it?'* And they might add, *'Not that I blame her, I'm sure I couldn't face it either,'* but nevertheless they would despise me, and I would despise myself.

It was a nice fantasy while it lasted, though. I even chose the tape I would play in the car on the M5, the Vivaldi wind *concerti*, with their sprightly, cheerful allegros.

TUESDAY 18TH FEB. I met my students for the first time this afternoon, in a rather bleak seminar room on the eighth floor of the Humanities Tower. We sat on moulded stacking chairs round a large table covered with a faint film of chalk dust. There were notices like road signs fixed to the wall with stylized pictures and diagonal bars across them, prohibiting smoking, eating and drinking. Do students nowadays have to be explicitly forbidden to eat and drink in class? Mine seem reassuringly nice on the whole. Of course it was an edgy sort of occasion, one of mutual appraisal. They had the advantage of already knowing each other well, having been taught for one semester by Russell Marsden. They are an established group, in which each has adopted, or been allotted, a role to play: the extrovert, the sceptic, the clown, the sophisticate, the malcontent, the mother, the naughty child, the enigma, and so on. They had only one person to weigh up this afternoon; I had a cast of twelve to memorize and distinguish between. Most of them are in their twenties, but only a few have come straight from doing a first degree. The majority have been working for a few years, and have given up jobs to take the course, supporting themselves from their savings, or by taking out loans, which makes it seem a dauntingly serious business and does nothing to lessen my anxiety. How, I wonder, can I possibly give them value for their money?

As an ice-breaker I thought I would read something of my own to them. This used to go down well at Morley College in the first class of the session, but I'm not sure it was a good idea on this occasion. I read from *The Eye of the Storm*. Not from work-in-progress, because I don't have any. I haven't been able to write anything except this journal since Martin died. I tried to start a new novel last September, but it just wouldn't come. I made myself physically sick trying to force it, so I gave up. Inventing fictitious characters and making up things for them to do seems so futile, so artificial, when someone real and near and dear to you has been suddenly, brutally snatched out of existence, like a candle flame pinched between finger and

[A hiatus there while I had a little weep. Bad sign: I thought I had stopped weeping. But I keep rediscovering what a void his death has left in my life, like the shockingly huge gap, as it seems, when you've had a tooth extracted and explore the space where it was with your tongue. Or like a phantom limb that, they say, still seems painfully present after it's been amputated.]

So I read from *The Eye of the Storm*, the kite-flying chapter. The students listened attentively and chuckled or smiled in the right places and asked intelligent questions afterwards. But I sensed a certain restraint, as if they would have liked to be more critical, but didn't dare. Perhaps it's just my paranoia.

WEDNESDAY 19TH FEB. Saw some of the students individually today, in Russell Marsden's office on the tenth floor of the Humanities Tower. My name has been stencilled on paper and rather crudely stuck over his nameplate on the door. He had cleared some of the bookshelves for me, and emptied the drawers of the steel desk, but locked the filing cabinet, and left his art exhibition posters on the breeze-block walls. Without them it would certainly be a rather drab, depressing little room, but surrounded by these emphatic statements of Dr Marsden's artistic taste (Mapplethorpe, Francis Bacon, Lucian Freud) I had to struggle against the feeling, never far away, that I am something of an impostor.

Simon Bellamy was the first to knock on my door. I took the opportunity to ask him why the group had seemed somewhat inhibited in the seminar yesterday. Simon is the group extrovert – handsome, cheerful, curly-haired, articulate. He has been elected (tacitly, almost unconsciously) as the group's spokesman, and I felt quite safe in putting the question to him. He explained that they hadn't been quite sure how to respond because Russell Marsden never read his work to them. 'I suppose,' he said, with a disarming grin, 'we thought that if we praised your writing it would look like toadying to the teacher and if we criticized it, it would seem rude.' He added, 'Actually I thought it was brilliant,' and we laughed together at the way he had undermined his own tribute in advance. And yet I believed him. Perhaps we always do believe in praise of ourselves. Even when we know it is not disinterested, we think it is deserved.

Marianne Richmond, Jasper's wife, phoned me this evening and invited me to dinner on Saturday, 'with a few friends', so that's something to look forward to. I'm dreading the weekend, especially Sunday – never my favourite day of the week. The loneliness. The vacancy.

It's very quiet here on Maisonette Row. The house adjoining mine is empty. Next along there's an African gentleman who goes out early in the morning and comes back late in the evening. I have seen him in the Social Sciences Reading Room in the Library, so I presume that's where he spends his days. Further along there's an elderly visiting professor of economics from Canada, who is pleasant enough but very deaf. The house furthest from me is occupied by a smiling but tongue-tied Japanese couple whose status and academic affiliation remain obscure. Not a lot of scope for social interaction. I still think longingly about running away, but of course with every day that passes this becomes more unthinkable, the probable consequences more serious, so I hang on, hoping that eventually I will pass the psychological point of no return and be reconciled to my fate. Meanwhile my mind insists on going back over the past and rewriting it: I apply for the job, and am offered it, but having walked around the campus and had a good think, I politely and gratefully decline, and drive back to London, humming along happily with the radio-cassette player, to resume my accustomed life. I take the aborted novel out of its drawer and find that it begins to flow after all. I have the basement of 58 Bloomfield Crescent converted (effortlessly) into a self-contained flat, and some delightful woman of my own age, another widow or divorcée, takes it and becomes a boon companion and devoted friend. I keep catching myself relapsing into this daydream. Sometimes the new tenant is a man, with narrative consequences too shamingly Mills & Boon to write down, even here. It's as if I am two people at once – the Helen Reed other people see, who is settling into her new job at Gloucester U, calm, efficient, conscientious; and another mad, deluded, disembodied Helen Reed living a parallel life somewhere else, inside the head of the first one.

The strain of keeping these two lives going at once is almost intolerable. I long for bed-time, when I can put them both to rest for a few hours. Sleep is bliss – but alas, a bliss one can't consciously enjoy, by definition. There's perhaps a brief moment of delicious languor, when you feel yourself dropping off, like when you're given an anaesthetic, but the next thing you know is that it's over, you've woken up, probably in the small hours, with your worries and regrets more oppressive than ever, and you can't recover the sensation of what it was like to be unaware of them. I'm tempted to go to the Health Centre and get a prescription for sleeping tablets, but I became so dependent on them in the months after Martin's death, and felt so zombie-like in the mornings when I was on them, that I'm determined to do without if I possibly can.

THURSDAY 20TH FEB. Second meeting with the students as a group. A workshop session, meaning that one of them reads from work in progress (in future it'll be circulated in advance) and the rest of them tear it apart, with me acting as umpire. That's the way the course is organized. Thursday afternoon is always a workshop session. The content of the Tuesday seminars is up to me: I can set them writing exercises or we can discuss some text or other that I prescribe.

Russell Marsden encouraged them to be candid in the work-shops, which I find rather alarming after the let's-all-be-supportive-of-each-other atmosphere of my evening classes at Morley. Rachel McNulty read a piece from her novel in progress about a young girl growing up on a farm in Ulster. I thought it was sensitive and convincing, if somewhat underwritten, but two of the others criticized it because there was no mention of the Troubles. The question was raised: is it possible to write about Northern Ireland without mentioning the political situation? I diplomatically suggested that the family tensions described in Rachel's fiction might be read as symbolic of the divisions in the community as a whole; but to her credit Rachel rejected this face-saving formula and said that some things were more universal than politics and they were the things she wanted to write about. Secretly I agreed with her.

FRIDAY 21ST FEB. As far as I can tell, few if any of my students live on campus. Most of them share flats or have bedsits in Cheltenham or Gloucester, and several have permanent homes in London or other places, and spend just three days a week here, sleeping over Tuesday and Wednesday nights in B&Bs or on the sofas of their friends. So I have a curious sense of living more like a student than they do. After yesterday's workshop we all went across to the Arts Centre Café for a cup of tea that was emended to an early drink, and I listened almost enviously to them all making their plans for the weekend away from the campus. The more I see of it, the more unsuitable it seems to me as a place in which to try and educate young people for life. If they don't have cars of their own it's difficult for students to travel to Cheltenham or Gloucester, and there's not much incentive to make the effort. All the necessities of life are provided on campus: there's a small supermarket, a launderette, a bank, a unisex hairdresser's, a bookshop-cum-stationer's, several bars, cafés and canteens. The Arts Centre puts on quite a good programme of concerts, touring productions of plays, art exhibitions and films. According to Simon Bellamy, who was an undergraduate here a few years ago, lots of students never leave the campus from one end of a semester to the other. They might be living in married quarters on some top-secret airbase ringed with electrified wire, or inhabiting a vast space-platform orbiting the earth, for all the contact they have with normal life. Simon assured me that they are quite content. 'Remember, for most of them it's the first time they've lived away from home. They can experiment with sex, drink, dope, without coming to much harm. Free contraception from the Health Centre. No drink-drive problem. No fuzz asking you to turn out your pockets. Nobody telling you when to go to bed or when to get up or to tidy your room. It's what most teenagers dream about. Pig heaven.' He grinned as he listed these attractions. Nevertheless I wonder if they don't pall after a while, and then what? One of the most depressing sights on campus is a drab, smoky, lino-tiled room on the ground floor of the Union full of pinball machines and computer games. It seems to be open twenty-four hours a day and there are always several catatonic figures inside, staring intently at the screens and displays, twitching

19

occasionally as they operate the buttons and levers. Was it for this that they swotted for A Levels, pored over UCCA forms, and drained their parents' pockets? How glad I am that Paul is at Manchester and that Lucy has a place at Oxford, real places with real people in them.

I can see myself acquiring bad habits from living here. My little house is equipped with a TV, and I've watched a lot this week. At home I seldom switch on before *The Nine O'Clock News*, and usually it's later than that, for an arts documentary or a film. This week I've been watching TV while eating my solitary dinner, and leaving it on afterwards because when I switched it off the silence seemed so deathly, and I can't stand listening to music on my tinny transistor radio. I've seen all kinds of programmes I never normally watch, soaps and sitcoms and police series, consuming them steadily and indiscriminately like a child eating its way through a bag of mixed sweets. For simple mindless distraction you can't beat early evening television. No scene lasts more than thirty seconds, and the stories jump from character to character so fast that you hardly notice how cardboard-thin they are.

SATURDAY 22ND FEB. Last night the film *Ghost* was on television after the News, and I decided to watch it, although I had seen it before, with Martin — or rather I watched it *because* I had seen it before with Martin. It was a surprise hit when it first came out and everybody was talking about it. We enjoyed it, I recalled, even as we rather despised its slick exploitation of the supernatural. I remembered only the bare bones of the plot: a young man is murdered in the street walking home with his girl, and tries to protect her from the conspirators who killed him, though as a ghost he is invisible and can only communicate with her through a medium. The few details of the movie that had lodged in my memory were the special effects when characters died: for instance, the hero gets up from the ground apparently unscathed and only realizes that he's dead when he sees his distraught girlfriend cradling his own lifeless body in her arms; and when the baddies die they are immediately set upon by dark gibbering shapes that drag them screaming off to hell (surprisingly satisfying, that). And I remembered that Whoopi Goldberg had been very funny in the role of the fraudulent medium who is disconcerted to find herself genuinely in touch with the spirit world. These things were just as effective the second time round. What I wasn't prepared for was the way the love story would overwhelm me. Demi Moore, whom I've always considered a rather wooden actress, seemed incredibly moving as the bereaved heroine. When her eyes filled with tears, mine brimmed over. In fact I spent most of the movie weeping, laughing at Whoopi Goldberg through my tears. I knew in my head that the film was cheap, sentimental, manipulative rubbish, but it didn't make any difference. I was helpless to resist, I didn't *want* to resist, I just wanted to be swamped by the extraordinary flood of emotion it released. When the ghostly hero reminds the sceptical heroine, through the Whoopi Goldberg character, of intimate and homely details of their life together that nobody else could possibly know, and it dawns on Demi Moore that her dead lover really *is* communicating with her, my skin prickled with goosepimples. When the hero (I've already forgotten his name, and that of the actor who played him) acquires the powers of a poltergeist and uses them to terrify the thug threatening Demi Moore, I crowed and clapped my hands in glee. And when, in a sublimely silly scene towards the end, Whoopi Goldberg allows him to inhabit her body so that he can dance cheek to cheek with Demi Moore to the smoochy tune they made love to at the beginning . . . well, I almost swooned with vicarious pleasure and longing. Afterwards I had a long hot bath and sipped a glass of wine as I replayed favourite scenes from the film in my head, and before I went to sleep I masturbated, something I haven't done since I was a teenager, imagining that Martin's ghost hand had inhabited mine and that he was making love to me.

When I woke in the small hours I felt depressed, as usual, but not ashamed. In a curious way it was a cathartic experience.

SUNDAY 23RD FEB. To the Richmonds' dinner party yesterday

evening – the social highlight of my first week at Gloucester U. It was quite an interesting evening. They have a nice house in a village about ten miles away – modern, but tastefully built in a traditional style out of Cotswold stone. I got lost in the dark country lanes and was the last to arrive. It was difficult to take in so many new faces all at once, but fortunately Jasper had given me a run-down of the guest list over morning coffee in the Senior Common Room on Friday.

Jasper himself opened the front door and took me somewhat by surprise by planting a firm kiss on my cheek. It was rather early in our acquaintance, I thought, for such a greeting – but I accepted it with good grace. He had a glass of white wine in his hand and I guessed it wasn't the first one he'd imbibed that evening. A teenage boy hovered nearby, bobbing and weaving restlessly.

'Oliver, take Helen's coat,' Jasper said to him, and introduced us. 'This is my son, Oliver. This is Helen Reed, Oliver. She's a writer. She writes novels.'

'Egg is writing a novel,' Oliver said, without looking at me.

'Is he?' I said, politely. 'Who is Egg?'

'Egg lives in London, with Milly and Anna and Miles.'

'They're characters in a TV series,' Jasper explained. He used his free hand to help me off with my coat. 'All about young lawyers who share a house.'

'I've been watching rather a lot of TV lately,' I said, 'but I must have missed that one.'

'I like Miles best,' said Oliver, looking over my head.

'Here, Oliver, hang up Helen's coat, will you?' Jasper said, handing the garment to him. 'Then you can go and watch TV. There's nobody else coming. Off you go.'

As Oliver took my coat away, Jasper said, 'Oliver's autistic. I should have warned you, but it slipped my mind.'

'That's all right,' I said.

'He thinks the characters in soaps are real people.'

'Well, he's not alone in that, I believe,' I said.

'True,' said Jasper, with a smile.

He ushered me into the drawing room and introduced me to Marianne, who was standing by the door in an irreproachable little black dress, relieved by an expensive-looking gold brooch, adjusting the lights. The room, handsomely proportioned, with a *trompe l'oeil* gas-fuelled log-fire burning in the open hearth, has lots of hi-tech spotlights and up-lights and down-lights controlled by dimmer switches which Marianne kept adjusting, so that one felt rather like being on a stage, perhaps in a musical by Stephen Sondheim: you'd be having a quiet conversation with somebody in a corner when suddenly you'd find yourself bathed in a pool of light and heads would turn as if expecting you to burst into song. Marianne used to be in publishing and we found we had one or two acquaintances in common. Now she works at home as a freelance editor. She is younger than Jasper and I presume his second wife. She is good-looking in a very groomed way (gold nail varnish to match her brooch), and has a bright, brittle social manner; her eyes glance all over the room, monitoring the other guests, while she talks to you.

The other guests were as follows: Reginald Glover, hairy-faced, hornrimmed marxist Professor of History, and his wife Laetitia, a music therapist, vegetarian, and (as later became evident) committed Friend of the Earth. Colin Riverdale, a fresh-cheeked young lecturer in the English Department, and his wife Annabelle. Colin seems to be Jasper's protégé and was anxious to make a good impression. He said several complimentary things about *The Eye of the Storm*, so specific in reference that I was fairly sure he'd been mugging it up in the last few days in preparation for meeting me. His own field is the eighteenth century, like Jasper's. Annabelle works in the University Library and seemed understandably exhausted by the effort of holding down her job and looking after three young children, the youngest of whom was upstairs in a carrycot on the Richmonds' bed. She said very little all evening and actually nodded off at one point. Nicholas Beck, silver-haired Professor of Fine Art, had been invited to make a pair with me, but only in the table-planning sense, because Jasper informed me that he is a celibate homosexual, on what authority I don't know. He moved to Gloucester fairly recently from Cambridge, and has that high-table trick of being able to make urbane conversation about any topic whatsoever without saying anything memorable or profound. Jasper kept asking him anxiously what he thought of the wine – apparently he used to buy the wine for his college. Beck was politely approving but implicitly critical of Jasper's offerings, *e.g.* 'Australian reds really have improved out of all recognition.'

The most notable guests, about whom Jasper had briefed me most thoroughly, were Ralph and Caroline Messenger. I knew of him already, of course, as someone who is often on radio and television, especially *Start the Week*, and as a reviewer of popular books about science and psychology in the Sunday papers. He's something of a star here, Professor and Director of the prestigious Holt Belling Centre for Cognitive Science, an odd-looking building, somewhat resembling an observatory, which Jasper pointed out to me from his office window on my first day. Messenger is in his late forties, I would say, with a big handsome head: thick, grizzled hair combed back from a broad brow, a hooked nose and a strong chin. In profile he reminded me of a Roman emperor on an old coin. Caroline, or Carrie as she is familiarly known, is American. She must have been stunningly beautiful in her youth, and still has a lovely face, with big cow-like eyes, and braided blonde hair, but her figure is too matronly by today's exacting standards. She was wearing a lovely billowing silk dress which flattered her ample form. They certainly make a striking couple. She addresses him as 'Messenger', which has a curious, ambivalent effect, half-deferential and half-ironic. In a way it seems to collude in placing him above ordinary mortals, who have their domestic first-name selves and their professional second-name personae; but at the same time the incongruous formality of a wife addressing her husband by his surname seems to mock his pretensions and set a cool distance between them. I only had time to exchange a few remarks with him before we were summoned to the dinner table. He has a frank, lively conversational manner, which combines the occasional American usage with a slightly plebeian London accent. That's why the media love him, according to Jasper: he doesn't sound like a dryasdust academic.

I sat opposite Carrie at dinner and found her very easy to talk to as well, open and friendly, as Americans often are. She said she loved my books but she didn't feel it necessary to demonstrate her familiarity by *viva*-ing me about them like Dr Riverdale. She gave me useful advice about shopping in Cheltenham, of which she seems to do quite a lot. Jasper told me that she has money of her own, adding, 'I think that's what keeps Ralph faithful to her, in his fashion.' What fashion was that, I asked. 'Well, Carrie told Marianne they have an agreement, that he's not to embarrass her on her own territory. He has plenty of opportunities to play away from home. At conferences, on his media jaunts. There was a reference to him in *Private Eye* once as a "Media Dong".' Jasper chuckled reminiscently, and asked me if I had seen Messenger's TV series on the Mind–Body Problem. 'Some of it,' I said.

The truth is that I saw only the last ten minutes of the last programme in the series, and that by accident. They were on too early in the evening for me, and I tend lazily to duck science programmes anyway, but now I wish I had watched them. I remembered that big Roman head turning away from a piece of apparatus (a brain scanner or something of the kind, with a supine patient being slid inside like someone about to be shot from a cannon) and leaning towards the camera in close-up saying almost gloatingly, '*So, is happiness   or unhappiness – just a matter of the hardwiring in your brain?*'

The head seems disproportionately large when you see him full-length, because his legs are on the short side. He has a thick, bull-like neck and broad sloping shoulders which thrust the head forward in a challenging, somewhat intimidating manner. Undoubtedly he has a kind of presence which no other man at the dinner party possessed – the sort that film-stars and international statesmen have. I kept stealing glances diagonally up the dining table at him to try and analyse it, that effect of being permanently lit by flashbulbs without flinching. Once I encountered his own gaze, and he smiled genially. We were too far away to talk. The table was too long, and the guests too many, for a single conversation. Down at our end, chaired by Jasper, we were discussing the current craze for screen adaptations of classic novels and comparing the two competing versions of *Emma* (Nicholas Beck complained pedantically that in both of them the lawns had obviously and anachronistically been mowed by machine) when voices were suddenly raised at the other end. Laetitia Glover and Ralph Messenger were having an argument about environmentalism. 'The earth doesn't belong to us, we belong to the earth,' she declared piously. 'The Red Indians knew that.' 'The Red Indians?' said Ralph Messenger. 'You mean the guys who would stampede a whole herd of buffalo over a cliff to get themselves steak for dinner?' 'I'm quoting a speech made by Chief Seattle in the mid-nineteenth century, when the American Government wanted to buy his tribe's land,' said Laetitia stiffly. 'I know that speech,' said Ralph. 'It was written by the script-writer of an American TV drama-documentary in 1971.' Annabelle Riverdale, who had been roused from her torpor by this exchange, gave a little splutter of a laugh, and then, in the ensuing silence, tried to pretend she hadn't. 'I don't know about any TV programme,' said Laetitia, reddening, 'I read it in a book. The script-writer probably did too.' 'He invented the whole thing,' said Ralph, 'and then people started quoting it in environmentalist tracts as if it were historical.' Laetitia glanced at her husband for support, but he kept his head down, perhaps unwilling to risk his academic reputation on such uncertain ground. Jasper gallantly came to Laetitia's rescue. 'Even if it isn't historical, Ralph, the sentiment could still be true.' 'On the contrary, it's quite false,' said Ralph. 'We don't belong to the earth. The earth belongs to us, because we're the cleverest animals on it.' 'That's so arrogant, so Eurocentric,' sighed Laetitia, closing her eyes to dissociate herself as completely as possible from this odious opinion. 'What do you mean, Eurocentric?' Ralph demanded, thrusting his head forward challengingly. One by one the rest of us fell silent and stopped eating.

'It was European colonialists who regarded the earth as something to be bought and sold and exploited,' said Laetitia. 'Indigenous populations have a natural instinct to preserve their habitat and use its resources sparingly.'

'On the contrary, only the limitations of their technology have prevented primitive peoples from destroying their environment on a scale that would appal us,' said Ralph.

'I don't know how you can be so sure of that,' she said.

'The Polynesians wiped out half the bird species on the Hawaiian islands long before Captain Cook ever got there,' he said. 'In New Zealand the Maoris butchered the entire population of giant moa birds and left most of the carcasses uneaten. To this day the Yuqui Indians in the Bolivian rainforest chop down trees to get at the fruit. Conservation is a concept of advanced civilizations.'

'Messenger, stop showing off,' said Caroline, and we all laughed with relief. 'I'm only trying to set Laetitia straight,' he said mildly. 'No you're not, you're haranguing her.' 'Yes,' said Marianne, who was sitting at the head of the table, with Ralph to her right and Laetitia two places down to her left. 'Leave Letty alone, Ralph, and help me carry out these dishes to the kitchen.' And he grinned and followed her out of the dining room with a stack of soiled plates, looking rather pleased with himself like a naughty but unrepentant boy, while Laetitia plaintively asserted that she could defend herself perfectly well.

Jasper opened another couple of bottles of Gum Tree Pinot Noir (or whatever it was) and went round the table recharging glasses. I took the opportunity to go to the loo, but must have misunderstood Jasper's directions because the first door I opened was a broom cupboard, and the second gave access to the back garden. I stepped outside to take a few welcome breaths of cold, fresh air, and found myself looking across a small paved yard into the brightly lit kitchen. Ralph Messenger had our hostess pinned against the kitchen door in a passionate embrace, and she was digging her gold-painted talons into his buttocks. Her eyes were closed – but in any case, she wouldn't have been able to see me standing in the darkness. It would seem that Jasper Richmond was misinformed about the Messengers' 'arrangement': either there isn't one, or it's being breached.

I woke this morning feeling slightly hungover and dyspeptic from last night's consumption of food and wine (I fear I was probably over the limit when I drove myself home, albeit very slowly and carefully) so I went for a walk after breakfast to get some fresh air. The sky was not promising – a quilt of dark grey cloud sagged from horizon to horizon – and it began to rain as soon as I left the house. Trudging round the campus on a wet Sunday morning was not a spirit-lifting experience, but I persevered, making it an occasion to master the geography of the place, and learn the locations of the various departments and faculties. The buildings erected in the sixties and seventies have not weathered well. Their concrete facades absorb the rain patchily, like blotting paper, and the brightly coloured panels and tiles with which they are trimmed, designed to relieve the dominant grey, are chipped and cracked or missing in many places. Ralph Messenger's Centre for Cognitive Science looks as if it was built more recently and to a higher standard. It's a round three-storey building with a domed roof that has a shallow indentation across the middle, very like an observatory except that there's no opening for a telescope. According to Jasper Richmond it was built with money from the Holt Belling computer people, after an international competition. The divided dome is supposed to represent the two hemispheres of the brain. The walls are made of mirror-glass. I wonder what that is supposed to represent – the vanity of cognitive scientists?

A little while later I came across another oddly shaped building – octagonal, this time. It turned out to be an ecumenical chapel and inter-faith meeting-place, shared by various Christian denominations and also (to judge by the notices pinned up in the lobby) used by Buddhists, Bahaists, Transcendental Meditators, yoga enthusiasts, Tai-chi devotees and similar New Age groups. What drew me into the building, however, were the strains of a familiar hymn, one we used to sing in my parish church when I was a girl. 'Oh Lord my God, when I in awesome wonder . . .' I checked a notice-board: yes, a Catholic mass had just begun. On an impulse I slipped into the chapel and sat down in the back row.

It's perhaps time I admitted to myself that I'm totally muddled and inconsistent about religion. I'm deeply grateful that I had a Catholic education even though I suffered unnecessary agonies of guilt, frustration and boredom on account of it in childhood and adolescence; and in retrospect I feel only nostalgic affection for the nuns who taught me even though most of them were more or less deranged by superstition and sexual repression, which they did their best to instil in me. I ceased to be a practising Catholic in my second term at Oxford, at the same time that I lost my virginity. The two events were connected – I could not with sincerity confess as a sin something I had found so liberating, or promise not to do it again. Intellectual rejection of the rest of Catholic doctrine quickly followed, whether as a consequence or a rationalization of this moral decision would be hard to say. Some years later, by dint of a certain amount of fudging and dissembling, I was married in a Catholic church, to avoid giving needless pain to my parents but also because when all's said and done I wouldn't have felt properly married in a registry office. When I had children of my own I had them baptized, again ostensibly to please Mummy and Daddy, but secretly because I should have felt uneasy myself otherwise. Also, it enabled us to send them to a Catholic primary school in due course. Martin didn't object, in spite of being a nonbeliever himself, because he recognized that the local Catholic primary school was better than the state ones and we couldn't afford private education at that stage of our lives. He thought there would be no harm in exposing our children to the more benign myths of Catholicism, like Christmas and guardian angels and people going to heaven when they died, as long as we were at hand to check any tendency to morbidity or fanaticism, and that they would grow out of any belief they acquired in due course, as indeed they did. Children are extraordinarily acute. Paul and Lucy seemed intuitively to know, even at the age of five or six, that they must pretend to believe things at school which weren't believed at home, and perhaps vice versa, and they managed this double life with remarkable aplomb. At their secular secondary schools they soon became as indifferent to religion as most of their peers, but I like to think that they acquired from their early education an above-average ethical sense, not to mention a priceless key to the literature and art of the last two thousand years. (I was shocked to realize that some of my students in the seminar last Thursday didn't understand Rachel McNulty's allusion to the New Testament story of Martha and Mary.)

After Paul and Lucy's first communions we never went to church as a family except for occasional weddings, funerals, and midnight mass at Christmas with my parents for old times' sake. But after Martin died I started going to Sunday mass again on my own, at the local parish church, out of a confused jumble of motives. I was desperate for some kind of consolation and reassurance, and perhaps I feared superstitiously that the Catholic God had punished me for my apostasy, and that I'd better get back on good terms with Him before He did something else terrible to me or my children. But the consolation never came and the fear seemed more and more ignoble as time passed. I was pleased to see girls serving at the altar, but otherwise not much had changed since I had last been in a Catholic church. The parish priest was an uncharismatic Irishman who celebrated mass as if it were a repetitive job which somebody had to do and the quicker the better, and his sermons were almost insultingly simple-minded. I didn't, needless to say, go to confession or communion, and after a few weeks I stopped going to church altogether.

Why did I go into the chapel today? My morale was at a very low ebb, and I suppose I thought the atmosphere would be different from that of a parish church, and so it was, but hardly more inspiring. The decor of the room itself was depressingly bleak and bare, having been purged of any trace of religious art or symbolism that might give offence to any of its users. A simple wooden table served as the altar, with chairs arranged in an irregular arc around it. It was a mainly youthful congregation, naturally enough, with a scattering of faculty and their families. I was surprised, and not particularly pleased, to see the Riverdales with their two infants on the other side of the room. I tried to make myself as inconspicuous as possible, but I caught sight of Colin smiling at me in the middle of the Gloria.

The style of the liturgy was informal: the altar server wore a tracksuit and trainers, and the music, led by a girl in jeans with a guitar, favoured folk tunes and rhythms. The young infants of the faculty were allowed to wander or crawl round the room pushing and pulling their Fisher-Price toys – or the young priest who was celebrating mass didn't have the courage to ask that they should be stopped from doing so. It was the Second Sunday of Lent, I discovered. (Lent! What a complex of forgotten emotions and memories that word summons up! Fasting and abstinence on Ash Wednesday, and the black smudges of ashes on foreheads of girls and teachers at school, piously left there all day . . . 'Giving up' sweets and sugar in tea . . . The joy of pigging oneself on chocolate on Easter Sunday . . . There are pleasures generated by self-denial that many young people will never know.) The First Reading was the story of Abraham and Isaac – a good story, but a rather horrifying one too, as Kierkegaard pointed out. One might have hoped for some allusion to *Fear and Trembling* in a homily on this text at a university mass, but no such luck. The young priest expounded it as a simple tale of obedience to the will of God and concentrated on the 'blessings' that accrued to Abraham in consequence. The Gospel was the story of the Transfiguration, ending with the apostles '*discussing among themselves what "rising from the dead" could mean*'. Indeed.

It was impossible to avoid speaking to the Riverdales afterwards. 'I didn't know you were a papist,' Colin said, smiling, and putting ironic quotation marks round the last word. If he had read any of my books apart from *The Eye of the Storm* he might have guessed that I was brought up as one. 'I'm not practising,' I said. 'I came in on impulse – just happened to be passing.' 'Well, lost sheep are always welcome,' he said, which I considered a bit of a nerve, even if it was passed off as a joke. 'Let me introduce you to Father Steve, our part-time chaplain,' he went on. 'No thanks,' I said coldly. 'I must be going.' Annabelle gave me a wistful, half-apologetic smile as I left them.

On the way back to *la maisonnette* I stopped at the supermarket to buy three bloated Sunday papers and spent the afternoon reading longingly about all the new plays, films, exhibitions *etc.*, on in London. Just before it got dark I went for another walk. The rain had cleared and there was a red winter sunset. The wire perimeter fence, reflecting the slanting light, glowed briefly like the element in an electric toaster, and then went out as the sun slipped behind a distant hill. I more and more feel as if I am in an open prison: I could easily walk out, I *long* to walk out, but the predictable consequences of doing so keep me here, on my honour. I must do my time.

3

ON the Wednesday of the second week of the semester, Ralph Messenger and Helen Reed happen to meet in the University's Staff House, at lunchtime. Helen is in the lobby, looking at an exhibition of paintings by a local artist. Ralph sees her as he comes in through the revolving door, and walks up behind her.

'What d'you think of them?' he says at her shoulder, making her jump.

'Oh! Hallo . . . I was thinking, if they were *very* cheap, I might buy one to brighten up my living-room.'

'Well, they're bright enough,' he says, surveying the pictures with his head cocked appraisingly. They are landscapes, boldly painted in lurid acrylic colours seldom, if ever, encountered in nature.

'Yes, and they're cheap enough, too. But somehow . . .'

'Somehow they're hideously ugly.'

She laughs. 'I'm afraid you're right.'

'Have you had lunch?'

'I was just on my way to the cafeteria.'

'Why don't we have it together?'

'All right. That would be nice.'

'But not in the cafeteria.'

'I don't usually eat much for lunch,' she says.

'Neither do I, but I like to eat it in comfort,' he says.

The dining room on the second floor is waitress service, and the tables have table-cloths and little vases of plastic flowers on them. They sit by a window with a view of the lake. Helen orders a salad, Ralph the pasta Dish of the Day, and they share a large bottle of sparkling mineral water.

'Actually, I was going to offer you coffee last Sunday morning,'

Ralph says. 'I saw you walking in the rain, looking as if you were at a loose end —'

'How did you see me?' She seems startled, and not particularly pleased, by this information.

'From my office window. You walked past the Centre, and I happened to be looking out.'

'What were you doing in your office on a Sunday morning?'

'Oh . . . catching up on work,' he says vaguely. 'I went out of the building to speak to you, but I couldn't find you anywhere. You seemed to disappear into thin air.'

'Did I?' She seems faintly embarrassed.

'Where were you?'

'I went into the chapel.'

'What for?'

'Why do people usually go into a chapel on a Sunday morning?'

'Are you religious, then?' There is a note of disapproval, or perhaps disappointment, in his voice.

'I was brought up as a Catholic. I don't believe any more, but —'

'Oh, good.'

'Why do you say that?'

'Well, it's impossible to have a rational conversation about anything important with religious people. I suppose that's why I didn't think of looking for you in the chapel. I had you down as an intelligent rational person. So what were you doing there, if you're not a believer?'

'Well I don't believe literally in the whole caboodle,' she says. 'You know, the Virgin Birth and Transubstantiation and the Infallibility of the Pope and all that. But sometimes I think there must be a kind of truth behind it. Or I hope there is.'

'Why?'

'Because otherwise life is so pointless.'

'I don't find it so. I find it full of interest and deeply satisfying.'

'Well, you're fortunate. You're healthy and comfortably off and successful in your work —'

'Aren't you, then?' he says.

'Well, I suppose so, up to a point. But there are millions who aren't.'

'Let's forget about them for a moment. What about you? Why isn't this life enough? Why do you need religion?'

'I don't need it, exactly. I mean, I've got along without it for most of my adult life, but there are times . . . I lost my husband, you see, about a year ago.'

'Yes, I heard about that.'

She waits for a moment, as if she expects him to add something like *'I'm sorry'*, but he doesn't.

'It was very sudden, totally without warning. An aneurysm in the brain. Our lives seemed to be going so well when it happened. Martin had just been promoted, and my last novel had just won a prize – we were planning to splurge some of it on a holiday. We were actually looking at brochures when . . .' She stops, evidently upset by the memory. Ralph Messenger waits patiently for her to resume. 'When he collapsed. He went into a coma, and died the next day, in hospital.'

'That was tough for you, but a good way to go for him.'

'How can you say that?' She looks shocked, then angry, angry enough to get up and leave him sitting at the table. 'He was only forty-four. He had years of happy life to look forward to.'

'Who knows? He might have developed some horribly painful degenerative disease next year.'

'And he might not.'

'No, he might not,' Ralph concedes.

'He might have had a long and happy life, and made lots of brilliant radio documentaries and had grandchildren and gone round the world and . . . all kinds of things.'

'But he doesn't know that now. And he didn't have time to think about it before he died. He died full of hope. That's why I say it was a good way to go.'

The waitress comes up with their food and they suspend the conversation for a few moments as she serves them. It is an opportunity for Helen to calm herself.

○ ○

'So you think that when we die we just cease to exist?' she says, when the waitress has gone.

'Not in an absolute sense. The atoms of my body are indestructible.'

'But your self, your spirit, your soul . . . ?'

'As far as I'm concerned those are just ways of talking about certain kinds of brain activity. When the brain ceases to function, they necessarily cease too.'

'And that doesn't fill you with despair?'

'No,' he says cheerfully, twisting creamy ribbons of tagliatelle on his fork. 'Why should it?' He thrusts the steaming pasta into his mouth and munches vigorously.

'Well, it seems pointless to spend years and years acquiring knowledge, accumulating experience, trying to be good, struggling to *make* something of yourself, as the saying goes, if nothing of that self survives death. It's like building a beautiful sandcastle below the tideline.'

'That's the only part of the beach you *can* build a sandcastle,' Ralph says. 'Anyway, I hope to leave a permanent mark on the history of cognitive science before I go. Just as you must hope to do in literature. That's a kind of life after death. The only kind.'

'Well, yes, but the number of authors who go on being really *read* after their death is minuscule. Most of us end up being pulped, literally or metaphorically.' Helen chivvies some limp lettuce leaves with brownish stalks to the side of her plate and cuts up the remainder. 'What *is* cognitive science, exactly?'

'The systematic study of the mind,' he says. 'It's the last frontier of scientific enquiry.'

'Really?'

'The physicists have pretty well got the cosmos taped. It's only a matter of time before they come up with a unified theory. The discovery of DNA has transformed biology once and for all. Consciousness is the biggest white space on the map of human knowledge. Did you know this is the Decade of the Brain?'

'No. Who said so?'

'Well, I think it was President Bush, as a matter of fact,' says

35

Ralph. 'But he was speaking for the scientific community. All kinds of people have got interested in the subject lately – physicists, biologists, zoologists, neurologists, evolutionary psychologists, mathematicians . . .'

'Which of those are you?' Helen asks.

'I started out as a philosopher. I read Moral Sciences at Cambridge, and did a PhD on the Philosophy of Mind. Then I went to America on a fellowship and got into computers and AI –'

'AI?'

'Artificial Intelligence. Once upon a time nobody was interested in the problem of consciousness except a few philosophers. Now it's the biggest game in town.'

'What's the problem, then?' Helen asks.

Ralph chuckles. 'You don't find anything surprising or puzzling about the fact that you are a conscious being?'

'Not really. About the *content* of my consciousness, yes, of course. Emotions, memories, feelings. They're very problematic. Is that what you mean?'

'Well, they come into it. They're called *qualia* in the literature.'

'Qualia?'

'The specific quality of our subjective experiences of the world – like the smell of coffee, or the taste of pineapple. They're unmistakable, but very difficult to describe. Nobody's figured out how to account for them yet. Nobody's proved that they actually exist.' Perceiving that she is about to protest, he adds, 'Of course they *seem* real enough, but they may just be implementations of something more fundamental and mechanical.'

' "The hardwiring in your brain"?' she says, putting quote marks round the phrase in her intonation.

Ralph smiles a pleased smile. 'You watched my TV series?'

'Only a little of it, I'm afraid.'

'Well, I don't go the whole way with the neuroscientists. OK, the mind is a machine, but a *virtual* machine. A system of systems.'

'Perhaps it isn't a system at all.'

'Oh, but it is. Everything in the universe is. If you're a scientist you have to start from that assumption.'

'I expect that's why I dropped science at school as soon as they let me.'

'No, you dropped it, I would guess, because it was doled out to you in spoonfuls of distilled boredom . . . Anyway, the problem of consciousness is basically the old mind-body one bequeathed by Descartes. My graduate students call our Centre, "the Mind/Body Shop". We know that the mind doesn't consist of some immaterial spook-stuff, the ghost in the machine. But what *does* it consist of? How *do* you explain the phenomenon of consciousness? Is it just electro-chemical activity in the brain? Neurones firing, neurotrans-mitters jumping across the synapses? In a sense, yes, that's all there is that we can observe. You can do PET scans and MRI scans nowadays that show different parts of the brain lighting up like a pinball machine, as different emotions and sensations are triggered in the subject. But how is that activity translated into thought? If translated is the word, which it probably isn't. Is there some kind of preverbal medium of consciousness – "mentalese" – which at a certain point, for certain purposes, gets articulated by the particular parts of the brain that specialize in language? These are the kind of questions I'm interested in.'

'And what if they are unanswerable?'

'There are some people in the field who take that view. They're called mysterians.'

'Mysterians. I like the sound of that,' she says. 'I think I'm a mysterian.'

'They believe that consciousness is an irreducible self-evident fact about the world that can't be explained in other terms.'

'Oh, I thought it was more like Keats's "negative capability",' says Helen. She sounds disappointed.

'What's that?'

' "*When a man is capable of being in uncertainties, mysteries, doubts, without any irritable reaching after fact and reason.*" '

'No, these guys are scientists and philosophers, not poets. But they're wrong to give up the search for an explanation.'

'What's yours, then?'

'I think the mind is like a computer – you use a computer?'

'I've got a laptop. I use it like a glorified typewriter. I have no idea how it does the tricks it does.'

'OK. Your PC is a linear computer. It performs a lot of tasks one at a time at terrific speed. The brain is more like a parallel computer, in other words it's running lots of programs simultaneously. What we call "attention" is a particular interaction between various parts of the total system. The subsystems and possible connections and combinations between them are so multitudinous and complex that it's very difficult to simulate the whole process – in fact, impossible in the present state of the art. But we're getting there, as British Rail used to say.'

'You mean, you're trying to design a computer that thinks like a human being?'

'In principle, that's the ultimate objective.'

'And feels like a human being? A computer that has hangovers and falls in love and suffers bereavement?'

'A hangover is a kind of pain, and pain always has been a difficult nut to crack,' says Ralph carefully. 'But I don't see any inherent impossibility in designing and programming a robot that could get into a symbiotic relationship with another robot and would exhibit symptoms of distress if the other robot were put out of commission.'

'You're joking, of course?'

'Not at all.'

'But it's absurd!' Helen exclaims. 'How can robots have feelings? They're just a lot of bits and pieces of metal and wire and plastic.'

'They are at present,' he says. 'But there's no reason why the hardware shouldn't be embodied in some kind of organic material in the future. In the States they've already developed synthetic electro-mechanical muscle tissue for robots. Or we may develop computers that are carbon-based, like biological organisms, instead of silicon-based ones.'

'Your Mind/Body Shop sounds like a modern version of Frankenstein's laboratory.'

'If only,' he says, with a rueful smile. 'We haven't got the resources to build our own robots. Most of our work is theoretical or simulated. It's cheaper — but less exciting. The nearest thing we've got to Frankenstein's laboratory is Max Karinthy's mural.'

'And what is that?'

'I'll show you now, if you're free. And give you a cup of the best machine-made coffee you've ever had.'

'All right,' says Helen. 'Thank you.'

When the waitress brings the bill, Ralph picks it up, but Helen insists on paying her share and he does not make an issue of it.

'You don't mind walking?' he asks, as they descend the stairs to the lobby.

'No, not at all.'

'There is a shuttle bus in . . .' He glances at a chunky stainless steel watch. 'About ten minutes.'

'No, I like to walk,' she says. 'It's the only exercise I get.'

'Me too. I always walk on campus unless its raining.'

It isn't raining outside, but looks as if it might soon. A damp wind is blowing across the campus under scudding grey clouds. They walk along the path that skirts the lake, moving into single file every now and again as a tinkling bell warns them of the approach of a cyclist. It being a Wednesday afternoon, there is evidence of sporting activity. Shouts and cries carry faintly from the playing fields on the eastern perimeter, and a rugby ball rises and falls in a spinning arc against the sky. On the lake, some students in wetsuits are windsurfing. The brightly coloured shards of their sails against the dark water make a pleasant picture, but the lake is hardly big enough for the purpose: no sooner have the craft got up some speed than they have to make quick turns to avoid hitting the bank, or each other. Capsizes are frequent.

'I know what this place reminds me of,' Helen says suddenly. 'Gladeworld. Have you ever been?'

'No, what is it?'

'A sort of up-market holiday village. I went with my sister's family last summer. It was in a biggish bit of wooded country, surrounded by a wire fence. You live in little houses built between the trees. In the middle there's a huge plastic dome with a kind of swimming-pool-cum-botanical-gardens underneath it with lots of water chutes and whirlpools and suchlike. And there's a supermarket and restaurants and sports halls – and an artificial lake for sailing and windsurfing that isn't quite big enough. That's what reminded me. That and the bicycles. You're not allowed to drive your car at Gladeworld once you've unloaded it. Everybody rents bicycles, or walks. Everything you need for your holiday is inside the fence. You never need to go outside.'

'It sounds ghastly.'

'My sister's children adored it, I have to say. But I felt a little trapped. There's a manned security barrier to stop unauthorized people getting in, but I couldn't help feeling that it was also there to discourage us from going out.'

They walk on in silence for a while.

'I get the impression you wish you hadn't come here,' he says.

'I'm probably just homesick,' she says. 'I daresay I'll settle down soon, and enjoy it.'

'Why did you apply for the job?'

'I need the money, for one thing.'

'But they pay you peanuts!' he exclaims, adding, 'I happen to know because I'm on the Senate Academic Appointments Committee. I saw the papers.'

'It may seem like peanuts to you, but I need it,' says Helen. 'I don't earn a great deal from my books, alas. And although Martin's life was insured, it only yields a modest annuity. But you're right, it wasn't just for the money. My daughter's having a gap year between school and university, she's in Australia. It was all planned before Martin died, and I didn't want to stop her. It's what they all do nowadays. And my son's in Iowa for his year abroad – he's doing American Studies at Manchester. The house seemed very big and echoey without them. And too full of memories. I thought a change of scene would do me good . . .'

She falls silent. Ralph gives a vague grunt of assent.

'What about you?' she asks. 'D'you like it here?'

'It's all right,' he says, 'but I'd go mad if I didn't get away from time to time.'

'To conferences, and on media jaunts?'

He glances at her quizzically, as if struck by her choice of words. 'That sort of thing, yes. There are worse places to be, but it's a bit sleepy and provincial. The University was fashionable in the seventies, but it was never given enough money to grow to a viable size, not for serious scientific research anyway. Now it's on the slide, to be frank. Like a football club desperately trying to avoid relegation from the Premier League. I didn't quite realize that when I was offered the directorship of the Centre. I was quite happy at Cal Tech, but this seemed like an offer I couldn't refuse, running my own show, in a purpose-built prize-winning building.' He points to the squat, cylindrical structure which has now come into their view, with its grooved dome and opaque glass walls.

'I'm told that the dome represents the twin hemispheres of the brain,' Helen says.

'That's right.'

'Why are the walls made of mirror glass?'

'Can't you guess?'

Helen smiles as if at some private joke, then frowns with concentration. 'Because you can see out of it but not into it? Like the mind?'

'Well done.' Ralph nods like a satisfied teacher. 'That's half the answer. But after dark, when the lights are on, you can see everything that's going on inside in the building from outside, symbolizing the explanatory power of scientific research. That was the architect's idea, anyway.'

'But if you draw the blinds —'

'Good point!' Ralph laughs. 'The architect explicitly excluded blinds and curtains from his design, but people found their offices intolerable in bright sunshine so he had to put them in, and some of us like to draw them when it gets dark.'

'Ruining the symbolism.'

'Not really. You can always draw the blinds on consciousness. We never know for certain what another person is really thinking.

41

Even if they choose to tell us, we can never know whether they're telling the truth, or the whole truth. And by the same token nobody can know our thoughts as we know them.'

'Just as well, perhaps. Social life would be difficult otherwise.'

'Absolutely. Imagine what the Richmonds' dinner party would have been like, if everyone had had those bubbles over their heads that you get in kids' comics, with *"Thinks . . ."* inside them.' He looks directly into Helen's eyes as he says this, as if speculating about her thoughts on that occasion.

She colours slightly. 'I suppose that's why people read novels,' she says. 'To find out what goes on in other people's heads.'

'But all they really find out is what has gone on in the writer's head. It's not real knowledge.'

'Oh? What is real knowledge, then?'

'Scientific knowledge. The trouble is, if you restrict the study of consciousness to what can be empirically observed and measured, you leave out what's most distinctive about it.'

'Qualia.'

'Exactly. There's an old joke that crops up in nearly every book on consciousness, about two behaviourist psychologists who have sex, and afterwards one says to the other, "It was good for you, how was it for me?" '

Helen has not heard this joke before, and laughs.

'That's the problem of consciousness in a nutshell,' Ralph says. 'How to give an objective, third-person account of a subjective, first-person phenomenon.'

'Oh, but novelists have been doing that for the last two hundred years,' says Helen airily.

'What d'you mean?'

She stops on the footpath, lifts one hand, and shuts her eyes, frowning with concentration. Then she recites, with hardly any hesitation, or stumbling over words: ' *"She waited, Kate Croy, for her father to come, but he kept her unconscionably, and there were moments at which she showed herself, in the glass over the mantel, a face positively pale with the irritation that had brought her to the point of going away without sight of him. It was at this point, however, that she remained; changing her place, moving from the shabby sofa to the armchair upholstered in a glazed cloth that gave at once — she had tried it — the sense of the slippery and the sticky."'*

He stares. 'What's that?'

'Henry James. The opening sentences of *The Wings of the Dove.*' Helen walks on, and Ralph moves into step beside her.

'Is it a party trick of yours — reciting chunks of classic novels from memory?'

'I started a DPhil thesis on point of view in Henry James,' says Helen. 'Never finished it, unfortunately, but some of the key quotations stuck.'

'Do it again.'

Helen repeats the quotation, and says, 'You see — you have Kate's consciousness there, her thoughts, her feelings, her impatience, her hesitation about leaving or staying, her perception of her own appearance in the mirror, the nasty texture of the armchair's upholstery, *"at once slippery and sticky"* — how's that for qualia? And yet it's all narrated in the third person, in precise, elegant, well-formed sentences. It's subjective *and* objective.'

'Well, it's effectively done, I grant you,' says Ralph. 'But it's literary fiction, not science. James can claim to know what's going on in Kate Whatshername's head because he put it there, he invented her. Out of his own experience and folk psychology.'

'There's nothing folksy about Henry James.'

He waves this quibble aside. 'Folk psychology is a term we use in the trade,' he says. 'It means received wisdom and commonsense assumptions about human behaviour and motivation, what makes people tick. It works fine for ordinary social life — we couldn't get along without it. And it works fine for fiction, all the way from *The Wings of the Dove* to *Eastenders* . . . but it's not objective enough to qualify as science. If this Kate Croy were a real human being, Henry James could never presume to say how she felt about that armchair, unless she'd told him.'

'But if Kate Croy were a real human being, your cognitive science could tell us nothing about her that we'd want to know.'

'I wouldn't accept "nothing". But yes, agreed, for the time being

43

we have to settle for knowing less about consciousness than novelists pretend to know. Here we are.'

They have reached the entrance to the Holt Belling Centre for Cognitive Science.

Sliding doors made of toughened glass, engraved with large entwined capitals, '*HB*', open automatically at their approach and slice the air silently behind them. The foyer is filled with a bluish, submarine light, filtered through the tinted windows. From inside it can be seen that the entire building is constructed mainly of steel and glass. The offices, workrooms and other rooms splay out from a central atrium. Their curved inner walls are made of glass, so the visitor can take in at a glance the various activities going on in each segment, though most of the people visible seem to be doing much the same thing, sitting at desks staring at computer screens and occasionally fingering key-boards. The three floors of the building are connected by a lift shaft situated at the opposite side of the atrium to the entrance, but also by an open spiral staircase, constructed of stainless steel and polished wood, that coils up from the centre of the ground floor, connected to the floors above by horizontal walkways and galleries.

'D'you notice anything unusual about the staircase?' Ralph asks.

'Well, it's extremely elegant, especially the banister,' says Helen.

'No, not that. It's left-handed, like the double helix of DNA. Spiral staircases usually go the other way.'

'Ah. I wouldn't have known.'

He shows her the accommodation on the ground floor: a general office, a small library, a lecture theatre with raked tip-up seats, postgraduate workrooms, with rows of identical computer terminals arrayed on tables, and an air-conditioned basement room which Ralph alludes to as the Brain of the building, full of computers of different shapes and sizes, humming and blinking to themselves, on whose discs and tapes most of the Centre's work is stored. A man in a white lab coat is studying a printout from one of these machines. Ralph introduces him to Helen as Stuart Phillips, his systems administrator. Helen remarks that the machines all have names

44

printed on white cards and attached to their casings: 'Haddock', 'Thompson-One', 'Thompson-Two', 'Snowy', *etc.*

Stuart Phillips says, 'It's easy to make mistakes if you refer to them by their technical designations – letters and numbers – so we give them nicknames.'

'Why all from the Tintin books?' says Helen.

'That was Professor Messenger's idea,' says Stuart Phillips, turning to Ralph.

'My kids were very fond of them,' he says. 'Still are, and so am I, for that matter.'

He leads her to the common room in the basement, furnished with low modern sofas and armchairs stained and threadbare from use, and a gleaming Swiss automatic drinks machine. Three young men dressed in jeans, sports shirts and trainers are chatting in a corner. Ralph introduces them to Helen as PhD students: Jim, Carl (from Germany) and Kenji (from Japan). She asks them what they are working on. Jim says robotics, Carl says affective modelling, Kenji says something indistinct that Ralph repeats for her benefit – 'genetic algorithms.'

'I can guess what robotics is,' says Helen, 'but what on earth are the others?'

Carl explains that affective modelling is computer simulation of the way emotions affect human behaviour.

'Like grief?' Helen says, glancing at Ralph.

'Exactly so,' he says. 'Though Carl is actually working on a program for mother-love.'

'I'd like to see it,' says Helen.

'I am not able to give a demonstration, I'm afraid,' says Carl. 'I am rewriting the program.'

'Another day,' says Ralph.

'And genetic whatsitsnames?' Helen enquires, turning to Kenji. The young man, whose English is not as good as Carl's, sweats and stammers through an explanation which Ralph tactfully summarizes for Helen's benefit: genetic algorithms are computer programs designed to replicate themselves like biological life forms. 'The programs are all set a problem to solve and the ones that do best are allowed to reproduce themselves for the next test. In other words, they pair off and have sex together' – so Ralph puts it, to the amusement of the students. 'We split each program in two and swap the halves. If you do this often enough, sometimes you end up with more powerful programs than a human programmer could have designed.'

'But they might get out of control,' says Helen, 'and take over the world.'

'More likely they'd end up in common rooms discussing whether human beings are conscious or not,' he says.

The young men laugh politely. Perhaps thinking that they ought to make some demonstration of industry and commitment to their research, they move off, leaving Ralph and Helen alone. He asks her what kind of coffee she would like and punches the appropriate buttons on the machine. He watches expectantly as she sips a cappuccino with chocolate powder sprinkled on top.

'Mmm, excellent,' she says. 'Only the polystyrene cup lets it down.'

'Ah well, the regulars have their own chinaware,' he says, going over to a wooden board where variously decorated mugs hang from cuphooks labelled with the owners' names. He takes a black mug with the word *BOSS* printed on it in white capitals, and positions it under the coffee-machine's tap to receive a double espresso with sugar.

'You don't have a separate common room for staff, then?' Helen comments. 'Very democratic.'

'Well, our students are all postgraduates. We don't run under-graduate courses, much to the University's displeasure.'

'Why is that?'

'I don't want my people wasting their time and energy teaching undergraduates elementary programming.'

'No, I mean, why is the University displeased?'

'There's money in student numbers. Higher education is a market nowadays, you know.' He looks at her over his coffee mug. 'It's a sore point with us at the moment, actually. I could easily bore you to death on the subject.'

'Try me,' she says.

'Well, briefly, this place was set up with an endowment from Holt Belling plc – the VC at that time was friendly with the Chairman of their Board. They provided the capital expenditure and half the running expenses, the University paying the other half. The agreement is renewed every five years. Next year will be the end of the second quinquennium, and Holt Belling aren't going to renew. They're full of admiration for what we're doing, but they just can't afford to support it any more. I can't blame them. Microsoft have taken a lot of their business away, and they have a cash-flow problem. In any case it was always assumed that eventually they would drop out and leave the University to take over full responsibility for funding us. But the University is short of cash too. The new VC and his Committee of Public Safety – that's what I call his team of administrators – tell me they can't afford to pick up the tab for the whole operation.'

'So what will happen?' Helen asks.

'In the worst-case scenario, we'll be closed down.' He smiles sardonically as he adds, 'Perhaps they'll convert this place into a Centre for Creative Writing. Jasper Richmond tells me he's running out of space in the School of English. And Creative Writing is very much approved of by the Committee of Public Safety.'

'Is it?' Helen sounds surprised.

'Oh yes. The courses are very popular, they attract lots of applicants, undergraduate as well as postgraduate. Americans choose to do their Junior Year Abroad here because they can get credits in Creative Writing. Lots of students, lots of fees. The School of English hires impoverished writers to teach them, on temporary, short-term contracts –'

'For peanuts,' Helen interpolates.

'For peanuts, exactly. Flat fees with no superannuation contributions, no sabbatical or maternity leave entitlements. The overheads of the course must be negligible. From a business point of view it's a high-yield, low-cost operation. Whether the world really needs more novelists is a matter of opinion.'

'Does it need more cognitive scientists?'

'*I* think so, obviously. The future's going to be dominated by computer science and genetic engineering. You need people who understand the fundamental problems and possibilities of those things, not just the applications. But our masters don't seem to understand that. It's always difficult to get money for blue skies research, in any field.'

'But you don't seriously think the University will close you down?'

'No. Well, only as a last resort, anyway. We're one of the few world-class departments in this place, rated 5 in the last research assessment exercise. It would be bad management, not to mention bad PR, if the University just pulled the plug. More likely we'll be asked to tighten our belts, or offer undergraduate courses.'

'Can't you find a new sponsor?'

'It's tricky. You see, it was a condition of the original endowment that this building would always be known as the Holt Belling Centre. You can't imagine a rival organization being happy with that. Even getting funding for specific projects is quite difficult, for the same reason. Our best hope at the moment is the MoD.'

'The Ministry of Defence?'

'They've shown interest in some of our work, and of course publicity is the last thing they want. Whatever happens, it'll mean more paperwork for me. But that's enough about boring administration problems,' he says, picking up Helen's empty cup and his own mug, and taking them across to the sink to dispose of the former and rinse out the latter. 'Let me show you the Karinthy mural.'

On their way there, they encounter the postgraduate Jim in a corridor, observing a small robot, about two feet high. It has three wheels, a rotating head with lenses for eyes, and a pair of mechanical claws.

'This is Arthur,' says Ralph. 'The latest addition to the Department strength. Bought off the peg.'

At that moment Arthur is motionless, facing into a corner, like a small boy who has been sent there for misbehaving in class.

'What is it doing?' Helen asks.

'Mapping out the space,' Jim says. 'Committing it to memory.'

Abruptly, Arthur swivels round on its wheels and sets off for the other side of the corridor where it bangs rather violently into the wall.

'Ouch,' says Jim, frowning. 'There must be something wrong with the program.' Arthur backs away from the wall, and contemplates it in a stunned sort of way.

'He looks as if he still has some way to go before he starts dating other robots,' Helen says to Ralph.

'Yes,' says Ralph. 'We shall be happy if we can teach him to pick up trash from the floor. Let's move on.'

Ralph leads Helen to the lift. Not only are its walls made of glass, but the floor too, so that you can look down between your feet at the cables and machinery in the shaft if so inclined, though Helen clearly is not. As they ascend smoothly and silently Ralph explains that Max Karinthy was a Hungarian-American philosopher and amateur painter who spent a year at the Centre as a Research Fellow a few years ago on sabbatical from Princeton, and amused himself, with Ralph's permission, and indeed encouragement, by decorating the second floor of the building with a mural illustrative of various well-known theories and thought experiments in cognitive science, evolutionary psychology and the philosophy of mind.

The lift stops at the second-floor gallery and its glass doors open with a mechanical sigh. 'Goodness!' Helen exclaims, as she steps out. The inner walls of the rooms on this floor are not made of glass like those on the two lower ones, but of solid brick and plaster, thus affording a curved painting surface, which runs around the circumference of the atrium. A series of overlapping scenes, figures, vignettes, painted in a bold, expressionist style, extend to left and right of the lift-shaft to meet at the opposite side of the gallery, making a kind of cyclorama. In contrast to the hi-tech austerity of the rest of the building, here is a riot of colours and forms.

'Quite impressive, isn't it,' says Ralph, looking satisfied with her reaction. 'Shall I give you the guided tour?'

'Please.'

He turns to his left, and Helen follows him. The first image to catch the eye is an enormous black bat with wings spread, flying towards the viewer at eye level like a Stealth bomber, encircled by fine concentric rings.

'In the early seventies a philosopher called Thomas Nagel wrote a famous paper called "What is it Like to be a Bat?"' Ralph explains. 'His argument was that there is absolutely no way we can ever know what it is like to be a bat – the only way to know is to *be* a bat. *Ergo* qualia are ineffable, *ergo* the scientific investigation of consciousness is impossible. A very simplistic argument, in my opinion, but it's had a surprisingly good run for its money. The choice of a bat for the thought experiment was inspired, though – they're such weird creatures. You know they navigate by echolocation, like radar?' He points to the concentric rings. 'When one of the guys who discovered this first described it at a scientific conference, some old prof came up afterwards and practically assaulted him, he thought the idea was so ridiculous.'

'What are those two bats doing in the background?' Helen asks, pointing to a pair of the creatures who seem to be kissing each other in some Disneylike parody of human courtship.

'They're vampire bats. One of them is regurgitating blood down the throat of the other.'

'Ugh! I wish I hadn't asked.'

'Apparently, when vampire bats come back from a night out, the ones that struck lucky will sometimes share their takeaway dinners with ones who didn't.'

'What's that got to do with the problem of consciousness?' Helen asks.

'It's got something to do with motivation. It looks like altruism at first glance, but a lucky bat will only share its blood with another bat with which it has a reciprocal arrangement should circumstances be reversed, so it's really a form of enlightened self-interest. The same is true of human beings – as the Prisoner's Dilemma illustrates.'

Ralph points to a picture of two men dressed in comic-book striped prison uniforms, sitting in two cells at each end of a row of empty ones, staring glumly through the bars. A warder stands guard between them. 'The situation is that they're both accused of a crime and they're both being invited to give evidence against each other. Note that they've been isolated and can't communicate. If each man betrays the other, they will both go down for a long sentence. If only one turns King's evidence, he will escape scot-free. If they both remain silent they may get lighter sentences for lack of evidence. It's a choice between cooperating and defecting. It can be applied to all kinds of situations: economics, politics, fishing rights, the school playground, whatever. The whole of life can be seen as a series of choices between cooperating and defecting.'

'Really?' says Helen.

'Take the University's latest cost-cutting exercise. Heads of Schools and Departments are faced with a choice between voting to spread the cuts as thinly as possible over the whole University – equal misery for all – or voting for drastic cuts in other Departments before somebody does it to them. Cooperate or defect. Mathematicians have spent thousands of hours trying to work out the most advantageous way to play the game. Whole conferences have been devoted to the subject. There was an international competition to devise the most effective strategy. Know what it turned out to be?'

'What?'

'Tit for tat. T.F.T. You cooperate with the other player unless and until they fail to cooperate with you, and then next time you defect. Only, as long as the other player knows that's what you'll do, you won't need to. That's what holds society together. That's the sum of human morality.'

'Hmm,' Helen murmurs, as if she might dispute this assertion, but chooses not to. She moves on to another section of the mural. 'And what is this?' She nods at a picture of a man seated at a desk which bears an In-tray and Out-tray, and a pile of books. The room in which he sits is otherwise bare and has no windows. The trays are filled with scrolls of paper inscribed with ideograms, and similar scrolls of paper are falling through a flap in the door.

'That's Searle's Chinese Room, a very famous thought experiment. The idea is that this guy is receiving questions in Chinese, a language he doesn't speak or read, and he has a kind of rule book containing logical procedures that enable him to answer them in Chinese. He sits there all day receiving questions and giving out correct answers, but he doesn't understand a single word. Is he conscious of what he's doing?'

'He'd be conscious of doing an incredibly boring job.'

'Good point,' says Ralph. 'But it's not Searle's. He argues that the man can't be conscious of the information he's processing, and inasmuch as he's acting like a computer program, neither can a computer program be conscious of the information it's processing. Therefore Artificial Intelligence must fail.'

'I presume you don't agree.'

'No, I don't. Because, even in a thought experiment, it's impossible to conceive of a computer program that would work as this one is supposed to work. Or if it could, then it would be conscious by any ordinary criteria.'

'And I suppose these are the Chinese asking the questions and receiving the answers,' says Helen, pointing to a vast crowd of Asiatic-featured people in Mao suits standing shoulder to shoulder with what look like mobile phones clamped to their ears.

'No, that was somebody else's thought experiment. It involved equipping the entire population of China with two-way radios to simulate the connections between human brain cells.'

'Why China?'

'Because it's the biggest population with a common language, I suppose. There are about a billion Chinese, I believe.'

'But the Chinese don't have a common spoken language,' Helen objects.

Ralph laughs. 'Is that right? I don't suppose the guy who dreamed up the experiment knew that. But there are about a hundred billion neurons in a single human brain, and more possible connections between them than there are atoms in the universe, so the experiment doesn't get anywhere near reality anyway.'

'What was the point of it?'

Ralph shrugs. 'I forget. Another anti-functionalist argument, I think. Most of these thought experiments are. Here's an interesting one.'

It is a picture of another windowless, cell-like room, but crowded with furniture and equipment – a desk, filing cabinets, bookshelves, computers, and a TV set. Everything is painted in black and white or shades of grey, including the young woman who sits at the desk. She wears black gloves, black shoes, opaque black stockings, and a white lab coat. The image on the TV screen is monochrome. But the room is built underground; above the surface, shown in cross-section, is a smiling pastoral landscape, full of brilliant colour.

'That's Frank Jackson's Mary, the colour scientist. The idea is that she's been born and raised and educated in a totally monochrome environment. She knows absolutely everything there is to know about colour in scientific terms – for example, the various wavelength combinations that stimulate the retina of the eye in colour recognition – but she has never actually seen any colours. Notice there are no mirrors in her room, so she can't see the pigmentation of her own face, eyes, or hair, and the rest of her body is covered. Then one day she's allowed out of the room, and the first thing she sees is, say, a red rose. Does she have a totally new experience?'

'Obviously.'

'That's what Jackson says. It's another argument for qualia being ineffable and irreducible.'

'It seems like a good one to me.'

'Well, it's better than most. But again the premise asks you to accept an awful lot. If Mary knew absolutely *everything* there is to know about colour – which is much, much more than we know at the moment – maybe she'd be able to *simulate* the experience of red in her brain. By taking certain drugs, for example.'

'Who are these people?' Helen asks, pointing to a group of figures sitting or standing or walking about. 'There's something odd about them, though it's hard to put one's finger on it.'

'Good for you,' says Ralph. 'And good for Karinthy. They're zombies.'

'Zombies!'

'Yes, we do a lot of work with zombies. Zombies are to philosophers of mind what rats are to psychologists and guinea-pigs to medical biologists. I wouldn't be surprised if there was a Zombie Rights Movement somewhere.'

'But they don't exist!' Helen exclaims.

'For a novelist you're very literal-minded,' Ralph says.

'I'm a realistic novelist.'

'For philosophical purposes, it's not necessary that zombies should exist, only that their existence is a logical possibility. They're useful for thought experiments because they're indistinguishable from human beings in appearance and behaviour, but they have no consciousness in the human sense. These long-haired chaps over here, for instance,' he says, pointing, 'are a young philosopher called David Chalmers and his zombie twin. But, as you see, it's impossible to tell which is which.'

'Talking of animal rights, what's happening to this cat?' Helen asks. She has paused in front of a picture painted horizontally across a door belonging to a Professor D.C. Douglass. In a series of frames, like a strip cartoon, a magician is shown placing a somnolent marmalade cat inside a wooden cabinet, followed by a piece of complicated scientific apparatus, and then closing the lid. In the last frame he has disappeared, leaving only the cabinet in view.

'That's Schrödinger's Cat, a famous puzzle in quantum physics. The apparatus in the box connects an instrument for measuring an electron's spin to a lethal injection device. The experiment supposes that the apparatus will kill the cat if the electron's spin is 'up'. But according to quantum mechanics the state of an electron is neither up nor down until someone observes it. Therefore the cat is neither alive nor dead until someone opens the cabinet.'

'The magician is Schrödinger?'

'No, that's Roger Penrose, the mathematician.'

'Any relation to Professor Robyn Penrose?'

'Who's he?'

'She. She's coming to give a lecture in the School of English this semester. I had a flier about it.'

'I don't think there's any connection. This Penrose thinks quantum physics holds the answer to the problem of consciousness.

Consciousness as the collapse of the wave function. Quantum collapses in microtubules.'

'You've lost me, I'm afraid,' says Helen.

'Well, it's not easy to explain,' says Ralph. 'It's been said that anyone who claims to understand quantum mechanics is either mad or lying.'

At this moment the door opens and a smallish man, clutching a sheaf of papers, appears on the threshold. He stops short, startled to find them in his way, and blinks at them through thicklensed spectacles. His greying hair suggests he is middle-aged, but his face is boyish.

'Ah, here's Duggers!' says Ralph. 'Duggers will explain it to you better than I can.'

'Explain what?' says the man.

'Quantum mechanics,' says Ralph. 'This is Helen Reed, she's a writer, teaching in the School of English this semester.' To Helen he says, 'This is my colleague Douglas C. Douglass, known to one and all as Duggers.'

'I have never approved that nickname,' says Duggers sourly.

'I'm pleased to meet you, Professor Douglass,' says Helen, extending her hand. His frosty expression thaws a degree or two.

'Did you want to see me, Messenger?' he asks Ralph.

'No, I was showing Helen the mural,' says Ralph. 'We had just got to Schrödinger's Cat when you popped out of your office like a quantum effect.'

'It's very interesting,' Helen says, gesturing at the art work.

'It would be whitewashed over, if I had my way,' says Douglass.

'Oh dear, why?' she asks.

'It's frivolous. And confusing to visitors.'

'Helen is confused about quantum theory, Duggers. Won't you explain it to us?'

'Not just now, if you don't mind. I've got some photocopying to do.'

He locks the door of his office and, with a curt nod, moves off.

'Then I'll have to try and explain it myself,' says Ralph, with a sigh.

But before he can do so, the door of the lift opens and one of the secretaries from the General Office steps out, calling, 'Professor Messenger!' She click-clacks up to them in her high heels, a little out of breath, her eyes wide with the importance of her message. 'Oh, Professor Messenger – Stuart Phillips has been trying to find you. Captain Haddock has crashed.'

Ralph grimaces. 'Oh dear.' He turns to Helen. 'I'm afraid you'll have to excuse me.'

'Of course,' says Helen.

'Captain Haddock is our Email server. If we don't get it fixed before the end of the afternoon my staff will begin to suffer from withdrawal symptoms.' He smiles faintly to show this is a joke, but perhaps not entirely a joke.

'It's time I was going, anyway,' Helen says. 'But thank you very much. It was most interesting.'

'Good. I hope you'll come again,' Ralph says. 'Shall we go down together?' He gestures towards the lift.

4

ONE, two, three, testing, testing . . . *[belches]* Pardon me! It's, what, 6.51 p.m. on Wednesday 26th February . . . I'm still in my office, instead of at home, warming my bum in front of the fire and enjoying the first drink of the day, because we have a problem in the Brain . . . I got a message this afternoon that Captain Haddock had crashed, but it seems to be a hardware failure or possibly wiring . . . there are technicians and sparks crawling all over the place at the moment trying to locate the source of the trouble and I don't feel like going home until I know that it's been fixed . . . the thought of an electrical fire breaking out in the Brain in the middle of the night is scary, unlikely as it is . . . So I called Carrie to say I'd be late and settled down to do some work on staff assessment I've been putting off . . . so many fucking forms these days . . . but when I unlocked the filing cabinet where I keep confidential material my eye fell on the old Pearlcorder and I couldn't resist listening to the tape I recorded last Sunday morning . . . Haven't got round to transcribing it yet . . . I really need one of those gadgets that audiotypists use with earphones and a footpedal to stop and start the tape . . . I know they've got one in the office downstairs but I feel shy about borrowing it, they'd wonder why I didn't give them the tape to transcribe . . . I've ordered a speech recognition software package called Voicemaster which I gather is the best on the market, but it hasn't come yet, and you have to train it to recognize your pronunciation before you can use it . . . Anyway, I played back the tape on the Pearlcorder just now, and I must say it was absolutely riveting . . . though of doubtful experimental value, alas . . . It's not just that the experiment itself partly determines the direction and content of your thoughts . . . it's that by articulating them . . . however informally . . . by articulating them in speech you're already at one remove from the phenomenon of consciousness itself . . . because . . . well because every phrase I utter, however fragmentary and inconsequential it may seem, is the output of a complex interaction . . . consultation . . . competition . . . between different parts of my brain . . . It's like a bulletin, an agreed text hammered out behind closed doors after a nanosecond's intense editorial debate, and then released to the speech centres of the brain for onward transmission . . . And that editing process is impossible to record or observe, except as a pattern of electro-chemical activity between millions of neurones, a pretty picture on a scanner . . . Never mind, it might be worth persevering with for a bit, the taping, something useful may emerge, perhaps about the nature of attention . . . not that I'll ever be able to quote much of it in a paper, it's far too personal, too revealing, not to say raunchy at times . . . but it was fascinating to . . . to as it were *eavesdrop* on one's own thoughts . . . I was almost sorry when the tape ended, when I was interrupted, or rather distracted, by the sight of Helen Reed wandering across the campus in the rain like a lost soul . . . It turns out that she went into the chapel, she was there all the time I was looking for her, she told me over lunch today . . . I happened to bump into her in the Staff House and we had lunch together . . . must have been the sauce on that pasta that's given me this indigestion . . . apparently she's a Catholic, or brought up as one . . . doesn't believe any more but can't bring herself to dismiss the whole boiling, still hankers after the idea of personal immortality, like so many otherwise intelligent people . . . even scientists . . . Some of Darwin's closest associates for instance whored after spiritualism . . . Wallace, Galton, Romanes, they all went to seances, consulted mediums . . . as if having destroyed the credibility of the Christian religion they were desperate to find some substitute for the Christian heaven . . . Galton even persuaded Darwin himself, it was in that biography I reviewed, to sit in on a seance once . . . but to his credit the old man walked out, left them sitting round the table holding hands in the dark, curtains drawn against the daylight, waiting for the spooks to do their stuff . . . George Eliot and her sidekick, whatsisname, Lewes, they were there too, I seem to remember, old horseface, she who pronounced God what was it . . . God inconceivable and immortality unbelievable, or the other way round . . . even she was prepared to give spiritualism a whirl . . . Having killed off God they started to panic at the consequences, even Darwin . . . incidentally, is that perhaps the second best known sentence in the history of philosophy, Nietzsche's '*God is dead*' . . . ? Even Darwin . . . wasn't his chronic ill-health psychosomatic? He was healthy and vigorous as a young man, how else could he have survived the voyage of the *Beagle*? But as soon as he gets hold of the idea of evolution, as soon as he writes *The Origin of Species* and begins to see the consequences it's going to have for religion, he develops all kinds of symptoms – boils, flatulence, vomiting, shivering, fainting . . . piles . . . tinnitus . . . dots before the eyes . . . every damn thing you can think of . . . none of his doctors could explain or cure any of it . . . one of them said it was suppressed gout, more like suppressed guilt . . . and he tried all kinds of quack remedies that no serious scientist should have contemplated for a moment . . . like, what was it, tying himself up in chains made of brass and zinc wire . . . drenching himself in vinegar . . . sucking the juice of two lemons a day . . . plunging into freezing cold baths . . . all to no avail . . . Wasn't all that nonsense a kind of self-punishment for having dealt a death-blow to religion . . . ? Though it wasn't evolution, it was the death of his beloved little Annie that did for his own belief in God . . . One has to remember there was a lot of death about in those days, much more than now, ordinary childhood illnesses could be fatal, childbirth too . . . it wasn't so much a desire for their own immortality that led Galton and Co. to spiritualism, it was the longing to meet their dead loved ones again, especially if they died young . . . No doubt that's why Helen Reed was drawn to the chapel last Sunday, she's still grieving for her husband . . . I tried a little shock therapy on her, refusing to be conventionally sympathetic when she played the bereavement card in conversation over lunch, and I thought for a moment she was going to walk away in a huff, but she kept her cool . . . and we had quite a lively conversation about dualism, consciousness, AI *etc.* . . . . I brought her over here afterwards to show her the Karinthy mural . . . She's smart, good-looking too, the figure that was largely concealed by the frock she was wearing on Saturday night was more in evidence today, under sweater and trousers, and distinctly shapely . . . also her skin is remarkably fine for a woman well past the bloom of youth . . . There's something melancholy about her though, she looks to me as if she badly needs a good seeing to, I shouldn't think she's had it since her husband died, she gives off a kind of aura of vowed chastity, like a nun . . . I wonder how long *I* would abstain from sex if Carrie were to die suddenly, not long I suspect, well I *know* it wouldn't be . . . It's rather shocking but . . . if I imagine Carrie dying the first thought that comes into my head is not a picture of myself distraught and grieving, but of being free to fuck other women, Marianne or Helen Reed or anybody else who might be available, without any qualms of conscience or fear of discovery . . . Of course I'm sure I'd be genuinely distraught and grief-stricken if it actually happened, and perhaps I might lose all interest in sex for a while, though I doubt it . . . more likely to go the other way, seek relief in another woman's arms, *'Please stay the night, I just want somebody to hold me,'* what a line, irresistible . . . And of course I'd inherit at least some of Carrie's money, I would be rich as well as free, no use pretending that doesn't occur to me too if I imagine her dying . . . It's a good example of what we were talking about this afternoon, the privacy of consciousness, the secrecy of thought, it's the filing cabinet to which only we ourselves have the key, and thank Christ for that . . . Carrie would be devastated if she knew I was thinking these thoughts now, she'd never forgive me . . . and yet for all I know she has similar fantasies about me dying suddenly, painlessly . . . imagines herself finding a new partner, falling in love again, perhaps someone younger, more romantic than me . . . Does that idea bother me? No, not really, because I don't really believe it, it's all hypothetical, I can't inhabit her fantasies as I do my own *[recording stops]*

Just had a phone call to say they found the cause of the problem . . . a mouse . . . not a computer mouse, a real mouse, with four legs and whiskers . . . it bit through a wire and electrocuted itself – they found the corpse. I'm off.

5

THURSDAY 27TH FEB. I ran into Ralph Messenger in the Staff House yesterday, at lunch time. Well, to be strictly truthful (and why not, since this is for no one's eyes but mine) I saw him through the plate glass windows, striding up the steps to the entrance, as I came out of the Ladies, and I loitered in front of some ghastly pictures on exhibition in the foyer in the hope that he might notice me when he came in – which he did, so we had lunch together. He mentioned that he had seen me from his office last Sunday morning, wandering about the campus in the rain – information I found disconcerting. I wondered how I had appeared to him. Bedraggled? Depressed? Deranged?

After lunch he showed me round his Centre, which proved unexpectedly interesting, especially something called the Karinthy mural – a kind of cycloramic wall painting on the second floor, illustrating various theories and 'thought experiments' about consciousness. Consciousness is apparently the sort of thing cognitive scientists study – indeed *the* thing at the moment, for scientists of all kinds. They have decided that consciousness is a 'problem' which has to be 'solved'.

This was news to me, and not particularly welcome. I've always assumed, I suppose, that consciousness was the province of the arts, especially literature, and most especially the novel. Consciousness, after all, is what most novels, certainly mine, are *about*. Consciousness is my bread and butter. Perhaps for that reason, I've never seen anything problematic about it as a phenomenon. Consciousness is simply the medium in which one lives, and has a sense of personal identity. The problem is how to *represent* it, especially in different selves from one's own. In that sense novels could be called thought experiments. You invent people, you put them in hypothetical situations, and decide how they will react. The 'proof' of the experiment is if their behaviour seems interesting, plausible, revealing about human nature. Seems to whom? To 'the reader' – who is not Mr Cleverdick the reviewer, or Ms Sycophant the publicist, or your fond mother, or your jealous rival, but some kind of ideal reader, shrewd, intelligent, demanding but fair, whose persona you try to adopt as you read and re-read your own work in the process of composition. I sort of resent the idea of science poking its nose into this business, *my* business. Hasn't science already appropriated enough of reality? Must it lay claim to the intangible invisible essential self as well?

I'm a self-taught two-finger typist, prone to error (for which reason I thank God – and science – for the invention of the word-processor). But some words I *always* seem to mistype. One of them is 'science', which invariably appears on the screen of my computer as 'scince', with a reproachful red wiggly line drawn under it by the automatic spell-checker. I duly correct it, but there is something onomatopoeically appropriate about 'scince' (pronounced *skince*) which I am sorry to lose: it expresses the cold, pitiless, reductive character of scientific explanations of the world. I feel this hard, cold, almost ruthless quality in Ralph Messenger. His reaction to Martin's death, when the subject came up in the course of lunch, was like having a bowl of icy water dashed in one's face. It shocked and angered me – I almost got up and left him at the table. But I'm glad I didn't. I might never have seen the Karinthy mural, for one thing. It provoked all kinds of ideas.

At the end of today's workshop I distributed copies of the *Encyclopaedia Britannica*'s article on bats to the students and told them to write a short piece on 'What is it Like to be a Bat?' in the style of a well-known modern novelist, for next Tuesday's seminar.

Reading through the above, it occurs to me that the only kind of fiction that wouldn't be open to Ralph Messenger's objections would be the kind that doesn't attempt to represent consciousness at all. The kind that stays on the surface, just describing behaviour and appearances, reporting what people say to each other, but never telling the reader what the characters are thinking, never using interior monologue or free indirect style to let us overhear their private thoughts. Like Ivy Compton-Burnett, late Henry Green, some of the *nouveaux romanciers* . . . But in the end that kind of fiction is dissatisfying – or at least it's enjoyable mainly as a bracing change from the norm. If novelists stopped trying to represent consciousness altogether, readers would soon get withdrawal symptoms.

I think I made quite an impression on Ralph Messenger with my word-perfect quotation from *The Wings of the Dove*. I didn't tell him that I had used that passage in my seminar the day before, so it was fresh in my memory.

FRIDAY 28TH FEB. I received today through the internal post an offprint of an article from an academic journal called *Cognitive Science Review*, and a compliments slip from Ralph Messenger, with '*This might interest you – RM*' scribbled on it.

The article is called 'The Cognitive Architecture of Emotional States with Special Reference to Grief', written (if 'written' is the word, rather than 'bolted together') by three male academics at Suffolk University. It begins with a definition of grief: '*An extended process of cognitive reorganization characterized by the occurrence of negatively valenced perturbant states caused by an attachment structure reacting to a death event.*' So now we know. That was what I went through in the months following Martin's death: just a spot of cognitive reorganiza-tion. The desolating loneliness, the helpless weeping, the booby traps of memory triggered at every step (we watched *that* TV programme together, we bought *that* reading lamp together, we – God help me – ate *that* type of Sainsbury's fresh-chilled chicken curry together just a couple of hours before the aneurysm struck. Even the newspaper falling through the letter box in the morning would remind me of how we divided it over breakfast, so I switched to another one which I don't like half as much).

Halfway through the article was a diagram purporting to represent the architecture of the mind, all boxes and circles and ellipses, thrown into frantic activity (a tangle of swirling arrows and dotted lines) by the reaction of an attachment structure to news of a death event. 'Attachment structure' is I suppose the cognitive science term for love.

SATURDAY 1ST MARCH. Went into Cheltenham today for a little shopping therapy, though heaven knows just getting away from the campus for a few hours is therapeutic enough.

I'd been in Cheltenham only once before, a few years ago, to do a reading at the Literary Festival, and was hardly there long enough to acquire much sense of the place. This morning I drove helplessly round the one-way streets for some time until I spotted the neoclassical hulk of the Town Hall where they hold the Festival events (a building of dingy brownish stone, with a pompous over-sized portico, that looks clumsy against the surrounding Regency terraces of white stucco) and then I knew where I was. I left the car in the first car-park I came to, and made for the town centre.

It was a cold day, but dry and sunny, and I spent an enjoyable hour or so strolling along the Promenade, browsing in Waterstone's, buying a blouse in Laura Ashley and a pair of trousers in Country Casuals, having a light lunch in a café served by waitresses in old-fashioned uniforms with little white aprons. I briefly explored a long, two-storied shopping mall discreetly hidden in a parallel street, but quickly retreated from its airless atmosphere and tinkling muzak. I followed a sign to the Art Gallery and Museum, which specializes in the history of domestic art and design − appropriately enough, because everywhere you go in Cheltenham you see restoration and refurbishment of old houses and terraces going on, inside and out, a kind of collective cult of the House Beautiful. There's some quite interesting stuff about William Morris and the Arts and Crafts movement in the museum, and I bought a few art nouveau posters in the shop to brighten up my living room.

I walked back along the Promenade, past the splendid Regency facade of the Municipal Building, past the Italianate Neptune fountain foaming and glistening in the sun, past the Imperial Gardens, past the Queen's Hotel, serene, white and majestic like a pre-war Cunarder at its moorings, to Montpellier Street, which Caroline Messenger had recommended to me, and which indeed proved to be charming, its boutiques, specialist shops and galleries snugly housed in a well-preserved Georgian thoroughfare. There's a wonderful rotunda at the top modelled on the Pantheon in Rome which has been very elegantly turned into a Lloyds bank.

I was thinking to myself, how agreeable this is, what a nice time I'm having, but there's one thing missing – someone to share it with, or report it to; and as I had that thought, gazing abstractedly into the window of a health-food shop, and feeling a cold qualm of incipient depression, who should emerge from the shop, heralded by the ping of an antique doorbell, but Carrie herself, like the answer to a prayer. She was dressed in a bright red topcoat, her blonde hair was long and loose under a mohair knitted cap, her cheeks glowed rosily, and her sickle lips opened on perfect teeth smiling broadly in recognition. She invited me back to her house for a cup of tea, and I accepted with only the polite minimum of hesitation.

Carrie had parked her car in a nearby residential street, Lansdown Crescent, a superb sweeping curve of terraced town houses. 'Nicholas Beck has bought one of these,' Carrie said. 'He's doing it up exquisitely. Very elegant of course, but not really convenient for modern family life. Lots of stairs, no garages, no gardens to speak of.' I said that was usually the case in spa towns, where everything was built for rental. 'You're absolutely right,' she said, as she drove away. '*Our* yard is rather small for the size of the house, but it serves its purpose. And we have a cottage in the country about half an hour away, near Stow, which we use at weekends. You must visit.'

The Messengers live in a part of the town called Pittville, after the developer Joseph Pitt who laid it out in the 1820s. 'Sounds like "Pitsville" to an American ear,' said Carrie. 'You can imagine how my friends back home laugh when I tell them where we live.' But I imagine she has the last laugh when they visit her. Pittville is a delightful garden-city estate of fine houses and elegant terraces, set in landscaped parkland surmounted by a vast neoclassical spa. Apparently you can still take the water in the Pump Room there, unlike in the Lloyds bank. The Messengers' house is a magnificent double-fronted detached villa in Greek Revival style, with a pair of massive Corinthian columns that rise through two stories. In gleaming white stucco it resembles a vast old-fashioned wedding cake, but there's nothing absurd or vulgar about it, the proportions are so perfect. In the drawing room Carrie poured Earl Grey from a Queen Anne teapot into Spode chinaware, and offered me toasted teacakes and home-made strawberry preserve. She is one of those impressive American women who seem to know how English life should be lived rather better than we do – and she has the means to set an exacting standard in practice. The house is beautifully decorated and furnished in appropriate style, right down to the repro brass taps in the downstairs cloakroom and the Early Victorian rocking horse in the family room. Carrie said Nicholas Beck helped her to acquire the choicest pieces of furniture, driving round the local countryside to auctions and antique shops being his favourite occupation. The numerous paintings on the wall, mostly American primitives and minor French impressionists, were however collected by Carrie herself. She did graduate work in art history, she told me, writing her dissertation on Berthe Morisot 'before she was rediscovered'. A small oil by Morisot, of a young girl reading, is her most treasured possession – and must indeed be worth a fortune now.

The youngest of their four children, Hope, was in the family room when we looked in, sprawled on a bean bag, watching a Walt Disney video on a portable television: a pretty, freckled, mopheaded eight-year-old in brightly patterned leggings, who grinned and said 'Hi' when I was introduced, exposing an orthodontic brace. The eldest child, Emily, seventeen, a tall, handsome, Californian-style blonde who takes after her mother, came in while we were having tea, with a new pair of shoes she had just bought. I wondered if the high heels and platform soles were really a good idea, given her height, but kept my counsel. Carrie didn't turn a hair when it transpired that the shoes had cost £89. Having noticed my shopping bags, mother and daughter persuaded me to display my modest purchases, and we had the kind of pleasantly trivial women's conversation about clothes and fashion which I haven't had since Lucy left home. When Emily was out of the room for a while, Carrie told me that she was her daughter by her first husband, from whom she is divorced. Emily has retained a perceptible American twang, whereas the other children speak with English accents.

As dusk turned to darkness outside, Carrie drew the heavy velour curtains and pressed a button at the side of the hearth to ignite the simulated-coal gas fire – a concession to modernity which she sought to mitigate by mentioning that they had a real hearth fire at 'Horseshoes', Horseshoes evidently being the name of their country cottage. Then Ralph came in with his two sons, Mark (fifteen) and Simon (twelve) – though they were introduced to me as 'Polo' and 'Sock'. All the children have nicknames whose derivations were explained to me in due course. 'Polo' is a contraction of 'Marco Polo', and 'Sock' is derived from 'Socrates', assigned to Simon because of his propensity for asking questions. Hope is known as 'Kitten' because of her petite build, and Emily as 'Flipper' because of a childhood passion for dolphins which she has long outgrown. Needless to say all these nicknames, like those on the computers in the Holt Belling building, were assigned by Ralph. It seems to be his way of stamping his personality on his domain. He also calls Carrie 'Blondie' from time to time. Perhaps she and the children call him 'Messenger' in mild retaliation.

Simon and Mark immediately went off to the kitchen to forage for food, unwinding long striped scarves from around their necks. They had been to Bath to watch a rugby match. 'Male bonding,' Ralph said to me with a grin. 'Carrie thinks it's very important.' He was in high good humour, and seemed pleased to find me in his house. 'You *like* going,' said Carrie, hitting him lightly on the shoulder. 'Well I used to play when I was young,' he admitted, and I could imagine him, head down like a bull, his broad shoulders locked in a scrum, thrusting and pushing in the mud. He is a very physical person – kissed Carrie when he came in, gave Emily a hug, and set Hope on his knee – and they responded with unselfconscious pleasure to his touch. I couldn't help comparing in retrospect the restrained body language of our own family life. Martin and I rarely hugged the children once they were out of infancy; they seemed to find it embarrassing – or was it we who were inhibited? We didn't hug each other much, either, now I came to think of it, unless we were actually making love. I was suddenly filled with regret and remorse at the thought of all the neglected opportunities for touching each other, lost now for ever. I envied the Messenger family their easy physical intimacy, touching, squeezing, patting, leaning against each other . . . Then I remembered seeing Ralph kissing Marianne Richmond, and reflected that there is a price to be paid for everything. At least I never had to worry about Martin's fidelity.

Ralph offered drinks and I accepted a small sherry, saying that then I would have to be off. I had no urge to leave the cosy room, but I didn't want to outstay my welcome. 'We're dining out tonight, otherwise I'd have invited you to take pot luck with us,' said Carrie, as if reading my thoughts, and I believed her. '*Are* we dining out, Blondie?' said Ralph, frowning. 'You know we are, Messenger,' said Carrie. 'At the VCs.' 'I forgot,' he groaned. 'Come to lunch at Horseshoes tomorrow,' Carrie said to me. 'Or next Sunday.' I would have loved to accept the invitation for tomorrow but some silly genteel principle of reserve made me defer the pleasure for another week. They really are an extraordinarily nice and hospitable couple. Perhaps when you're so rich and fulfilled it's easy to be nice to other people. Or perhaps – an even more cynical thought – it's a way of converting other people's envy into gratitude.

When I rose from my chair to go, Ralph asked me where I was parked, and insisted on driving me there, warmly seconded by Carrie. I submitted gracefully. In the car (a big Mercedes estate) I thanked him for sending me the offprint. He asked me what I thought of it. I said I had found it rather alienating, the jargon and the diagrams seemed so remote from the actual experience of grief.

'It's only a model,' he said.

'But if you want to make a robot that really feels grief . . .'

'Oh, that was just a debating point.'

'You mean it's not really possible?' I said.

'It's possible,' he said. 'But it would be a hugely expensive and time-consuming project, and what use would it be – a robot whose cognitive functions could be drastically disturbed by random events – just like a human being?'

Then what was the point of the article, I asked.

'The mind is a virtual machine. Sometimes you can learn a lot from studying a machine when it's malfunctioning, even in theory.'

'Is that what grief is, then?' I said. 'A malfunction?' I didn't really want to get into an argument after receiving so much kindness from him and Carrie, but I couldn't keep an ironic tone out of my voice, and he gave me a quick appraising glance.

'Well,' he said. 'It's hard to see what it's *for*, in evolutionary terms. I mean, compared say with jealousy – which is equally disabling, equally unpleasant, but has an obvious function. Ensuring that no other male impregnates your mate.'

'What about female jealousy?' I asked

'Very similar: it secures the male's exclusive interest in feeding and protecting her offspring. You could say, I suppose,' he continued, as if thinking aloud, 'that the desire to avoid the pain of bereavement is an incentive to look after one's mate and offspring. But there are already enough other powerful incentives to do that. And anyway, knowing that you did everything possible to avoid being bereaved doesn't seem to alleviate the pain when it happens.'

'And sometimes there is nothing you could have done to avoid it,' I said with feeling, but he didn't seem to register my allusion to Martin.

'Quite so,' he said. 'All these funerals you see on television after terrorist bombs, earthquakes, and so on. People beside themselves with grief. Weeping, wailing, thrashing about. It's all so *excessive*, so disproportionate to any possible evolutionary payoff. As Darwin said, "Crying is a puzzler." '

I was struck by the phrase: '*Crying is a puzzler.*' Ralph said it was in Darwin's notebooks somewhere. He promised to look up the passage for me.

When we reached the car-park he politely got out of the car and offered to escort me to mine, but I said it wasn't necessary and this time I got my way. We shook hands, and I had a fleeting

○ ○

presentiment that he was going to kiss me on the cheek, but he didn't.

6

ONE, two, three, testing, testing . . . There's no need to test this gadget, you can see the words appearing right in front of your eyes on the screen, but I'm making an audiorecording at the same time so I can go over the text later and put in the dots for pauses . . . I'd no idea this voice recognition software was so good . . . You'd think a Centre for Cognitive Science would have the latest dope on such things but to my amazement when I asked around there wasn't anyone on the staff who actually owned such a program or had any experience of using one . . . They seemed to think it was some kind of toy, something you might buy at Dixon's for your kids at Christmas but nothing of serious interest, just shows you how conservative and blinkered academics are . . . Anyway, Voicemaster arrived on Friday and I spent a few hours training it. I had to start by reading a couple of passages, one from Lewis Carroll another from the *Times*, so it could learn my accent . . . It produces a fair amount of gibberish at first, but you correct it on screen and gradually it learns your way of pronouncing vowels, which is the main variable, and by the end of the day it was only making about one mistake every other line, which isn't bad, in fact a lot more accurate than my typing . . . The software works by matching your input of phonemes against a database of frequently occurring collocations . . . so a free association monologue is just about the most difficult possible task because the context keeps changing . . . The program is also a bit prudish . . . refused to transcribe the word 'fuck' at first . . . came up with all kinds of alternatives, 'suck', 'ruck', 'tuck' *etcetera* . . . but I've taught it to talk dirty. So here we are . . . It's Sunday 2nd March, 8.45 a.m., yes 8.45 . . . because Carrie got a bit stroppy when I told her on the way home from the VC's last night that I . . . God what a boring evening that was . . . the Richmonds were there but no opportunity for a quick snog with Marianne . . . at one point she gave me the eye as she went out to the toilet but I took no notice, what did she think I would do, follow her out and knock on the door of the loo to be let in . . . ? She's getting reckless, Carrie might easily have intercepted that glance, fortunately she was gossiping with Lady Viv at the time . . . I was talking to Stan . . . Sir Stan and Lady Viv, what a pair of names for a Vice Chancellor and his consort, sounds like a music hall act . . . But he told me that Donaldson has accepted the honorary degree which is good news, highly chuffed apparently, that should help with our funding . . . Anyway . . . I'm here at this ungodly hour because Carrie got a bit stroppy when I mentioned I was coming in again this morning to continue the experiment. *'Don't you spend enough hours in that place already, for God's sake?'* Fair point I had to admit, but I was itching to try out this software on a stream of consciousness exercise, so I promised I'd go in first thing, be back home by ten in time to drive to Horseshoes, the kids are never up before then anyway on a Sunday . . . Of course I could load the software on to my computer at home and use it there, but I would feel inhibited, afraid someone might overhear, given the sort of thing that seems to pop into my head when I'm idly ruminating . . . even though they'd have to creep up the staircase and put their ear to the door . . . the fact is you feel very vulnerable, exposed, speaking your private thoughts aloud, you need to be quite confident nobody could possibly overhear . . . So here I am at my desk in my office at the Centre once again, a mug of cappuccino with cinnamon no sugar beside me, but this time wearing a headset with microphone just in front and to one side of my mouth as per instructions and ready to go . . . I'll only correct major errors as I go along, the text can be tidied up later . . . In the car just now it occurred to me that it might be interesting to do not another random dip into the stream of consciousness, but a specific exercise of memory. Of course in a sense all consciousness is memory, we can't be conscious of the future, though we might try to predict it, and we aren't even conscious of the present strictly speaking, because mind states always lag behind brain states as that chap, neuroscientist, what's his name . . . Libet, he showed that conscious awareness of a decision to act always lags behind the associated brain activity by about half a second . . . so in a sense every moment of our lives is already in the past when we experience it . . . you might say consciousness is a continual action replay . . . But I'm talking about long-term memory, I'm going to try and recall an experience distant in time and see or try to see from the transcript how the mind recovers . . . recuperates . . . reconstructs the past and the extent to which shorter-term memories triggered by association interfere with or interact with this process . . . So what shall it be? What long-term memory shall I try to activate?

My first fuck, how about that, yes, no problem, her knickers . . . The first thing I think of is her easing her knickers over her hips . . . looking at me slyly from under her hair falling forward across her face, I was transfixed, I'd never seen a woman undress before . . . except in films of course . . . but in those days you never saw a woman actually taking off her knickers on the screen, come to that I'm not sure I've ever . . . I mean you might see them sailing through the air or a close-up of them on the floor, but not the woman actually . . . perhaps it's too awkward or homely an action, difficult to do gracefully or erotically, stooping and bending and standing on one leg then the other . . . Strippers for instance always have some kind of snap fastener or velcro so they can whip them off in a single movement . . . hah, that girl in that place in Soho what was it who took her g-string off before her bra . . . she wasn't thinking, or rather she was thinking of something other than stripping, daydreaming, it was mid-afternoon, a dead hour, with only a few punters in the place, Christ knows what I was doing there, between meetings perhaps, a bit boozed and randy after a business lunch perhaps, I can't remember, but there I was with half a dozen solitary wankers, slumped in our chairs in the violet-tinted half-darkness watching this girl in a cone of spotlight going through her routine like a sleepwalker, shedding bits and pieces of her costume as she shuffled her feet and rocked her hips to recorded disco music, until she was down to her bra and g-string . . . and then absent-mindedly she took off the g-string before the bra, hah . . . and we men in the audience all sat up as if we'd had a mild electric shock . . . a look of acute embarrassment came over her face and she faltered in her dance and lost the tempo as she realized what she'd done and she blushed, she actually blushed, and muttered '*Sorry*', the first time she'd spoken on that or I bet any other stage, strippers never speak, and then she *put the g-string back on again* and went on with her robotic routine . . . Robotic, yes, if you could embed the hardware in convincing synthetic flesh it would be relatively easy to make a robot stripper, I mean the program would be so simple . . . But for a moment, just for a moment, she'd seemed like a real human being, unpredictable, fallible, vulnerable . . . somebody laughed in the darkness, a short, barking guffaw, which provoked a few other chuckles in the scattered audience, and the mood of gloomy onanistic eroticism was broken . . . Because the protocol of striptease is strict, a certain order must be observed in the exposure of parts . . . any deviation will break the frame of the event, make it seem *natural* . . . like undressing for bed at home . . . everybody has their own way of doing that, their own order, and sometimes you change it if it suits you . . . Carrie for instance will sometimes take off her knickers, panties she calls them, before her bra, and walk around the bedroom like that if she's going to use the bidet, at least she used to, doesn't walk around naked so much any more, getting selfconscious about her figure . . . Martha took her knickers off last, but then that was a kind of striptease, she was looking at me all the time, enjoying her power over me . . . I was sitting on the bed with an erection making a peak like Everest in my Y-fronts, my eyes wide, hardly breathing, mouth dry but unable to swallow . . . my ears pricked for sounds from outside, even though I'd seen Tom Beard drive away that morning in his old pick-up truck with Sol in the passenger seat and a trailer full of ewes past their prime he was disposing of at the market, what was it they called it . . . '*casting for age*', yes, even though I knew he was going to be away till late that night still I was afraid that something might happen, a breakdown for instance or an accident and he might come back unexpectedly . . . '*Don't worry, love,*' she said, as she led me by the hand from the kitchen to the stairs. '*You can hear a car coming from miles away, and that old gate squeaks like the devil . . .*' She led me upstairs to her bedroom and drew the curtains but they hardly darkened the room, the afternoon sun shone through the thin material bathing her in a soft pink light, like a stripper on a stage . . . and she began to undress, taking off each item and folding it carefully over the back of a windsor chair . . . '*What you waiting for then?*' she said and I gawped at her like an idiot. '*Don't be shy, it won't be the first time I seen you with no clothes on,*' she said, meaning that afternoon when she saw me swimming in the stream with the dogs . . . A sweltering day, we'd just moved the flock to a new pasturage, the sheep were eagerly cropping the succulent fresh grass, Tom had gone off on his tractor to see to a broken fence, and there was this deliciously cool stream which we'd forded with the flock further up, running clear over pebbles and slabs of slate with a place under a ledge deep enough for swimming . . . I couldn't resist, threw off all my clothes and plunged in, delicious . . . the two Border collies watched me enviously from the bank, panting in the heat, their tongues lolling from their mouths but too well-trained to stir until I called them to join me, '*Come!*' and they dashed barking into the water and paddled towards me with their noses in the air and circled round me as if I was a stray sheep . . . I fooled them by diving and popping up behind them and laughed with glee at their surprise and turned on my back and floated staring up into the endless blue of the summer sky, drifting with the current until I reached the shallows and felt the stones on the stream's bed gently graze my back . . . I stood up and began to wade upstream towards the deep place with the dogs gambolling and splashing at my heels and then I was suddenly aware of Martha on the far bank, sitting on her bicycle with one foot on the ground, watching me with a smile on her face which broadened to a grin as I stopped and hastily covered my crotch with my hands like a footballer facing a free-kick . . . She called out where was Tom and when I told her she pedalled off with a wave . . . I stood stock still in the water with my hands over my cock till she was out of sight . . . it began to rise and thicken as I wondered how long she had been watching me with that smile on her face and after a quick look round to make sure nobody else was watching I jerked myself off, shooting my seed into the sunny air and the fast-moving stream, observed only by the patient, incurious, uncensorious dogs. Because I fancied Martha oh yes, but I hadn't dared hope till that day that she might reciprocate, though she was always nice to me, serving me choice tidbits of food at table and asking if I had any washing, ironing my shirts better than my mother did, I knew she liked me all right, but after all she was a married woman twice my age . . . Tom though was older than her and according to Martha not much interested in sex or much good at . . . *'Ten minutes on a Saturday night is about his limit . . .'* He'd taken a young wife in middle-age hoping to beget a son to leave the farm to and when no children came he lost interest, blamed Martha for being barren, so she told me one day, refused to consider that the problem might be his, refused to have any tests of his sperm-count, refused to discuss the matter, even though he spent – or perhaps *because* he spent most of his working days organizing the copulation of sheep . . . So it was the classic situation, the older husband, the frisky young wife, the young lodger brimming with spunk, only seventeen, still a schoolboy but, as Martha said, or rather whispered, *'big for your age, love,'* a schoolboy from South London who had been sent to live on a sheepfarm in the Dales for his health, for fresh air and exercise after a spell of glandular fever . . . our GP's idea, Tom was a distant relative of his . . . and not a bad idea, either, I grew strong and fit from the work, walking miles a day over the Dales, striding up twenty per cent inclines, wrestling with sheep for foot-rot inspection, holding them down as Tom cut out the infected tissue . . . my muscles hardened, my shoulders straightened, I must have looked pretty good to Martha wading stark naked in the stream, in fact she told me so later, *'Like a statue in a museum, like one of them Greek gods made out of white marble . . .'* I saw the frank admiration in her smile as she watched me from her bicycle, so it wasn't entirely a surprise when that day in the kitchen . . . though I could still scarcely believe my luck, for that matter I can hardly believe it now, imagine, a seventeen-year-old schoolboy whose body was a testosterone power station constantly on the edge of melt-down and his mind . . . his mind a pornographic theatre that never closed . . . but whose sexual experience extended no further than french-kissing girls from our sister grammar school up the road in the lunch hour and maybe squeezing their tits under their serge uniform blazers if you were lucky . . . to lose my virginity to an experienced, warm-blooded fully grown woman . . . who laughed and told me not to worry when I came prematurely as inevitably I did . . . but I'm getting ahead of myself . . . where was I, ah yes, that day Tom and Sol his shepherd went off to the market and I was left alone on the farm with Martha and came in to eat my lunch in the kitchen, sitting at the deal table, the wood's grain worn into grooves by years of scrubbing, as she served me and then sat and watched me eat, I was aware, inexperienced as I was, I was aware that the air was heavy with sexual invitation . . . it was in the sway of Martha's hips as she moved about the kitchen, it was in the absence of the faded flowered pinafore she usually wore, allowing me to see the shape of her brassiere under her tight blouse and the faintest suggestion of cleavage where a button that might have been done up had been left undone, it was in the smell of shampoo from her freshly washed hair as she bent over my shoulder to put a plate of ham and cheese before me, it was in the faint smile that played over her lips as she sipped a cup of tea and watched me eat from the other side of the table, making casual conversation which I scarcely took in . . . No, I wasn't entirely surprised that when I got up to go back to work she detained me, using one of the oldest tricks in the book, '*I think I've got something in my eye, Ralph, would you have a look?*' making me stand very close to her, staring into her eye, tentatively pushing back her eyelid with my finger, feeling her breath on my cheek, feeling her bosom pressing against my chest, feeling her hands on the small of my back drawing me closer and hearing her murmur, '*Give us a kiss, Ralph, for the love of God . . .*' I kissed her and she kissed me back and I swayed and lost my balance and staggered and she laughed and said, '*Come upstairs and lie down, we'll be more comfortable,*' leading me towards the staircase by the hand, and when I said what if Tom comes back, '*Don't worry, love,*' she said, '*you can hear a car coming from miles away in this god-forsaken place,*' . . . but it wasn't just fear it was guilt too, because I liked Tom, dour and taciturn as he was . . . he was very decent to me, taught me the rudiments of sheep-farming and how to command the dogs, '*Come,*' '*Stay,*' '*Sit,*' '*Come bye*' to go left, '*Away to me*' to go right, '*That'll do*' to finish . . . It was a thrill to control the flock that way, by remote control, as if the dogs were connected to your brain like limbs . . . I didn't want to cuckold the man who had taught me that, not

77

that I knew the word then, but once we were in her bedroom and she began taking off her clothes there was no going back . . . '*What are you waiting for then?*' she said. '*Don't be shy, it won't be the first time I seen you with no clothes on,*' but I *was* shy, and turned my back on her as I hastily undressed down to my underpants so I missed her taking off her stockings, when I turned round she had her hands behind her back undoing her brassiere, an old-fashioned type, heavily stitched and sharply contoured, and as she shrugged it off her breasts tumbled out of the cups and spread themselves across her rib cage, outlined by half-moons of shadow . . . I sat down on the edge of the bed and watched as she scratched herself comfortably and then stooped to take off her knickers, old-fashioned knickers like the bra, French knickers I think they're called, with wide legs, lace-trimmed, peach-coloured silk or maybe satin, she must have put them on specially . . . Funny, I never thought of that until now, thirty-odd years after the event . . . they weren't the sort of knickers a sheepfarmer's wife would wear every day of the week . . . She stepped out of them, straightened up, dropped them on to the seat of the chair and stood before me, a naked woman in all her glory . . . not that she was classically beautiful, Martha, or girlie-magazine beautiful, her breasts sagged a bit, her waist was too thick and her legs too short, but she was the first naked woman I had ever seen in the flesh, and when she said, '*Well, d'you like what you see, Ralph Messenger?*' I whispered hoarsely *yes* in all sincerity, and she laughed softly and came over and stood in front of me so I was staring straight at her crotch sparsely fleeced with ginger pubic hair veiling but not concealing the pinky-brown crease of her cunt . . . '*Are you going to take your pants off or shall I do it for you?*' she said, and I stood up to take them off, having to pull the elastic waistband out like a catapult to get it over my tumescent cock . . . In fact I'm having a little trouble here with my Ralph Lauren trunks right now . . . recalling all this has given me a tremendous hard-on . . . I'll have to stand up for a moment, adjust my . . .

Ah that's better . . . The campus looks deserted, nobody about, no sign of Helen Reed this morning . . . intriguing woman, smart, quick on the uptake, a good arguer, prepared to stand up for herself, I like that, too many people think arguing about things that matter, arguing to win, is in bad taste somehow . . . good legs too I saw as she got out of the car last night, she was wearing one of those slit skirts which fell open as she swivelled on the seat showing a nice bit of thigh . . . I thought about giving her a kiss on the cheek when we said goodbye but decided against . . . there's something about her, a kind of ironic detachment . . . an alertness to the least hint of bullshit . . . made me think she wouldn't welcome it, would think I was taking liberties . . . Well no hurry, we'll be seeing plenty of her I think, Carrie seems to like her and she must be lonely as hell stuck in that maisonette on campus, I saw her eyes light up when Carrie said come to lunch next Sunday . . . *'Crying is a puzzler,'* I promised to look it up for her . . . not now though, back to the desk and Martha . . .

I told Carrie the story of Martha once, thinking it would turn her on, but we ended up having a row instead because she said it was abuse, sexual abuse . . . I said, rubbish, I was eager, willing . . . *'It doesn't matter,'* she said. *'She was a sexually frustrated adult who used your adolescent dick as a dildo . . .'* I said on the contrary she was a warm-blooded, big-hearted woman who taught me things about sex it took my contemporaries years to learn, if they ever learned them . . . Every boy should have a Martha, I said, she taught me to be a good lover . . . *'you mean she made you into a sex addict,'* Carrie said and turned over and went to sleep, we were in bed at the time, in the house in Pasadena . . . *'sex addict'* . . . typical Californian psychobabble, what could it possibly mean, addicted to sex, men are biologically programmed to want as much sex as they can get with as many women as they can get . . . only culture constrains our urge to copulate promiscuously . . . sometimes suppresses it completely of course, as with priests and monks, poor deluded sods, or almost completely, as in the case of Tom Beard . . . *'Ten minutes on a Saturday night is about his limit . . .'* He'd been a bachelor too long, a celibate bachelor, living with his widowed mother on an isolated farm, his only recreation the male camaraderie of the local pub, beer and tobacco, darts and dominoes . . . but Martha was different, she grew up in a market town in the Midlands where there were dances and cafés and a cinema and plenty of boys . . . she'd just been jilted, she told me, when she met Tom at a wedding and married him on the rebound, she was getting fed up with living at home with five siblings, sharing a bedroom with her youngest sister, Tom offered her a house of her own with a colour telly and carte blanche to order a modern fitted kitchen, and something about his slow silent dark good looks attracted her like the hero of a Western, but the physical side of the marriage was a disappointment from the outset . . . *'Comes of spending too much time with sheep, it's just tupping to him, a quick in and out,'* with no thought of Martha's pleasure . . . thought being the operative word, because what distinguishes human sex from animal sex is precisely that we are able to think about it, that's why we enjoy it, and enjoy each other's enjoyment . . . Watch two dogs copulating in the street or two monkeys in a cage or a ram serving a ewe, the males are getting some relief perhaps, like scratching an itch, like shitting or pissing, but pleasure is not the word that comes to mind, while the females seem to be just putting up with it . . . Do female animals have orgasms? I doubt it, must ask somebody in Zoology, but I bet the female orgasm was a discovery of *Homo sapiens* . . . or *Mulier sapiens* . . . and we developed bigger penises than the apes by natural selection, women tending to choose mates with big ones . . . not that there was anything the matter with Tom in that respect, as I knew from watching him piss out on the hillside, he had the equipment but he just didn't know how to use it to give a woman pleasure . . . Martha taught me that and I'm eternally grateful to her, as were many women subsequently who didn't know who they had to thank for the good times I gave them . . . you can't call it abuse, if she'd just been exploiting me she'd have been angry when I came all over her the moment she took my penis in her hand, but she just laughed and said *'Don't worry, love,'* and caressed and stroked me until I was hard again . . . by the end of my stay I could keep it in her for fifteen minutes without coming by reciting physics formulas silently to myself . . . incidentally even if there is some randy species of chimp that has discovered the female orgasm, I bet the males don't deliberately delay their ejaculation to prolong the female's pleasure . . . Martha got such pleasure out of the act there were tears of joy in her eyes afterwards . . . I think perhaps I like fucking mature women

80

more than young girls because of my first experience with Martha . . . they're so grateful it makes you feel proud . . . and physiologically they have a greater capacity for orgasm . . . we did it six or seven more times, in the evenings when Tom went down to the pub . . . as soon as the sound of his pick-up truck faded as it passed over the brow of the hill we went upstairs . . . But one evening it happened just as I'd feared, the truck broke down on his way to the pub and he walked back to the house to phone the AA and we heard the gate squeak when we were both at it on my bed, Christ that was a narrow escape, she just got her clothes back on in time and told me to stay in bed and pretend I wasn't feeling well . . . after that we were too scared to do it any more, at least I was . . . I had little doubt that Tom would've given me a thrashing if he'd caught us *in flagrante*, and I had visions of being sent back home in disgrace and having to confess to my parents which was even worse to contemplate . . . After the holidays I told my best friend at school all about it and he refused to believe me, he thought I was making it all up, '*You lying bastard, Messenger,*' he said. I didn't argue, I was quite relieved in a way . . . it seemed a kind of betrayal of Martha to tell, of Tom too, and yet I had to tell somebody, I was bursting with the knowledge of what I had experienced, but it suited me not to be believed because there was less chance of the story being circulated and perhaps getting back to my parents . . . or our GP. I wrote to Tom and Martha thanking them for my stay and we exchanged Christmas cards for a couple of years, but then we lost touch and I never saw or heard from either of them again . . . Christ it's a quarter to ten [*recording ends*]

7

MONDAY 3RD MARCH. Spent all yesterday and most of today reading the students' work-in-progress, their major projects for the year, novels (or in two cases collections of short stories) which they started last semester under Russell Marsden's supervision, or brought up to the University with them, already under way. I feel rather jaded by the experience. It's not that they're badly written – on the contrary, the general level of ability is high – it's just that there are too many of them, too many to take in all at once. Every time I open another folder there's another imagined world to be inhabited, a whole new set of characters with names to be memorized and relationships of consanguinity and affinity to be sorted out, times and seasons to be noted, physical appearances to be pictured, connections of cause and effect to be inferred . . .

There's Rachel McNulty's glum chronicle of going through the menarche on a dairy farm in County Armagh; Simon Bellamy's deft satirical comedy about a group of young people starting up a style magazine in Soho; Robert Drayton's memory monologue of a condemned prisoner on the eve of execution in some imaginary African state ruled by a mad dictator; Frieda Sinclair's unflinching tales of young women dancing, drinking, shagging and puking in clubs from Inverness to Ibiza; Gilbert Baverstock's novel about a pathologically shy insurance clerk who falls in love with a girl in his office and communicates with her by Email, pretending to be a hip screenwriter in Los Angeles; Thomas Vaughan's gritty historical novel about a strike in the Rhondda Valley coalmines in the nineteenth century; Chuck Romero's *Bildungsroman* about a young man losing his virginity and finding his vocation in Providence, Rhode Island (where Chuck comes from); Farat Khan's interlinked short stories about cultural and generational conflict in the Asian community of

Leicester (where she comes from); Saul Goldman's Oedipal ding-dong between self-made Jewish businessman and gay artistic son; Franny Smith's funny and appalling multi-viewpoint portrait of a Liverpool sink school; and Aurora da Silva's kinky fabulation about a New Age Institute on a Greek island that runs courses on sado-masochism, body-piercing, tantric sex, and recreational drug-taking. That's eleven self-contained fictional worlds. There should be twelve, but Sandra Pickering hasn't submitted her folder yet. Eleven is quite enough to go on with, however. Already they're becoming confused in my mind, and I'm afraid that I'll make some frightful blunders when I see the students individually, getting the names of characters wrong and the story lines muddled up.

It's a very unnatural way to read, of course, jumping from one unfinished story to another, but it made me think about the prolific production of fiction in our culture. Is it over-production? Are we in danger of accumulating a fiction-mountain – an immense quantity of surplus novels, like the butter mountains and milk lakes of the EEC? I remember Ralph Messenger's dry remark, '*Whether the world needs more novelists is a matter of opinion.*' His own opinion was pretty obvious.

Of course one can argue that there's a basic human need for narrative: it's one of our fundamental tools for making sense of experience – has been, back as far as you can go in history. But does this, I ask myself, necessarily entail the endless multiplication of *new* stories? Before the rise of the novel there wasn't the same obligation on the storyteller – you could relate the old familiar tales over and over, the matter of Troy, the matter of Rome, the matter of Britain . . . giving them a new spin as times and manners changed. But for the last three centuries writers have been required to make up a new story *every time*. Not absolutely new, of course – it's been pointed out often enough that at a certain level there are only a finite number of plots – but the plot must be fleshed out each time with a new set of characters, and worked out in a new set of circumstances. When you think of the billions of real people who have lived on this earth, each with their unique personal histories, that we shall never have time to know, it seems extraordinary, even perverse, that we should bother to invent all these additional pretend-lives. And it *is* a bother. So much that in reality is simply 'given' has to be *decided* when you're writing fiction. Facts have to be represented by pseudo-facts, laboriously invented and painstakingly described. The reader must register and memorize these facts in order to follow your story, but they are flushed away almost as soon as the book is finished, to make room for another story. Before long nothing remains in the reader's memory but a name or two, a few vague impressions of people, an indistinct recollection of the plot, and a general sense of having been entertained, or not, as the case may be. It's frightening to think of how many novels I must have read in my lifetime, and how little I retain of the substance of most of them. Should I really be encouraging these bright young people to add their quotient to the dust-heap of forgotten pseudo-lives? Would they perhaps be more profitably occupied designing computer models of the mind in Ralph Messenger's Centre for Cognitive Science?

TUESDAY 4TH MARCH. No mail today. I haven't had a letter from Lucy since I got here, although I wrote to tell her the address. Maybe she didn't get it in time – she said she was going off with some friends on a trip to the Barrier Reef. I did arrange with the Post Office to have my mail redirected, but perhaps one slipped through the net. Probably there's a letter from her lying on the doormat in the hall at 58 Bloomfield Crescent under a heap of junk mail addressed to the Occupier, fliers for local shops and free samples of shampoo. My tenants haven't arrived yet – departure delayed by illness – so I can't ask them to check. Paul hasn't written for ages either, but then he always was a hopeless correspondent. And anyway he's a man. I worry about Lucy so far away from home, and reading all these novels about young people hasn't helped. There's so much about drugs, casual sex, getting drunk. Of course I made sure she knew all about the facts of life, contraception *etc.* at an early age, but I don't actually know whether she's still a virgin or not. Is that a good thing or a bad thing? Carrie confided on Saturday that Emily is sleeping with her boyfriend and tells her all about it, which I suppose shows an admirable degree of mutual trust, but something in me recoils from such intimacy between parent and child.

WEDNESDAY 5TH MARCH. Answer to Monday's concluding question: a resounding 'No.'

I ran into Ralph Messenger in the campus bookshop today, and mentioned that I was a little worried about Lucy. 'Don't you have Email?' he asked, and I had to admit that I didn't, and anyway Lucy doesn't have a computer. 'I bet she has access to one,' he said, and he's probably right, since she's working in an office. 'You should get yourself wired,' he said. I think I shall.

Talking about Lucy reminded me of his German postgraduate student's project on mother-love, and he invited me back to the Centre to see it. It was a great anticlimax: nothing but a glorified computer game, really. There was this woman-shaped icon on the screen representing a mother, and three smaller icons representing her children, all demanding to be fed and clothed and looked after, and encountering various hazards like falling in the fishpond, or getting scalded by a cooking pot, or running out of the house and into the road, and the mother was having to make decisions all the time about directing her attention to where it was most urgently needed – putting hungry child A on hold while she pulled child B from under the wheels of an advancing bus *etc., etc.* The poor woman was in constant skittering motion, coping with one emergency after another. I was reminded of the video games in the arcade in the Students' Union. Anything further removed from the emotional experience of motherhood would be difficult to imagine. I'm afraid I laughed out loud. Carl looked downcast, and Ralph a little irked. He said it was only an experimental model, and at an early stage of development.

As I was leaving, he gave me directions to their cottage near Stow-on-the-Wold, and said, 'Bring a swimming costume. We have a hot tub.' I presume it's one of those big jacuzzi things they have in the open air in California. Must be a bit chilly in Gloucestershire in early March, surely?

My faith in the Creative Writing course, or at least in my own ability to teach it, has been strengthened considerably by a very good response to the 'What is it Like to be a Bat?' exercise. I've just looked at the work handed in yesterday, and there are some excellent, if rather ribald, parodies or pastiches. The best ones are by Simon Bellamy, Frieda Sinclair, Aurora da Silva and Gilbert Baverstock. I'm going to photocopy them and send them to Ralph Messenger.

THURSDAY 6TH MARCH. My tenants have arrived at Bloomfield Crescent and have been phoning me on and off all day with questions about the house. Where is the timer clock for the central heating? What do they do with 'trash'? Where is the instruction manual for the washing machine? (answer: lost) How do you light the gas fire in the lounge? (answer: with a spill, the automatic spark is broken) Is there another 'icebox' apart from the very small one in the kitchen? (answer: I'm afraid not) And so on. I suppose I should have written out more exhaustive instructions for them. They sound quite nice, Professor Otto Weismuller and his wife Hazel, if a little tone-deaf to English humour. When I told Professor Weismuller that 'You just have to be firm' with the flush handle in the downstairs loo, and 'Don't take no for an answer,' he thought I was telling him to call a plumber.

However, one bit of good news: there are two airmail letters from Australia which they are going to forward to me soonest.

FRIDAY 7TH MARCH. Long article in the paper today about Jean-Dominique Bauby, a French writer, journalist, editor of *Elle* magazine, aged forty-three, who had a kind of stroke that left him in a condition called 'locked-in syndrome', conscious but unable to move a muscle – except for one, his left eyelid, which he used to communicate and – astonishingly – to dictate a book about his experience. He worked out with a friend a system of blinking this one eye to semaphore letters of the alphabet, to make up words and sentences. Incredibly laborious and time-consuming, but it worked.

The book has just been published to critical acclaim, and apparently there was a TV documentary about him that had a huge impact. No wonder. It's an extraordinary story, even in the newspaper report, both tragic and inspiring.

In a way it seems the worst thing that could happen to a human being – to be locked inside your body, completely helpless, unable to speak or gesture, unable to even nod or shake your head. Apparently he was in a coma for four weeks, and it was some time before the staff at the hospital realized that he had regained consciousness. They had written him off as being in a vegetative state. It must have been like being buried alive, hearing people walking about above your grave and not being able to attract their attention. Jean-Dominique Bauby himself compares it to being in a diving bell. His book is called *The Diving Bell and the Butterfly*, the butterfly being his thoughts that flutter about inside the diving bell, unable to get out – until he invented the eyelid code. That's the inspiring side of the story: that he did in the end find a way to communicate his plight. It's tremendous testimony to the strength and resilience of the human spirit, its refusal to be silenced.

Of course I can't help thinking of poor Martin, whose aneurysm was by the sound of it rather similar to the Frenchman's stroke, and might have had the same effect, perhaps. In fact . . . the horrible thought occurred to me that perhaps Martin wasn't dead when they let me in to see him at the hospital but suffering from locked-in syndrome, but of course that's nonsense, he was dead, his heart had stopped and he wasn't breathing. I can't wish it had been otherwise, I don't think I could have coped with looking after someone in Bauby's condition. Selfish of me, but that's the truth.

SATURDAY 8TH MARCH. I brought a swimming costume with me from London, thinking that I might take some exercise at the Sports Centre pool here (a good resolution so far not acted upon), but when I got it out and looked at it this morning it seemed a shabby, faded thing, so I went into Gloucester to buy a new one. Gloucester rather than Cheltenham because I had a silly fear of running into Carrie in

○ ○

the shop by some bizarre coincidence and having to reveal that I was buying a new swimming costume specifically to cut a good figure in her hot tub.

A somewhat anxious business always, for a woman, buying a swimming costume, especially as one gets older. No garment exposes so cruelly the increasing imperfections of the body. Looking at myself in the angled mirrors of the changing cubicle, I was dismayed to see a network of indigo veins, like hairline crazing in old china, or the lines in Danish Blue cheese, spreading from behind both knees.

After much searching I found a plain black one-piece with a halter neck that I thought looked quite becoming, but I tried it on over my knickers, as very reasonably requested by the store for reasons of hygiene, and when I put it on again at home, sans underwear, behold: tendrils of pubic hair sprouting luxuriantly from under the cutaway crotch. So now I must shave myself. What a bore. I feel punished for my vanity.

One redeeming feature of the expedition was that I saw Gloucester Cathedral for the first time. It's not huge, but beautifully proportioned, built of mellow Cotswold stone, with a remarkable square Perpendicular tower that has delicate fretted stonework running round the top like a balustrade. The cloisters are exquisite – among the finest in the country my *Visitor's Guide* claimed, and with justification, I should say. Edward II is buried here. All I know about him is from Marlowe's play, which may not be reliable, but makes him seem like a real person who once lived and breathed, not just a name in a history book. It seemed extraordinary to stand beside the remains of somebody who lived seven hundred years ago, and know who he was. If Ralph Messenger is right, the atoms of his dust are indestructible. But it is my mind that preserves his identity, and makes a connection between us.

As I trod the worn paving of the ancient aisles, pausing at intervals to admire fine brasses and carved statuary, another literary association came to mind. In *The Golden Bowl* Charlotte and the Prince begin their adulterous affair at Gloucester, delaying their return to London

from a country houseparty on the pretext of viewing the cathedral –
and there's a reference to the tomb of Edward II, I'm sure. Did they
really visit it, to give circumstantial plausibility to their story when
they returned to their respective spouses, or did they spend every
stolen moment in their room at the inn selected by the resourceful
Charlotte? I don't have the novel to hand to check. James probably
doesn't say, anyway.

I had lunch afterwards at the Cosy Pew Café, just round the
corner from the Cathedral, poring over every word in the guide
because I had brought nothing else with me to read. I wondered
despondently if this was the spinsterish future that awaits me:
collecting cathedrals and reading at the table in twee restaurants.
Perhaps buying the new swimming costume was some kind of
instinctive gesture of resistance to such a fate. In which case, let us
shave ourself uncomplainingly.

8

What is it Like to be a Freetail Bat?
By M★rt★n Am★s

WELL, we hang out a lot during the day. We hang out in caves, crevices, under eaves, inside roofs, anywhere that's dark and warm. Caves are favourite. We hang from the ceiling and crap on the floor, only it seems like we're hanging from the floor and crapping on the ceiling because we're upside down. Crapping when you're upside down is an art. The crap generates heat as it decomposes; also, of course, a smell.

When it gets dark we go out to eat, insects mostly. We gobble them up on the wing, using our radar equipment. *Beep, beep, beep, beep, beepbeepbeepbeep POW!* It's cool. I can zap two fruitflies inside a second, flying blind. Tom Cruise, eat your heart out.

Then we go back to the cave and crap on the floor. We also crap during flight, to reduce the weight we're carrying. You could say that crapping was one of our chief occupations in life. Eating insects and crapping.

Sex is not so hot, to be honest. We only fuck for six weeks in the year – the whole colony is on heat at the same time. You can imagine the scene: thousands of guys milling about in the cave frantically trying to cram twelve months' screwing into a lousy six weeks. You can seriously damage your health.

The women are only interested in one thing: your sperm. They have some sort of gynaecological trick of secreting it inside their snatches until such time as they want to get pregnant. Then they all fuck off to a nursery cave in some warm spot to have the kids. Only women and children are allowed inside. Back in the male cave we hang out and make do with clawjobs.

I wouldn't mind if the women looked after the newborn kids properly. But when they go out to eat they leave the kids on their own, in unsupervised playgroups, rolling about and fighting with each other, amongst all the bat poo and insect corpses and fruit husks on the cave floor. Or else they hang them in rows on the walls and ceiling and sometimes the poor little fuckers fall off their perches and onto the deck, or they try to fly before their radar is properly tuned and have accidents, crashing into the walls and each other. Our infant mortality rate is a disgrace.

If you survive the nursery, though, life expectancy is quite good. You can expect to live for ten years. I'm nine and a half.

What is it Like to be a Vampire Bat?
By Irv*ne W*lsh

We goat back to the auld cave aboot the same time, Gamps n me, jist is the sun wis rizin. Scotty wis back already, hangin from the ceiling feelin sorry for hisself. Ah hud goat ma fix from one ay they Highland bullocks that feel like shagpile rugs on legs, n Gamps hud foond a sheep wi its throat torn oot by a fox, the jammy cunt, but Scotty hud goat fuckall.

'There wis this field full ay coos,' Scotty said, 'but the cunts kept wakin up fore I cood sink ma teeth into em.' I kenned well thit Gamps didna believe him. 'Gie us soom ay your blood, Gamps,' Scotty sais. 'Ye mustve goat gallons oot ay that sheep.'

'Fuck oaf, Scotty,' sais Gamps. 'Ye wouldna gie fuckall to *me* the other night when I wis skint.'

'I tole ye, Gamps, ah couldna, ahd digested it by the time ah goat home.'

'Lyin cunt,' said Gamps. 'N I doant believe you went oot last night neither. Ye've bin skivin here waitin fir us tae bring hame the blood.'

'Tha's nae true, Gamps, ah wiz oot all night, ah jist dinnae have any luck.' Scotty turns tae me. 'Dannyboy,' he sais, 'gie's soom ay yirs, fir the luv ay Goad.'

'No way, Scotty,' ah sais.

'Och c'moan, Dannyboy, ah'm disprit,' he sais. 'Ah'll pay ye back double next time I score.'

He wiz shakin all ower fit tae shed his wings, n his fangs wis chatterin together like chopsticks, sae I took pity on the radge and sicked up aboot fifteen mill ay blood intae his gob. He gulped it doon n collapsed on a pile ay auld shite on the flair wi a sigh of relief. 'Goad bless ye, Dannyboy,' he seis. 'Ye saved ma life.'

'Whit's the matter wi yir technique, Scotty?' ah sais. 'Whir did ye try t' bite them coos?'

'In the neck,' he sais.

'That's nae guid,' ah sais, geing Gamps a wink. 'Ye have tae go fir the arsehole.'

'The arsehole?' he sais wonderingly.

'Aye the wee ring ay soft tender flesh between the pelt n the hole issel,' I sais. 'Ye creep up behind yir bullock n lick his arsehole with yir tongue, likesay its one ay his mates rimmin him. Then ye sink yir fangs in very gentle. The cunts love it.'

'Heh, heh,' Scotty laughs. 'Them bullocks must be queer as fuck.'

'Ay course they are,' says Gamps. 'Every cunt kens thit. They're all HIV positive.'

'Whit?' Scotty started tae shake again. 'Are ye tellin me thit blood's infected?' he sais.

'Why d'ye think I wanted to git rid of it?' I sais.

'Ye cunt! Ye've murdered me!' he screamed, n he started gaggin n retchin n stickin his claws down his throat to try and sick up the blood. Gamps n me wiz pishing oursells laughin.

'Ye daft radge,' sais Gamps to Scotty at last. 'How cood bullocks be bufties when they've hud thir bollocks cut off?'

What is it Like to be a Bat?
By S*lm*n R*shd**

What kind of question is that, sir? With all due respect, what would you say if I asked *you*, 'What is it like to be a man?' You would undoubtedly reply, 'It all depends on what kind of man.' What race, what colour, what class, what caste, what situation in life? Likewise with bats. We are of many kinds. There are short-tailed bats and long-tailed bats, several varieties of free-tailed bats, the spotted bat, the pallid bat, the Western mastiff bat, the slit-faced bat, the hollow-faced bat, the Old World leaf-nosed bat, the mouse-tailed bat, the horseshoe bat, the bulldog bat, the funnel-eared bat, the smoky bat, the disk-winged bat, the Old World sucker-footed bat, the Dobson's moustache bat, and the common bat, to name but a few. We all have our distinctive habits and habitats.

Myself, I am a temple bat. I belong to a colony inhabiting the Surya Deula temple at Konarak, on the Bay of Bengal. How I come to be hanging from the coat hook of a toilet in the first-class cabin of this Air India jumbo jet is a long story, involving a tourist's camera-case, an errant sleeping tablet, and a faulty airport X-ray machine. The camera-case was carelessly left open and empty on the pedestal of one of the carved columns of the Surya Deula last Wednesday evening, that dusky time when we temple bats emerge from our nooks and crannies in the crumbling sandstone and sift the warm silky air for tasty midges, crunchy mosquitoes, juicy fruitflies and other entomological dainties . . . The bats' Happy Hour, you might say. But, alas, no hour is happy for me. What is it like to be a temple bat? Bloody hell, as far as I am concerned, if you will pardon the expression, sir.

My fellow bats, you see, are perfectly content with their existence because they don't *know* they are bats. As you have observed, I possess the gift of speech, whereas my brothers and sisters have only the gift of squeaks. Furthermore, I have a memory, whereas they do not. They don't know that they were men and women in their previous incarnations, and that they have been relegated to this level of the great chain of being for the sins they committed in their former existence. But because of some accident, some blip or slippage in the

93

normal process of transmigration, I am cursed with consciousness, a human mind in a bat's body, making my punishment a million times worse.

Contrary to popular belief, sir, bats are not totally blind, we can distinguish day from night and the vague shapes of things, but the rich detail of the world's forms and colours is a closed book to us. So I can only 'see' the interior of this toilet by reconstructing it from memory: the stainless steel hand basin, the subtly lit mirror reflecting coloured bottles of complimentary after-shave and *eau de Cologne*, the horseshoe-shaped tissue-paper covers thoughtfully provided to pro-tect one's buttocks from contact with the common toilet-seat – you are availing yourself of this convenience at the moment, perhaps. No, I beg you, sir, please don't discommode yourself, there is no need to be embarrassed – your bare knees are just a faint pale blur to my limited vision . . . I am able to picture the interior of this cubicle in every detail only because I was once a frequent flyer in these gleaming machines myself. A film producer frequently shuttling between Bollywood and Hollywood, I lolled in the sumptuously upholstered seats of Nabob Class, cosseted by smiling supple-hipped sari'd air hostesses plying me with champagne, caviare and hot towels. The most delectable and gullible of these young ladies I would arrange to meet in their off-duty hours after landing, promising them roles in my upcoming productions, though not revealing that these had titles like *Asian Babes – Sex Slaves, Pussy Vindaloo,* and *Pilau Talk.* Yes. I was a producer of porn movies aimed at the Indian market – Simla Pinks' stag nights, Bombay businessmen's after-hours entertain-ment, video rentals for sad, frustrated bachelors . . . Nothing really filthy, I hasten to say, no cum-shots, no violence, just simulated consensual sex and a little masturbation. But nothing would turn my customers on more readily than the sight of an obviously well-brought-up Indian girl degrading herself in this fashion. Nothing would turn *me* on more readily, to tell you the truth (I was what you might call a hands-on producer). I'm afraid I lured many an innocent maiden into a life of shame, with flattery and bribery and trickery. And now I suffer for it . . . You have visited the Surya Deula, perhaps? Yes? You remember the sculptures? Yes, I am told that they are unforgettable. Unfortunately I omitted to visit the site myself in my previous incarnation. You can perhaps imagine the frustration for someone of my tastes and background, of having the eyesight of a bat in the presence of the greatest monument of erotic sculpture in the world?

What is it Like to be a Blind Bat?
By S★m★★l B★ck★tt

Where? When? Why? Squeak. I am in the dark. I am always in the dark. It was not always so. Once there were periods of light, or shades of darkness. Squeak. There would be a faint luminosity from the mouth of the cave. When it faded I knew it would soon be time to leave the cave, with the others, to go flittering through the dusk. Squeak. Now it is always dark, uniformly dark. Whether at any given moment it is dark outside my head as well as inside, I do not know. All I know, if know is the word, and it is not, is that I can see nothing. I can feel, hear, smell, but not see. Squeak. I can feel the ledge which the claws of my hindlegs grip. I can hear my squeaks as they depart and rebound, and distinguish them from the constant din of other squeaks tintinnabulating around the walls of this place. Squeak. I can smell the reek of ammonia rising from the floor, if floor is what it has. Perhaps I am suspended above a lake of ammonia, but I think not, for I have never heard anything like a splash after voiding my bowels, unless the surface of the lake is so far beneath me that the sound of ordure hitting it does not carry to my ears.

I can feel with my foot-whisker that there is another beside me. He has a foot-whisker too, I feel it brush against me from time to time. Squeak. I say he, it could be a she for all I know, there is no way of telling, unless I were to fumble under its folded wings with my foreclaw to ascertain whether there are two holes there, or a hole and a prick, and such an action might be misinterpreted. Squeak. Better to remain in a state of uncertainty. Uncertainty is unpleasant, but certainty can be worse. I would prefer to be uncertain that I am blind, but that is the only thing I am certain of, because it was not always uniformly dark. Squeak. Once there were shapes, I'm sure there were shapes. Dark shapes against a less dark background. When I was very young my mother took me with her when she went hunting, in her pouch. Squeak. I clung to her nipples as she soared and swooped through the gloaming, scooping up insects, and I remember the shapes of things that she flew between, above, beneath. Now there are no more shapes, only touch, smells, sounds. I have lost shapes for ever. When? Why? How? Squeak.

9

'THEY may be quite clever as parodies,' Ralph says. 'I really can't judge, because I don't read much contemporary fiction. I haven't got the time. But –'

'You should read Helen's novels, Messenger,' says Carrie. 'They're very good.'

'I'm sure they are,' says Ralph. 'And one day I shall make up for the omission.'

'I'd much rather you didn't,' says Helen. 'But go on.'

'I was going to say, as attempts to answer the question they're hopelessly anthropomorphic.'

'What's anthropo – what's it mean?' Simon asks.

'*Bzzzz!*' Mark makes a noise like the interrupt buzzer in a TV quiz show. 'Treating non-human things as if they were human.'

'Very good, Polo,' says Ralph. 'It's like the animals in Walt Disney films, Sock.'

'What was the question?' Carrie asks.

'"What is it Like to be a Bat?"' says Helen. 'It's the title of a philosophical article.'

'Yes, it sounds like one,' says Carrie.

'Another philosopher recently posed the question, "What is it Like to be a Thermostat?"' says Ralph.

'It's cool, on and off,' says Mark, raising some chuckles.

'Good one, Polo,' says Ralph.

'He was joking, I presume, this philosopher?' says Helen.

'No,' says Ralph. 'He was perfectly serious. If consciousness is information processing, then perhaps anything that processes information, in however humble a way, should be described as conscious. Pan-psychism, it's called in the trade. The idea is that consciousness is a basic component of the universe, like mass and energy, strong force and weak force. I don't really buy it myself.'

'Why not?' Helen asks.

'It has a whiff of transcendentalism about it. People who are keen on it tend to be kindly disposed towards oriental religion.'

'Why don't you want Messenger to read your books?' Emily asks Helen, with frank curiosity.

Helen seems a little discomfited by the question. 'It's just that when people read your books because they know you, it tends to distort the reading experience. Especially if they don't normally read literary fiction.' She turns to address Ralph. 'I'm surprised you don't, though, since you're so interested in consciousness. It's what most modern novels are about.'

'Oh, I read some when I was younger,' Ralph says. 'The early chapters of *Ulysses* are remarkable. Then he seemed to get distracted by stylistic games and crossword puzzles.'

'What about Virginia Woolf?'

'Too genteel, too poetic. All her characters sound like Virginia Woolf. My impression is that nobody has improved on Joyce in that line. Am I right?'

'Probably,' says Helen. 'The stream of consciousness novel as such is rather out of fashion.'

'I'm getting out, I've had enough,' says Carrie.

'Of the tub, or of consciousness?' says Ralph.

'Both,' says Carrie.

The conversation is taking place in the hot tub in the back garden of the Messengers' country cottage. The ground slopes quite steeply away from the rear of the house, and a timber balcony has been constructed with steps that lead down to the garden. Halfway down there is a kind of mezzanine deck in which a redwood tub, some seven feet in diameter and five feet deep, has been fitted flush with the surface. A bench runs round the inner circumference, on which Helen and the Messenger family are companionably seated, hip to hip. The hot water bubbles up between their legs and sends wraiths of steam into the cold air. It is late afternoon, or early evening, and already dark. The only illumination comes from the blue lights fitted inside the tub below the waterline, and the lanterns with thick amber glass cowls fixed at intervals on the staircase and along the decks.

Carrie clambers out of the tub, steadying herself with a hand on Ralph's shoulder. The water streams from her tight, dark swimming costume and pallid heavy limbs. She wraps herself in a towelling robe and thrusts her feet into a pair of rope-soled mules. 'Time you kids got out too,' she says.

'Oh Mum . . .' they complain.

'I mean it. Come and help me set the table for tea.'

One by one the children get out of the tub, wrap themselves in towels, and mount the stairs to the house. Emily is the last to go. 'I guess I ought to help Mom,' she sighs.

'I really should be going,' says Helen, without stirring from her seat. 'I came to lunch, not tea as well.'

'Oh stay,' Ralph says. 'You seem to be enjoying yourself.'

'It's blissful,' she says, tilting her head to look up at the sky. 'Lying in a hot bath looking straight up at the stars! My mother would have a fit if she could see me. "*You'll catch your death of cold*," she'd say.'

'You won't,' Ralph assures her.

'Can you buy these tubs in England?'

'Not made out of redwood, as far as I know. We shipped it from California, at enormous expense, and had our local builder plumb it in.'

'Well, it's a wonderful invention,' says Helen, stretching out her legs and letting them float to the surface. 'I suppose it must have a thermostat. Does that make it conscious?'

'Not self-conscious. It doesn't know it's having a good time – unlike you and me.'

'I thought there was no such thing as the self.'

'No such *thing*, no, if you mean a fixed, discrete entity. But of course there are selves. We make them up all the time. Like you make up your stories.'

'Are you saying our lives are just fictions?'

'In a way. It's one of the things we do with our spare brain capacity. We make up stories about ourselves.'

'But we can't make up our own lives,' Helen objects. 'Things

99

happen to us, or don't happen to us, outside our control. Did you read about that poor Frenchman with, what do they call it, locked-in syndrome?'

'Yes, interesting.'

'You can't say he's making up his ghastly situation.'

'He's constructing a particular response to it,' says Ralph. 'A pretty heroic one, I grant you.'

'But doesn't it make you believe there is some such thing as the soul, or the human spirit?'

'No, why should it?'

'Well, the courage of the man, his determination to communicate . . .'

'Yes, it's very admirable . . . but it's still just information processing by his brain. There's nothing supernatural about it. No ghost in the machine.'

'That's such a loaded word, "ghost",' says Helen. 'It has connotations of superstition and fantasy. I don't believe in ghosts, but I believe in souls.'

'Immortal souls?'

'I'm not sure,' Helen says, stirring the water with her foot.

'Oh well, I'll grant you a *mortal* soul, it's just another way of describing self-consciousness. But Descartes believed he had a soul because he could imagine his mind existing independently of his body. Isn't that what ghosts are reputed to do?'

'Well, isn't that what the Frenchman, whatshisname, Bauby – isn't that what he's doing, going on thinking independently of his body? His body is totally paralysed.'

'He can still see with one eye, I believe. And hear. And anyway, his brain is part of his body.'

After a pause, Helen says, 'What did you mean about our spare brain capacity?'

'Well, the human brain is much bigger than that of any other animal on the planet. Our DNA is only about one per cent different from that of chimps, our nearest relatives, but our brains are three times bigger. Obviously that gave our primitive ancestors a great advantage in the evolutionary stakes. We learned to make tools and weapons, to communicate through language, to solve problems by running various options through our mental software, instead of just reacting instinctively. We got beyond the four Fs.'

'What are they?'

'Fighting, fleeing, feeding and . . . mating.'

'Oh . . .' Helen sniggers.

'But the greater size of the human brain is way out of proportion to the evolutionary advantage we gained over other species. That's what I mean by spare capacity. Primitive man was like a guy who's been given a state-of-the-art computer and just uses it to do simple arithmetic. Sooner or later he's going to start playing with it and discover that he can do all kinds of other things as well. That's what we did with our brains, in due course. We developed language. We reflected on our own existence. We became aware of ourselves as creatures with a past and a future, individual and collective histories. We developed culture: religion, art, literature, law . . . science. But there's a downside to self-consciousness. We know that we're going to die. Imagine what a terrible shock it was to Neanderthal Man, or Cro-Magnon Man, or whoever it was that first clocked the dreadful truth: that one day he would be meat. Lions and tigers don't know that. Apes don't know it. We do.'

'Elephants must know,' Helen interjects. 'They have graveyards.'

'I'm afraid that's a myth,' says Ralph. '*Homo sapiens* was the first and only living being in evolutionary history to discover he was mortal. So how does he respond? He makes up stories to explain how he got into this fix, and how he might get out of it. He invents religion, he develops burial customs, he makes up stories about the afterlife, and the immortality of the soul. As time goes on, these stories get more and more elaborate. But in the most recent phase of culture, moments ago in terms of evolutionary history, science suddenly takes off, and starts to tell a different story about how we got here, a much more powerful explanatory story that knocks the religious one for six. Not many intelligent people believe the religious story any more, but they still cling to some of its consoling concepts, like the soul, life after death, and so on.'

'I think that's what really irks you, isn't it?' says Helen. 'That most people go on stubbornly believing that there *is* a ghost in the machine however many times scientists and philosophers tell them there isn't.'

'It doesn't "irk" me, exactly,' says Ralph.

'Oh yes it does,' says Helen. 'It's as if you're determined to eradicate it from the face of the earth. Like an Inquisitor trying to root out heresy.'

'I just think we shouldn't confuse what we would like to be the case with what *is* the case,' says Ralph.

'But you admit that we have thoughts that are private, secret, known only to ourselves.'

'Oh yes.'

'You admit that my experience of this moment, lolling here in hot water, under the stars, is not exactly the same as yours?'

'I can see where this argument is going,' he says. 'You're saying, there's something it is like to be you, or to be me, some quality of experience that is unique to you or to me, that can't be described objectively or explained in purely physical terms. So one might as well call it an immaterial self or soul.'

'I suppose so. Yes.'

'And I'm saying it's still a machine. A virtual machine in a biological machine.'

'So everything's a machine?'

'Everything that processes information, yes.'

'I think that's a horrifying idea.'

He shrugs, and smiles. 'You're a machine that's been pro-grammed by culture not to recognize that it's a machine.'

Carrie's voice calls from above. 'Messenger! Are you two going to stay out there all night?'

'We'd better go in,' says Helen.

'Yes, perhaps we should,' says Ralph.

They climb out of the pool and ascend the wooden steps that lead to the rear of the house. In a dark angle of the staircase, where a lightbulb has failed, Ralph detains her with a hand on her arm.

'Helen,' he murmurs, and kisses her on the lips.

She does not resist.

10

MONDAY 10TH MARCH. I've been trying to read students' work-in-progress today but finding it hard to concentrate, thinking all the time about THAT KISS. I was taken totally by surprise – we'd been having such a lofty intellectual discussion, not to say ding-dong argument . . . I felt his foot touch mine once or twice in the hot tub, but I thought it was just accidental, it never crossed my mind that he had any amorous intentions. Can you argue, really argue, argue to win – and flirt at the same time? Surely not. Though I remember thinking that he was going to kiss me when we parted outside the car-park in Cheltenham after a similarly sharp exchange of views . . . Perhaps he finds it sexually stimulating, a woman standing up to him in debate. But I didn't anticipate anything more than a friendly social kiss on that occasion, a light brush of the cheek, whereas yesterday's kiss was firmly mouth on mouth – not passionate, not intrusive, but definitely sexual. And I accepted it. At least, I didn't resist it. I didn't slap his face or push him away, or ask him what he thought he was doing. I didn't say a word. Perhaps I even responded a little. I certainly enjoyed it – my whole body twanged like a harp that's been plucked. I feel moistly aroused now, as I revive the moment. Goodness, how can one kiss have such an impact?

Of course, my life has been rather sparsely furnished with kisses for some time. Remember that, dear, won't you? You're very susceptible, very vulnerable, at the moment. Do you mean sex-starved? Well, yes dear, perhaps you are a little bit, and he's a very attractive man, whatever you think about his opinions and his morals. Just keep your head, don't do anything foolish. Right then, I won't.

But to begin at the beginning: I went to the Messengers' cottage yesterday for lunch, as arranged. It's situated in the middle of pretty, picture-postcard Cotswold country – pretty even at this time of year, when there isn't a leaf to be seen on the deciduous trees. The road wound and undulated between dewy meadows and green hump-backed hills dotted with sheep, through villages embalmed in a Sunday morning hush, past ancient churches and neat farmhouses and snug thatched cottages. 'Horseshoes' has a thatched roof, but it's more of a house than a cottage – double-fronted, built of mellow Cotswold stone, its walls covered with wisteria which one can imagine dripping with mauve blossom in May. It has low, raftered ceilings, and a bumpy flagged floor covered with rugs, and a huge open fireplace in the living-room. Needless to say it's provided with central heating and other mod cons, all tastefully integrated into the eighteenth-century fabric.

Here the Messenger family simulates the life of English country folk for one or two days a week: Carrie bottles fruit and makes preserves on the oil-fired Aga, Emily rides the pony she keeps at a local stable, and Ralph chops wood for the open fire or takes the younger children out for rambles and bike-rides. At the back of the house, however, a more exotic and sybaritic note is struck: a balcony, or 'deck' as they call it, has been constructed on two levels, with a redwood hot tub on the lower level. The effect is rather bizarre as you pass from the English eighteenth century of the house to twentieth-century California in the back garden, like walking through different film sets in a studio.

After lunch (a superb leg of local lamb, roasted to perfection, with slivers of garlic and sprigs of rosemary delicately inserted into its layer of fat) we went for a walk around a circuit of lanes and footpaths in the neighbourhood, I in borrowed Wellington boots (they have several sizes for visitors to choose from). And then, as the red winter sun was setting, we changed into swimming costumes, wrapped ourselves in towels and bathrobes and sallied out to the hot tub. I must say it was most enjoyable, sitting in the open air, immersed up to one's neck in bubbling hot water, looking up as the stars came out in the darkening sky. The whole family squeezed in and sat round in a circle.

It wasn't long before Ralph mounted his hobby horse. I suspect the rest of the family is bored with consciousness as a conversational topic, but it's new to me and extremely interesting. After the others had got out and returned to the house, he and I lingered for some time, talking about the existence – or non-existence – of the soul. He has this utter confidence in the evolutionary, materialistic explanation of everything that is difficult to resist, certainly with the kind of faltering half-belief in the transcendental that is all I possess now. Then Carrie called us from the house to come in for tea, and as we were going up the steps, he kissed me.

I didn't, of course, tell Carrie about it later. So it's there, now, a secret between us, something he and I know, and she doesn't. When he passed me the honey and the butter at the tea-table, and our eyes met, the knowledge passed between us silently and invisibly – not merely that we had kissed, but also that we had agreed to conceal it. We did not betray to the others what had happened by so much as the flicker of an eyelid or slightest tremor of the voice. How adept at deception we human beings are, how easily it comes to us. Did we acquire that ability with self-consciousness?

I have absolutely no intention of embarking on an affair with Ralph Messenger, for a whole host of reasons. Let's be quite clear about that. Nevertheless I was left with a small irreducible feeling of guilt about the episode, which I tried to assuage by helping Carrie to clear up the kitchen after the meal. As we were stacking the dishwasher she mentioned casually that she was writing a book, a historical novel set in San Francisco at the time of the great earthquake in 1906. Apparently she has some old family papers – letters and diaries – from the period, to draw on for material. She thinks it will have a ready-made readership in contemporary California where everybody is obsessed with earthquakes. 'The trouble is, I don't know how much historical background to put in,' she said. 'It's basically a family story.' Somehow I found myself offering to read the manuscript – which, to use one of Emily's expressions, is something I need like a hole in the head. Another fictional world to assimilate! Carrie eagerly accepted the offer. Was I trapped into it – was that why I'd been invited to Horseshoes – is that why Carrie has been cultivating my acquaintance all along? Or was it my own guilty conscience about the kiss that prompted this act of supererogation? I couldn't – I can't – decide. But why do I always have to look for devious motives for everything? Why shouldn't Ralph's kiss have been just a spontaneous, unpremeditated action, a simple piece of gallantry, a frank admission that he finds me attractive and enjoys my company, nothing more than that, setting the seal on a pleasant shared experience, arguing about metaphysics in the hot tub. And why shouldn't Carrie have mentioned her novel by chance, and why should I distrust my own generosity in offering to read it? I suppose it comes of being a novelist, that one always prefers a complicated explanation to a simple one.

My 'lunch' invitation had been stretched inordinately, and in the end we all left the house together at about seven o'clock. Suddenly the pace of life speeded up. Everybody bustled about, supervised by Carrie, picking up things and putting them away, resetting thermostats and turning off lights, drawing curtains and fastening shutters, making the house secure for another week. It was as if the curtain had come down on some dreamy pastoral idyll, and the company was suddenly galvanized into action, shedding their costumes and packing up their props before moving on to the next venue. We parted in the lane outside the house as we got into our respective cars. I said goodbye and thanked them sincerely.

'Come again,' said Carrie. 'Make a habit of it . . . I hate to think of you spending your Sundays on campus.' Ralph grinned at me over her shoulder. 'Absolutely,' he said. 'We'll see you next Saturday, anyway,' said Carrie. She meant at Ralph's fiftieth birthday party, to which I have been invited.

LATER. I heard on the news tonight that Jean-Dominique Bauby has died, just days after his book was published. Very very sad, but at least he lived long enough to know it was a huge success. Perhaps that's what kept him going, the determination to see his book through to publication, and once that was achieved his exhausted spirit gave up the struggle. So where is he now? Nowhere, according to Ralph Messenger, he has just ceased to exist – except in the minds of readers of *Le scaphandre et le papillon*, and in the memories of those who knew him personally. But those minds and memories are themselves allegedly constructs, fictions, tied to decaying brain cells, doomed to eventual extinction too.

There's something horribly plausible about Ralph's arguments, religion arising out of man's unique awareness of his own mortality, *etc.* I checked in the *Encyclopaedia Britannica* about elephants' graveyards, and he's right, dammit. Animals brought to the slaughter-house sense their impending fate, one is told – they kick and struggle and shit themselves as they are chivvied towards the abattoir; probably they can sniff the taint of blood in the air long before human nostrils would detect it, or perhaps they smell the fear of the animals that preceded them. But they don't know *why* they are distressed; they fear death without knowing what it is. We are the only creatures that know, and know *all the time*, after infancy. Was that the terrible price of self-consciousness?

In fact – when you think about it in this light – the story of Original Sin in Genesis could easily be a myth about the advent of self-consciousness in evolutionary history. *Homo sapiens*, by virtue of his sudden surge in brain-power, apprehends his own mortality, and is so appalled by the discovery that he makes up a story, as Ralph said, '*to explain how he got into this fix and how he might get out of it*'. A story about having offended some power greater than himself, who punished him with death for his transgression – and, in later elaborations of the story, offered him a second chance of immortality. It's all there in the first five lines of *Paradise Lost*:

> *Of man's first disobedience, and the fruit*
> *Of that forbidden tree, whose mortal taste*
> *Brought death into the world, and all our woe,*
> *With loss of Eden, till one greater man*
> *Restore us, and regain the blissful seat . . .*

Strip away the mythology and the theology and the baroque poetry, and you find there perhaps a faint trace of primitive man's first dismayed discovery that he is mortal, that he lives in time and will die in time. In the myth, the forbidden tree is the tree of knowledge, the knowledge of good and evil. Eat of its fruit, God warns Adam and

Eve, and you will die. But perhaps in reality the knowledge was *of* death, and all the existential angst it brought in its train. The fall of man was a fall into self-consciousness, and God a compensatory fiction. QED.

And yet, as somebody said, the idea of the universe existing without a Creator seems just as far-fetched as the idea that a God created it, especially when you're looking up at the stars at night. We know they weren't always there. You can trace everything back to the Big Bang, but where did the ingredients for the Big Bang come from?

Perhaps our mistake is to imagine that the God behind it all must be like us, that 'He made us in his own image and likeness,' as the Catechism has it. Suppose God is omnipotent and eternal, but has no more self-consciousness than a lion? Or an ocean? That would explain a lot – the existence of evil, for instance. Perhaps God didn't intend it because He, or rather It, didn't intend anything. Suppose we are the only creatures in the universe with self-consciousness and intentionality and guilt? A chilling thought. Yet one would be loath to renounce self-consciousness, to return to the unreflective animal existence of pre-lapsarian hominids, swinging from the trees or loping though the broad savannahs, responding simply to the imperatives of the four Fs.

> *for who would lose,*
> *Though full of pain, this intellectual being*

as Milton put it. Belial speaking, of course. Or as John Stuart Mill said, 'better to be a dissatisfied man than a satisfied pig.' It was one of Martin's favourite quotations.

Martin. Do I think he has ceased to exist? No, but he seems to be getting somehow . . . fainter, more distant. In the weeks after he died I used to talk to him a lot, sometimes aloud. I would be reading the newspaper over breakfast and come across something that would have interested or amused him and I'd say, 'Listen to this' – and then look up and see the empty chair on the other side of the table. But I'd read it out anyway, as if he could hear, wherever he was. And I'd have conversations with him in my head, and sometimes out loud. If some decision that had to be made was worrying me, about money or repairs to the house, for instance, I'd ask him what I should do. I'd say, 'Shall I take the lump sum or convert it into an annuity? Shall I get three estimates for the re-roofing or will two be enough?' Martin was always the one who looked after those things, and I found it useful to work out decisions in this way, like a child discussing its problems with an imaginary friend. But one day Lucy came home early from school, let herself into the house and heard me talking in the kitchen about renewing an insurance premium. She gave me a worried look when she came into the room and found I was alone. After that I was more careful.

One reason why I found it hard to accept, really accept that Martin was dead, was that he died so suddenly, utterly without warning. One minute he was there, and the next he was gone. It was as if he'd just left the room on some trivial errand and not come back: you kept thinking there must be some mistake, some misunderstanding, and he'd soon reappear, smiling and apologizing . . .

Another reason was the ghastly funeral. Martin was an agnostic, his parents are nominally C of E, but not churchgoers, and his sister Joanna is a militant atheist who works in Family Planning and deeply disapproved of our having the children baptized and sending them to a Catholic primary school. 'I hope you're not going to have a religious service,' she said sharply, when I phoned her to tell her the time and place of the cremation. 'Martin wouldn't have wanted it.' 'Well, not a Catholic one, if that's what you mean,' I said with equal sharpness (Joanna and I never got on). There was no question of that, anyway, since neither I nor the children had been practising Catholics for years and I wasn't in touch with any friendly priest who might have stretched a point and agreed to officiate. We decided on a small private family funeral, with a memorial service later for his friends and colleagues. But, in spite of Joanna, we agreed that Martin's parents, not to mention mine, would be upset by a totally secular occasion, so settled for a very basic Christian service conducted by a minister provided, for a fee, by the undertakers. He didn't know Martin from

Adam, of course, and made no attempt to disguise his boredom with the occasion and his impatience to get it over with. The undertakers were polite and efficient, but you could sense a certain professional disappointment at the meagreness of our numbers and the austerity of our service (with only eight mourners, one of whom announced that she would take no part in the service, we didn't attempt any hymns; and I had requested donations to medical research instead of flowers). It was a dark, wet, November day. The crematorium looked exactly like what it was for, a grim structure of sooty brick, with sodden wreaths and bunches of flowers from previous funerals wrapped in plastic spread out over the forecourt for mourners to admire and evaluate. The chapel was overheated but cheerless, bare of any religious decoration which might exclude or offend. The service was got through with almost indecent haste. The minister gabbled out the prayers, we muttered the occasional 'Amen', and then he pressed the button, the piped music came on and the coffin began slowly to descend, like an old-fashioned cinema organ. Lucy burst into tears, and I put my arm round her to comfort her, but I felt nothing. I was only able to endure the whole horrible experience by distancing myself from it, so it did absolutely nothing to help me with the grieving process.

A few months later, Martin's friends at the BBC organized a memorial service in a Wren church in the City, and I went to that more hopefully, even eagerly. But it was a dissatisfying occasion, a queer mixture of the sacred and the profane: the sounds of Martin's favourite modern jazz tracks bouncing off the white and gold walls and Ionian columns, reminiscences by colleagues full of in-jokes and allusions which I couldn't follow, extracts from Martin's award-winning documentaries on pollution and deep-sea fishing, a render-ing of 'Ave Maria' by a well-known soprano who had figured in his programme about Covent Garden . . . It was a large gathering, but I had never met many of the people present before. Afterwards there was a sort of party in the upstairs room of a nearby pub, and several people got drunk, including Lucy, who was sick in the car on the way home . . . I didn't feel that the occasion had been much more efficacious than the funeral in reconciling me to Martin's death, or allowing his spirit to rest in peace.

TUESDAY 11TH MARCH. Good seminar this afternoon: readings and discussion of the 'What is it Like to be a Bat?' pieces. Lots of laughter and general good humour. I think people feel less anxious, less sensitive about having their work dissected in public when it's a set exercise. Real writing is inevitably a kind of self-exposure. Even if it's not overtly autobiographical, it reveals indirectly your fears, desires, fantasies, priorities. That's why hostile reviews are always so wounding, so difficult to shrug off. You wonder, even if they're wrong about your book, whether they might be right about you. The students must feel the same in the workshop sessions, but there is much less at stake in a set exercise. And the parody-pastiche element gets them to stretch their literary muscles – trying things they wouldn't risk in their own work. It seemed worth repeating, so I told them the story of Mary the colour scientist coming out of her monochrome world, and asked them to do something similar with that. Only this time there are to be no clues to the models – I've got to be able to identify them from the style alone. (*Groans.*)

I happened to hear Ralph Messenger on the radio this morning – some kind of popular science magazine programme. He was being interviewed about 'wearable computers'. I switched on in the middle of the discussion, but as far as I could gather somebody's just written a book suggesting that as computers get smaller and cheaper in the future they could easily be worn on the person or actually implanted in the body, to monitor your pulse rate, temperature, blood pressure, muscular tension, blood sugar level, *etc.*, *etc.*, and anyone with access to this information on their own wearable computers could tell from it what you were thinking and feeling. *Is this feasible?* he was asked. 'Well, it's technically feasible,' he said. 'Computer chips are getting smaller and smaller and more and more powerful all the time. They're improving faster than any other machine in history. It's been calculated that if cars had developed at the same rate as computers over the last thirty years, you'd be able to buy a Rolls-Royce today for under a pound, and it would do three million miles to the gallon . . . So there's no reason why wearables shouldn't become cheaply available in the not-too-distant future.' *But why would anybody submit to being fitted with them?* he was asked. 'Well, one suggestion is that domestic appliances could respond to the information and anticipate your needs – when you came in tired from work, say, the Teasmaid would make you a cup of tea and the TV find you a suitably relaxing programme without your having to lift a finger,' he said. 'But wearables could also be made compulsory in certain contexts. For instance, suppose there was a wearable that triggered a red light on the roof of your car when your blood-pressure and pulse rate went above a certain level.' *A sort of road-rage meter?* 'Exactly. It could prevent a lot of accidents. Wearing one might be made a condition of holding a driving licence.' *But could these wearables allow us to know what other people are actually thinking?* 'No,' Ralph said, 'because our thoughts have a semantic content that is much too complex and fine-grained to be identified through physical symptoms. The proposal is based on a rather simplistic behaviourist psychology.'

Interesting that he was so dismissive of the wearables. Perhaps he doesn't like the idea that philandering might be electronically monitored in the future – that Carrie might be able to tell by glancing at a little gadget like a wristwatch exactly the level of lust he felt for another woman at a dinner party. If they *are* feasible, these wearables could put an end to adultery.

11

ONE, two, buckle my shoe . . . It's Wednesday 12th March, 5.30 p.m. . . . I've got the Voicemaster up and running and it's brilliant, not only does it take direct dictation, but I can also feed pre-recorded tapes directly into it by wire, which means I can still use the old Pearlcorder, anywhere I like. I'm dictating this while driving home from the University, or rather while being stuck in a traffic jam on the A435, some kind of bottleneck ahead, roadworks or an accident . . . So there's no need for me to go into the Centre on Sunday mornings any more to continue the experiment, which will improve relations with Carrie no end . . . and in any case it no longer seems such a secure and private place for the purpose since I met Duggers entering the building last Sunday just as I was leaving . . . We clocked each other simultaneously through the glass doors, he was outside, using his swipe card to open them, as I approached from inside . . . we were equally taken by surprise, glared at each other like two burglars coming face to face on the stairs of an empty house . . . he looked slightly flustered . . . no doubt I did too, but by the time he got the door open we'd recovered our poise . . . Hello Duggers, I said, what are you doing here on a Sunday morning? 'I often come in at the weekend to catch up on work,' he said frostily. 'It's the only time you can be sure of getting some peace in this place.' I know what you mean, I said, with false camaraderie. 'And what about you, Messenger?' he said. 'Escaping from the joys of domesticity?' What would you know about them? I nearly asked him. Duggers lives with his widowed mother and unmarried sister in a square redbrick Victorian villa in one of the few villages in this part of the world that are totally devoid of charm. Not many people have ever been invited inside this house, certainly not us, but I have driven past occasionally, and 'joy' and 'domesticity' are not words you would immediately associate with it. Oh no, just collecting some papers I forgot to take home, I said, patting the briefcase I was carrying. I instinctively concealed the fact that I'd been in my office for the past hour, perhaps because I was thinking queasily that he might easily have arrived earlier and been in the building without my knowledge . . . pausing outside my office as he heard the murmur of my voice . . . pressing his ear to the door . . . no, he wouldn't stoop to that, but he gives me the creeps, Duggers, always did from the first day I met him, when I came to look the place over and be looked over in my turn, they flew me from California, I spent two days meeting the faculty and graduate students, I gave a lecture, the VC gave a dinner . . . the usual drill . . . I remember the cold dislike in Duggers' eyes behind his round schoolboy spectacles when we were introduced . . . I knew at once that he must be the leading internal candidate for the job, and he knew at once that I was going to get it . . . well, I understand how he felt, still feels, up to a point, his research record is outstanding, narrower than mine, but more original . . . but this isn't just a research job, it's just as much a financial management job, and a leadership job and a PR job – it requires charisma as well as brainpower . . . and Duggers has got about as much charisma as the adolescent schoolboy swot he resembles . . . poor old Duggers . . . I wonder what he's working on that's so interesting he can't stay away from it on a Sunday morning, eh? Of course I know in general terms, evolutionary systems that can teach agents how to use them, write their own instruction manuals, so to speak, because that's what he's been into for the last two years . . . but has he made a really important breakthrough . . . ? If so, it could have huge commercial potential as well as theoretical significance . . . *That* would be a test of my professional objectivity, I have to admit – if Duggers were to hit the headlines with a sensational new discovery . . . it would be good for the Centre, it could be decisive in preserving our identity as an élite research institute, so I ought to be delighted . . . but could I bear such glory going to him? Suppose he got an FRS out of it . . . No, I don't think I could bear that . . . My God, just the thought of having to congratulate him, forcing the words through your teeth when you'd like to bite his ear off, shaking his hand when you'd like to dislocate his arm . . . No, no, not an FRS for Duggers, please . . . I'm pretty well resigned to not getting one myself . . . well not really resigned, but I know what they say about me, *'a popularizer, a media don, one flashy book to his credit but no serious original research . . .'* it's partly envy of course . . . and very few people in cognitive science are Fellows anyway . . . The subject is too amorphous, perhaps, overlaps with too many other disciplines to have an identity of its own . . . is it maths, is it philosophy, or psychology . . . or engineering? All those things actually, that's what makes it so fascinating, but it's regarded with suspicion by the scientific establishment, as a kind of mongrel subject . . . hard to imagine a cognitive scientist ever getting a Nobel Prize . . . even if somebody cracked the problem of consciousness tomorrow, what prize would they give him? Physics? Chemistry? Physiology? It doesn't fit any of the categories . . . wonder what it's like, really like, to win a Nobel . . . the qualia of Nobelness . . . it must be like, what's the word for becoming a god . . . *apotheosis*, yes . . . suddenly you become invulnerable, immortal . . . not literally of course, but you've achieved something that death can't take away from you . . . and you don't have to struggle any more while you live . . . any further achievement is a bonus, your cup overflowing . . . you have nothing to fear from others . . . you are above competition . . . let Duggers have his FRS by all means, let everybody in the Science Faculty have an FRS . . . there is only one Nobel . . . You simply bask in its glory, its glamour surrounds you like a halo wherever you go . . . you fall asleep every night smiling with the knowledge that you are a Nobel prizewinner and you wake happy, not knowing why immediately, but then remembering . . . every day of your life that is your first conscious thought . . . *I won the Nobel* . . . Is that what it's really like, I wonder? Or are Nobel prizewinners just like the rest of us, still dissatisfied, still ambitious, always hankering after more discoveries, more honours, more fame? Well, I'll never know . . . not even an FRS in realistic prospect . . . Perhaps I love the life of the body too much, women, food, wine . . . especially women . . . your true scientist only thinks about his science, he lives and breathes it, he begrudges every moment that he is distracted from it . . . that story about the scientist whose wife knocks on the door of his study . . . *WIFE: Alfred, we must talk. SCIENTIST:* (looks up from desk, frowns): *What about? WIFE: I have a lover. I'm leaving you. I want a divorce. SCIENTIST: Oh.* (pause) *How long will it take?* If you could imagine Duggers married you could imagine him behaving like that . . . if he were to dictate his stream of consciousness into the Voicemaster it would be all genetic algorithms . . . algorithms and the occasional gripe about the Centre in general and me in particular . . . Or take Turing, a truly great mind, a genius, changed the course of civilization, well accelerated it anyway, somebody else would have invented the computer sooner or later, but he was incredibly ahead of his time . . . but a totally screwed-up human being, a lonely, repressed, unhappy homosexual, eventually killed himself in a dreary flat in Manchester . . . if I was offered the chance of coming back to live my life again either as Turing or Ralph Messenger, I wouldn't hesitate . . . Would anyone *choose* to be a homosexual I wonder, if they had the choice? It's not that I'm homophobic, I just feel sorry for them. What a deprivation, not to find the bodies of women attractive, their curves and their cunts and all the other fascinating differences from men . . . to be constantly lusting after bodies just like one's own seems so . . . boring . . . And then, let's face it, the adult male arsehole is not a thing of beauty . . . no wonder Nicholas Beck is celibate . . .

Ah, good, the traffic's beginning to move at last . . . a blue light flashing up there so it must be an accident . . . looks like it's the crossroads where I take the shortcut to Horseshoes . . . I kissed her . . . Helen . . . after the others had gone back to the house we stayed on in the tub chatting, or rather discussing, quite heavy stuff actually . . . that's what I like about her, she doesn't think it's pretentious to talk about serious subjects . . . until eventually Carrie called us to come in for tea, and as we were climbing the steps I kissed her . . . I took a chance, but my instinct is usually right with these things . . . like when I kissed Carrie in the elevator at MIT . . . I could tell she was having a good time, liked the house, loved the hot tub . . . her body in a swimming costume fulfilled every expectation, I had time for a quick appraisal as she shrugged off her robe and climbed into the tub, poor Carrie enviously eyeing her slender waist and sleek thighs

... the tits are a little low slung and wide apart, but shapely and firm ... they bounced perceptibly – with their own elasticity, not the cotton latex, as she stepped down into the tub ... when she clambered out I had an excellent view of her bottom ... and a very nice bottom it is, ample but not wobbly ... just ample enough for the cheeks to escape in two plump crescents from the costume, which was cut high at the leg ... in fact only a tiny strip of material, not much more than an inch wide, prevented me from staring right up her fanny ... Funny things, swimming costumes ... how little they cover, and yet what a difference they make. It's always a complete surprise when you see a woman naked for the first time ... sometimes a pleasant one, sometimes a disappointment ... I wonder if she would be up for a nude tub one day, not *en famille* of course, but an adults-only session like people used to have sometimes in California ... sipping beakers of Napa Valley Zinfandel with the smell of barbecue smoke in the air and the strains of a raga coming from the portable stereo ... great times ... Carrie won't go nude in the tub when the kids are around ... fair enough I suppose, they'd be embarrassed as hell, the boys would anyway ... And we're all so conscious these days of sexual abuse, terrified of giving any grounds for suspicion or feeding a future false memory syndrome ... and Emily not being my daughter complicates matters ... though I'm not sure it would bother *her* ... That time I saw her naked about a year ago, when I walked into the family bathroom, looking for something, and she was having a bath, '*Oh! Sorry!*' Just glimpsed her taut adolescent breasts gleaming wet with big brown aureoles and pointed nipples before I turned on my heel and walked out, yelling through the door, '*Lock the door when you take a bath, please*' ... She grinned at me a little sheepishly when she came out of the bathroom later, '*Sorry about that, Messenger*' ... but she didn't seem upset ... *I* was, though ... because I'd like to fuck Emily ... I'm not *going* to, of course, it would be unthinkable – no, that's exactly what it is, thinkable ... there's no sexual act however perverse or bizarre that can't be thought, that hasn't been thought by somebody ... but I have no intention of doing it, none at all ... Even though the idea of that acne-ravaged, gangling boyfriend of hers, Greg, having the privilege is almost unbearable . . . I'd never do it . . . It's one of those thoughts that we keep locked in the confidential filing cabinet of our minds . . . no use trying to shred it or burn it, or deny its existence, you can only hide it, from your own sight as well as other people's . . . which isn't made any easier when you surprise your nubile step-daughter in her bath . . .

How did I come to unlock this particular drawer of the filing cabinet anyway . . . ? Helen Reed, yes, I'd like to fuck her too, but that isn't just thinkable, it's conceivably doable, no taboo there . . . I kissed her, and she didn't object . . . she didn't respond exactly, but she didn't resist . . . it's been a good week for illicit kisses . . . I snogged Marianne yesterday, in Sainsbury's car-park of all places . . . I was in the store getting the wine for the party, she was doing the weekly grocery shop on her own, we met in the aisle pushing trolleys in opposite directions, between the soft drinks and the Phileas Fogg Tortilla Chips . . . we chatted for a while, innocently enough, but as we parted I asked her where she was parked and after a moment's hesitation she murmured, 'By the bottle bank' . . . When I'd filled my trolley with booze and paid at the checkout I pushed it out into the car-park and unloaded it into my car . . . it was dark and wet, a fine invisible drizzle falling on the rows of cars, misting their windows . . . I sat in my car watching until she came along, pushing her own trolley piled high with food . . . when she'd unloaded it into the boot of her Volvo she got into the driving seat but she didn't start the engine or turn on the lights. It was a nice dark spot beside the bottle bank, with no other cars parked near. I walked up to the car opened the front passenger's door and got in, she had the seat back down in the recline position . . . we fell on each other . . . wordlessly as always, tongues in each other's mouths, hands groping under each other's clothes . . . I was thinking we might actually do it right there and then in the car, like a prostitute and her trick, but there was a sudden explosion of broken glass as somebody tossed a salvo of bottles into the bottle bank and it startled her, she broke away, turned aside, and started the engine . . . without a word . . . she put the car into reverse . . . I had to scramble out in a hurry . . . she left me standing there

° °

beside the bottle bank, panting for breath and with an erection like a broomstick . . .

Oh yes, a nasty accident, VW camper turned over, MG in the ditch, police cars, ambulance . . . Thank you, officer . . . I'm out of here, as the Yanks say . . . *[recording ends]*

12

THURSDAY 13TH MARCH. I've encountered a strange and rather disturbing problem with one of my students, Sandra Pickering. I had already cast her as the Enigma of the group, because she said very little in class – just stared at me in a slightly disconcerting way, impassive, unblinking. She's in her late twenties, with a smooth oval face, straight shoulder-length blonde hair, and a full bust, usually concealed under a black leather blouson. Her lips are full and fleshy, the upper protruding over the lower, giving her a slightly sulky expression in repose. There's nothing remarkable about her appearance except that she has a metal stud in her tongue – silver I suppose, or perhaps stainless steel. You glimpse it now and again on the rare occasions when she speaks, winking and gleaming inside her mouth. It must be very uncomfortable when eating, one imagines.

She's one of the students who have given up jobs to do the course – hers was in advertising, she vouchsafed, when I went round the group on my first day questioning them about their backgrounds. In fact she never says anything to me unless I specifically address a question to her, and then she replies briefly and non-committally. I wondered whether she was depressed or had some other personal problem, and discreetly sounded out Simon Bellamy on the subject. He admitted that she seemed subdued this semester, but said she had never been a very demonstrative or talkative member of the group, always 'keeping herself to herself'. She has attended all the seminars and workshops, but she was the only student who didn't submit a piece on 'What is it Like to be a Bat?' (admittedly it was voluntary) and she didn't have anything to say about anyone else's, giving the impression that she considered the whole thing a rather trivial parlour game. More significantly, she was the last one in the group to show me her work-in-progress. She handed in a couple of chapters of a novel entitled *Burnt* on Tuesday, after I had sent her a sharpish note, and I read them yesterday.

The novel is about a young woman called Laura who works in an advertising agency as personal assistant to an older, married man called Alastair. She is attracted to him, and it's obvious that they're going to have some kind of affair in due course. It's a familiar, not to say banal story, enlivened by some shrewd observation of office politics, and a deft, sardonic handling of the contrast between the heroine's turbulent inner life – all romantic longing, erotic fantasy and self-doubt – and her composed, professional outward behaviour at work. It's written in the second person: '*You put on the white blouse. You take off the white blouse because it makes you look like a school prefect. You put on the black silk bustier. You take off the black silk bustier because it makes you look like a tart. You put the white blouse back on, leaving three buttons undone at the neck . . .*' I expect she got the idea from Jay McInerney, but no matter. So far, so good, I thought at the end of the first chapter.

But then, as the character of Alastair was developed in the second chapter, I had a very strange feeling of *déjà vu*. In several respects he resembles the character of Sebastian in *The Eye of the Storm*. He is tall and gangly, absent-minded and untidy, often turning up for work with odd socks, or with his shirt buttons done up askew. He has a habit of leaning back in his swivel chair and putting his feet up on the desk and vibrating a pen or pencil between his teeth when thinking. He answers the telephone with an impatient 'Yes?' He is forever banging into people and furniture because he walks around with his head down. And there are other, less tangible similarities, harder to pin down, but very apparent to me.

I was, to use an ugly but expressive word, gobsmacked. I didn't know what to make of it. Was it some kind of joke? If so, I didn't get it. Or had she read *The Eye of the Storm*, assimilated the details about the character of Sebastian into her creative subconscious, and recycled them without knowing it? That seemed the most likely explanation.

When she attended my breeze-block cell of an office for her tutorial, I came straight to the point: 'Have you read *The Eye of the Storm*'? She said she had, over the Christmas break. That surprised me: it meant she must have written the second chapter very recently, and she couldn't possibly have been unconscious of her borrowings. 'You do realize, I suppose,' I said, 'that a lot of Alastair's character traits correspond exactly to those of my character Sebastian?' 'Yes, I noticed that,' she said coolly. 'You *noticed*?' I repeated blankly. 'When did you notice?' 'When I read your book,' she said, looking equally blank. 'But you must have written this second chapter after you read *The Eye of the Storm*,' I said. 'Oh no,' she said, 'I wrote both those chapters last summer, before I started the course.' I stared at her. 'Have you revised them while you've been here?' I asked. 'Yes,' she said, 'in November, after I showed them to Russell.' 'Are you telling me,' I said slowly, 'that you wrote every word of this' – I held up the second chapter, and looked her straight in the eye – 'before you read *The Eye of the Storm*?' She didn't look away – she hardly blinked. 'Yes, of course,' she said. 'Then how do you explain the extraordinary similarities between my character and yours?' I listed some of them. 'Just coincidence, I suppose,' she said, with a shrug. The suggestion of a scowl passed over her smooth features, like a pond ruffled by the wind. 'You're not suggesting I copied your character, are you?' she said. 'I thought perhaps you reproduced some details from my book without being aware of it,' I said. 'Oh no,' she said, shaking her head emphatically, 'that's impossible. I told you – I started my novel before I read yours.' 'Perhaps somebody else told you about it? Perhaps you read a review?' I said, trying desperately to find a face-saving explanation which we could both agree on, even if I didn't believe it. 'No,' she said flatly, 'I'd remember it.' 'Well then,' I said, throwing up my hands, 'I don't know what to say. I'm totally at a loss.' I should report that throughout this conversation, while I shifted uncomfortably in my seat, and swivelled my chair from side to side, and fiddled with things on my desk, as if *I* were the accused party, she sat in her chair quite still and composed, with her knees and feet together and her hands joined demurely in her lap. 'I don't see the problem,' she said. 'They're quite common, men like that. We can't be the only writers to have invented a character who sometimes wears odd socks.' She added cheekily, 'It's a bit of a cliché, actually.' 'Of course the details are not significant if you take them one by one,' I said irritably.

'It's the same *combination* that's so extraordinary.' We were both silent for a few moments. 'What did you think of it, anyway?' she said, as if we had disposed of the problem. 'I find it hard to judge, in the circumstances,' I said. 'Have you written any more?' It turns out that she has written drafts of two more chapters. I said I would be very interested to see them, and brought the tutorial to a rather abrupt end.

I was thrown completely off-balance by this encounter, and have been unable to think of anything else all day. I'm afraid I was a very ineffective chair of the workshop session this afternoon – fortunately it was Simon Bellamy's turn to present his work, and he was quite capable of running the discussion himself. While it proceeded I kept glancing at Sandra Pickering, often finding myself, disconcertingly, looking straight into her opaque brown eyes. Once she made a comment on Simon's piece, and I glimpsed the little metal stud gleaming in the dark hollow of her mouth, like a jewel in the forehead of a toad. There is something faintly reptilian about this young woman – her impassivity, her repose, her unblinking gaze. No doubt I'm just projecting my own insecurity on to her. Suppose she is telling the truth. Is it possible that two different writers could independently invent the same character? Only, surely, if the character were a complete stereotype. I suppose that's what rattled me – the implication that both Sebastian and Alastair are stereotypes, composed of the same clichés.

The point is, I know that Sebastian *isn't* a stereotype, because I based him partly on Martin. Martin recognized the resemblance, and didn't mind – was rather tickled in fact – and so did most of our friends. But perhaps in the actual writing, in the process of turning the real Martin into the fictional Sebastian, I somehow lost the sense of felt life (as Henry James called it), I fell back lazily on familiar tricks of 'characterization', I failed to find a language that would give familiar traits and mannerisms a unique individual quality, and ended up producing something indistinguishable from the apprentice efforts of Sandra Pickering. A humbling, not to say humiliating, thought. I wish I had the folder of reviews of *The Eye of the Storm* with me here to browse through, to reassure myself that there was real originality in that book. Pitiful, really, that one's self-confidence should be so fragile, but there it is, it never took much to undermine mine. How often did Martin come home from work to find me long-faced and red-eyed because I'd lost faith in what I was writing. Once — it must have been before I had a computer, or even a photocopier — he had to go out into the back garden and recover a whole manuscript from the dustbin where I had thrown it in a fit of despair, and brought it back all stained and smeared, but smelling rather pleasantly of the potato and apple peelings adhering to it. He sat me down at the kitchen table with a glass of wine and made me read the first couple of chapters aloud to him, and convinced me that it was worth going on with. That was *Mixed Blessings*, so he was right. Oh Martin, how I miss you.

FRIDAY 14TH MARCH. Went into Cheltenham today to buy a present for Ralph Messenger. Choosing something appropriate was not easy. They've both been so kind to me that I wanted it to be more than a token, but not *too* expensive, or it would look like a bribe to make them go on being kind. In the end, after much hesitation, I settled on an executive toy, a little abacus made of brushed stainless steel. It was actually quite pricey, but I hope it will be received as merely witty.

I also bought myself a new dress for the occasion, a nice A-line frock in crushed velvet with a scoop neckline. I didn't want to wear the same skirt and top that I wore to the Richmonds' dinner party, and the other evening outfits I brought down here no longer please me for one reason or another. As usual I thought about going for something coloured and ended up getting black. It's safe and versatile and still in fashion. And after all, I *am* a widow.

13

'IF I were you, I would separate the historical stuff from the story of Alice and her family,' says Helen. 'Having Alice think so much about local politics and the architecture of the city, and so on, seems rather unnatural.'

'I know what you mean,' says Carrie. 'But how?'

'There's no reason why you shouldn't use an omniscient narrator, simply addressing the reader over the head of the character,' says Helen.

'Wouldn't that make the book seem rather old-fashioned?'

'You can give it a modern spin,' says Helen. 'Drop in a lot of references to the present day. You know *The French Lieutenant's Woman?*'

'Oh yes, I loved that book,' says Carrie.

'Or frame Alice's story with a contemporary one: somebody like yourself going over family papers, trying to reconstruct the history of her great-grandmother, researching the historical background . . .'

Carrie stops peeling prawns. 'That's a brilliant idea, Helen.'

'Well, don't rush into it,' says Helen. 'It would involve a lot of re-writing.'

'What would?' says Ralph, coming into the kitchen.

'Go away, Messenger,' says Carrie. 'Helen is giving me a tutorial.'

'Oh, have you been reading Carrie's book?' Ralph says to Helen. 'What's it like? She won't let me see it.'

'It's very promising,' says Helen.

'Am I in it?'

'Of course, that's the first question you *would* ask,' says Carrie.

'I don't think so,' says Helen.

'What do you want, Messenger?' says Carrie.

'The Screwpull,' says Ralph, grinning at Helen as if inviting her to see an innuendo in the name of this device. 'The host's best friend.'

'It's in the drinks cabinet.'

'No it's not.'

'Then it's where you last left it. Try the sideboard drawers.'

'OK.' Ralph plunges his index finger into a bowl of guacamole, licks it, gives an approving grunt, and goes out.

'I wish I was taking your course, Helen,' says Carrie.

'You might not like it,' says Helen. 'Some of the students are pretty rough with each other's work.'

It is the evening of Ralph's birthday party. Helen has arrived early, by prior arrangement, to help with the food preparations. Most of the serious food – the poached whole salmon, the farm-cured ham on the bone, the variegated salads – has been supplied by a local catering firm, and is already laid out in the dining room beside stacks of plates and sets of cutlery wrapped in thick paper napkins. But Carrie likes to prepare her own canapés. Helen has been entrusted with the task of chopping and slicing *crudités* for the savoury dips. Carrie herself is peeling fresh prawns and impaling them on toothpicks, separated by cubes of ripe pimiento, like miniature shish kebabs. In the large square hall, with its floor of black and white flags, a table has been placed to serve as a bar, with bottles of red and white wine arranged in two symmetrical phalanxes, separated by a large tray of gleaming wineglasses. Shortly after Ralph has left the kitchen the two women hear the regular *pop! pop!* of corks being pulled with the aid of the Screwpull. More distantly the strains of cool instrumental jazz percolate from the hi-fi in the drawing room, where Emily is placing little bowls of nuts and pretzels in strategic places. The Messengers are experienced party-givers, and everyone knows their function and how to perform it. The front doorbell rings.

'The first guest,' says Helen, superfluously.

'I guarantee it's Duggers,' says Carrie, glancing at the kitchen clock. 'Nobody ever explained to him that a party invitation is not a test of punctuality. Be a sweetheart and talk to him, would you Helen?'

'Now you can explain quantum mechanics to me, Professor Douglass,' says Helen.

'This hardly seems an appropriate moment,' he says, smiling primly.

'But it's lovely and quiet,' she says. 'Soon this room will be full of people and noise and it won't be possible to have a serious conversation.' They are alone in the drawing room, standing in front of the simulated coal fire. Helen holds a glass of Californian Sauvignon Blanc, Douglass a glass of orange juice. Helen proffers a bowl of macadamia nuts. Douglass takes one and nibbles it with a rapid movement of his front teeth, like a squirrel.

'Why are you interested?' he says.

'Ralph said it had something to do with the theory of consciousness,' she says. 'I'm interested in that.'

'Very small particles behave like waves, in random and unpredictable ways,' says Douglas. 'When we make a measurement, we cause the wave to collapse. It's been suggested that the phenomenon of consciousness is a series of continuous collapses of the wave function.'

'Is that the same as chaos theory?' says Helen.

'No.'

'I just thought . . . "collapse" and "chaos" . . .'

'They are quite different concepts.'

'But they make science sound terribly exciting, don't they?'

Professor Douglass evidently finds this remark too girlishly trivial to be worthy of a response. 'Some quantum physicists argue that we create the universe we inhabit by the act of observing it. That it is only one of many possible universes that might have existed, or, in an extreme formulation, actually do exist parallel to the one we inhabit.'

'Do you believe that?' Helen asks.

'No,' says Professor Douglass. 'The universe is certainly there, independently of ourselves, and was there before we existed. But it is possible that we can never know it as it really is, because of the uncertainty principle.'

'The uncertainty principle, yes . . .' says Helen. 'I've heard of it of course, but . . .'

'Heisenberg demonstrated that you cannot accurately specify

both the position and the speed of a particle. If you get one right, you get the other wrong.' He looks round at the empty room and then at his watch. 'Did I make a mistake about the time of this party?' he says.

'No. Somebody has to be the first to arrive,' says Helen. 'You created the party, you see. Out of all the many possible parties there might have been! If somebody else had arrived first, it would have taken a completely different course, because I would have spoken to them instead, and perhaps never spoken to you at all, or not about the same thing, and every conversation that will now take place would have been different if you hadn't come first. How's that for a quantum theory of parties?' She laughs, pleased with her conceit.

'It's more like chaos theory, actually,' says Douglass pedantically.

'Oh, why?' says Helen.

'Chaos theory deals with systems that are unusually sensitive to variations in their initial conditions or affected by a large number of independent variables. Like the weather, for instance.'

'Oh, I know, you mean when a butterfly flutters its wings on one side of the world and sets off a tornado on the other.'

'That is an oversimplification, but basically, yes.'

'Oh good,' says Helen. 'At last I got something right.'

The front doorbell rings, and there is a sudden hubbub in the hall.

'There, some more independent variables have arrived,' says Helen.

The house begins to fill up. The curtains on the long Georgian windows have not been drawn, and light streams out on to the drive and footpath. Approaching guests can see the throng inside, chatting and laughing and drinking and chewing animatedly but silently, like actors on television when the sound is turned down. The door has been left on the latch, so there is no longer any need to ring the bell, but Ralph hovers just inside the door to welcome his guests, and receive their congratulations, birthday cards and gifts. Men are directed to hang their coats in the downstairs cloakroom, where some linger to examine the wall-paper with its pattern of illustrations reproduced from *La Vie Parisienne*; women are invited to spread their coats on the twin beds of the guest bedroom, which has an *en-suite* bathroom convenient for last-minute adjustments to hair and make-up. Divested of their outdoor attire, the guests provide themselves with red or white wine, beer or soft drinks from the bar-table in the hall, tended by Mark Messenger in an electric blue shirt and black Dockers, then pass into the large drawing room, where Simon and Hope wriggle through the crush bearing plates of canapés, darting back occasionally for replenishments to the kitchen, where Carrie is warming up the ciabatta and focaccia and organic wholemeal rolls in the electric oven for supper, while chatting to some women friends who are enviously inspecting the new modular kitchen units and work surfaces imported from Germany and fitted just a few months ago.

In the drawing room knots of guests form, loosen and reform. Conversational topics are carried from one group to another like viruses: the sad case of Jean-Dominique Bauby; Dolly the cloned sheep; crashes on the motorway in fog earlier in the week; the defeat of England by Italy in a World Cup qualifier at Wembley; the schoolteacher in nearby Cheddar shown by a DNA test to be the direct descendant of a prehistoric hunter whose skeleton was found in one of the caves; the impending General Election.

'May Day, a good omen for Labour,' somebody says.

'We don't need omens,' says another. 'We've got polls. We've got by-election results. If the Wirral result is replicated in May, Labour will have a majority of over two hundred and fifty.'

'That's pure fantasy, of course.'

'Maybe . . . but even if it's only half true . . .'

Laetitia Glover is in a state of exasperated indecision over the election, which she explains to Helen. 'Of course I want the Tories out, that's a priority,' she says. 'And the best way to achieve that in Cheltenham is a tactical vote for the Lib Dems – they took the seat off the Tories at the last election. But it goes against the grain to actually *work* for the Lib Dems. I'm condemned to watch from the sidelines.'

'Couldn't you work for Labour in another constituency?' says Helen.

'Well, I *could* . . .' Laetitia says, drawling the last word, and not looking particularly grateful for the suggestion.

'But one hardly feels like working for the party under Blair and Brown,' says Reginald Glover.

'Exactly!' says Laetitia. 'They've hamstrung any future Labour government by promising not to increase income tax.'

'Do you want to pay more income tax, Laetitia?' Ralph asks her, as he comes up with a bottle of wine in each hand, red and white.

'If it's necessary to save the Health Service,' she says stiffly. 'But it's the fat cats in the privatized industries who should be squeezed.'

'I see Bill Gates is now the richest man in the world,' says Ralph, topping up her glass. 'He's worth twenty-nine billion dollars and every day he makes another forty-two million.'

'It's simply obscene that one man should have such wealth,' says Laetitia.

'Just think,' says Ralph. 'If we could persuade him to move to Britain, and reintroduced supertax, he could probably fund the National Health Service all on his own.' He winks at Helen and moves away.

'What was that supposed to mean?' Laetitia demands.

'I think it's about high taxation being a disincentive to enterprise,' says Reginald Glover, with a slight curl of his hairy lip. 'I'm afraid Ralph always had a soft spot for Mrs Thatcher. Not surprising really. What was Thatcherism but Darwinian economics? Survival of the fittest.'

Helen detaches herself from the Glovers and joins a little huddle of Ralph's graduate students who seem, surprisingly, to be discussing Zola. 'Which of his novels do you like best?' she asks Jim. But it transpires that they are discussing a footballer who scored a decisive goal against England on Wednesday. Not having much to contribute on this subject, she turns aside to greet Jasper Richmond, who is working his way back to the bar.

'Hallo,' he says. 'Come and get another drink.' He leads her out into the hall, and recharges his glass and hers. 'I'm glad you were invited. The Messengers give the best parties around here.'

'They certainly seem to know how to do it,' says Helen.

'They have the money, and the space. And you get a mixture of arts and sciences you don't get anywhere else. That's mainly Carrie's doing. Nice house isn't it?' He gestures largely with his free hand.

'Lovely.'

'They've got another one, you know, in the country near Stow.'

'I know, I've been there.'

'Have you?' He looks surprised, and impressed. 'That's quick. Congratulations.'

'What for?' Helen asks.

'You've obviously been adopted . . . Only very special friends are invited to the cottage. They do that every now and then, or rather Carrie does. She takes a fancy to someone, a woman, usually a newcomer . . .' He sniggers. 'I don't mean to suggest that she's a lesbian.'

'Oh good,' says Helen lightly.

'It happened to Marianne when we got married. It happened to young Annabelle Riverdale, when Colin was appointed. It happened to a lot of the women here tonight. For a while you're the favourite, until another candidate comes along. Did you go in the hot tub?'

'Yes.'

'It's a kind of baptism,' he says, nodding. 'But I'm delighted – it's just what you need while you're at GU. Wealthy hospitable friends.'

'Yes, they've been very kind,' says Helen.

'Marianne thinks Carrie does it to pre-empt any extramural interest on Ralph's part. Consciously or unconsciously.'

'What do you mean?'

'Well, when an attractive new woman arrives on campus, Carrie makes her a friend of the family. It makes it difficult for her to become a special friend of Ralph's.'

'I see,' says Helen.

'There's the VC,' says Jasper, looking over her shoulder. 'Come and meet him.'

Jasper Richmond introduces Helen to the Vice Chancellor and his wife, Sir Stanley and Lady Hibberd. 'Stan and Viv, that's what our friends call us,' the VC says cheerfully, in a Lancashire accent. 'We're not lah-dee-dah, are we, Viv? Very glad to have you on board, Helen. You don't mind if I call you Helen?'

'Not at all,' she says.

Colin Riverdale comes up and hovers, smiling, with Annabelle at his side holding a large goblet of white wine in her two hands like a communion cup. Sir Stan nods a greeting to them but carries on speaking to Helen.

'I'll be honest with you,' says Sir Stan, 'I didn't rate creative writing as an academic subject when I came here. But when I looked at the books, I was converted.'

'You mean, books by former students?' says Helen.

'No, no! I mean the accounts,' says Sir Stan, laughing heartily. 'I don't have much time for reading, I'm afraid. Viv's the reader in our house, aren't you ducks?'

'I did so enjoy your book, *The Eye of a Needle*,' says Lady Hibberd to Helen.

Helen smiles, murmurs something indistinguishable.

'That's by Margaret Drabble,' says Annabelle Riverdale, 'and it's called *The Needle's Eye*.'

'Oh,' says Lady Hibberd.

Colin looks daggers at his wife. 'Sorry,' she says. 'It comes of being a librarian.' She bows her head contritely and drinks from her goblet of wine.

'Well, it was the Eye of something,' says Lady Hibberd.

'I wrote a book called *The Eye of the Storm*,' says Helen.

'That's it,' says Lady Hibberd. 'It begins with a man in an off-licence.'

'Well, no, actually that's *The Needle's Eye*, I'm afraid,' says Helen apologetically.

Annabelle Riverdale chokes on her wine. Colin leads her away like a naughty child.

'You know Patrick White wrote a novel called *The Eye of the Storm?*' Jasper says to Helen, to distract the company from this incident.

'Yes. I found out too late to change the title of mine,' says Helen. 'Anyway, I'd become attached to it.'

'Ah well, no wonder you got confused, Viv,' says Sir Stan to his wife. 'Is that allowed?' he demands of Helen.

'Yes, there's no copyright in titles,' she says.

The decibel level of the conversational roar in the drawing room is rising. Most of the guests have had two or three glasses of wine by now. Ralph and Carrie exchange a glance. Ralph raises an interrogative eyebrow; Carrie nods. She begins to direct guests towards the dining room, where a line soon forms around the long mahogany table, cooing and exclaiming over the appetizing dishes. The guests take their laden plates back into the drawing room or scatter to other rooms on the ground floor – the breakfast room, the television room, the family room – which have been opened up and tidied for the occasion, with chairs and cushions and stools arranged invitingly in small arcs.

Ralph sees Marianne Richmond slipping out into the back garden for a smoke. After a minute or two, he picks up a carton of empty wine bottles from the hall and follows her. He sees the red tip of her cigarette glowing in the shadow of the patio wall and goes over.

'Did anyone see you come out?' she says.

Ralph stands still, but does not speak.

'Did anyone see you?' she repeats.

'I brought some empty bottles with me as an alibi,' he says, putting his clinking burden on the ground. After a short pause, he adds, 'I thought we weren't to speak. I thought that was the first rule of this game.'

'The game's up,' Marianne says. 'Well, over, anyway.'

'What do you mean?'

'Oliver saw us in Sainsbury's car-park on Tuesday.'

'I didn't know Oliver was with you!'

'He wasn't,' says Marianne. 'It was an unlucky coincidence. He was on independence training. He does it every Tuesday afternoon at the F.E. College. Special Needs. They take them out, teach them to use public transport, take them shopping. They went to Sainsbury's on Tuesday, Oliver got separated from the group somehow, got lost, was wandering about the car-park looking for the minibus, when he saw us, in my car.'

'How do you know?'

'He said to me yesterday, "I saw you kissing Ralph Messenger in your car." '

'Christ!' says Ralph. 'He knows me by name, does he?'

'He never forgets a name. Especially anyone who's been on television.'

'Christ,' Ralph says again.

'I'm terrified he'll mention it to Jasper.'

'Can't you tell him not to?'

'He wouldn't understand.'

'Well, if he does, you'll just have to deny it,' says Ralph. 'After all, it sounds a pretty tall story doesn't it? Nobody would believe it if it was your word against his.'

'Oliver doesn't tell lies,' says Marianne. 'He doesn't understand the concept.'

'No, of course he wouldn't,' says Ralph thoughtfully. 'No T.O.M.'

'What?'

'Theory of mind. Knowing that other people may interpret the world differently from yourself. The ability to lie depends on it. Most children acquire it at the age of three to four. Autistics never do.'

'Well, that's very interesting, but not much help,' says Marianne. 'Jasper knows that Oliver doesn't tell lies.'

'You'll just have to say he must have been mistaken,' says Ralph. 'After all, it was dark, raining.'

'But we were there, the three of us, at the same time,' says Marianne. 'Jasper could establish that if he wants to be forensic about it. Suspicious circumstances, wouldn't you say?'

Ralph thinks for a moment. 'OK. Suppose Oliver saw us, separately, in the store, then he gets separated from his group, he's wandering round the car-park in a state of some distress, looking for his mates, and he sees a couple who look like us, wearing the same sort of clothes perhaps, snogging in a car, the windows are all misted up, and he thinks it's us. But of course the idea is preposterous. Ralph Messenger and Marianne Richmond snogging in Sainsbury's car-park? You just laugh it off. No problem.'

'Well, I hope you're right,' says Marianne, taking a last drag on her cigarette and stamping it out on the flagstones. 'We'd better go back indoors,' she says. 'But not together.'

'What about a kiss, first?' he says, reaching out for her.

'No Ralph.' She pushes him away firmly. 'It was a stupid game, and now it's over.'

Marianne turns on her heel and walks back to the house, clutching herself and shivering a little from the cold.

Ralph picks up the box of empty bottles and carries them to the dustbins at the side of the house.

Helen finds Professor Douglass buttoning up his overcoat in the hall.

'Must you go so soon?' Helen asks him.

'I'm afraid so,' he says. 'My womenfolk become uneasy if I'm out very late at night.' It is ten-fifteen by the grandfather clock in the hall. 'And to be frank with you, I'm not excessively fond of parties. One never finishes a conversation properly.'

'I know what you mean,' says Helen.

'Not that that would bother our host,' says Douglass, putting on a pair of black kid gloves, and flexing his fingers. 'The master of the scientific sound-bite.' He exposes his teeth in a smile to make this seem like a genial jest. 'Tell him and Mrs Messenger that I had to leave, would you? I couldn't find them to say goodbye.'

'Of course.'

'Goodnight, then.'

With two clicks of the press-studs on his gloves, he is gone.

Helen goes into the drawing room, where Laetitia Glover is having an argument with Colin Riverdale about birth control. 'The Catholic Church has a lot to answer for,' she says. 'Opposing contraceptive programmes in the Third World is criminally irresponsible.'

'It suits the capitalist countries of the northern hemisphere to keep populations down in the southern hemisphere,' says Colin. 'By raising the standard of living in the Third World in a purely material sense they create new markets for their consumer goods.' This point silences Laetitia for a moment, because it enlists an argument she has used herself in other contexts.

'I'm not just talking about poverty and malnutrition,' says Laetitia. 'There's also the question of AIDS. African women need to be protected against the consequences of male promiscuity.'

'It's no use distributing condoms to African women if African men won't use them,' says Colin.

Annabelle Riverdale, who is listening silently and despondently to this discussion, raises her empty glass, squints at it, and moves unsteadily towards the door, evidently bent on getting a refill. Helen follows her and catches up with her at the table in the hall. 'Are you feeling all right?' she asks.

'Yes thanks,' says Annabelle. 'I just thought I'd edge away before Colin starts on the joys of periodic abstinence.'

Helen smiles sympathetically. 'You mean the Rhythm Method? My sister tells me it's lots of bother and it doesn't work anyway.'

'It works for us,' says Annabelle.

'Oh, good,' says Helen, slightly confused.

'Because I take the pill as well,' says Annabelle. She raises a forefinger and taps it against her lips. 'Don't tell Colin.'

'No, of course not,' says Helen, gaping a little.

'I think I'm going to be sick,' says Annabelle. 'Where's the nearest loo?'

'Over here,' says Helen, taking her arm and guiding her towards the downstairs cloakroom.

Returning to the house with his empty box, Ralph encounters Helen.

'Oh, hallo,' she says. 'Colin Riverdale has taken Annabelle home. She wasn't feeling well.'

'Oh dear. I hope she's not pregnant again.'

'She's not.'

Ralph looks surprised by her emphatic tone.

'And Professor Douglass was looking for you,' says Helen. 'He had to leave.'

'That's Duggers. Always the first to arrive and the first to go. I don't know why he bothers to come. He hates parties anyway.'

'So he said.'

'Did he . . . ? I haven't opened your present yet. Shall I now?'

'If you like,' she says.

There is a small table beside the front door where the gifts and cards have been deposited. Ralph unwraps Helen's present, and draws the stainless steel abacus from its box. 'Ah, what I've always wanted,' he says. 'Thank you very much.'

'I thought it might come in useful when the millennium bug strikes,' says Helen.

'I saw a cartoon the other day, with two ancient Romans looking at one of these,' he says, sliding a few ball-bearings along the top wire of the abacus with his forefinger, 'and one is saying to the other, *"I'm afraid it's going to crash when we move from BC to AD."* '

'Seriously,' says Helen. 'Aren't you worried? I read somewhere that on January 1st 2000 everything will stop. Planes will fall out of the sky, ships go round and round in circles, operating theatres will go dark, supermarkets will run out of food and nobody will get paid their wages or their pensions.'

'Alarmist talk and millennial fever,' says Ralph. 'There *is* a problem with some of the big old main-frame computers, but it'll be sorted out.'

'I'm rather sorry to hear you say that,' says Helen. 'There's something rather poetically satisfying about the idea of modern civilization being undone by its own technology.'

'Well, you wouldn't much enjoy being pushed back into the

Middle Ages overnight, I can tell you,' he says. 'By the way I looked up that Darwin reference for you: "*Crying is a puzzler.*"'

'Oh, thanks. I'd forgotten all about it.'

'It's in my study – upstairs. Perhaps you'd like to see it? The study, I mean. Most people think it is worth the climb.'

'Well, all right, thank you,' says Helen after a moment's hesitation.

Carrie happens to pass from the kitchen to the dining room at this moment, carrying a large bowl of chocolate mousse, with Nicholas Beck in tow bearing a similar dish of fruit salad. 'Just going to show Helen my study,' Ralph says to Carrie. 'Keep me some chocolate mousse.'

'No,' she says, without breaking step. 'It's first come, first served.' Nicholas Beck gives a little smirk over his shoulder as he follows Carrie into the dining room.

'Do you want to have your pudding now?' Helen says to Ralph.

'No, she's only kidding. There's another bowl in the fridge, I bet. Come on, we'll avoid the feeding frenzy.'

He leads her up two flights of stairs. 'There are two schools of thought about studies,' he says. 'One is that it should be on the ground floor, so that you can keep in touch with what's going on in the house, pop in and out easily to make the most of every scrap of spare time. The other is that it should be at the top of the house, as far away from the domestic action as possible, somewhere you retire to, where you won't be disturbed.'

'A lonely tower,' says Helen.

'Exactly. I'm a lonely tower man.'

Ralph Messenger's study has been constructed out of what were originally servants' quarters, making a large room nearly half the floor area of the house, with a deep fitted carpet, extensive bookshelves, a vast desk and swivel chair, a round table with two upright chairs, a Charles Eames chaise longue, numerous reading lamps, standard lamps and spotlights, wood veneer filing cabinets, a computer tower and large-screen monitor, several other electric and electronic appliances – printer, scanner, fax machine, a combination TV-VCR, a hi-fi system – and a telescope mounted on a tripod under a skylight.

All the furniture is made of cherrywood and stainless steel, and upholstered in black leather.

'I wouldn't call this a lonely tower,' says Helen. 'It's a cross between a luxury bachelor pad and Mission Control.'

Ralph chuckles. 'It's rather nice, isn't it? But this is the finishing touch it's been waiting for.' He places the abacus on the desk-top, beside a set of brushed stainless steel cylinders welded together as a container for pens and pencils.

'It matches!' says Helen, pleased.

'Yes. I assumed you'd asked Carrie's advice.'

'No, it was just chance. Or my sixth sense. But you probably don't believe in a sixth sense.'

He smiles. 'No, I don't.' He goes across to one of the filing cabinets, pulls out a drawer on noiseless bearings, and extracts from one of the suspended files a single sheet, the photocopy of a page from Darwin's *Notebooks*. 'Here you are.'

He puts the sheet under the reading lamp on the desk top so that they can both look at it. 'It's a passage from the 1838 notebook. Darwin is thirty. The voyage of the *Beagle* is two years behind him. He has the idea of evolution firmly by the tail. Hah, no pun intended . . . He's convinced that man is descended from apes, but he hasn't gone public yet – he knows all too well what an uproar it will cause. He's been thinking about laughter – that when humans laugh they expose their canine teeth, just like baboons. He speculates that our laughter and smiling might be traced back to the way apes communicate the discovery of food to the rest of their tribe.' Ralph underlines the quotation with his index finger as he reads aloud: ' "*This way of viewing the subject important, laughing modified barking, smiling modified laughing. Barking to tell other animals in associated kinds of good news, discovery of prey. – no doubt arising from want of assistance.*" Then comes the afterthought. He can't think what crying might be a modification of. "*Crying is a puzzler.*" '

' "*Sunt lacrimae rerum,*" ' says Helen.

'My Latin's a tad rusty,' Ralph says.

' "There are tears of things." Virgil. It's almost untranslatable, but one knows what he means. Something like, "Crying is a puzzler." '

'Actually laughter is a puzzler too,' says Ralph. 'Darwin's explanation doesn't really cut it.'

'Could you design a robot that would laugh at another robot's jokes?' Helen asks.

'It would be a challenge,' says Ralph. 'But I don't see why not.'

'I don't believe a machine could ever feel amused,' says Helen. 'Or happy, or sad – or bored.'

'Bored?' Ralph smiles, as if he had never considered this possibility, or impossibility, before.

'Yes. If my Toshiba laptop were a human being it would be bored stiff because I only use it to do word-processing. I don't suppose I use even ten per cent of its brainpower. But the computer doesn't mind.'

'Absolutely,' says Ralph. 'That's why computers are so liberating for mankind. We can abolish boredom! Why would you want to reproduce it artificially? Is boredom an essential feature of human nature?'

'Well, I think perhaps it is. Happiness and sadness are, anyway. I want to see a robot that can laugh and cry and sulk before I believe it's conscious.'

'You may not have to wait long. Computers are evolving at incredible speed.'

'I know, I heard you on the radio the other day.'

'Did you?' Ralph looks pleased. 'Well, it's true. Your little laptop probably has as much memory as the University's first main-frame. A megabyte of memory cost half a million in those days. Now it costs about two pounds.'

'But you don't need megabytes of memory to get a joke,' says Helen. 'Even an infant can recognize something that's funny. Ever played "Peep-bo" with a baby?'

'True,' Ralph says. 'But I was thinking of identifying the logical structure of events perceived as funny, so you could build that into the architecture. Suppose one got a computer to crunch millions of jokes instead of numbers? It might discover the mechanism behind laughter. Did I tell you what a very fetching dress that is you're wearing?'

'No,' says Helen, 'but thank you. Shouldn't we rejoin the party?'

'OK,' he says. 'Would you like to take this with you?' He folds the sheet and slips it into an envelope.

'Thanks,' she says as she takes it from him.

'Well, thanks for the abacus. Do I get a kiss as well?'

'I don't think so,' says Helen, after a momentary pause.

'Didn't you enjoy it last time?'

Helen seems unwilling to answer this question. 'I don't want to have an affair with you, Ralph,' she says at length.

He opens his eyes wide, spreads his hands, and grins. 'Hey, who said anything about an affair? All I had in mind was a friendly kiss.'

'Really?' She looks him challengingly in the eye. 'Are you telling me that it has never crossed your mind that you would like to go further than that?'

He stares at her for a moment, mouth open a little, then laughs. 'Well, sure. But men think that all the time about the women they meet, attractive women. It doesn't mean they intend to do anything about it.'

'Isn't kissing doing something about it?'

'Not necessarily. There are all kinds of kisses. Some are passionate, some are . . . just friendly.' He smiles. 'The qualia of kissing are infinitely various.'

'Well, you should know,' she says. 'You seem to do a lot of research.'

Ralph stops smiling. 'What d'you mean?'

'Oh, nothing.'

'Come on. Tell me.'

Helen looks away and then back at Ralph. 'I happened to see you kissing Marianne Richmond at their dinner party . . . through the kitchen window . . . I wandered out into the back yard by mistake. I wasn't spying.'

'I'm not having an affair with Marianne,' says Ralph.

'It's really none of my business,' says Helen. 'I wish I hadn't mentioned it. Shall we go down?'

'We were just fooling around. It was a game we used to play, a kind of dare-game. But it's over now.'

'As I say, it's none of my business.' She moves towards the door. 'I'm going down now.'

'Hang on.' He turns off the desk lamp and a standard lamp. 'I hope this doesn't mean we can't be friends any more,' he says.

'No, on the contrary. It's to ensure that I can go on being friends with both of you.'

'Oh good.' He joins her at the door. 'Er, you haven't . . . you wouldn't . . . say anything to Carrie about . . . ?' She gives him a slightly contemptuous look. 'Sorry,' he says.

Helen walks out of the room. Ralph turns out the remaining lights from the master switch by the door, and closes it behind him. The roar of conversation rises to meet them as they descend the staircase.

14

MONDAY 17TH MARCH. Another weekend has passed in thrall to the Messengers.

It had been agreed that I would stay the night after the party on Saturday, so that I could drink without worrying about driving myself home. I felt a little self-conscious, standing beside Ralph and Carrie in the hall and saying goodbye to the last departing guests, as if I were a member of the family — but that is what I seem to have become. 'Adopted', was Jasper Richmond's word. I was somewhat disturbed by his remarks, but he's a rather malicious gossip, and probably everything he says should be taken with a pinch of salt. If Carrie is being nice to me just to keep tabs on Ralph, it seems a risky strategy. He's already managed to kiss me once, and would have done again on Saturday night if I'd let him.

After the final stragglers had gone, I helped collect the soiled plates and glasses from various rooms on the ground floor, and to stack them in the kitchen ready for the domestic help, who was coming in next morning specially to attend to them. Carrie made the three of us (the children had long ago retired to their bedrooms to watch TV or sleep) a delicious nightcap, a Mexican drink of hot chocolate with brandy and a touch of chilli in it, and we sat round the kitchen table sipping this concoction and discussing the highlights of the party before we retired to bed.

The guest bedroom still smelled faintly of the mingled perfumes of the evening's female guests. I opened the window to air it before I went to bed. And I locked the door. Why? Did I think Ralph might try to sneak into my bed in the middle of the night? An absurd idea of course; and yet, as I entertained it, tossing and turning under the duvet (something in the Mexican drink seemed to be acting as a stimulant rather than a soporific), I wondered what I would do if I had left the door unlocked and he did sneak in. Supposing Carrie took a pill and was sound asleep, and he crept out of their bedroom and into my room and slipped under the covers – would I scream and struggle? Bring Carrie and the children running from their bedrooms? Denounce Ralph in a scene of excruciating embarrassment, and leave by taxi in the middle of the night? No, I wouldn't. So what would I have done? Protested and remonstrated in whispers? *'Are you mad? Get out of my bed at once or I'll, I'll, I'll . . .'* What? *'I'll never speak to you again.'* A feeble threat. So what – do I let him have his way? Of course not – and yet I had to ask myself whether this train of thought wasn't a variation on the famous female rape fantasy the pop psychologists tell us about, the desire to abandon oneself to sex without having to take moral responsibility for it. Why else was I imagining this scenario? I'm not going to have an affair with Ralph Messenger because I don't wish to be a party to adultery, not because I don't find him attractive. I do find him attractive, alas.

Mulling wakefully over our conversation in his study, I regretted (and still regret) that I spoke so bluntly: *'I don't want to have an affair with you, Ralph.'* He had the grace to admit that some such thought had crossed his mind. But now he knows that it has crossed *my* mind too, something I would rather have kept to myself. And then I stupidly blurted out that I'd seen him kissing Marianne Richmond – it must have been all the wine I had drunk that loosened my tongue and dissolved my usual discretion. As soon as the words were out of my mouth I wished I could suck them back in and swallow them. He looked really rattled, then angry, before he recovered his usual poise.

Recalling all that when I woke the next morning, I felt some uneasiness about meeting him and Carrie at breakfast, and took my time washing and dressing. Fortunately I'd brought a pair of jeans and a sweater with me, so I didn't have to appear in my new party frock among the comfortably *deshabillés* Messengers. Carrie was still in her dressing gown, her hair tousled and her face shiny with moisturiser, and Ralph was wearing a CAL TECH tee-shirt and a pair of tracksuit trousers. The children who were up were still in pyjamas. They were eating waffles with maple syrup – apparently an established Sunday morning treat – at the long kitchen table. Ralph greeted me cheerily, without a hint of embarrassment, and Carrie poured me freshly squeezed orange juice and coffee.

She said that they were going to spend the day at Horseshoes, and why didn't I come with them. I had anticipated this invitation and was going to excuse myself on the grounds of all the manuscripts I have to read, but I weakly changed my mind and accepted. It was a bright crisp morning and the thought of a day in the country was inviting, certainly more inviting than solitude and a TV dinner on Maisonette Row.

So I spent another agreeable day with the Messengers, helping Carrie prepare the vegetables for lunch, helping Emily with her French homework, playing Trivial Pursuit with the younger kids, while Ralph retired to his study to read a book he is reviewing for one of next Sunday's papers. I felt a little like a governess to a rich family in a nineteenth-century novel, sharing some of the perks of affluence in return for making myself invaluable, but I didn't really mind.

When the time came for the hot tub I excused myself – rather wistfully because the sky had clouded over in the course of the afternoon and a few snowflakes were beginning to fall. The idea of sitting in the hot tub while it was snowing was exciting, but I hadn't brought a swimming costume with me. Ralph rather cheekily suggested I wore my underwear, and put it in the tumble drier afterwards, but Carrie found me an oversized tee-shirt and an old pair of cotton shorts belonging to Emily which served the purpose admirably, practical without being alluring. It was a magical experience, lying back in the hot tub, watching the feathery flakes flutter down, dark against the sky, then white when they reached eye level, then melting into the steam and the hot water. By the time we got out, the snow had settled in a thin layer on the deck, and we left our warm wet footprints in it as we climbed back to the house. I made sure that I didn't get left behind in the tub with Ralph this time.

I have new neighbours: a young couple have moved into the

maisonette next door. When I got back from Horseshoes yesterday evening I saw there was a car in the drive and lights on behind the curtains. This morning I saw the new occupants go off for a jog together, and popped out to introduce myself when they returned, glowing and panting from their exercise. Ross and Jackie, they're called. He has just been appointed to a lectureship in Sports Science, whatever that is, in the School of Community Studies, whatever they are, and she is a physiotherapist, hoping to get a job in a private clinic in Cheltenham or Gloucester. I invited them in for a coffee, but Ross said they were 'running late'. I said it seemed quite early enough for running to me, but the quip failed to register. But when Ross said they had better go and get showered, Jackie giggled as if at something risqué. I get the impression that they haven't been living together for very long. They have a honeymoon air about them. Ross had his arm round Jackie's waist as we talked, and patted her bottom fondly as they went off to take their shower, no doubt together. I'm afraid they're unlikely to become bosom pals of mine.

I saw Annabelle Riverdale at the Library this morning. She was on duty at the Reader Services Desk, and gave me a slightly panic-stricken look as I went by, so I stopped to say hallo. 'I'm afraid I disgraced myself on Saturday,' she said. 'Don't worry about it,' I said, 'I don't think anybody noticed.' 'Colin did,' she said gloomily. 'I get nervous at parties and then I drink too much.' She eyed me speculatively. 'You mustn't take any notice of what I say in my cups.' 'I can't even remember what you said,' I said airily. She gave me a timid, grateful smile.

WEDNESDAY 19TH MARCH. Students handed in their 'Mary the Colour Scientist' pieces yesterday. Some excellent work again. Sandra Pickering did a surprisingly good imitation of Fay Weldon. But she hasn't given me the next chapters of her novel yet. I reminded her at the end of the class and she mumbled something about needing to do more work on them. I suspect she's trying to make her Alastair less like my Sebastian, and finding it difficult. It seems obvious to me now that she must have read *The Eye of the Storm* when it first came out, borrowed from it unconsciously when she came to start her own novel, then read it again last Christmas because I was coming to teach the course, and realized what she'd done. If she'd only admit it I could do something to help her.

I haven't seen much of my new neighbours, though I do hear them through the party wall, laughing and shouting to each other, and thumping energetically up and down the stairs. Sometimes a sudden silence falls after a series of shrieks from Jackie, and I wonder if horseplay has turned into what I'm sure they call 'bonking'. I imagine Ross catching Jackie on the stairs, pulling down her tracksuit bottoms and taking her incontinently on the landing. Once I pressed my ear to the wall and listened for the sounds of sexual congress, but heard nothing except the beating of my own heart.

15

MARY had a little lamb . . . testing, testing . . . It's 9.10 a.m Monday 17th March and I'm driving to work. Progress is painfully slow on the Inner Ring this morning, a combination of rain and roadworks, so I got out the old Pearlcorder to pass the time . . . It seems to have become a habit . . . like keeping a diary, though I never kept a diary before, couldn't be bothered, but dictating to Voicemaster makes it easy . . . and perhaps it's middle age, you begin to feel rather possessive, protective about your thoughts, anxious to get them down on paper before they fade away . . . the brain cells are decaying inexorably, the neural networking is getting slower, you generate fewer new ideas . . . Or you forget the ones you've had – spend hours, days, working through an argument or a theory and then when you finally get it into shape you realize it's an idea you had yonks ago . . . This is a cheerful train of thought for a wet Monday morning . . . comes of passing the fifty mark no doubt . . . The party was . . . interesting . . . Marianne, yes, I'm not sorry she's called off our little game, it was getting too risky, and all for what, a bit of *frottage* every now and then . . . I hope to Christ whatsisname, Oliver, keeps his trap shut . . . or nobody pays any attention to his babblings . . . So Marianne's going back into purdah and Helen doesn't want to take her place . . . Though she jumped at the chance to come to Horseshoes next day, and Christ that outfit she wore in the tub, the tee-shirt clinging to her tits and the white cotton shorts were semi-transparent when she stood up and climbed out with Carrie and the others, I could see the dark crack of her arse through them, Jesus . . . I had to stay behind in the tub until my hard-on subsided . . . There's no doubt that sexual *[recording stops]*

It's 9.35 and I'm in a layby on the A435, parked behind a Dutch juggernaut whose driver is presumably having a kip since there's no coffee-bar on wheels to tempt anyone to stop here, or other attraction apart from an overflowing garbage bin . . . I interrupted the recording on the Inner Ring because I noticed a passenger in the front seat of a Mondeo level with my car in the traffic jam was staring at me and I became a bit self-conscious, especially given what I was . . . interesting that usage, by the way, *'to become self-conscious'*, as if we're not self-conscious all the time . . . What it really means is second-order self-consciousness, or you could call it *reflected* self-consciousness . . . when we become conscious of ourselves as perceived by others, or rather we feel others are conscious of our self-consciousness, as if they've accessed what is usually private and known only to ourselves . . . I wondered if this bloke could lip-read he looked so interested, twisted round in his seat to stare at me dictating . . . I gave him a cold fuck-off look and he hastily turned his head away, but I didn't feel like going on with the dictation, so I closed down the Pearlcorder . . . and quite soon the traffic cleared and I was on my way . . . But having a bit of time in hand I thought I'd pull in here for a few minutes and put my *pensée* on record while I can still remember it . . . What I was going to say was that sexual desire is a tough nut for AI to crack, though I'm not aware that anyone has even thought of how to build it into the architecture . . . that curious and uniquely human combination of physical stimulus-response and mental activity . . . that rich intoxicating brew of blood-filled tissue and pheromones and obsession and calculation . . . It's a puzzler, as Darwin would say.

Yesterday evening, after we got back from Horseshoes, I decided to look for that tape of Isabel Hotchkiss . . . something about the shape of Helen's breasts moulded by the saturated tee-shirt reminded me, especially the nipples, blunt and protuberant, they reminded me of Isabel's tits, and I was suddenly seized with a strong desire to listen to the tape of us having sex in that hotel room in San Diego . . . Not to jerk off, but just to recover the sensation of a wild one-night stand, something I haven't had for some time . . . Carrie was watching TV with the kids, some heritage melodrama with horses and carriages and crinolines, never my cup of tea . . . I went up to my study to hunt for the tape . . . didn't take long to find it . . . I wore headphones so nobody else in the house could possibly overhear anything, dimmed the lights and stretched out on the chaise longue . . . and pressed Play . . .

It was, what, at least eight years ago, and I hadn't listened to the tape since then, so I had only a vague memory of what was on it, and it was a big disappointment at first . . . the Pearlcorder wasn't quite up to the job, too far away perhaps, or more likely the sound was muffled by my clothing, I hid the machine under my shirt, I think . . . I could hear occasional faint sexual noises, giggles and grunts and moans, but mostly it was a hissing silence, like radio noise from deep space . . . Then there was a passage of conversation between us, but I couldn't distinguish any words, only the intonations of statements and questions . . . it was very frustrating . . . Then suddenly we raised our voices and I could hear everything . . . we were shouting at each other, shouting 'Fuck me!' and 'I love you!' and moving towards some tremendous volcanic orgasm . . . Isabel screamed and I howled 'YESSSS!' as we came together . . . and then there was the sound of someone knocking indignantly on the wall of the room next door and Isabel and I burst out laughing, happy heedless triumphant laughter. Listening to it was incredibly exciting. The whole episode came back to me in all its detail, including the conversation that was only an unintelligible murmur on the tape . . .

It was the penultimate day of the conference, we'd both given papers in the late afternoon in the same session, papers which had been well received, so we were both feeling pleased with ourselves, high on the adrenaline of the occasion . . . ready to let off steam . . . for a little R&R . . . The conference was taking place in one of those vast American hotels with fountains and waterfalls and a small rain-forest in the atrium . . . express elevators that nail you to the floor with G force . . . thousands of identical rooms on corridors stretching to infinity, and any number of themed bars, coffee shops and restaurants . . . There was no need for the conferees to venture out into the streets of San Diego, and not much opportunity if you were conscientious, because the programme ran continuously from

9 a.m. to 10 p.m. . . . Isabel and I had a couple of drinks with some other people who had been at our session . . . and either I was being particularly witty or Isabel was already making a play for me, for she chuckled and nodded at everything I said, and smiled at me over her glass . . . I manoeuvred through the crush to stand next to her, and then as the others moved off to eat, taking little *carnets* of meal tickets out of their wallets and frowning at them, I quietly suggested to Isabel that we should skip the evening's plenary session and dine out somewhere for a change. She jumped at the idea, and went off ostensibly to powder her nose. Ten minutes later we rendezvoused in the air-conditioned lobby and emerged into the muggy Californian night giggling like a couple of truant schoolkids. I told the cab driver to take us to the best Mexican restaurant in town, which looked like a hangout for the local mafia but turned out to be terrific . . . we had a hot spicy feast of *burritos* and *enchiladas* and *chimichangas* dripping with salsa and sour cream, sluiced down with a couple of bottles of robust Californian red. The second bottle was probably a mistake, though it didn't seem so at the time because the more Isabel drank the less inhibited she became. We talked shop at first, research and professional gossip, then the conversation became more personal. She was in her mid-thirties, I would say, and not particularly good-looking – she had somewhat equine features, wore thick-rimmed glasses, and her hair was drawn back into a bun at the back of her head, so tightly it made your head ache sympathetically to look at it . . . I had no intention of seducing her when I suggested the date, I just felt like having some admiring female company and she was to hand. But when, about two glasses through the second bottle, I made some light-hearted reference to the severity of her hairstyle she reached up to the back of her head, tugged at a comb, and shook out her hair. It was long and shiny and fell forward over her shoulders, suddenly making her look ten times more feminine and desirable, something she was obviously well aware of. The signal was unambiguous. She was an associate professor at one of the Illinois State campuses, separated from her husband, who worked in the same neurobiology department . . . According to Isabel, they split because she'd got tenure and he hadn't – 'He just couldn't handle it . . .' They

had one child with shared access – hubby was looking after the kid while she was attending the conference. And was she seeing anybody else, I asked. 'No,' she said, 'I'm leery of long-term relationships now . . . I don't want to get involved again. What I'm looking for,' she said, eyeing me boozily through a curtain of hair, 'is a physically gratifying, emotionally empty, one-night stand.' 'I'm sure that could be arranged,' I said, immediately on fire with lust. The Martha syndrome kicked in – the chance to bring sexual bliss to a mature woman gagging for it. I caught the waiter's eye and wrote a cheque in the air to summon the bill.

We necked lubriciously in the cab back to the hotel, and in the elevator to her room on the twenty-eighth floor . . . We tore each other's clothes off as soon as the door was shut behind us and I foxtrotted her over to the bed but she said she had to go to the bathroom and while she was in there I draped my clothes over a chair and on a whim set the Pearlcorder to record . . . When she came back we lay on the bed and did all the things . . . we sucked and licked and fingered and fucked . . . and at first I was preening myself on how long I was managing to keep going without coming, but then I started to get a bit worried as to whether I was going to come at all . . . I regretted that second bottle of Californian red . . . meanwhile Isabel was sighing and moaning and purring with apparent pleasure, but she wasn't showing any real signs of coming either . . . I raised the question as delicately as I could, lying on top of her and supporting myself on my forearms . . . 'I guess I was wrong,' she said. 'You're a wonderful lover, Ralph, but I guess I'm not cut out for recreational sex after all.' She paused for a moment. 'If you could say, "*I love you*,"' she said, 'it might do the trick. You don't have to mean it.' I cottoned on instantly. 'Of course I love you,' I said earnestly, without betraying the slightest hint of insincerity, and I felt a kind of shudder go through her body. 'Oh boy,' she murmured. 'I love you and I love fucking you,' I said, suiting the action to the word. 'I love you fucking me,' she said. I said, 'I love you and I love to hear you say that word.' 'Oh fuck me, darling,' she said. And so we went on, chanting a counterpoint of 'love you' and 'fuck me', until we reached a crescendo and a climax that had our neighbour hammering furiously on the wall.

I listened to the tape again, and it was even more exciting the second time . . . I felt extremely horny . . . I went looking for Carrie . . . Emily and Mark, watching the TV in the lounge, said she'd gone to bed . . . I hurried upstairs again . . . I was glad to find her still awake, reading. I brushed my teeth and slipped under the bedclothes beside her, naked, and put my hand on her belly. 'What do you want, Messenger?' she said. 'What do you think?' I said, reaching down and lifting the hem of her nightdress. She sighed and put down her book. 'All right, but don't make a noise, the kids are still up.' 'I think they know we have sex,' I said. 'Even so . . .' she said. She pulled her nightdress over her head. Her breasts are awesome . . . *Sunday Sport* readers would come in their trousers just looking at them. I climbed on top of her, sank into her, wallowed in her . . . making love to Carrie these days is like fucking a Bouncy Castle . . . but I worked hard and after a while she began to respond and to make the little mewing noises she makes . . . 'Say "fuck me,"' I said. 'Shsh. Fuck me,' she whispered. 'Louder,' I said, 'as if you mean it.' But she wouldn't. 'I love you,' I said. Her eyes opened wide with surprise. It's a long time since I said that to her. 'I love you too, Messenger,' she said. 'Then say "fuck me" aloud,' I said. But she wouldn't. I closed my eyes and tried to think of Isabel. But it was Helen Reed that I saw in my mind's eye, in her wet tee-shirt and her sopping shorts. As I was saying, lust is a puzzler.

16

Mary Comes Out

SHE sat, Mary Willingdon, in the grey vestibule, windowless like every other room in the extensive subterranean apartment, with her hands folded in the lap of her grey serge skirt, and watched the minute-hand of the wall-mounted ebony clock move through the last segment of its circular sweep. Now it was exactly aligned with, and eclipsed, the hour-hand which pointed to the Roman numeral eleven. When the longer of these two indicators had measured five more units, the clock would strike eleven solemn, sonorous notes; the black baize door which gave access to the outside world, via a long dark corridor terminating in another door massive and studded, would swing silently open on its oiled hinges; and her master would appear on the threshold.

He would be dressed, she was confident, in his usual immaculate black suit and gleaming black boots, with a crisp white shirt-front and a grey silk cravat at his throat. But he would not be wearing over his abundant black beard and side-whiskers the slitted face mask of dull steel that customarily concealed from her view the colour of his eyes and lips. And perhaps today he would be carrying, rather than wearing, the tight supple black gloves, made of the finest kid, that always concealed his hands in her company.

She glanced down at her own hands, clasped together in a misleading attitude of tranquil repose, and sheathed in serviceable pigskin which she was permitted to remove only at night, in total darkness, with the assistance of the blind maidservant, Lucy, thus preventing any inadvertent glimpse of the pearly pinkness that – so she understood – tinted the translucent plates covering the dorsal surfaces of her finger-ends.

Well, she would soon see her fingernails along with many other things, but mingled with that agreeable reflection was the apprehension, at once vaguer and more exciting, that it was not only her sense of sight that would be enhanced by 'coming out' into the world of colour, but also her sense of touch. She might take Professor Hubert Dearing's naked hand in her own when he greeted her in future — though 'naked' was not of course the right word, neither was 'bare' nor 'unclothed'. She finally settled on 'divested of its customary leathern integument', but not before the more expressive epithets that presented themselves to her mind as candidates had caused her to blush. That is to say she experienced a burning, tingling sensation in her cheeks which she knew was caused by a sudden flooding of the blood vessels in her facial dermis, though the visual effect of this phenomenon, like every other alteration in her complexion, was something she knew only theoretically. There was not a single looking glass or other reflective surface in the entire suite of rooms she inhabited, and even the surface of Professor Dearing's mask had been carefully roughened so that it would not give back to our heroine even a distorted image of her own face.

Was she pretty? Was she beautiful? She hoped, at any rate, that she wasn't altogether plain, if only for Hubert Dearing's sake, since he was professionally required to spend so much of his time in her company. She couldn't ask poor Lucy's opinion on this matter, and she dared not enquire from Miss Calcutt, the forbiddingly helmeted matron who supervised her activities in the hours of artificial light. It is hardly necessary to add that she would have died rather than put the question to Hubert Dearing himself — the very thought was enough to send another blush surging through her cheeks. He praised her intelligence, her diligence, her eager and rapid assimilation of scientific knowledge. He had said to her once, when she was fourteen — she had commemorated the remark in her diary — 'You are a remarkable girl.' But he studiously avoided any observation about her person, perhaps fearing to excite her curiosity, or even vanity — weaknesses the female sex was apparently predisposed to in the great world outside — about the colour of her eyes, hair and lips; thus tempting her to obtain some forbidden piece of mirrored glass which might compromise the whole experiment. He need not have disturbed himself on that score, Mary thought, stiffening and straightening her back at this hypothetical suspicion. The long minute-hand moved a centimetre nearer to the apex of the clockface.

For her part, she already considered Hubert Dearing the handsomest of men, having seen several photographic portraits of him in black and white, but she looked forward with eager expectation to seeing him, as it were, in the flesh. Indeed it seemed to our young friend that nothing could more appropriately present itself first to her starved apprehension of colour than the visage of the great man who had presided over her upbringing and education for so many years. Heroically bearded and whiskered as he was, however, it was likely that at first glance the chief points of colour in his face would be his eyes. Would they be brown, or blue, or grey? Grey would certainly be disappointing – she had already had a surfeit of grey. She had a fancy they would be brown, because the sound of the word matched the timbre of his voice. But what would brown *look* like? Soon she would know.

Or would she? She recalled, with a slight qualm of fear, the warning note he had sounded at their last interview, only the day before. 'It's possible, you know, that you won't see anything.'

'Anything?' She gave it back to him as a question.

'I mean anything in the way of colour. It's possible that after so long a confinement in a monochrome environment . . .' He let the consequence make its own way to her lively intelligence.

'I might be literally colour-blind,' she concluded.

He fidgeted with his gloves, flexing his fingers and pushing the tight leather down between them. 'It's possible,' he said. 'If it should turn out so, could you ever forgive me?'

'I should still be an object of some interest to medical science, would I not?' she said bravely. 'That would be a compensation.'

'You're wonderful,' he said simply, and a thrill coursed through her entire body as she took the full measure of his esteem. 'I only stated the worst possible case because it is my duty to do so,' he went on. 'I have no doubt that tomorrow will be the happiest day of your life.'

'I think so too,' she said.

That day had dawned – whatever dawn looked like – and now it was the eleventh hour. The minute-hand twitched forward to point to twelve. The clock began to strike. Even louder it seemed to Mary was the beating of her own heart, always prone to palpitations at moments of strong emotion. She heard the sound of bolts being drawn on the other side of the door. She rose from her seat and clasped her bosom with an involuntary movement of one gloved hand.

The door swung open, and there on the threshold stood Professor Hubert Dearing, smiling through his beard.

'Well, my dear,' he said, 'are you ready for your great experience?'

She stared, and her face was deathly pale. She was not staring at his beard-fringed lips, however, or into his dark brown eyes. Her own eyes had been drawn to a brighter spot of colour on the lapel of his jacket, where a red rosebud, plucked from his garden that morning, and framed by a green leaf or two, was pinned to his buttonhole. Dearing observed the direction of her gaze and glanced down complacently at the flower, fingering the lapel of his jacket. 'This is –' he began. But before he could say more she had collapsed at his feet.

'Mary!' he exclaimed in horror. He knelt swiftly beside her, felt her pulse, ripped apart the bodice of her dress, loosened the tight lacing of her corset, and pressed his ear to her breast. But to no avail. The redness of the rosebud had penetrated her brain like an arrow, and her fragile heart, overcharged by the intensity of the sensation, had stopped.

Mary's Rose

So this is the story of how Mary saw color for the first time when she was a young woman, because she did not see color when she was a baby like you and I, though nobody knows exactly when babies first see colors, because they see them when they cannot tell you that they see them, but babies certainly do see them, and when they begin to learn to talk they learn the names of the different colors, and the color they nearly always learn the name of first is red.

Mary learned the names of the colors when she was an infant but she did not see the colors themselves, she was not allowed to see any colors in the place where she was living, only black and white and all the shades of grey in between, so the names of colors when she was learning them did not mean the same as what they meant to you and to me when we were learning them, they were like words in a foreign language to Mary when she was a little girl learning them, she could only guess at the thing that happened in your head when you saw something that was red or yellow or blue or one of the other colors. She was not allowed to play with colored bricks or colored balls or colored toys of any kind. She was not allowed to use colored paints or colored pencils or read books with colored pictures. She lived underground in a house with no colors in it at all except black and white and all the shades of grey in between, and there were no mirrors anywhere so she could not see the color of her own lips, eyes and hair. All day and every day she had to wear clothes that covered every inch of her body so she could not see the color of her own skin, and the clothes were black or white or one of the shades of grey in between. And she was never allowed out of doors so she never saw a green field or the blue sky or a rainbow. As she grew up she learned more about color, but she was never allowed to see any things that were colored. All this was to find out what would happen to a person who knew everything about color except what colors looked like, to find out what they would feel inside themselves when they finally saw a color, as Mary did on the day which I am going to tell you about.

Before the day when Mary saw color for the first time she would try and discover what the different colors were like by just thinking about them. When she was young she used to say the color-words aloud to herself and try to imagine what the colors would be like from the sounds of the words when you said them, but when she was older she discovered that there were many languages in the world and that the same color could have different names with entirely different sounds in the different languages, so that for instance 'yellow' was '*jaune*' in French and '*gelb*' in German and '*żołty*' in Polish, though a yellow object, say a lemon, or a pat of butter, would look the same to an English person or a French or a German or a Polish, so there was no way you could tell what a color would be like from its name. Then she tried to guess what the different colors were like from phrases and expressions she met in her story books, phrases and expressions like 'he was red with anger' or 'I'm feeling blue' or 'she was green with envy' and she would try to will herself into these moods and wait for a color to suffuse her mind and tint her vision of the black and white and grey world she inhabited but it did not happen that way and then she read in other books that people were sometimes red with embarrassment or blue with cold or green with nausea so she concluded that there was no correspondence between a particular color and a particular state of mind or body.

What is color? Well it is a very strange thing, it is a kind of light, in fact what we call light is made up of all the colors of the rainbow mixed together, color is light that has been broken up into its separate parts, it is waves of light hitting different objects and bouncing off them to hit the inside of your eye and sending different signals to your brain. Mary learned all about that in science lessons as she grew up, she learned all about the different lengths of the waves of light and the different frequencies of the waves that belonged to the different colors, and she learned about the different cells in the eye that received the different waves, and how some people could not see some colors because they didn't have a full set of receptor cells, she learned about the various kinds of color-blindness, about deuteranopia and protanopia and tritanopia, but she herself had never seen any colors at all until the day I am going to tell you about. She learned everything there was to know about color from blackboards with diagrams drawn in white chalk and from scientific textbooks with black and white illustrations.

So the great day came when Mary was let out of her underground home and allowed to see color for the first time. You can imagine how excited she was, but the scientists and philosophers who had brought her up and educated her and taught her everything there was to know about color were nearly as excited because they were going to get answers to questions that had puzzled them for a long time and about which they had argued among themselves for a long time, questions such as what is it *like* to see color for the first time, because as I was saying you cannot ask a baby what it is like to see color for the first time because they cannot talk so they cannot tell you but Mary would be able to tell them, and is color something that just happens in your brain or is it something that exists on its own in the world, and is color something you can imagine in your head without seeing it or do you have to see it, and is a particular color the same for everybody or is it different for each individual, and could a color-scientist like Mary, for that is what she had become by now, who knew all about wavelengths and frequencies, identify the first color she saw just by taking measurements with a spectrophotometer or would she have to be told what it was? These were some of the questions the scientists and philosophers hoped Mary would be able to answer for them when she saw a colored thing for the first time on the day that I am telling you about.

The scientists and philosophers argued among themselves about what thing this first colored thing that Mary was to see should be, because of course they were not going to let Mary walk out into the outside world with all its multiplicity of colors, she would be overwhelmed, she wouldn't know where to start, it would be impossible to monitor her responses with scientific precision, so it had been decided that on the first day she would see just one colored thing and that thing would be a red rose. They chose red because it is the most common color concept in the world, not counting black and white, that is to say every known language has a word for red though not all the languages in the world have words for all the colours there are in the world. And they decided on a rose, rather than a red brick or a red flag, because a rose is a natural object and its red a natural red.

So when Mary came out of her underground home for the first time, on the day I am telling you about, carrying her spectrophotometer, she did not find herself in the open air, but in another windowless room painted a uniform pale grey and lit by white light. The walls had observation holes drilled in them through which the scientists and philosophers could observe Mary and grilles through which they could speak to her, and in the middle of the floor was a white plinth and on the plinth was a single red rose in full bloom and that was the only thing that was in the room.

Mary dropped her spectrophotometer on the floor and went straight to the rose. 'What do you see, Mary?' the chief scientist asked her, and all the other scientists and philosophers held their breaths. 'A rose,' she said. She knew it was a rose because she had seen black and white drawings and photographs of roses in her botanical textbooks. But she had never seen a real rose in three dimensions before and she had never held a real rose in her hand before and she had never smelled the perfume of a real rose before. She picked up the rose by its stalk very carefully between finger and thumb and stroked its velvety petals and buried her nose in its centre and inhaled its perfume and she seemed like someone in ecstasy. 'What color is the rose, Mary?' asked the chief scientist, and again all the other scientists and philosophers held their breaths.

'I don't know,' Mary said, 'and I don't care.' 'You don't care?' the scientists and philosophers all cried together. 'I don't care what colour it is,' said Mary. 'A rose is a rose is a rose is a rose.'

Mary Sees Red

'Well, today's the day, Dickinson!' Professor Horatio Stigwood rubs his eternally cold hands together expectantly. He is wearing a bright red tie under his white lab coat as a sign of his confidence.

'Quite so,' Professor Giles Dickinson dourly replies. The two men are waiting for the elevator on the ninth floor of the Centre for Consciousness Studies, Stanstead Airport Science Park, on this bright and breezy April day in the year 2031.

'You don't want to raise your stake?' says Stigwood.

'No.'

'Do I detect a note of apprehension?' Stigwood enquires, with a thin, dry-lipped smile.

'I don't approve of betting,' says Dickinson. 'Certainly not betting on the result of a scientific experiment. I was persuaded into that wager against my better judgement.'

An electronic *ping* announces the arrival of the elevator. The doors slide open and the two men enter the padded cube.

'I'll release you, if you like,' says Stigwood.

'No, let it stand,' says Dickinson. 'I'm quite confident of the outcome.'

The elevator slows to stop at the fourth floor. Dickinson moves closer to the doors.

'See you in the observation room at eleven, then,' says Stigwood.

'At eleven,' says Dickinson, leaving the elevator without looking at him.

Oh, the wonderful world of scientific research! Such patience, such dedication, such attention to detail! For thirty-one years Mary X has been incarcerated in her underground cell ('suite', the experimenters prefer to call it). Taken as a new-born infant straight from the darkened delivery room, her eyes bandaged on the journey from the hospital so that no possible inkling of the coloured nature of the world would have an opportunity to reach her brain through her still undeveloped optical nervous system. Nourished and played with and educated by a team of masked assistants dressed from head to foot in black and white clothing. Introduced to the wider world via virtual reality machines programmed to operate exclusively in monochrome. Instructed in physical sciences by distance learning, tutored in optics and neuroscience by Nobel prizewinners, furnished with the very latest research into the phenomenology of colour perception – she knows everything it is possible to know about colour without having had the actual experience of colour. All coloured illustrations in her books and periodicals have been removed and replaced with monochrome replicas. There are no mirrors or reflective surfaces in her living quarters in which she might see the pigmentation of her lips and eyes and hair. As it happens, she has raven-black hair, and full red lips, and her eyes are cornflower blue; she is actually a very beautiful young woman, though of course she doesn't know it. Poor Mary! Mary, Mary, solitary, how does your garden grow? With grey, grey grass and black, black shrubs, and dead white flowers all in a row.

But now her life is about to change. The experiment, begun in the year 2000, with a grant from the National Lottery's Millennium Fund, is all but complete. The momentous day has come: Mary is to be released from her long colourless hibernation to settle the great debate about qualia. Are they, as neuroscientists like Stigwood maintain, merely electro-chemical reactions in the brain; or are they, as philosophers like Dickinson assert, irreducible subjective experiences of the individual human *gestalt* interacting with its environment? For months now, Stigwood has been artificially stimulating Mary's brain with electrodes, replicating the pattern of brain cells firing in his own brain when perceiving the colour red, as revealed by positron emission tomography and magnetic resonance imaging. She reported a sensation which he told her was red. Whether it corresponded to the ordinary perception of red there was no way of knowing. That is exactly what they are about to find out. When Mary steps out of her colourless habitat at precisely eleven a.m., she will find herself in a bare, white-painted anteroom with just one spot of colour: on a glass-topped table in the centre of the floor is a single red rose in a transparent glass vase. The question is, will Mary know when she sees it that it is a *red* rose?

At one minute to eleven o'clock, Stigwood and Dickinson are poised tensely behind the one-way window that separates the observation room from the anteroom. Stigwood glances at his watch and nods to an assistant, who presses a button on a console. A trap-door in the floor opens automatically. Slowly Mary's head and shoulders appear, then the rest of her body, as she climbs the spiral staircase that leads from her dungeon. She looks around, blinking in the bright reflected light, and sees the rose. She gasps, and puts her hand to her heart; then tip-toes towards it, as if it is a living creature that might run away if startled. The scientists watch her, scarcely daring to breathe. It is not the paltry bet of a hundred pounds that concerns them; it is the prospect of professional triumph or failure.

'Mary.' Stigwood speaks to her through a PA system, making her jump.

'Yes?' She looks round the room, trying to identify the location of the speakers, not realizing that the opaque panel in the wall is a one-way window.

'What do you see on the table?'

'A rose.'

'What colour is it?'

A pause. The longest pause either man has ever experienced in their lives.

'Red,' she says.

Stigwood punches the air. Dickinson looks stricken. He snatches the hand mike from Stigwood.

'How do you know?' Dickinson asks.

'It's the colour of blood.'

'Blood?' It is Stigwood's turn to look dismayed. 'How do you know the colour of blood?'

Mary blushes. 'Every woman knows,' she says.

Stigwood beats his head with his fist. 'Dammit, we forgot about that!' he wails.

'The question remains open,' says Dickinson with visible relief.

'Mary,' says Stigwood, 'I'm afraid we're going to have to repeat the experiment with a different colour. Would you please return to your suite.'

'You said I was going to go out into the world today.'

'It will only take a few months more.'

Mary takes the rose out of the vase, pours the water on to the floor, and smashes the neck of the vessel against the edge of the table. She holds the jagged edge against her throat. 'If you bastards don't let me out of here this minute,' she says, 'I'll show you the colour of my blood.'

17

'YOU need an algorithm for self-preservation,' says Ralph Messenger. 'Mother must love herself as well as her kids if she's to function effectively. You follow me?' He is in his office at the Centre for Cognitive Science, giving a supervision to Carl, the German postgraduate student. It is mid-morning on Friday 21st March. Carl nods gravely and makes a note. The telephone rings, and Ralph answers it. 'Helen!' he says, in a tone of pleased surprise. 'Just one moment.' He covers the mouthpiece with his hand. 'I think that's about it for today, Carl. See you same time next week. OK?'

'Yes, of course, Professor Messenger. Thank you,' says Carl. He looks a little put out, however, as he gathers up his papers and files.

'Is this an inconvenient time?' Helen says anxiously in Ralph's ear. 'I'll call back later.'

'No, no, it's OK.' He waits until Carl has left the room, and closed the door behind him. 'Just finishing off a supervision,' he says. 'What can I do for you?'

'Well I applied to the University's Central Computing Services for Email facilities, as you suggested. Lucy *does* have an Email address at her office, by the way . . .'

'Good.'

'And now they've sent me a letter with a password and a lot of instructions I don't understand.'

'Where are you?' Ralph says.

'At number five, Maisonette Row.'

He laughs. 'Is that what they call it?'

'No, it's what I call it.'

'I'll come round and sort it out for you,' he says.

'You must be far too busy . . . But I thought perhaps one of your young men –'

'I'll come in the lunch hour. You'll need a modem and some software. What's the make and model number of your computer?'

'It's a Toshiba something – let me look . . . "Satellite 210". Listen, I feel awful, taking up your lunch hour.'

'Have you got some bread and cheese in your maisonette?'

'Yes . . .'

'Then you could give me lunch.'

There is a slight pause, then, 'Well, all right,' she says.

At 12.45 Ralph knocks on the front door of Helen's maisonette and is admitted. She leads him from the minimal lobby into the living-room. He puts down his briefcase, and looks round. 'I don't think I've been in one of these before,' he says. 'It's quite cosy, isn't it?'

'I've done my best,' she says, gesturing at the rubber plants, the art nouveau poster prints on the walls, the brightly coloured cushions and throws on the sofa and easy chair. 'But it has severe limitations.'

'Won't you show me round?'

'This is it, really. It's open-plan.'

'But there's an upstairs,' he says, peering up the open staircase that rises from one side of the living-room.

'It's hardly worth seeing,' she says. 'But if you want to . . .'

'Well, as a member of Sonato, I should know what kind of accommodation we offer visitors like you.'

Helen leads him up the staircase, and stands on the tiny landing. 'My bedroom,' she says, opening a door. He crosses the threshold and looks round a small room furnished with a dressing table, a fitted cupboard, and a double bed placed against the wall under a sloping ceiling and dormer window. The bed is neatly made and the doors and drawers of the furniture closed. Apart from a small pile of books on the bedside table, few of Helen's possessions are visible.

'All very tidy,' he says. 'If I were living here on my own it would be a complete tip within a week.'

'Habit,' Helen says with a shrug. She indicates the second door off the landing. 'Bathroom and loo in there.'

'May I see?'

Helen opens the door of the bathroom for his inspection, catches sight of a pair of panties on the floor beneath the towel rail and darts in to snatch them up. Ralph smiles but does not comment.

'That concludes the tour,' she says, dropping the panties into a cylindrical polyamide container with a cork lid that doubles as a laundry basket and stool. He turns and precedes her down the stairs.

'D'you want to have lunch now, or do the Email first?' Helen says, indicating with one hand the table, already laid for lunch on a red linen cloth, and with the other the desk, with her laptop open and switched on, weaving a lazy screensaver pattern.

'Let's do the Email first,' he says. 'Then we can relax.' He takes a boxed modem and two floppy disks from his briefcase and sits down at the desk.

'Shouldn't I pay you for this stuff?' she asks.

'No. The software is free.'

'The modem, then.'

'Compliments of the Centre.'

'I think I should pay.'

'It would cause me, or rather Stuart Phillips, an awful lot of trouble to invoice you.'

Helen gives in. 'All right, then. Thanks.'

'What password did they give you?' Ralph asks.

Helen consults a sheet of paper. ' "Highjump" for the dialup service, and "lipstick" for the Email.'

'Hmm, quite good.'

'Good?'

'Easy to remember.'

'What are yours?'

'I don't need a dialup password,' he says, 'because I have direct access to the network, even at home. And I shouldn't really divulge my Email password.'

'Oh, I'm sorry,' she says, embarrassed. Then she adds, 'But you know mine, now.'

'I couldn't demonstrate how it works otherwise. You can always change it later.'

'No, I'm not really bothered.'

'It's "backpack", actually,' he says.

'I really didn't want to know,' she says. 'I wish you hadn't told me.'

'I wouldn't want you to think I don't trust you,' he says.

'"Lipstick" and "backpack",' Helen muses. 'It sounds as if Computer Services are prone to gender stereotyping.'

'No, it's quite random,' Ralph says. 'They have a list of words and just dish them out on demand.'

He shows her how to dial up the University network, and how to send and receive Emails. He enters Lucy's Email address in Helen's Nickname file, and then his own. 'D'you want to call me "Ralph" or "Messenger"?' he asks.

'"Messenger",' she says, after a moment's thought.

He watches and guides her as Helen hesitantly sends a two-line message to Lucy, asking her to confirm that it has been received. Helen presses the 'Send' button and the text of her message disappears in the blink of an eye.

'Theoretically it could be in Australia already,' Ralph says. 'Though probably it will be held up by congestion in the system. She should get it today, though.'

'It's amazing.'

'And all for the cost of a local call. By the way, always write your letters before you dial up. You'll save a lot on your phone bill that way.' He shows her how to do this.

'Thank you very much,' she says. 'I think that's about as much as I can take in at first go. I'll put the soup on for lunch.'

'I hope you haven't gone to a lot of trouble,' says Ralph. 'When I said "bread and cheese" I meant just that.'

'Well, basically that's what it is,' Helen says. 'With a little pâté, and a green salad.'

'And soup.'

'And soup. While I'm heating it up, you might like to look at some new work by my students,' says Helen. She gives him the three best pieces about Mary the Colour Scientist.

Ralph sits in the easy chair and reads through the manuscripts, chuckling occasionally, as Helen goes to and fro between the kitchenette and the table. 'You've certainly got a lot of mileage out of the Karinthy mural,' he says, as he finishes his reading.

'So have the students,' she says. 'I must say I'm quite impressed by the way they've responded. Some of them have made a real effort to research the scientific stuff – this batch in particular.'

'Up to a point,' he says. 'But they're pure fantasy.'

'Well of course they are,' says Helen. 'But isn't the original thought experiment a fantasy?'

'Well, yes,' Ralph says. 'But it makes a serious philosophical point which these stories don't begin to address.'

'They're not trying to address it. I didn't ask them to address it,' says Helen. 'They're using the story of Mary to defamiliarize something we take for granted, the perception of colour, which is what good writing always does. And they're also rather cleverly imitating certain literary models, by the way . . .'

'Yes, I did recognize the Henry James . . . And I got the Gertrude Stein at the end . . . They're very well written, I grant you. But they all demonize science – did you notice? The scientists are always the baddies – imprisoning, exploiting, depriving poor Mary. Even killing her in one case.'

'But it's inherent in the original thought experiment,' Helen says. 'That's the first thing any normal person would think when they heard it for the first time – the terrible plight of this poor girl, shut up in a totally monochrome world from infancy to adulthood, just to satisfy scientific curiosity. The soup's ready if you'd like to sit down.'

The soup is tomato and basil, served with a whorl of sour cream on top and warm ciabatta.

'Mmm, delicious,' Ralph says, after his first sip. 'This isn't out of a tin, or a carton.'

'No,' says Helen. 'The kitchen is equipped with a blender, fortunately.'

'And what a selection of cheeses!' he exclaims, glancing at the cheeseboard.

'It's just what I happened to have in the fridge,' she says. 'What would you like to drink? Mineral water?'

'Have you got a beer by any chance?'

Helen looks downcast. 'I don't keep beer, I'm afraid. I don't drink it myself. There's a bottle of Beaujolais, if . . .'

'Why not?' he says. 'I don't usually drink wine in the middle of the day, but what the hell – it's Friday. And I think it would be an insult to drink mineral water with that Stilton.'

So Helen fetches the bottle of Beaujolais Villages, and Ralph opens it with an old-fashioned corkscrew and pours two glasses. 'Cheers,' he says.

'Cheers,' she says. They eat in silence for a few moments. Then, 'How's Carrie?' Helen asks.

'Very well, thank you. Is her novel any good? You can be quite honest, I shan't tell her what you say.'

'I think it's promising,' Helen says. 'Definitely promising.'

'Great,' says Ralph. 'It's just what Carrie needs, a project of her own that's really fulfilling. This Beaujolais is really very decent. May I?' He lifts the bottle.

'Of course.'

Ralph tops up their glasses. 'Are you working on anything yourself at the moment?' he asks.

'No.'

'Not writing anything at all?'

'Nothing. Apart from my journal.'

'A journal?'

'I haven't been able to write fiction since Martin died,' she says.

'I see.' Ralph cuts himself another slice of Stilton. 'So you're keeping notes on all of us, then?'

'No, no,' says Helen, looking slightly flustered. 'Certainly not.'

'You mean to say that there's nothing about me in your journal?' he says, smiling and looking her in the eyes. 'I should feel quite humiliated if I believed that.'

'Well, inevitably . . . there are references to people whom I've met here . . . people who've been kind to me, as you and Carrie have, but . . .' Helen lets the sentence die. 'It's just a way of keeping my writing muscles exercised. They atrophy otherwise. I try to write something every day. It doesn't matter what it's about.'

'I started keeping a kind of journal too, recently,' he says.

'Did you?' It is Helen's turn to look intrigued.

'It began as a bit of research into consciousness, as a first person phenomenon. The idea was to generate some raw data. I just dictated my thoughts into a taperecorder as they occurred to me.'

' "*Let us record the atoms as they fall upon the mind in the order in which they fall.*" '

'Just so. Who said that?'

'Virginia Woolf.'

'I bet she didn't, though. I bet she jiggled the order about to suit herself.'

'Yes, she probably did.'

'And described it all in very beautiful, much-revised prose.'

'Yes. But she aimed to produce the illusion –'

'Ah well, I wasn't trying to produce an illusion, I was after the real thing,' says Ralph. 'It's difficult though – impossible, really. The brain does a lot of ordering and revising before the first words come out of your mouth.'

'So you abandoned the experiment?'

'No, I still dictate something every now and again. It's become a habit.'

'Are you keeping notes on me?' she asks.

'Yes,' he says, without hesitation.

'Then we're even,' she says, draining her glass. Ralph stretches across the table to refill it. 'No more,' she says, but does not prevent him. He empties the remainder of the wine into his own glass.

'I'm glad you invited me round today,' he says. 'I thought you were offended with me.'

'Why should you think that?'

'Well, after our conversation at the party, in my study . . . And then the next day at Horseshoes you seemed to be avoiding me.'

'I would hardly have come to Horseshoes if I had wanted to avoid you.'

'Yes, I cheered myself up with that very thought,' he says.

There is a brief pause while Helen digests this remark. 'Would you like some coffee?' she says.

'In a minute. Let's enjoy the last of the wine.'

Helen sips and swallows. 'I'm not going to be fit for anything this afternoon,' she says. 'I shall fall asleep.'

'What a good idea,' says Ralph, smiling cheekily. 'I wouldn't mind a siesta myself.'

'Haven't you got work to do this afternoon?' she says in the same light tone.

'All I've got is a boring committee meeting which I should be very glad to skip,' he says. 'We could go upstairs into that cosy little bedroom of yours and have a nice lie-down.'

Helen swirls the wine round slowly in her glass. 'I told you, I don't want to have an affair with you, Ralph.'

'Why don't you?'

'I don't approve of adultery.'

'Well, as long as it's not because you don't find me attractive,' he says. Helen is silent. 'I find *you* very attractive, Helen. In fact, I think I'm falling in love with you.'

'You must fall in love very easily,' she says dryly. 'Were you in love with Marianne?'

'That was just fooling around, I told you. We started to snog once at a party, when we'd both had a bit to drink, and then it became a kind of private game between us, to do it every time we met socially. We never spoke about it. It made the dullest dinner party quite exciting. It was the emotional equivalent of bungee jumping – you had the sensation of reckless abandon, but really we were both safely tethered. There was no question of our going further than snogging. When I fall in love, I want to *make* love,' he says, looking earnestly into her eyes. 'And I believe I'm a good lover.'

'I don't think we should go on with this conversation,' says Helen, but without moving from her chair.

'We could go upstairs and take off our clothes and lie down on your bed and make slow, very enjoyable love, and fall asleep in each other's arms, and wake refreshed and renewed. Nobody else would ever know about it.'

'No,' Helen says. 'I won't.'

'Why not? You know we're attracted to each other. It happened that first evening we met, at the Richmonds, as soon as I set eyes on you. It's unmistakable. That sudden feeling of buoyancy, a simple delight in the existence of this captivating other person . . . You felt it too, don't deny it. I caught your eye several times at dinner.'

'We can't just do what we want without regard to other people,' Helen says.

'If it's Carrie you're referring to . . .'

'Yes, it is.'

'She won't mind as long as we're discreet.'

'What d'you mean?'

'Carrie's not dumb. She knows most men are not one hundred per cent faithful to their wives. She knows I'm a highly sexed man. But she doesn't check up on me. She doesn't go through my pockets. That's why our marriage has survived.'

'Carrie's my friend,' says Helen. 'I wouldn't want to deceive her.'

Ralph sighed. 'We deceive each other all the time, Helen – you know that. There are a thousand things you wouldn't tell Carrie under any circumstances. Why make a fetish of this one?'

'That's the way I am. It's probably my Catholic upbringing.'

'But you don't really believe all that nonsense any more. You don't believe you'll go to Hell just because one afternoon, after a very pleasant meal, you went upstairs with me to your bedroom and very pleasantly fucked? Do you?'

'No, but . . .'

'It's no big deal, Helen. People are fucking all the time, all over the world, and a lot of them, perhaps most of them, are not married to each other. It's just a very nice thing to do with someone you like. It's the supremely human act, freely to fuck, not because you are on heat, or in oestrus, like an animal, but to give and receive pleasure.'

Helen stands up and begins stacking the soiled plates. 'I'll make coffee, and then you'd better go to your committee meeting,' she says.

Ralph glances at his wristwatch. 'If I'm going to the committee meeting, I'll have to skip the coffee.'

'As you wish,'

'You're sure you don't want me to skip the committee?'

'Quite sure.'

'Well, I'm sorry. I think it would have been . . . memorable.' He gets up from his chair and gathers his belongings together. 'I'll see you on Sunday, then.'

'I don't think I shall come to Horseshoes this weekend,' Helen says.

'But you're expected! You're invited. You're . . . an institution.'

'I'll see,' Helen says.

'Thanks for the lunch.' He extends his hand, and Helen takes it. He raises her hand to his lips and plants a kiss on her knuckles. 'See you on Sunday,' he says.

18

Friday 21st March. Ralph has just left, after trying and failing to get me to go to bed with him. It was a close call – closer, I suspect, than he had any inkling of. If he had seen me this morning, frantically preparing for his arrival, he would have really fancied his chances.

I phoned him at about eleven o'clock this morning, asking for help in getting fixed up with Email, and he promptly invited himself to lunch. Just bread and cheese, he said. There was a heel of old Cheddar in my fridge and not much else, so I dashed over to the campus supermarket and stocked up with Stilton, Gruyère and chèvre, Ardennes pâté, salad stuff, and enough tomatoes to make soup. Then I tore round the house with the vacuum cleaner, tidied the living-room, plucked my drying underwear from the line over the bath, changed the sheets on the bed (why? because they show under the slightly-too-small duvet and looked as if they needed changing, or so I told myself, but who knows what ideas were simmering in my subconscious – and anyway, why should I suppose that he would see the inside of my bedroom? Though as it happened he insisted on a thorough tour of the accommodation as soon as he arrived, including the bathroom, which had a pair of discarded knickers on the floor that had escaped my notice.)

By this time I was sweating profusely from all the exertion, so took a shower for the second time today, and decided to wash my hair while I was about it, and changed my clothes – twice, because the skirt and blouse I first put on seemed too dressy for the occasion, especially crowned with my freshly washed hair, so I adopted a more casual look, a loose denim shirt worn outside a pair of trousers. I wanted to make a pleasing impression without sending any seductive signals. Not that he needed any encouragement. I'm quite sure he came here with every intention of trying to seduce me, and that the request to see over the house was just a pretext for learning the relevant domestic geography – casing the joint, as burglars say, or used to say in novels.

'Seduce' is another word that sounds terribly old-fashioned and literary now, suggestive of deflowered maidens and ruined women, of Richardson's Pamela defending her 'virtue' against Mr B, but I can't think of a better one at the moment. After all, he was trying to get me into bed and I was resisting temptation. And there's no doubt that I *was* tempted. He's the first man I've met since Martin died that I have felt physically attracted to – that I can imagine myself naked and entwined with, without the image seeming ridiculous or repellent. There've been a few occasions in the last year, literary parties and suchlike, when I've been chatting away to some man, and perhaps got carried away a bit by alcohol so as to seem more flirtatious than I really felt, and then I would realize with alarm that he was calculating the chances of getting off with me and I would immediately freeze up, or wave to some non-existent friend on the other side of the room and rush off to greet them, or find some other excuse . . . once I left some poor mutt, a middle-aged bookseller with yellow teeth and hairy ears, holding my wineglass while I went to the lavatory, but instead of rejoining him I took my coat from the hall and crept away and hailed a cab and rode home alone giggling guiltily to myself.

After the long years of monogamous sex with Martin it seemed unthinkable to start all over again with another, strange man. We had become so used to each other, we had aged together, we were patient of each other's imperfections, understanding of each other's needs, we knew each other's preferences and proclivities and dislikes, and if it happened that on occasion he lost his erection, or I couldn't achieve an orgasm, it didn't matter, he didn't let it bother him, I didn't fake it, for we knew there would be other occasions. It takes time to build up that kind of relationship, it's like a language that you have to learn. What would one do, face to face, naked body to naked body, with a stranger who didn't speak it, who had another language of his own? It was no use thinking back to one's mildly promiscuous youth for a model of how to behave. Those excited, shy, solemn, anxious, drunken couplings in college bedrooms and sordid bedsits, seem pathetically shallow in retrospect. How eager the young men were, how impatient their quivering erections, how quickly they finished, how disappointing, on the whole, one's own sensations were, though one hardly admitted it to oneself, so tremendous was the sense of liberation, of achieved adulthood, of just *knowing* at last what sex was. Martin was the first man who made love to me slowly, the first to give me a proper orgasm – and the only one, to date. He had a capacity for sensuality. You could see it in his eyes when the mood was on him, and in the faint play of a smile at the corners of his mouth. I sense the same capacity in Ralph Messenger.

Yes, I was tempted – all the more because he wooed me with words, like a Renaissance poet to his coy mistress. He didn't attempt to kiss me, though I kept thinking he might, perhaps I was half-hoping he would – perhaps he knew that I was half-hoping he would, and was deliberately disappointing me to provoke desire . . . But he didn't kiss me when he came in, he didn't make a grab at me when we were upstairs together, he didn't suggest a move to the sofa when we had finished our lunch. He behaved like a perfect gentleman. Except that he coolly proposed that we should go upstairs and, as he put it, 'very pleasantly fuck'. Oh dear, just writing those words down makes me wet.

Is he right? Have I pointlessly denied myself a pleasant experience – one from which I might have arisen 'refreshed and renewed'? God knows I could do with some refreshment of that kind – my body craves to be held and stroked and comforted. Sometimes I think I'm struggling with Ralph Messenger for my soul – literally, because according to him, it doesn't exist. Not in the sense of an immortal, essential self answerable to its creator for its actions. '*Oh, I grant you a* mortal *soul. It's just another way of describing self-consciousness.*' And self-consciousness is a fiction, an epiphenomenon of surplus brain-capacity. So why be good? Why deny oneself pleasure? '*If there is no God, everything is permitted,*' says one of the Karamazovs. Is that true? Then why don't we all kill, rob, rape, and deceive each other all the time? Enlightened self-interest, the materialists say – the recognition that we increase our personal chances of survival by accepting social constraints and sanctions. Civilization is based on repression, as Freud observed. But not in sex, not any more, the godless say. There is no need to pretend that sex for pleasure should be confined to monogamous marriage. True? Not if contemporary fiction is to be believed. There seems to be just as much anger, jealousy, bitterness generated by sexual infidelity as there ever was.

If I could be 100 per cent sure that Carrie would never find out, and therefore never be hurt, perhaps I would sleep with Ralph, but such mathematical certainty can never be guaranteed in human relations. And it's not only her feelings that weigh in the balance. In a curious way I feel it would dishonour Martin's memory, or the memory of our marriage, if my first sexual experience after his death were to be an adulterous one. If that's irrational, even superstitious, so be it.

19

MARY had a little lamb . . . or should I say spectrophotometer . . . and what was that other one? *Mary Mary quite contrary* – no, *solitary*, it was Helen who was contrary, alas . . . I thought I was going to get lucky when she called me this morning and invited me to lunch . . . well I suppose technically I invited myself, but still . . . it was a kind of a come-on, please mister computer scientist can you help poor little me with my Email . . . and she phoned from home not her office . . . I'd deliberately not contacted her since the weekend. Once I saw her on campus in the distance and waved but didn't stop, pretended I was in a hurry . . . I was waiting to see if she would make the first move, and she did . . . Appearances were promising when I arrived at her house, she'd obviously been cleaning it in my honour, everything neat and tidy like a show home, cushions plumped on the sofa, crisp clean sheets on the bed – a double I was glad to note . . . and a pair of knickers left accidentally on purpose in the bathroom . . . or so I surmised at the time, but perhaps I was wrong, maybe it was a genuine oversight. She certainly whipped them away smartly enough, I just had time to see they were a pair of plain white cotton pants, nothing like Martha's peach satin hanky-panky kit . . . There's no doubt she wanted to see me, but unfortunately she has scruples about fucking me . . . Pity, I really fancy her . . .

So instead of love in the afternoon I had three hours of crucifying boredom at the Senate working party on interfaculty modular compatibility, meaning we're supposed to come up with a formula to ensure that a course in say the School of Community Studies requires as much work and deserves the same weight as a course in say Electrical Engineering, so that the University can put its new degree in Interdisciplinary Studies on the market . . . our Pick 'n' Mix degree as the Registrar likes to refer to it, which is supposed to give us a competitive edge in the annual applications bazaar and save the University's fortunes . . . Market research has apparently established that there's an unfilled niche for a degree course that would allow the student to combine courses across the whole university curriculum, nuclear physics with soap-opera analysis, molecular biology with medieval mystery plays . . . I daresay it looks quite enticing on paper, especially the glossy, colour-illustrated paper of the University's brochure, but some of these subjects are harder than others and most of them can't be studied properly in isolation, but I didn't make myself any friends this afternoon by pointing this out . . .

It's 5.30 on Friday 21st March and I'm in my office killing time till I meet Carrie at six for a quick bite in the Arts Centre Café before a concert we're going to . . . Haydn and Mozart, I think . . . Carrie booked the tickets . . . a waste of time, really . . . I like listening to music as background, while I'm doing something else, but not sitting in a concert hall . . . After a few bars, I'm away, daydreaming, free-associating . . . no doubt I don't know enough about music, but I wonder how many people actually *think* music when they're listening to it . . . very few I bet . . . Imagine if you could put a wire into every brain in a concert hall and watch the scan patterns – would they all be the same? I very much doubt it . . . and if you could actually download the semantic contents of their brain activity digitally and decode them and print them out, five hundred people all listening to the same piece of music, I bet you'd get five hundred totally different totally unique thought streams as wild and incoherent and surprising as dreams . . . all kinds of thoughts, trivial, serious, erotic . . . *did I lock the back door I like that woman's scarf the lead violin's nose is dripping he must have a cold I've got a bit of indigestion mustn't fart I like this bit it's on that CD she gave me last Christmas I must remember to buy her a birthday card that cellist something very sexy about a woman playing the cello right up between her thighs why does the conductor keep flicking the hair out of his eyes why doesn't he get himself a fucking haircut I need one myself actually must make an appointment that travel agency next door where shall we go next year not Majorca again what about Portugal* and so on and so on . . . Hmm, not bad that, but I cheated of course . . . I'm dictating this straight on to the computer via Voicemaster so am able to correct and revise as I go . . . it took me quite a while to put that little sequence together . . . Like Virginia Woolf . . .

Interesting that Helen keeps a journal . . . I'd give anything to see what's in it . . . Suppose I offered to swap mine for hers, hah! there's an idea . . . my secret thoughts for hers . . . would she be tempted, I wonder? Of course it would put a definitive stop to any hopes of bedding her, once she'd read my lurid memoirs . . . Or on the other hand perhaps not, you never know, she might be turned on by them . . . And who knows if her own journal isn't equally sexy? I would find out anyway if she really fancies me or not, and how strong her principles are . . . No this is silly, I wouldn't dare show this stuff to anybody . . . though on the other hand . . . if I had her own journal, there's bound to be something compromising in it . . . there would be a kind of guarantee of confidentiality in the act of exchange . . . the threat of tit-for-tat . . . mutually assured destruction . . . no . . . too risky . . . anyway she wouldn't do it . . . Would she?

20

From: R.H.Messenger@glosu.ac.uk
To: H.M.Reed@glosu.ac.uk
Subject: Email
Date: Mon, 24 Mar 1997 9:08:31
----

helen, hi, just checking that your email is working ok. have you had a reply from your daughter?

we missed you at horseshoes yesterday. i hope you're getting over that cold. it must have come on quitesuddenly - you looked fine on friday. many thanks for the lunch.

best wishes, ralph,

From: H.M.Reed@glosu.ac.uk
To: R.H.Messenger@glosu.ac.uk
Subject: Email
Date: Mon, 24 Mar 1997 10:31:13

Dear Ralph,
Thank you very much for your kind enquiry. Yes I've heard from Lucy and we've already exchanged two long letters. It's marvellous to be effortlessly in touch with her like this. Many thanks for helping me to get 'wired' (is that the phrase?)

My cold is improving, thanks.

Best wishes, Helen

P.S. What does the 'H' stand for?

○ ○

From: R.H.Messenger@glosu.ac.uk
To: H.M.Reed@glosu.ac.uk
Subject: dark secret
Date: Mon, 24 Mar 1997 10:50:10

----

helen,
herbert i'm afraid, a dark secret i do my best to conceal, but the uni
payrollinsists on full intials and email addresses are based on that. it
was my dads name. what does M stand for?

'wired' is cool but you're going to have to loosen up your prose style
for email. speed is the essence for instance dont bother with caps
because they take up time unnecessarily, two keystrokes instead of one
and dont bother correcting typos.

since your cold is improving, what about lunch tomorrow? staff house
at 12.45?

ralph

H.M.Reed@glosu.ac.uk
To: R.H.Messenger@glosu.ac.uk
Subject: Tuesday
Date: Mon, 24 Mar 1997 12:17:11

Dear Ralph,
Thanks, but I have a seminar on Tuesday afternoons, and I like to have
a quiet hour to myself immediately before it.

I can't lose a lifetime's habit of correct spelling and punctuation, I'm
afraid. 'M' stands for Mary.

Best wishes, Helen

From: R.H.Messenger@glosu.ac.uk
To: H.M.Reed@glosu.ac.uk
Subject: M, lunch
Date: Mon, 24 Mar 1997 12:40:03

----

ah that explains your emotional identification with Mary the colour
scientist.

what about wednesday then? we could go off campus to a country pub
if you prefer. ralph

From: H.M.Reed@glosu.ac.uk
To: R.H.Messenger@glosu.ac.uk
Subject: your invitation
Date: Mon, 24 Mar 1997 16:42:18

Dear Ralph,
I think it would be best if we didn't meet for a while, certainly not 'a
deux' (I can't seem to do italics in Email). You have made your feelings
very plain. I won't pretend that I find them repugnant, but I can't
reciprocate, for reasons you know.

Best wishes, Helen

From: R.H.Messenger@glosu.ac.uk
To: H.M.Reed@glosu.ac.uk
Subject: ridiculous
Date: Mon, 24 Mar 1997 16:50:49

----

helen, that's ridiculous. i can take no for an answer, I'm not going to
harrass you. i admire your mind as well as your body. i enjoy your
company. i like kicking ideas around with you.

ralph

From: H.M.Reed@glosu.ac.uk
To: R.H.Messenger@glosu.ac.uk
Subject: ideas
Date: Mon, 24 Mar 1997 17:31:02

Dear Ralph,
Can't we kick them around by Email?

Helen

From: R.H.Messenger@glosu.ac.uk
To: H.M.Reed@glosu.ac.uk
Subject: a proposal
Date: Tue, 25 Mar 1997 09:21:25

----

ok I was going to put a proposal to you over lunch but here it is.
suppose we swap journals? i show you mine and you show me yours –
complete, uncensored, unedited. what do you say?

ralph

From: H.M.Reed@glosu.ac.uk
To: R.H.Messenger@glosu.ac.uk
Subject: your proposal
Date: Tue, 25 Mar 1997 11:21:19

Dear Ralph,
What an extraordinary idea. I wouldn't dream of it. My journal is
private. I have no intention of ever publishing it. I may draw on it one
day for fiction, but very selectively, and with all kinds of disguises and
transpositions. It's not intended for anyone's eyes but mine.

Helen

From: R.H.Messenger@glosu.ac.uk
To: H.M.Reed@glosu.ac.uk
Subject: my proposal
Date: Tue, 25 Mar 1997 12:26:53

----

helen, the same is true of my journal. when i started it i thoiught i
might use it as research data, to illustrate my work in progress on
consciousness but i soon realised i could never publish any substantial
chunk of it, its too compromising. i think this may be a fundamental
difficulkty in consciousness studies, nobody daring to bring the third
person discourse of science to bear on the first-person phenomenology
of their own consciousness in a raw state . . .

we,ve spoken before about the essential feature of c. being its secrecy,
the fact that our thoughts are known only to ourselves. sometiems this
is a source of satisfaction, it gives us a sense of our own unique
identity, I think therefore I am. sometimes it leads to solipsism, the
rather frightening idea that perhaps only my own thoughts arereal . . .
either way it works against the AI project which must assume there are
regularities in the architrcture of the human mind which can be
replicated. It seems to me that there is a kind of opportunity here in
the coincidence that we have both been keeping journals over the
period when we made each other#s acquaintance. If we swap we would
each have a unique insight into the workings of another person's mind,
we could compare our responses to the same event. I could literally
'read your mind' and you mine.

ralph

From: H.M.Reed@glosu.ac.uk
To: R.H.Messenger@glosu.ac.uk
Subject: your proposal
Date: Tue, 25 Mar 1997 18:45:29

Dear Ralph,
I can see what's in it for you. What's in it for me?

Helen.

From: R.H.Messenger@glosu.ac.uk
To: H.M.Reed@glosu.ac.uk
Subject: my proposal
Date: Tues, 25 Mar 1997 22:53:02

----

surely a novelist, especially a woman novelist, should jump at the
chance to look inside a man's head, to really see what goes on in there.
i,m taking a trremendous risk, much more than you would be i'm sure.
you'll be shocked, disgusted by a lot of the things bobbing about in my
stream of consciousness. it's more like a sewer most of the time. it's
possible that when you've read my journal you'll nver want to see me
or speak to me again. i sincerely hope not of course. i hope that like
me you value the truth above all else. if we do this we shall 'know'
each other more completely than lovers ever know each other. they
penetrate each others bodies to the depth of a few inches or so, with
tongues, fingers, etc, but we would get inside each other's heads, we
would possess each other as no two people have ever done before.
doesn't that idea excite you?

ralph

From: H.M.Reed@glosu.ac.uk
To: R.H.Messenger@glosu.ac.uk
Subject: your proposal
Date: Wed, 26 Mar 1997 10:24:42

Dear Ralph,

You're very eloquent, but no thanks. Of course as a novelist I'm curious about other people's minds, and what goes on inside them, and a lot of the business of writing fiction consists of trying to imagine what X or Y would be thinking in this or that imaginary situation. And yes, OK, perhaps reading your journal would give me some insights into the male psyche in general and yours in particular. But ultimately I feel that the privacy of our thoughts is essential to human selfhood and that to surrender it would be terribly dangerous. We all have bad, ignoble, shameful thoughts, it is human nature, what used to be called Original Sin. The fact that we can suppress them, conceal them, keep them to ourselves, is essential to maintain our self-respect. It's essential to civilization.

Why is torture so horrible, so morally repugnant? Not just because of the pain it inflicts, but because it uses bodily pain to prise secrets from the mind, which should be inviolable.

Helen

From: R.H.Messenger@glosu.ac.uk
To: H.M.Reed@glosu.ac.uk
Subject: my proposal
Date: Wed, 26 Mar 1997 11:10:12

----

helen, hey i'm not trying to torture you, i'm just offering you a deal, your thoughts for mine, to further our respective researches into human nature.

ralph

○ ○

From: H.M.Reed@glosu.ac.uk
To: R.H.Messenger@glosu.ac.uk
Subject: your proposal
Date: Wed, 26 Mar 1997 12:24:42

Dear Ralph,
I'm sorry, but there seems to me something distinctly Faustian about
your contract. I smell a whiff of brimstone about it.
The answer is no.

Best wishes, Helen

From: R.H.Messenger@glosu.ac.uk
To: H.M.Reed@glosu.ac.uk
Subject: my proposal
Date: Wed, 26 Mar 1997 12:40:12

----

well it was worth a try.

I hope you won't have any objection to joining us at horseshoes next
weekennd. as its easter we're making a long one of it. You could come
sunday and stay overnight. carrie seconds this invite.

ralph

From: H.M.Reed@glosu.ac.uk
To: R.H.Messenger@glosu.ac.uk
Subject: your invitation
Date: Wed, 26 March 1997 17:55:32

Dear Ralph,
Thank you (and Carrie) very much, but I have promised to visit my
parents at the Easter weekend. I hope to see you both sometime after
the break.

Best wishes, Helen

21

THURSDAY 27TH MARCH. Just got back from a workshop. It was Franny Smith's turn to present her stuff – a chapter from the novel in progress, provisionally entitled *Class Notes*. I circulated it in advance, but she asked if she could read it aloud, which was a good idea, because the Liverpool accent made the dialogue really come alive. I wonder if I should encourage her to write for radio. I didn't go across to the Arts Centre Café for a drink with the students as usual, because it's the Easter weekend and most of them are going home or off for a short holiday and were anxious to get away. The University closes tomorrow for four days. I'm going away myself, to spend a few days with Mummy and Daddy. It was arranged ages ago, at Christmas in fact, and I was glad to have an excuse, genuine this time, to decline another invitation to Horseshoes. I shall have a duller weekend, but more peace of mind, out of Ralph Messenger's reach for a while, even by Email (I'm leaving my laptop and modem behind).

I'm not going to Southwold till Saturday, however. I pretended to Mummy and Daddy that I was tied up here tomorrow, but the rather shameful fact is that I don't want to spend Good Friday with them. I never did like Good Friday, even as a child. It always seemed a queer uncomfortable day. A holiday of a kind – most of the shops shut in those days, though they don't seem to any more – but you weren't supposed to be happy or enjoy yourself. In the afternoon we went to church, its statues shrouded in purple drapes, standing out against the white walls like ink blots shaken from a giant pen; to the bleak Good Friday service with its interminable prayers and Veneration of the Cross (how I hated pressing my lips against the ceramic feet of Jesus on the big wooden crucifix after a long line of other people had done the same; even if the altar server did wipe away the spittle each time with a white linen cloth – what kind of hygienic protection did that give after the hundredth wipe, I squeamishly wondered). And it was a day of fasting and abstinence – still is, I presume, about the last one left in the Church calendar – so you felt hungry much of the day; and Mummy held the view that our one proper meal shouldn't be positively enjoyable, so we had an almost flavourless repast of steamed fish, boiled potatoes and cabbage. And the television set wasn't turned on in the evening unless for a religious programme, or at least something very serious and improving. As far as I know they still observe Good Friday in the same austere fashion, and I respect them for it; but I don't want to go to the Good Friday liturgy or to upset them by declining to go. The Easter Vigil is a different matter, I can handle that. So I'm planning to make an early start on Saturday morning – it's a horrendously long drive, right across the thick waist of England, but hopefully the worst of the holiday traffic will be over by then.

At the end of the workshop this afternoon Sandra Pickering came up and thrust an A4 envelope of a substantial weight and thickness into my hand. 'This is what you asked to see,' she said. 'Oh, thank you,' I said. 'I'll look at it over the weekend.' We were the last to leave the seminar room, so I made conversation as we walked along the corridor together. 'By the way, I enjoyed your piece on Mary the Colour Scientist. Very clever.' 'Oh, good,' she said. 'Are you going anywhere interesting this weekend?' I asked. 'I'm going to Spain,' she said. 'I may miss next Tuesday's seminar actually. I'm coming back that morning, and if the flight is delayed I won't get back here in time.' 'Oh, well, don't worry. Enjoy yourself,' I said. 'Thanks,' she said, without returning my smile, and we parted.

The envelope is on the desk beside me, unopened. Now that, after badgering her for a fortnight, I've finally got my hands on the continuation of her novel, I feel strangely hesitant about reading it, almost apprehensive. What am I going to do if her male character continues to resemble Sebastian in *The Eye of the Storm*? I haven't the faintest idea. I think I'll leave it till tomorrow. Have my supper and half a bottle of wine and watch television instead.

GOOD FRIDAY, 28TH MARCH. It's been a horrible, horrible day. Sometimes I thought I should go mad.

I opened Sandra Pickering's envelope after breakfast and settled down to read the contents – two chapters, about fifty pages of neat double-spaced typescript in all. At first I felt relieved, if anything. The character of Alastair still reminded me intermittently of Sebastian (and indirectly of Martin) but I put this down to my memory of the first two chapters, for there were no new character-traits that were obviously derivative from *The Eye of the Storm*. And the story itself rattled along in a quite lively fashion – I was almost enjoying it. And then . . . the thunderbolt struck. I could almost smell burning. No that's the wrong metaphor. I felt a sudden chill. I froze with a kind of terror. I was reading a passage about the heroine, Tina, and Alastair making love for the second time. Only it wasn't Alastair. It was Martin.

I've been turning this over and over in my mind all day, but most of the time in a kind of delirium, and only now, as darkness is falling, do I feel capable of writing down, lucidly, coherently, rationally, what I felt as I read that passage and why I felt it.

The sexual act is such a common, banal act, endlessly repeated by millions of people every day, as Ralph observed; but everyone has their own individual way of leading up to, performing and disengaging from it, as unique and unmistakable as a signature or a thumbprint. It's made up of several things – tempo and sequence, for instance, as well as the kind of foreplay or coital position that is favoured. If you are in a long-term relationship you become familiar with your partner's pattern of stimulus and response, and he with yours. It's not that every sexual act is exactly the same; but there is a kind of repertoire which you build up together, elements of which you combine in different ways on different occasions. It is, as I wrote here the other day, a kind of language which lovers learn. A certain movement of the limbs speaks for itself: *touch me here, stroke me there, come into me now*. And of course there may be unusual or perverse elements in the repertoire which make it particularly distinctive.

When two people start a new relationship they both bring to it habits and preferences acquired with their previous partners, but it's likely that the more experienced partner will dominate the creation of the new repertoire, at least at first. That was certainly the case with Martin and me. Sandra Pickering's heroine is much younger than Alastair and her sexual experience has consisted of unsatisfactory short-term affairs and one-night stands. Their first attempt at intercourse is in fact a comic disaster, which I found quite amusing. Alastair sees Tina home one night after an office party, declines her coded invitation to 'come up for a coffee', Tina prepares despondently for bed, takes a sleeping pill, Alastair has second thoughts, turns back and rings her doorbell. Tina lets him in and calculates that she has fifteen minutes to get him into bed and have sex before she falls irrecoverably asleep, so acts like a nymphomaniac, unbuttoning his shirt and unzipping his trousers, drags him into the bedroom demanding instant intercourse, but passes out in his arms 'in mid-shag', as she elegantly puts it. Alastair, concerned, stays the night, and in the morning, in the early hours, they wake together and she confesses her folly. He proceeds to make love to her in his own way.

I tried to persuade myself that this next passage replicated erotic descriptions in a thousand contemporary novels, but the tempo, the sequence, the combination of caresses and muttered endearments, the delicate attentions of Alastair's tongue and fingers to Tina's erogenous zones, were all like a replay of my own experience with Martin. The final piece in the jigsaw, the final tap of the hammer (for I felt stifled, trapped, like someone being nailed into a coffin still alive), was from the post-coital phase of our repertoire. Martin had an odd and rather endearing habit − not always, but often − of rolling on to his stomach and asking me to lie on top of him, to spread my limbs symmetrically over his splayed form, fitting my pelvic bone into the soft curve of his buttocks, relaxing and allowing my whole unsupported weight to press him into the mattress. We would lie like that for minutes on end, half asleep, breathing in and out like a single body. When I came to the description of this action in Sandra Pickering's manuscript, I flung the pages to the other side of the room with a howl of pain and dismay.

Needless to say, there is nothing in *The Eye of the Storm* about Martin's sexual habits, proclivities, and mannerisms. I don't write explicit sex scenes in my novels, and even if I did I wouldn't have done so in a book which already took some indulged liberties with Martin's character, nor would he have countenanced it. So where did Sandra Pickering get this material from? Putting aside supernatural or ESP explanations (and I did desperately entertain them from time to time in the course of this horrible day – Sandra Pickering as some kind of a witch or psychic who was able to read my mind and appropriate my memories), putting all irrational theories aside, there was only one possible source: Martin himself. Sandra Pickering must have had an affair with my husband.

More than anything in the world I wanted to confront Sandra Pickering. I wanted to have her pinned against the wall, tied to a chair, my hands on her throat, ready to tear the truth out of her. But she was gone from the campus, from England, for four days. I had a phone number for a flat she shared in Cheltenham, which I tried just in case she hadn't left yet or had changed her plans, but a voice there confirmed that she had left the previous evening and no, they didn't have a contact number for her in Spain.

What was particularly maddening was that I knew so little about Sandra Pickering, no facts which might corroborate – or blessedly falsify – my suspicion. Then I thought to myself: files. There must be a file on her in the School of English Office with some personal information in it. I went out into the almost deserted campus. It was like a graveyard or a ghost town. Everybody had left for the weekend except foreign students who had nowhere else to go, or had been unprepared for the sudden exodus. They looked baffled and despondent, as if wondering what was supposed to be good about this Friday, that had emptied the campus like a rumour of plague. A cold wind was blowing across the flat acres of grass and ruffling the grey waters of the artificial lake. There were hardly any signs of spring, except for the occasional scattering of daffodils and crocuses shivering in the wind. I met the Japanese couple from the end house on my terrace, in tightly buttoned topcoats, evidently taking a walk. They smiled and bowed their heads, and looked as if for once they actually wanted to chat, but I was in no mood for socializing – I forced a smile and made noises and gestures suggestive of an urgent errand and pushed on to the Humanities Tower.

There I encountered an obstacle. The main doors were locked, and I had no key. I hurried over to the Security Centre near the main gate and asked if someone would let me into the building. The men on duty, who belong to some private security firm, were polite but uncooperative. Did I have a pass authorizing me to enter the building outside normal hours? No, I did not, I wasn't aware that I needed one. Then they were afraid they couldn't help me. I raged and expostulated, and they grew less polite and even less cooperative. In the end I stormed out of the office, threatening wildly and futilely to make a complaint. I went back to the maisonette, made myself some lunch, clumsily, boiling the soup and burning the toast, forced down the food without tasting anything, tried to read – hopeless. Then I had another idea: Jasper Richmond, as Head of the School of English, would have keys, keys to everything. I rang him up, and Marianne answered. Jasper had gone out for a walk with Oliver. Could she help? No, I said, I'll call again later. 'Very well,' she said. 'I'll tell him when he comes in.' Her tone was cool, guarded. Perhaps she had picked up a hint of hysteria in my own.

Jasper called me at about three. I had had time to rehearse a reasonably plausible story about why I needed to borrow his keys to the Humanities Tower and the School of English Office and the filing cabinets containing student records. He offered to drive over to the campus to assist me, but I insisted on going to fetch the keys and promised to return them this evening. I arrived at his house half an hour later. On the way I passed through several villages with clusters of parked cars round their churches and chapels, indicating that services were in progress inside, but otherwise the roads were clear and quiet. Oliver opened the door. 'Hallo Helen Reed,' he said, before I had identified myself. 'Have you written any novels lately?' 'No I haven't,' I said. 'Neither has Egg,' he said, 'because Milly is going out with O'Donnell. And Miles is jealous because Anna is being nice to Jerry.' He proceeded to tell me a great deal more about the state of play in *This Life* before Jasper came out of his study to rescue me and hand over the keys. I declined the offer of a cup of tea, and drove straight back to the University.

I parked near the Humanities Tower and stayed in my car, concealed by its tinted windows, until a patrolling security guard had passed by, afraid that he might stop me from using my borrowed keys without a pass. Then I slipped into the building like a thief, and took the lift to the tenth floor. I felt deeply uneasy in the huge empty building, in which every sound I made seemed amplified – my footsteps on the lino-tiles, the thud of the fire-doors slamming shut behind my back, the click of the key in the lock of the School Office door, the metallic rumble of the filing cabinet drawers. I took deep breaths and struggled to remain calm.

I found Sandra Pickering's file after a few minutes' search. There wasn't much in it – her application form, her CV, Russell Marsden's report on her first term's work – but it was enough. There in her CV was all the evidence I needed. From 1993 to 1994, Sandra Pickering had been employed as a contract research assistant by the BBC in London, working on radio documentaries.

MONDAY 31ST MARCH. Just got back from Southwold after a long, tiring drive on roads congested with returning holiday traffic. It wasn't much of a holiday for me – I wasn't in the mood – though I was glad to get away from Stalag Glosu for a few days, and Southwold is a pretty little place which I usually enjoy visiting. It's certainly the ideal retirement location for Mummy and Daddy. They've been 'retired' most of my adult life, but now they really are beginning to look old.

I was born when my mother was forty – a 'mistake' I presumed, perhaps one of the many failures of the Rhythm Method of birth control. It was always a mystery to me how they managed to limit the number of their offspring to two before I came along, since they belonged to a docile and obedient generation of Catholics, who accepted the Church's teaching on this matter unquestioningly. I didn't enquire, of course. We never discussed sex in a personal way at home. I suspect that they didn't have a great deal of it – that much libido was sacrificed on the altar of Faith in their married life, and that the act which led to my conception was a fairly rare event by that time in their marriage. It would be fascinating to know what provoked it. Some happy family celebration? Some euphoric holiday excursion? Some sexy film seen accidentally on television? No, definitely not that – when I lived at home my mother would always tell Daddy to 'turn over to the other side' if anything even mildly salacious appeared on the box, and it wasn't just to preserve *my* innocence. God knows my novels are pretty reticent by contemporary standards, but I can tell from the odd comment that Mummy and Daddy find them rather shocking, '*a little . . . you know, dear . . . outspoken . . . of course we're very old-fashioned . . .*' I don't pursue the matter. I never discuss my books with them – I would prefer that they didn't read them at all, for reasons I explained to Emily the other day.

When I was growing up, Mummy and Daddy always seemed significantly older than the parents of my friends – more like other children's grandparents. And now they hardly seem to belong to the modern world at all – the world of mobile phones and body-piercing and serial cohabitation and recreational drugs . . . Southwold, with its rows of brightly painted beach-huts facing the sea, its quaint old-fashioned tea-shops, its horse-drawn brewery drays, its by-laws against dogs and radios and ice-cream vans and anything else which might make a noise or a mess, its promenade where in high summer you will see ladies wearing stockings with their flowered dresses, and gentlemen wearing folded handkerchiefs tucked into the breast pockets of their blazers – Southwold, which has successfully created the illusion that time stopped there at some moment in the nineteen-fifties, suits them perfectly. It even has a fine medieval church which Daddy has the satisfaction of regarding as only on temporary loan to the Protestant persuasion. Of course we went to the much less impressive Catholic church for the Easter Vigil mass on Saturday evening, which was however crowded – 'five times as many people as you'll see in St Edmund's this weekend,' Daddy boasted, and he was probably right, though the congregation was smaller than I remembered from previous years.

The symbolism of the Easter fire, lit in a brazier outside the church, and carried into the sanctuary as lighted candles, never fails to impress, and some of the readings in the service, especially from the Old Testament, are magnificent. All day there had hardly been a minute when I wasn't thinking privately about Martin and Sandra Pickering, but for a while I was lifted out of my own preoccupations by the power and eloquence of the scriptures. It seemed a good and wholesome thing to be sitting there, listening to the word of God. But then came the Renewal of Baptismal Promises: *'Do you reject Satan?* **I do.** *And all his works?* **I do.** *And all his empty promises?* **I do . . .** *Do you believe in Jesus Christ, his only Son, our Lord, who was born of the Virgin Mary, was crucified, died and was buried, rose from the dead and is now seated at the right hand of the Father?'* No, I didn't, not really, honestly. I couldn't bring myself to utter the responses, and I sensed that Mummy and Daddy were aware of my closed lips. And needless to say, I stayed in my seat when they went up to the altar to take communion.

Mummy could tell that I was depressed and preoccupied, and attributed it to grief for Martin. We often used to go to Southwold for Easter, and she obviously presumed that my visit had stirred up poignant memories. She made several references to the healing effect of time and the advisability of not 'brooding' on the past. 'Of course, it would be easier if you still had your faith, dear,' she sighed. 'But I pray for you, and for Martin, every night.' She assumes Martin must be in Purgatory, expiating his sins in this world before being admitted to eternal bliss. As an agnostic he clearly can't have gone straight to Heaven; on the other hand it would be distressing to suppose one's son-in-law had gone to Hell, and modern theology allows salvation to be possible outside the Church. So he must be doing time in Purgatory, and she supposes that her prayers will help him gain some remission. 'Don't bother, Mummy,' I felt like saying. 'Let him burn for a good while yet.' But of course I didn't – not just because I wouldn't dream of shocking her with the story of Sandra Pickering, but because I can't be *absolutely* certain that he was unfaithful to me with her until I hear it from her own lips. All weekend I have been living in a horrible indeterminate state between righteous indignation and self-doubt, which won't be resolved until I confront her tomorrow. Please God let her plane not be delayed. I don't think I could bear another twenty-four hours of suspense.

TUESDAY 1ST APRIL. April Fool's Day, appropriately enough. I certainly feel that I have been made a fool of – though for years, not just a day.

Sandra Pickering got back in time for the seminar this afternoon – straight from the airport, evidently, for she was toting her holiday luggage. After the class had ended, I asked her if I could see her in my office. She said she was tired and asked if it could be postponed till tomorrow, but I insisted. I marched her in silence, like a prisoner, to the tenth floor. I think she guessed what was coming. She certainly didn't seem surprised by my questions, once we were seated in my office, and she didn't prevaricate in her answers. Yes, she said, she had known Martin at the BBC. She worked with him on two programmes in 1993. He had taken her with him on research trips, which sometimes entailed staying in hotels overnight, and on one such occasion they had started an affair, which lasted about six months, mainly conducted in snatched hours during the day, in her studio flat in Paddington. She said he made it clear to her from the beginning that he wasn't going to leave his family for her, and she mustn't imagine that he ever would. She was sufficiently under his spell to accept this condition. She read my novels, 'naturally', but *The Eye of the Storm* wasn't published until after the affair had ended, and she had left the BBC to work in advertising. Then she chose not to read it, because she was planning to write her own novel, and didn't want to be intimidated or distracted by reading anything by me. 'I was always a bit jealous of you, actually. The clever, successful writer-wife-mother whom he was never going to leave.' She went on an Arvon long-weekend course, and made an impression on Russell Marsden, who was one of the tutors, and he encouraged her to apply for the MA in Creative Writing here. She started *Burnt* in the summer before she came up, never dreaming of course that she would be taught by me. It wasn't until halfway through the semester that Russell Marsden announced to the group that I had been appointed to replace him while he was on study leave. 'I knew there was a risk that you would recognize Martin in Alastair,' she said, 'especially when I read *The Eye of the Storm* over Christmas. But there was nothing I could do about it. I couldn't start again from scratch, with a completely different character.' 'You could have started a completely different novel,' I said. 'What, halfway through the course?' she said. 'Why should I? I've given up a good job to do this course, I've drawn out all my savings and borrowed to pay for it. Why should I throw away all the work I've done just to avoid hurting your feelings?' I had no answer to this. My remark sounded weak to my own ears, as if I should have preferred to live on in ignorance. Perhaps part of me *would* have preferred that. I asked her why the affair had ended. 'It ended when he got another research assistant.' There was something about the way she said it, a slight curl of her fleshy upper lip, a stress on the word *another*, which warned me there were more revelations to come. 'I wasn't the first,' she said, 'or the last.'

It seems that Martin had a reputation for sleeping with his research assistants. Most of his close colleagues must have known this, including some whom I met socially. Many of the people at the Memorial Service must have known. Sandra herself had been in the church that day, though she avoided meeting me afterwards, and so, she assured me, had been the girl who supplanted her in Martin's affections.

I felt dizzy and hardly able to breathe. The raw breeze-block walls of the poky little office seemed to swell and contract, the gross, meaty nude on the Lucian Freud poster, and the black, burnished figure on the Mapplethorpe, seemed to ripple and move obscenely. I struggled to conceal my dismay, to retain some dignity and professional poise. When she said, 'I hope this isn't going to prejudice my mark for the course,' I wanted to scream and throw things at her, but I just said coldly, 'That's what external examiners are for.' Then I terminated the interview.

I sat there at my desk for perhaps an hour, hardly moving, slowly turning back the pages of my married life and re-reading them in the light of what I had just learned. I had been completely deceived.

There was a whole dimension to my husband's character and behaviour that I, with my famous novelist's insight and intuition, had never suspected or guessed at. How was it that I never smelled the perfume or body scents of those young sluts on him? Never found a trace of lipstick on his collars or a compromising note or pair of ticket stubs in his pockets? He must have been very, very careful. Or perhaps it was just me who was very stupid, very unobservant, very trusting. Now I knew without a shadow of a doubt that he had been chronically unfaithful to me, a number of little incidents and enigmas, that I had hardly registered at the time, suddenly came back sharply into focus, charged with implication. A shirt or two of his that unaccountably disappeared. Phone calls that went dead when I answered. Messages that he would have to work late. How easily I had been fooled.

I wondered how long his philandering had been going on. As soon as I posed the question I thought I knew the answer: since the time of my big depression, seven or eight years ago. For six months I languished at the bottom of a deep hole, like the shaft of a waterless well, while kindly, puzzled people, of whom Martin was one, peered down at me over the rim of the parapet and tried to cheer me up, or lowered drugs and advice in a bucket. During that time I was unable to write, or even read fiction. My own novels seemed worthless, banal, phoney. I read the gushing compliments in the fan-letters I occasionally received with a kind of listless wonder that people could be so easily taken in. I read a lot of non-fiction – history, biography, letters – not with any real pleasure, but just to fill up the days. I was unable to take pleasure in anything, including sex. Especially sex. We made love occasionally, on Martin's initiative, but I couldn't pretend to enjoy it. I said I was sorry, there was nothing personal about it, and he was patient and understanding – or so I thought. Well, he understood all right, but he wasn't so patient after all, apparently.

Then after six months, for no discernible reason, except perhaps sheer boredom with being miserable, but not miserable enough to end it all, my depression began to lift. Recovery was helped, though not caused, by a number of lucky breaks and happy events in quick succession: the French translation of *Mixed Blessings* won a prize,

Martin accompanied me to Paris to collect it, and we had a delightful weekend in a luxury hotel at someone else's expense; Lucy passed the entrance exam to North London Collegiate with flying colours . . . Life suddenly seemed good again. The sun shone inside my head once more. I started a new novel. We resumed normal married life. Our love-making was not as frequent as it used to be, but I put this down to a natural decline of libido as we grew older. Now I know differently. Martin had plenty of libido left, but not so much to spare for me. He had developed a taste for younger flesh while I had been turned off sex.

Can I blame him? Yes, of course I blame him. Not just because he polluted our marriage by intimate contact with other, foreign bodies, but because he deceived me, he cheated on me, he made a fool of me. If he were still alive I would divorce him. But death has divorced us already. There is nothing I can do with this knowledge, no way I can relieve my anger, except to write it down.

Carrie called this evening. She asked me how I was and I said, 'Fine, thanks,' as one does, and she said, 'No you're not, I can tell from your voice.' I admitted to feeling in low spirits, but not the reason. 'I know just what you need,' she said. 'An afternoon at the Droitwich Brine Baths. I'll take you.' This didn't sound at all enticing to me, but she insisted it would do me a world of good. 'When things get too much, I always take time out at the Brine Baths,' she said. 'You won't regret it.' She arranged to pick me up tomorrow. Ralph is away, apparently, in Prague, for a few days. I can't help wondering what might have happened the Friday before last if I had known then about Martin and Sandra Pickering.

WEDNESDAY 2ND APRIL. Carrie came to the maisonette to pick me up, at about 1.30. I was on the watch for her, so that as soon as her car drew up outside I was able to pop out of my front door, fully dressed and ready to go. I wanted to avoid having to invite her in and show her round the house, in what would have been a rather queasy replay of Ralph's tour of inspection. I couldn't decide whether or not to mention his visit to Carrie. If he had already mentioned it himself, it might seem strange if I didn't. On the other hand, if he *hadn't* mentioned it to her, and I did, she might wonder why he had concealed it from her. It vexed me to be involved in all this calculation and deception about what had been essentially a non-event. As it happened Carrie solved my dilemma by remarking, as we drove off, 'Ralph tells me you have a neat little pad there.' 'Yes, he came round the other day – he very kindly helped me to get fixed up with Email,' I said. I didn't mention that he stayed for lunch, and neither did Carrie, so perhaps she doesn't know.

We whizzed up the M5 to Droitwich Spa in Carrie's sporty Japanese car in no time. Apparently Droitwich is built on the biggest, deepest deposit of salt in Europe, and the hot springs bubble up from this source. People have been bathing in the water for centuries on account of its alleged medicinal and restorative properties, but the present-day baths are surprisingly and agreeably modern, Inside, the ambience was not, as I had feared, that of an antiquated municipal baths, with draughty changing rooms and slimy cracked tiles, but more like a private health club. You change into your swimming costume, put on a white towelling robe, and shower in the main bathing area, a light, airy space with long windows all down one side. They tell you to smear Vaseline over any scratches or cuts on your skin to avoid a stinging effect from the brine, and on no account to try and swim, because any splashing could be dangerous to the eyes.

The bath itself is like a medium-sized swimming pool, though. You descend a flight of shallow stone steps into the warm, almost hot, water, which is quite clear, and sink gently into what feels like a huge liquid cushion. You float effortlessly, with half your body above the surface, buoyed up by the dense salinity of the water. It's most comfortable to lie on your back. Shaped polystyrene pillows are available to keep the back of your head out of the water. Supported by one of these, you can float in total relaxation.

Swimming pools are usually such noisy places, echoing with the shrieks of children and the splashes of divers, but here the loudest noise was the murmur of conversation from the café area at the far end of the pool where you are served with complimentary tea and biscuits after your immersion. The bathers in the water do not talk much. They lie entranced, spreadeagled on the water, drifting gently on the occasional ripple that passes over its surface, or moored to the edge of the pool by their feet, hooked under the handrail that runs all around it. If it weren't for their serene expressions you might imagine they were corpses from some marine disaster.

I closed my eyes and drifted until I bumped gently against the end of the bath. A slight push with my foot sent me back into the middle of the water. I licked my finger experimentally: it tasted unbelievably salty. I thought of Alice in Wonderland swimming in the deluge of her own tears with the Mouse and the Duck and the Dodo, and it struck me that perhaps they didn't drown because tears are salty. The brine bath was like a tank brim-full of fresh warm tears. Then I suddenly thought: I will never weep for Martin again.

You are advised to bathe for not more than forty minutes. I lost all sense of time, but when I saw Carrie rise majestically from the water, like some beautiful hippopotamus, her sleek lycra costume stretched over her voluptuous breasts and hips and her hair covered by a tight rubber cap, I followed her out of the pool. We showered, dried off, put on our robes, and relaxed on loungers for a while. Then we went to have our tea and biscuits. I thanked her for introducing me to a fascinating experience, and said that I already felt better for it. She asked me why I had been feeling depressed, and rather to my surprise – having sworn her to secrecy, and without revealing the source of my information – I told her.

22

'WELL, I can understand how you feel,' says Carrie, pouring another cup of Darjeeling for herself. 'But look on the positive side. He told her from the start that he wasn't going to leave you for her, right? That shows he really loved you.'

'Not necessarily,' Helen says. 'It might mean that he simply didn't want to be bothered with the mess and expense of a divorce. Especially the expense – his salary at the BBC wouldn't have stretched to support two *ménages* comfortably.'

'Well, at least it means he didn't love *her*,' says Carrie. 'It was just sex. And who knows, maybe she threw herself at him. Not many men can resist that.'

'I can't believe young women were queuing up to throw themselves at Martin,' says Helen. 'He wasn't *that* attractive.'

Carrie sighs. 'You'd be surprised. Whenever you have a situation where the men have power and the women have youth and beauty, there's a trade-off. The men exploit their power to get sex, and the women exploit their looks to get promotion, or good grades, or just a good time. I should know, I did it myself.'

'You did?' Helen sounds surprised, almost shocked.

'Sure. When I was a co-ed at Berkeley, I only slept with faculty. And they had to be assistant professors, at least – not just graduate instructors. I wouldn't even look at the boys in my classes.' She giggles reminiscently. 'I was a real bitch. But I was beautiful in those days.'

'You still are, Carrie,' says Helen.

Carrie shakes her head sadly. 'It's sweet of you to say so, Helen, but I lost the battle against cellulite some time between the third and fourth babies. If we were living in the age of Rubens, it might be a different story, or even Renoir . . . But today's ideal of feminine beauty is the body of an adolescent boy, with tits like apples stuck on the front. Check it out in *Vogue*. Messenger has a theory about it.'

'Oh?' Helen angles her head interrogatively.

'Yeah. When fertility was the most desirable attribute of a woman, big hips and huge bosoms were an index of good childbearing potential, so got selected. Now that sex has become primarily recreational, men favour lithe, athletic partners that can do all the positions in *The Joy of Sex* without breaking sweat. In a few hundred thousand years, all babies will be made in test tubes and the pear-shaped woman will be as obsolete as the dinosaur.'

'You're not pear-shaped, Carrie,' says Helen, 'you're . . . magnificent. You're Junoesque.'

'Well, thank you, honey,' says Carrie, smiling. 'But when I was twenty-one . . . Boy, I could fall in love with myself just looking in the mirror. If I fancied a teacher, I only had to sit in the front row of the classroom in a pair of shorts and a tight-fitting top and look at him admiringly and he would like, melt visibly. I could guarantee that the next time I went to see him in his office hours he would suggest we continued the discussion of my paper over a coffee, and before the week was out we would be in the sack together. It was the nineteen-seventies, you know, before AIDS and Political Correctness, and everybody on campus was screwing like there was no tomorrow. Was it like that at Oxford?'

'A bit,' says Helen.

'Fortunately the climate had changed by the time I met Messenger,' Carrie says. 'I don't have to worry about gorgeous young graduate students – not that there are that many in Cognitive Science, but they do show up occasionally – I don't have to worry about Messenger that way. There've been too many sexual harassment cases in universities. Faculty have learned to be wary of getting involved with students – and quite right too. Berkeley in the seventies was like Sodom and Gomorrah. Even Harvard was swinging – I went there to do graduate work. Naturally I set about seducing my dissertation adviser. Ironically enough he turned out to be an old-fashioned honourable guy who insisted on marrying me.'

'Who was he?' Helen asks.

'Alexander Higginson. You heard of him?'

'No, I don't think so.'

'He's written several books about nineteenth-century French painting, and a whole load of articles. Alex was quite a bit older than me. It was a kind of Dorothea Brooke and Casaubon thing – I was in awe of his fine mind and his beautiful French accent. My folks tried to talk me out of it. My father thought Alex was just after my money – my granddaddy left me quite a bit, you know. I don't think Alex was, actually, but anyway Daddy insisted on a marriage contract drawn up by his lawyer which put a ring fence round my personal income, so I suppose I should be grateful to him, the way things turned out.'

'This is all quite fascinating,' says Helen. 'How did you meet Ralph?'

'At a party in Cambridge – Cambridge, Mass. Messenger was at MIT. I'd never met anyone like him before. Most of our friends at Harvard were humanities faculty, and at home my folks mixed mainly with wealthy business people and patrons of the arts. I'd met very few scientists and I thought of them as dull, nerdy types obsessed with boring and incomprehensible things like electrons and neutrons. Messenger was totally different from the stereotype. For one thing he looked more like a rock star than a scientist – he wore his hair long in those days, and dressed in flares and bright silk shirts. He talked to me in this funky Michael Caine accent about computers and artificial intelligence in a way that made sense to me. He talked like a man who had the future in his bones. He also seemed incredibly sexy. My marriage wasn't going too well by then. The age gap was taking its toll. Things had picked up a little when Emily was born, but after the novelty had worn off it was clear that Alex didn't really like babies. And I was no longer in awe of his intellect. I'd figured out that all his books were variations on the same theme, and even that was borrowed from Gombrich. I was through with the Dorothea role and ripe for Madame Bovary . . .'

'You had an affair with Ralph?'

'Yeah. He invited me over to MIT to see some computer-generated art, and he kissed me in the elevator on the way out. It was some kiss. We never looked back. I used to have to get a baby-sitter for our assignations – that's how Alex found out. I guess he could have made something of that if he'd wanted custody of Emily, but he didn't. It was quite a civilized divorce. Shortly afterwards Messenger got a job at Cal Tech and we moved to Pasadena. Would you like some fresh tea?'

'Yes please.'

Carrie summons a waitress and orders more tea. The waitress says apologetically that only one complimentary pot is included in the price of admission. Carrie says she will gladly pay for it later, but hasn't any money on her at the moment. The waitress looks worried and offers to bring fresh hot water for nothing. Carrie settles for that. 'England, I love it,' she says, as the woman trots off. 'So what's your story,' she says to Helen. 'How did you meet Martin?'

'At a play, in the quadrangle of an Oxford college,' Helen says. 'On a summer evening, with swifts flying through the air.'

'Sounds wonderfully romantic. Were you students together?'

'No, Martin went to Durham. I was a postgraduate when I met him, he was a trainee with the BBC in London. He was the brother of a friend of mine who was playing Titania in a student production of *A Midsummer Night's Dream*. She invited him up to see it and asked me to sit next to him and keep him company. It was rather like you meeting Ralph actually. We hit it off immediately. He was only a couple of years older than me, but he seemed much more mature than any of the boyfriends I'd had. We went to the cast party afterwards and sat in a corner talking, until it was time for him to catch his late-night bus back to London. I got to know that bus service very well. We started seeing each other regularly, spending alternate weekends in Oxford and London. I think it was the happiest time of my life, looking back at it. Working in the Bodleian Monday to Friday, every hour it was open, and making love at the weekends. Until I got pregnant.'

'Accidentally?' Carrie asks.

'Of course,' says Helen. 'I didn't want a child, not when I was still on the very bottom rung of the academic ladder. But I didn't want to have an abortion – my residual Catholic conscience, I suppose.

Fortunately Martin didn't want me to, either. He suggested we got married, which frankly was a huge relief because my parents would have found the idea of a grandchild born out of wedlock rather hard to swallow.'

'Is that why you married him?' Carrie asks.

'No, I was in love with him, I was hoping we would get married one day, and have children, the usual things. It was just all happening a bit sooner than I'd envisaged. I moved down to London. I thought I could go on with my research at the British Museum, and travel up to Oxford occasionally to see my supervisor. I managed it for a few months, but once Paul was born, things got difficult. I couldn't really cope with a baby and a husband in our cramped flat in Balham. I got post-natal depression.'

'Oh, that's tough.'

'I got over it in time, but I abandoned the DPhil, and my academic ambitions.'

'But you became a novelist instead,' says Carrie. 'Which is a much better thing to be.'

'Well, perhaps.'

'I never finished my PhD either,' Carrie says.

'Do you regret it?'

'Not really. I didn't want an academic career. I was always uncomfortable with the competitive atmosphere of the Harvard graduate school. I could sense the other students were thinking all the time, *"What's she doing this for? She's so rich she doesn't need a job."* Which was true actually. But I'd like to do something, apart from raising the family and managing Messenger . . . Hence the novel.'

The waitress brings the hot water and, with a conspiratorial wink, more biscuits. Carrie pours the water into the two pots and nibbles a biscuit thoughtfully. 'Were you always faithful to Martin?' she says when the woman is out of earshot.

'Of course,' says Helen, bridling a little. 'Otherwise I wouldn't feel so hurt. I'd have no right to be.'

'Sure,' says Carrie. 'I didn't mean to . . . It's just that, well, your novels have quite a lot of infidelity in them.'

Helen laughs, a little self-consciously, and tugs at the belt of her robe. 'Well, so have most novels, I'm afraid. There's not a great deal of narrative mileage in the stable monogamous marriage.'

'Yeah. Like Tolstoy says at the beginning of *Anna Karenina*, "All happy families resemble each other . . ." '

' "But unhappy ones are different in their own ways." I'm not sure that's true, actually, the first part,' says Helen, frowning. 'Happy families are not all alike. The trouble is, they're not very interesting – unless of course you happen to belong to one. Fiction feeds on unhappiness. It needs conflict, disappointment, transgression. And since novels are mainly about the personal, emotional life, about relationships, it's not surprising that most of them are about adultery. Infidelity, I should say, because lots of couples don't get married nowadays – but it doesn't seem to make much difference to the sense of betrayal, does it, when one partner cheats on the other?'

'No. But how did you get your insight into that? In *Mixed Blessings*, for instance?'

'There was quite a lot of chopping and changing in our circle of friends in London. I kept my eyes and ears open. Then my women students at Morley, in the creative writing course, would talk to me about their intimate lives at the drop of a hat . . .'

'Really?' Carrie laughs. 'How did they feel when their stories turned up later in one of your books?'

'Of course I took very good care not to use anything in a way that would embarrass anyone,' says Helen, a shade defensively. She pours herself another cup of tea. 'Sometimes you only need a tiny detail from real life to set your imagination working in a completely different direction from the original anecdote, so that the person who told it to you won't even recognize it in the finished novel. Don't stare, but there's something rather interesting going on behind you.'

Looking over Carrie's shoulder, Helen has caught sight of an elderly woman being winched into the pool in a kind of cradle suspended from a small crane. Carrie adjusts the angle of her chair so that she can see too. The woman is thin and bony, her swimming costume droops on her withered flesh, her joints are swollen with arthritis, and her limbs tremble as if she is afflicted with Parkinson's Disease. Her hollow features are twisted in a grimace that is meant to be a smile but expresses only embarrassment and discomfort. A friend or nurse stands in the water, speaking reassuringly, ready to receive her as she is gently lowered into the water. Then she is released from her harness, and allowed to float free, her companion holding up her head. Her limbs slowly unfold, the trembling diminishes, and a genuine smile settles on her lips.

'That's a neat bit of machinery,' Carrie remarks. 'I wonder if it would take my weight. I may need it one day.'

'Don't,' says Helen.

'You too. You never know.' She turns to face Helen. 'Look, since you've told me all this stuff, I'll tell you what I think. I understand the pain you're feeling. You trusted Martin and now you discover he wasn't the person you thought he was. But you can't do anything about it, you can't even bawl him out, because he's not around any more. You thought you were safe inside a little citadel of happy marriage, observing all the sexual strife going on outside, taking notes, counting the casualties, without getting hurt yourself. But now you've been wounded, you really have something to write about. From the heart. That's the way to relieve your anger.'

'I don't want to write a revenge novel,' Helen says.

'Why not?'

'Good writing never comes out of purely negative feelings,' Helen says. 'Maybe in time, when the wound is not so fresh . . .'

'Right. Take your time. Meanwhile, get a life, as the saying goes.'

'What do you mean?'

'You've been grieving for Martin ever since he died, right? It's time to quit.'

'I already have. It just came to me, as I was floating in the pool. I shall never weep for him again.'

'Great. It's time you started thinking about making a new relationship. You're beautiful, charming, intelligent −'

'Oh, come off it, Carrie!'

'No, you come off it, Helen. No false modesty, please. It's time to get happy again.'

'Oh, "happy",' says Helen with a sigh. 'Sometimes I think I'm hardwired for unhappiness, to use one of your husband's expressions.'

'Messenger? When did he say that?'

'On television,' says Helen.

'Oh yeah,' says Carrie. 'Well, *he's* hardwired for happiness, I guess. That's probably why I married him.'

23

GOOD King Wenceslas looked out . . . OK . . . Battery light looks a bit dim but it seems to be working . . . It's Sunday afternoon, 6th April, I'm in the British Airways Executive Lounge at Amsterdam airport . . . waiting for a plane to Birmingham because I missed my connecting flight to Bristol by minutes due to a delayed departure from Prague, in spite of running the entire fucking length of Schiphol, which is under reconstruction and a complete shambles . . . running with my head back and my briefcase tucked under my arm like a wing-threequarter having a bad dream trying to score a try on an infinitely receding pitch . . . the Schiphol terminal must be a kilometre at least from end to end . . . jinking and weaving through defensive lines of travellers porters builders painters plasterers . . . only to be told at the gate that the flight had closed and was already taxiing to the runway, though the Departure monitors said it was still boarding . . . I was royally pissed off, especially when I discovered there were no more flights to Bristol today . . .

I flew to Prague from Bristol via Amsterdam rather than take a direct flight from London to avoid the tedious journey to and from Heathrow or Gatwick, but now Carrie has to meet me at Birmingham and drive me to Bristol so I can pick up my car which I left there . . . I just phoned her to make the arrangement and she wasn't too pleased, can't say I blame her . . . She's at Horseshoes with the kids and Helen and it's going to cut their day short . . . I suppose Helen felt easy about going out there knowing I was away . . . I hope she's not going to keep avoiding me, for one thing Carrie will notice and wonder what's been going on . . . perhaps it's just as well she didn't take me up on that offer to swap journals . . . God knows what would have happened if she'd agreed . . . and yet in a way that was part of the attraction, the element of risk . . . As soon as the idea popped into my mind that Friday . . . walking back to the Centre from her house . . . I couldn't stop thinking about it, it obsessed me all weekend, especially as she didn't join us at Horseshoes . . . she called Carrie on Saturday to say she had a cold coming on, I didn't believe it for a moment . . . then at Easter she was away . . . I must try and resume friendly relations when I get back . . .

I've got a two-hour wait here so I got the old Pearlcorder out of my briefcase to fill up some of the time and stayed put in this soundproofed telephone cubicle where nobody can overhear me, though the lounge is as quiet as a graveyard . . . not many businessmen travel on Sundays . . . Whew . . . I've only just recovered my breath, and a normal pulse . . . Still got indigestion though . . . effect of four days eating Czech food, which seems to consist entirely of saturated fat and carbohydrates . . . the Czech idea of a well-balanced meal is, say, goulash soup with dumplings, followed by half a roast goose with fried potatoes and dumplings, and for dessert cranberry dumplings smothered in whipped cream. Washed down with a few litres of Pilsner beer. How do they survive this diet? Why aren't they falling down in the street in droves with cardiac arrest? Well, you do see a lot of overweight people, especially middle-aged men, but also a surprisingly large number of slim, elegant young women . . . like Ludmila for instance, she must have a twenty-inch waist and her belly is as flat as a . . . Not a pancake, not a Czech pancake anyway, stuffed with preserved plums and whipped cream . . . though she ate one . . . she ate two, she ate anything that was put in front of her while I was with her . . . How do these girls do it? Perhaps they only eat socially, when someone else is paying, and starve themselves the rest of the time . . . or stick their fingers down their throats after a blowout . . . it's not anorexia, though, or bulimia, there's no lack of self-esteem involved, quite the contrary. It's a shrewd assessment of what will help them to get on in, or out of, the Czech Republic . . . It's not enough to be smart and speak English, you have to look like Kate Moss too . . . I imagine these young women all over Prague, living at home in cramped apartments in crummy concrete tower blocks, sharing a bedroom with a younger sister, a bathroom with the whole family, with no privacy, no money,

215

just one really good dress in the wardrobe and a figure which they tend carefully like a priceless plant, knowing their prospects depend on not getting to look like their mothers . . . Because in spite of the Velvet Revolution, or rather because of it, there's a lot of what you might call genteel poverty in the country. Superficially Prague seems to be a lively prosperous place, but it's mainly tourists, entrepreneurs and crooks (if you can tell the difference between the last two) who are having a good time . . . a lot of people are worse off than they used to be under communism, especially if they work in the state sector. Ludmila's parents, for instance, both professionals, her father's a pathologist, her mother's a hygienist, but she told me they have to coach schoolkids in the evenings to make ends meet, because their fixed salaries have been devalued by inflation . . . Not surprisingly there's a slightly weary cynicism in people's reaction when you speak approvingly of the Velvet Revolution. 'Sure we're free to travel now,' Ludmila said to me. 'But we can't afford to.' We were in bed at the time, having a post-coital chat. I was longing to go to sleep but it didn't seem polite to turf her out, and there wasn't room for us both to go to sleep, it was a single bed hardly big enough for us to lie side by side . . . The British Council booked me into a quaint old inn overlooking the Charles Bridge, with its thirty-one statues of saints gesticulating like petrified bookies all along the parapets . . . I suppose they thought I would like the historic ambience of the place, its crooked staircases and low headbanging doorways and dark panelled walls and cabin-like rooms, when actually what I really like when I'm away from home is something like a Hilton or a Hyatt – space, luxury . . . a bath big enough to float in, a shower powerful enough to drill holes in your skin . . . a well-stocked mini-bar, a choice of porn channels on the TV . . . and a bed big enough to do sixty-nine without the likelihood of falling on to the floor or stubbing a toe on the bedside table. Not that I attempted anything of the sort with Ludmila, it was a very basic sort of fuck . . . no oral sex and I used a condom, so it was safe enough, but . . . somewhat mechanical . . . Not a night to remember with any great satisfaction . . . I'm supposed to have given up that sort of thing, anyway, one-night stands on trips abroad, especially with women half my age . . . It was partly boredom, partly gallantry, because of that remark I made, '*I can think of several things,*' which she misinterpreted. Funny that, but I thought she might be insulted if I didn't make a pass as the evening drew to a close . . . it was that, and boredom with dragging round Prague . . . Everybody raves about the place, but it seemed to me like a rather superior sort of heritage theme park, overcrowded with the same sort of people you see at Disneyland, tourists in trainers and baggy shorts and tee-shirts . . . because the weather was warm, spring has arrived in central Europe, almost a heat-wave . . . and that was another thing, I was too hot most of the time, brought the wrong clothing with me, too much wool, I felt itchy and sweaty, especially sitting in stuffy restaurants shovelling down the goulash soup and roast goose with dumplings, or for a change beef broth with dumplings and roast pork with sauerkraut and dumplings . . . the trouble is I actually like that kind of food and I'm naturally greedy so I eat too much of it . . . especially on a trip like this where people keep taking you out to restaurants twice a day, lunch and dinner, three or four courses every time . . .

I think I preferred Eastern Europe when it was communist and there wasn't so much to eat, not much of anything actually, even if you were a visitor carrying hard currency . . . There was a kind of bracing satisfaction to be got from exposing yourself temporarily to a life of privation. I remember walking the streets of Łódź one winter afternoon, it must have been in the seventies, in a kind of ecstasy at the total unrelieved miserableness of everything, the grimy dilapidated apartment blocks, the dirty frozen snow heaped in the gutters, the trams packed with grey-faced passengers grinding and groaning round the corners on their metal tracks, the lines of shapeless, expressionless women in boots and topcoats queuing stoically outside food shops with totally empty windows and bare shelves . . . it made you appreciate the ordinary taken-for-granted luxuries of life back home . . . it made you profoundly grateful for the British passport and airline ticket tucked safely in your inside pocket . . . there's not the same exhilarating contrast any more . . .

The original invitation for this trip came from my Czech publisher to go out for the publication of their edition of *The Mind*

Machine . . . I suppose I was flattered that they considered my ten-year-old book worth translating and thought they deserved to be encouraged, so I accepted . . . then the publisher immediately applied to the British Council for funding and they agreed on condition I gave a lecture and a seminar at the University, so I said all right, and in the end it developed into a very busy programme, what with the lecture and the seminar and press interviews and book signings and even a three-minute interview on the national networked TV news . . . My publisher, Milos Palacky, whom I'd never met before, turned out to be a typical product of the new spirit of postmarxist entrepreneurial capitalism, a genial but wily character who had conjured up all this publicity without laying out a single *koruna* himself apart from picking up the bill for lunch one day (cauliflower soup with dumplings, roast wild boar with dumplings, fruit dumplings with dumplings) . . . According to a Czech writer I met Palacky is notorious for not paying royalties when they're due, and I shouldn't expect to get any more money than the rather modest signature advance I've received . . . I wasn't reassured when I was introduced to my translator, a middle-aged lady who didn't speak English very well and seemed to have no scientific background, but I wasn't able to probe Palacky about this because he doesn't have much English either . . . everywhere he went he was accompanied by two broad-shouldered heavies in black suits and dark glasses who opened doors and held people back when he walked from his car into a building . . . presumably they were there to protect him from assault by angry creditors . . . Well it didn't take me long to realize that I was being exploited, but I soldiered on, did my stuff with the media and the booksellers like a pro, gave my all-purpose oft-repeated survey-lecture on The Problem of Consciousness to a full house at the Charles University . . . Levine's Explanatory Gap, Crick's Astonishing Hypothesis, Chalmers' Hard Question, Dennett, Searle, Minsky, Penrose, the usual suspects, a little dig at neuroscience as the new phrenology, a little dig at behaviourism – '*How was it for me?*' always gets a laugh . . . finally a plug for AI complemented by phenomenology, building models of affective as well as cognitive processes, working from the bottom up rather than the top down . . . That was on Friday afternoon . . . followed by a reception and a dumpling dinner . . . then on Saturday morning I gave a closed seminar to the Philosophy and Psychology faculty about our experimental work at the Centre and afterwards the prof in charge introduced me to Ludmila Lisk, a young research assistant in Psychology . . . The rest of my day was slated as 'free time – sightseeing' on my itinerary prepared by the British Council, and Ludmila had been appointed to act as my guide. At that moment what I really wanted to do was bugger off back home on the first available flight . . . but there was this eager, smiling, not-bad-looking and incredibly slim young woman holding out her hand for me to shake . . . it would have been cruel to refuse her services . . . I swear I didn't calculate then how far these services might extend . . .

She'd been given a sum of money to cover our expenses so the first thing she did was take me to a 'typical Czech restaurant' where we had a typical Czech lunch . . . then I dragged my bloated stomach round old Prague in the heat of the afternoon and followed Ludmila in and out of the Cathedral and the Castle and churches and art galleries and admired Gothic this and Rococo that and art nouveau the other until Ludmila said it was time to have an early dinner because she had tickets for the opera, something by Janáček . . . 'Would you mind very much if we didn't go to the opera?' I said . . . She looked worried. 'You do not like it?' she said. 'I hate it,' I said. She bit her lip to suppress a smile, as if I had something naughty. 'What do you like to do instead?' she said . . . 'Well, I can think of several things,' I said, smiling . . . at least I intended to smile, but maybe it came across as a kind of leer, because she blushed, thus converting my innocent remark into a *double entendre* . . . 'For instance,' I said, trying to disperse this misunderstanding, 'we could find a nice cool bar and have a few ice-cold beers and then perhaps we might go to a movie in an air-conditioned cinema and then perhaps I might be ready for a light supper somewhere.' So that's what we did. We found a bar with a jazz guitarist grooving quietly in the background . . . and then an old Woody Allen movie with English dialogue and Czech subtitles . . . and then a little Vietnamese restaurant that served meals without compulsory dumplings . . . Over supper and a very decent bottle of Hungarian Riesling Ludmila told me about her research, a team-project modelling the learning process, trying to build into the model the accumulation of knowledge through experience, dialogue with and imitation of other learners, as well as the acquisition of rules, using simulations of children's games like Animal, Vegetable or Mineral . . . it sounded pretty hopeless to me, too many variables, but I was politely encouraging . . . and of course she grovelled before my reputation, flattered me like hell, but she'd done her homework, knew *The Mind Machine* well enough to quote it . . . and all the time hovering over our conversation, like *'Thinks'* bubbles in a cartoon, were our respective speculations about how the evening would end. 'Does he want to sleep with me?' and 'Does she expect me to sleep with her?' Officially the plan was that she would see me back safely to my hotel before taking a cab home . . . It was a warm balmy night . . . we strolled through Old Town Square and had another look at the Astronomical Clock, which happened to be just striking midnight, with its moving figures, the Turk, the Rich Man and Vanity, all shaking their heads at Death, who nods 'Yes' . . . and lingered on the Charles Bridge to gaze at the floodlit Castle or Palace or whatever it was on a high ridge overlooking the city, apparently floating in the night sky like a mirage . . . At last the place began to work its spell on me, and it seemed natural to imitate the other couples canoodling in the shadows cast by the thirty-one saintly statues so I put my arm round her waist and commented on how slender it was and wondered whether I could make my finger-tips join round it and she laughed and invited me to try . . . I couldn't, but I held her young body between my hands, hard and springy and supple like a sapling, and drew her towards me and bent back her head with a kiss . . . and one thing led to another . . . She didn't waste any time once we were inside my room, she was out of her clothes in a flash, not that she was wearing many – a cotton dress, a pair of briefs, no bra, she didn't need one her breasts were so small, too small for my taste . . . the opposite of Carrie . . . what was that ad when I was a kid, I forget what it was for, '*Not too little, not too much . . . but just right . . .*' She slid between the sheets and lay there watching me undress, which I found disconcerting . . . my body seemed gross and lined and blemished compared to her lean white torso and limbs . . . I turned out the light and drew back the curtains to open the windows on the grounds that it was stuffy in the room but really to conceal my embarrassment and lack of visible ardour . . . I rose to the occasion in due course . . . but I couldn't swear that she didn't fake her orgasm . . .

No, it was definitely not a lay to remember with any great satisfaction . . . it was all too easy . . . If it had been the nineteen-seventies I might have suspected a plot, taperecorders and cameras hidden in the woodwork, to blackmail me into becoming a spy . . . Though there *was* a sort of payback time in the end . . . during the day I'd carelessly mentioned the conference at the end of May and when she was getting dressed to go home she asked me if she could give a paper because then she could apply to the British Council for a travel grant . . . I said that the programme was already full (a lie) but she could do a poster if she liked . . . I could hardly say less having just fucked her . . . but the Council won't think a poster is worth a travel grant . . . I trust . . .

24

SUNDAY 6TH APRIL. I've just returned from Horseshoes after dropping off the Messenger children at Pittville Lawn. While we were having lunch, Ralph phoned from Amsterdam airport to say he'd missed his connection to Bristol and was flying to Birmingham instead, so Carrie has had to go there to pick him up. I offered to take the children home to save Carrie some driving and she gratefully accepted. I was glad of the opportunity to do *her* a favour for a change.

The change of plan cut short our day at Horseshoes, which was a pity, because it was glorious weather, warm enough to sit out on the deck. It's six p.m. now and still light. The clocks went forward last weekend, but I was too preoccupied then to notice or take any pleasure in the extra daylight in the evening. I'm feeling calmer about the Martin business now. It was a relief to talk to somebody about it, and Carrie was a sympathetic listener, though there was an irony in the advice she gave me to find another man, since the only one who is interested in me at the moment is her husband.

One consequence of the revelations about Martin is that he has finally 'gone'. He's no longer an invisible presence hovering on the margins of my consciousness. I have no urge to conjure up his spirit to accuse or reproach him. Nor do I seriously want him to burn in purgatory, still less in hell. I can't imagine him going on existing anywhere, in fact, because he turned out to be a kind of impostor, whose real self I will never know. In a way I'm glad I found out the truth here rather than at home, with the children and friends around. By the time I am back in London it will seem quite natural that I should have stopped grieving for him, or even mentioning him.

MONDAY 7TH APRIL. Spring seems definitely to have arrived. Another fine day, and the sun was distinctly warm on my back as I walked across the campus. The sap is visibly rising everywhere. The pink cherry blossom is out on the trees around the Library, and the students were out on the steps, sunning themselves with straps down and shirts off, flirting, kissing and holding hands, helpless participants in the rites of spring.

The sexual instinct, what a puzzle it is, what an enormously wide spectrum of emotions it generates. Ecstasy at one end, terror at the other. There was a horrifying story of a gang rape in the newspaper I read over coffee in the senior common room – it happened last September but the case has just come to trial. An Austrian woman, a tourist in London, got chatting to some youths aged fourteen (*fourteen!*) to seventeen, they seemed to her friendly and she went for a walk with them. Which was a bit naïve of her, perhaps, but it was broad daylight, and she probably thought of them as children (she is thirty-two herself, it said) and being a foreigner she probably didn't understand their conversation too well, or read the signs in their body language, tone of voice, facial expressions, *etc.*, for they must have been nudging and winking at each other, exchanging glances, sniggers, *sotto voce* comments. They led her to some deserted spot where they stripped her and raped her, 'repeatedly' the newspaper report said, then flung her naked into a canal, though she pleaded with them not to, and told them she couldn't swim – which probably saved her life, actually, because she could, and managed to drag herself out of the canal on the other side. I pictured her, sobbing and shivering, bruised and bleeding, streaked with mud and slime, staggering along the towpath until she found somebody to help her. What struck me was that she said she survived this ghastly ordeal by 'separating her mind from her body as much as she could'. I wonder what Ralph Messenger would make of that. It seems to me a good argument for dualism.

Jasper Richmond came into the SCR while I was there, escorting a porter and a trolley loaded with cases of wine and boxes of wine glasses for the reception this evening. Professor Robyn Penrose of Walsall University is coming to give the H.H. Crosbie Memorial Lecture, an annual event endowed by the widow of some former member of staff here. I've been invited to the reception and to have dinner with her afterwards. The lecture is entitled, 'Interrogating the Subject'. 'It may be heavy going, I'm afraid,' Jasper said. 'Lots of jargon. She's one of these Theory people.' 'Why did you invite her?' I asked. 'It wasn't my idea,' he said. 'But some of my younger colleagues were keen to have her.' He bared his teeth in a reflex leer. 'I mean, as a speaker. Though I understand she's quite good-looking too.'

The news is dominated by Election coverage. Labour are holding on to their twenty-point lead in the polls, suggesting a landslide on May 1st. I find I have left it too late to register as a postal voter, and since Election Day is a Thursday, a teaching day for me, it looks as if I shall forfeit my vote. Though it would be theoretically possible to travel up to London and back in the morning, it would be an awful fag, and to be honest I'm not sufficiently motivated to make the effort.

I've always voted Labour since I was a student, when nearly everybody I knew was automatically left-wing, but with decreasing enthusiasm and conviction as time went on. If Martin hadn't kept me toeing the line I might have defected to the SDP, which he used to describe sneeringly as 'the party for people who don't really like politics'. New Labour seems indistinguishable from the SDP, which is fine by me, but my constituency is already a Labour seat, and they'll hardly need my vote to win this time. Even Daddy, who has voted Tory all his life except for 1945, is talking about voting Lib Dem this time, or at least abstaining. He is thoroughly disgusted with the incompetence of this government and the sleaze with which it is tainted. Mind you, if Southwold goes Labour, the world really will be turned upside down.

TUESDAY 8TH APRIL. The 'Subject' in Robyn Penrose's lecture title turned out to be a kind of multiple pun, meaning the subject as experiencing individual, the subject of a sentence, the subject of a political state, and the subject of English Literature in the university curriculum. As far as I could follow it the general argument was that the Subject in all these senses is a Bad Thing, that there is some kind of equivalence between the privileging of the ego in classical psychoanalysis, the fetishization of formal correctness in traditional grammar, the exploitation and oppression of subject races by colonialism, and the idea of a literary canon: they are all repressive and tyrannical and phallocentric and have to be deconstructed . . . It was quite a dazzling discourse in its way, juggling all these conceptual balls in the air, especially when delivered by a tall, handsome, youngish woman in a smart black velvet trouser suit, her flaming red hair swept up at the back with a silver comb, and long silver earrings swinging and glinting as she swept the audience with her confident gaze. But it depressed me that the awed-looking young people in the audience were being given such a dry and barren message. Where was the pleasure of reading in all this? Where was personal discovery, self-development? But the argument didn't allow for the self, the very idea of the self is a miss-reading or 'mister-reading' (or myster-reading?) of subjectivity, apparently. The individual is constructed, deconstructed and reconstructed continuously by the stream of semiosis into which she is thrown by the acquisition of language (I think I got that right, I was taking notes). The metaphor of the stream reminded me of the poor Austrian woman flung into the canal by the louts who had just raped her, and I thought it wouldn't be much consolation to her to know that this was in some obscure and indirect way the fault of compulsory Shakespeare in English Literature syllabuses . . . Towards the end of her lecture Professor Penrose began to invoke analogies from computing. The Windows that allow you to move effortlessly between different programs running at the same time was offered as a metaphor of the decentred self. It struck me as I listened that there was a queer kind of correspondence between what she was saying and what Ralph Messenger says. Both of them deny that the self has any fixed identity, any 'centre'. He says it's a fiction that we make up; she says it is made up for us by culture. It's alarming that there should be so much agreement on this point between the most advanced thinking in the sciences and the humanities.

I sat next to Professor Penrose at dinner (a fairly horrid meal in a private dining room in Staff House) and found her much more sympathetic than I expected. I don't *think* this was because she had read some of my novels and spoke intelligently about them. She has a daughter aged four whose father doesn't seem to be in the picture, and is much preoccupied with the logistic problems of being a single parent and head of Communications and Cultural Studies at Walsall. It's one of the new universities (odd to think that Gloucester once had that status, its buildings now seem so worn and weathered on the outside, scuffed and threadbare inside) that were created from the old polytechnics. Robyn Penrose was appointed there just a couple of years ago with what she described as 'a mission statement to upgrade their quality assessment in research and teaching'. She deployed this management jargon with the same smooth competence as she had displayed in literary theory. I got the impression that she cracks the whip over a recalcitrant and resentful staff of mostly older men, spurring them on to achieve higher and higher productivity, like an old-fashioned factory boss. But she seemed more interested in discussing infant ailments and gender stereotyping in nursery schools with Annabelle Riverdale, who was sitting opposite her at dinner. There are curious contradictions between her literary theory and her professional practice and between both and her personal life. But she probably regards consistency of character as an exploded concept.

Marianne Richmond accosted me at the reception after the lecture and persuaded me to buy a £5 ticket for a duck race she's organizing next Sunday at Bourton-on-the-Water, to raise money for some charity connected with Oliver. It's a more developed form of Pooh Sticks. Lots of numbered plastic ducks are tossed off a bridge into the river to float downstream, and the first one to pass the finishing post wins a prize for the person with the corresponding number on their ticket. It sounds more fun than the average raffle, and I coughed up my fiver cheerfully. We exchanged opinions about the lecture and I said I wished Ralph Messenger had been there, because I would have liked to know what he thought of it, at which she looked at me rather sharply, as if I had revealed a closer acquaintance with him than she was aware of. She has no idea, of course, that I know about her 'game' with him – nor, I trust, that he has since turned his attentions to me. The Glovers were there, unable to talk about anything but the Election. Now that Blair looks likely to win by a landslide, Laetitia is speaking more approvingly of New Labour, positioning herself to bask in the glory of victory. They are having an Election Night Party and she promised to send me an invitation.

WEDNESDAY 9TH APRIL. Ralph Messenger rang me up this morning – I was working at home. 'Don't you check your Email?' he said. 'Every other day,' I said. He roared with laughter. 'Most of my colleagues check theirs every twenty minutes,' he said. 'I sent you a message yesterday morning.' 'I'm sorry,' I said, 'shall I look it up?' 'No, don't bother,' he said, 'it was just to suggest we had lunch today. I want to ask you a favour.' 'What kind of favour?' I asked warily. 'Nothing you could disapprove of,' he said.

After a moment's hesitation, I agreed. It seemed to me that to refuse would be an exaggerated gesture. Enough time has passed since he propositioned me, and I made myself perfectly clear then, and in our subsequent Email correspondence. Now that the air has been cleared, there's no reason why we shouldn't resume a friendly relationship. 'Staff House or pub?' he said, and I prudently opted for the former.

LATER. Pity about the choice of Staff House. Apart from the food it was an agreeable and interesting lunch. Ralph was very amusing about the excessively rich cuisine in Prague, but at least it sounded enjoyable as well as indigestible. The favour he wanted to ask turned out to be my participation in a conference his Centre is hosting at the end of the semester. It's something called the International Conference on Consciousness Studies, known as Con-Con to its habitués, which Ralph described as a travelling circus that sets up its tent every summer in a different location, and this year it's Gloucester's turn. 'It's not a straight academic conference where you get specialists in a single subject chewing the fat with each other,' he said. 'It's genuinely interdisciplinary, and you get some fringe people, nutcases and cranks, as well as some of the biggest wheels in cognitive science. I think you might find it interesting.' Apparently it's the custom to invite somebody to give a short address at the very end of the conference called 'Last Word', summing up their impressions of the event, and he wanted me to do it. I was quite flattered, but said I wasn't qualified, I wouldn't be able to understand what half the speakers were saying. 'That doesn't matter,' he said. 'The idea of the Last Word is to get a view that hasn't already been heard at the conference. Last year, for instance, it was a Buddhist monk. Another year it was a zoologist. We've never had any literary input before.' 'That certainly seems a serious omission for a conference on consciousness,' I said, 'but why don't you invite a proper academic, like Robyn Penrose?' I told him about her lecture.

'Oh I can't stand those people,' he said, 'postmodernists, or poststructuralists, or whatever they call themselves. They've infiltrated Con-Con lately, caused no end of trouble.' I was surprised he was so hostile, and asked him why. 'Because they're essentially hostile to science. They've picked up some modern scientific ideas without really understanding them and flash them about like a three-card trick. They think that Heisenberg's Uncertainty Principle and Schrödinger's Cat and Godel's Theorem license them to say that there is no such thing as scientific proof and that science is only one interpretation of the world among others equally valid.' 'Well, isn't it?' I said, just to be provocative. 'Certainly not,' he said. 'Its explanatory power is of a quite different order from, for example, animism or Zoroastrianism or astrology.' 'Well, I grant you that,' I said, 'but those examples are rather extreme.' 'Choose your own examples,' he said, with a challenging lift of his chin. I couldn't think of any off the top of my head. 'Since the Enlightenment,' he said, slipping into lecture mode, 'science has established itself as the only true form of knowledge. This has created a problem for rival forms – they've had to either take it on board, try to make themselves scientific, and run the risk of discovering that there's no foundation to their conceptual world – like serious theology, for instance – or put their heads in the sand and pretend science never happened – like fundamentalist religion. These postmodernists are mounting a last-ditch defence of their disciplines by saying that everybody is in the same boat, including scientists – that there are no foundations, and no sand. But it's not true. Science is for real. It has made more changes to the conditions of human life than all the preceding millennia of our history put together. Just think of medicine. Two hundred years ago doctors were still bleeding people for every ailment under the sun. If you had cancer, would you consult a postmodern oncologist who thought reflexology and aromatherapy were on a par with surgery and chemotherapy?' 'Not when you put it like that,' I said. 'But aren't there areas of human experience where scientific method doesn't apply?' 'Qualia, you mean?' he said. 'I suppose so,' I said. 'I was thinking of happiness, unhappiness. The sense of the sublime. Love.' 'Of course that's the big unsolved problem,' he said. 'How to connect brain states, which can be observed, to mind states which, at present, can only be reported. But if you're a scientist you must believe there's an answer to be found. That's what the Centre is for.' I asked him if he thought that one day somebody, a new Einstein, would wake up in the morning and have an idea like Relativity which would solve the problem of consciousness at a stroke. 'To be honest, no. I think it's more likely that the problem will be solved by a computer than a human being. The question is, will we recognize it when we see it?'

THURSDAY 10TH APRIL. Good workshop this afternoon. Saul Goldman presented a chapter in which his hero takes his father to a gay bar for the first time. Very funny. But the best thing about the session from my point of view was that Sandra Pickering attended it. She had been absent for the two previous meetings – ever since the

229

showdown of last week – and I was beginning to fear that she was in a depression or sulk or had dropped out of the course completely, and that there would be a fuss in which the whole story would come out. But she reappeared today – not only that, but she actually contributed an intelligent remark or two. The metal stud on her tongue winked and gleamed inside her mouth when she spoke. I entertained some thoughts about its possible application as a sex aid, but these were satirical rather than jealous. I no longer have an overwhelming desire to scratch her eyes out.

Altogether, things seem to be calming down. Ralph behaved himself impeccably on Wednesday, so I don't have any qualms about joining him and Carrie at Horseshoes for lunch on Sunday. In the afternoon we're all going to watch Marianne Richmond's duck race at Bourton-on-the-Water. And I'm making a little excursion of my own tomorrow. Now that the weather has turned fine, and the days are longer, I've decided that I ought to get off the campus more often and explore some of the many interesting places there are in the locality. I've been reading a new collection of Henry James's letters, and was particularly intrigued by one he wrote to Charles Eliot Norton in the spring of 1870 from Malvern, which isn't far from here. He went there for his health, after spending some time in Florence (it was his 'Grand Tour' year in Europe, paid for by his father). I was particularly struck by this passage:

> Yesterday morning if I had thought of Florence it would have been almost in charity. I walked away across the country to the ancient town of Ledbury, an hour of the way over the deer-cropped slopes & thro' the dappled avenues of Eastnor Park (Earl Somers's –) a vast & glorious domain & as immensely idle & charming & uncared for as anything in Italy. And at Ledbury I saw a noble old church (with detached *campanile*) & a churchyard so full of ancient sweetness, so happy in situation and characteristic detail, that it seemed for me (for the time) – as so many things do – one of the memorable sights of my European experience.

A church with a detached campanile sounds very quaint and un-English and I am immensely curious to see it for myself, so I am going there tomorrow. Fingers crossed that it is still as James saw it.

FRIDAY 11TH APRIL. A very extraordinary thing happened today. Just when I thought my life had settled back into a humdrum, unexciting routine, an event occurred that throws everything into question again, and makes me wonder whether anything in human behaviour is ever what it seems. Not the least remarkable aspect of the experience is that what began as a kind of Jamesian pilgrimage turned into a scene that might have come from one of his own novels. So let me record it with the 'solidity of specification' that the Master would have approved.

Ledbury is a very simple journey by car from here: you just follow the A438 all the way from exit 9 on the M5. I caught a glimpse of the magnificent Norman abbey as I passed through Tewkesbury and resolved to stop and have a closer look on my way back. From there it's a fast open road through pleasant rolling country (less lush and groomed than the Cotswolds) that in due course launches you up a long hill like a ramp into the town centre of Ledbury. This is, architecturally speaking, black-and-white country, and Ledbury has some fine specimens in its High Street – notably the Market House, a beautifully proportioned Tudor building balanced on stilt-like wooden columns, and 'The Feathers', a Tudor inn with a wonderfully irregular facade, which I mentally noted as a possible place for lunch. I called in at the little Tourist Information Centre and provided myself with some leaflets about the town. It turned out to have lots of literary associations far more rooted and substantial than James's fleeting visit (which was not recorded in the tourist literature). William Langland is thought to have been born in Ledbury. John Masefield definitely was, and lived there until he ran away to sea. Elizabeth Barrett was brought up nearby, in an extraordinary house with Turkish minarets (since demolished, unfortunately, but photographs have survived), and there is a hideous Victorian red brick and timber Institute with a clock tower named after her, situated almost opposite the Market House. A plaque set in the wall records that it was opened by Sir Rider Haggard in 1898.

I loved all this. I metaphorically hugged myself with glee. I love to feel connected with the great, and not so great, writers of the past by walking the ground they walked and seeing the things they saw. A lot of my London friends like to mock the heritage industry, but I'm enormously grateful that so much money and effort is expended on preserving the fabric of the past. The approach to Ledbury's parish church, for instance, must have looked much the same to James as it did to me – not so spick and span, perhaps, in his day, and no doubt smellier – but essentially it has been preserved from modernization. As you climb the crooked, cobbled lane that leads from the High Street, with low black and white houses crowding in from each side, you can see at the top, soaring above the roofs, the steeple of St Michael and All Angels, with its 'golden vane surveying half the shire', as Masefield wrote (according to my guide – I don't know much Masefield off by heart). James's word '*campanile*' had misled me into imagining a tower in Italian Renaissance style, something like Siena's on a reduced scale, but of course it's a steeple, originally Norman, with a spire that was replaced in the eighteenth century. It *is*, however, detached from the main body of the church, as James said, freestanding amid the green grass and weathered tombstones, and I don't think I have seen anything quite like it elsewhere in England. The church itself is full of historical and architectural interest. The big wooden doors are pockmarked with bullet holes from the Battle of Ledbury (whatever that was, my leaflets didn't say) and there is a small red window set above the big East Window, supposed to have been put there in the sixteenth century as a kind of substitute for the sanctuary lamp banned by Protestant Reformers (something to tell Daddy about, it's the sort of nugget he delights in).

After a thorough inspection of the church, and a leisurely wander among the tombstones, reading the inscriptions, I strolled back down the lane, feeling thoroughly pleased with myself, and with an appetite for lunch. The Feathers turned out to be just the ticket. Sometimes a woman on her own can feel uncomfortable eating bar food in a pub, but this place was more like a large, informal restaurant. The whole ground floor had been opened out, and most of the walls removed, but the thick vertical beams left standing like pillars, creating a large irregular space, with alcoves and bays. Logs smouldered in the big open fireplace, and there were spring flowers on every table – solid, unpolished wooden tables, with comfortable Windsor armchairs. Blackboards over the long bar listed an enticing and adventurous menu. I ordered garlic and herb tagliatelle with chilli prawns and sun-dried tomatoes, reserving the possibility of an orange truffle pot with Grand Marnier sauce for dessert. A smiling motherly waitress took my order, to which I added a large glass of the house Chardonnay. The first course, when it came, was as mouth-watering as its description promised. I could hardly believe my good fortune.

And then it happened. I had just finished my tagliatelle and prawns; the waitress had removed my plate and taken my order for dessert. I swallowed the last mouthful of wine, settled back into the curve of the Windsor chair with a sigh of satisfaction, and idly looked up and across the floor of the restaurant. On the other side of the room, in one of the cosy-looking bays with upholstered seats, a table that had been empty when I came in, with a 'Reserved' card on it, was now occupied – by Carrie Messenger and Nicholas Beck.

My first reaction was: what a delightful surprise, what a happy coincidence, to meet friends unexpectedly in this charming place. The explanation for their presence flashed into my mind at the same instant (it's extraordinary how fast the brain works in these situations) as I recalled Carrie mentioning on my first visit to the house on Pittsville Lawn that Nicholas Beck had helped her acquire period furniture by driving her round the country to auctions and antique shops. They must be on just such an expedition today, I presumed.

My next impulse was to go over and greet them, perhaps even to join them for a while, to share my discovery of Ledbury's enchanting church and steeple. No doubt they were already familiar with it, but they wouldn't know about the Henry James connection and I was eager to impress them with this little crumb of knowledge, in the way one is with cultured friends. But just as I was about to rise to my feet, Nicholas Beck took Carrie's hand, leaned across the angle of the table, and kissed her full on the lips.

It was a lover's kiss. There was no doubt in my mind about that. Immediately my brain went into turbodrive again (it must be because of my conversations with Ralph that I have begun to picture my own thought processes in the language of engineering) scanning possibilities, resolving contradictions, revising assumptions, making deductions. The unavoidable inferences were that Nicholas Beck was neither celibate nor homosexual, as Jasper Richmond had confidently informed me, and that Carrie was no more faithful to Ralph than he to her.

What to do now?

What I wanted to do was to flee at once, before they saw me. But could I recall the waitress, cancel my pudding and settle my bill, without drawing attention to myself? As I hesitated, Carrie, who had gently detached her crescent lips from Nicholas's, but kept her head close to his for a moment, now turned away, leaned back in her seat, and surveyed the restaurant, with a complacent amorous smile still lingering on her face. The smile faded abruptly, like a light being switched off, as she caught sight of me staring at her from the other side of the room.

Oh, it was so like the scene in *The Ambassadors* where Lambert Strether, at the riverside inn in the country outside Paris, identifies what he at first took to be a pair of anonymous young lovers in a rowing boat as Chad Newsome and Mme de Vionnet, and realizes that their relationship, which he has believed and staunchly declared to be platonic, is after all an illicit sexual liaison. There was the same momentary dismay and confusion on both sides, quickly covered up by good manners and quick improvisation. Carrie recovered her smile almost at once, though it was a very different and distinctly forced one that she beamed at me, as she mimed surprise and pleasure and waved to me to join them. I waved and smiled back with, I'm sure, equally obvious artificiality, like Strether 'agitating his hat and stick' on the riverbank. Nicholas had by this time turned his eyes sharply in my direction as Carrie murmured something to him. To spare his, and my own, embarrassment, I ducked my head and groped under my chair for my handbag. Then I got up and walked across to their table, placing one foot in front of the other as carefully as a model on a catwalk.

By the time I reached them, Nicholas had recovered his composure. He rose from the table, greeted me suavely and offered me a seat. Carrie and I exchanged a kiss on both cheeks – curious, that, because we never did so before, but it was an instinctive mutual gesture, which, if I try to analyse it, was designed to draw the erotic charge from the kiss I had just witnessed: to place it, as it were, in a code of purely social behaviour, as if we were theatrical types who went around embracing each other at every opportunity.

Well, we performed well enough in the scene that followed, feigning joy and astonishment at the coincidence of our meeting in the quaint little town. I asked if they were on the antique trail, and Carrie quickly took the cue, describing just the sort of chest of drawers she was in search of, while I burbled enthusiastically about the church and trotted out my Henry James anecdote. Mercifully, our ordeal was not as extended as that of the characters in *The Ambassadors*, obliged to dine together in strained conviviality, and then return to Paris by train together, to preserve the fiction that Strether's friends were only out for the day, when they had clearly planned to spend the night in some rustic love-nest. Whether Carrie and Nicholas Beck had booked a bedroom in the Feathers for the afternoon, I have no idea, and didn't linger to ascertain. When the waitress brought their first course, I made a move to return to my table, but Carrie insisted on my eating my pudding with them. But I skipped coffee, and departed as soon as I decently could. I hurried to my car, and skedaddled out of Ledbury as fast as my wheels would carry me. I drove straight back to the campus, quite forgetting my intention to visit Tewkesbury Abbey, replaying the scene in the restaurant in my mind and giggling aloud in a mildly hysterical fashion from time to time.

For there *was* something funny as well as shocking about what I had inadvertently discovered. Adultery, as one knows, can be a subject for both comedy and tragedy in literature, from a Feydeau farce at one end of the spectrum to *Anna Karenina* at the other, and the same is true in life, depending on the context and your point of view. I certainly hadn't seen anything amusing in Martin's betrayal of me with Sandra Pickering. But the idea of Ralph Messenger, of all people, being cuckolded by Nicholas Beck, of all people, was irresistibly comic. Had Beck, I wondered, deliberately encouraged the rumour that he was a celibate homosexual? What a wonderful cover story — it was as good as Horner's putative impotence in *The Country Wife*. Perhaps he was swiving all the wives on campus under the noses of their husbands. But common sense reasserted itself. I recalled a number of little incidents which suggested a proper *affaire* that had been going for some little while. Carrie's car parked outside Nicholas Beck's town house in Lansdown Crescent on that February afternoon when I ran into her in Cheltenham. The strange little complacent smirk on Nicholas's face as he crossed the flagged hall behind Carrie, carrying a pudding dish for her at Ralph's party. And the casual recurrent dropping of his name, in her conversation, as a connoisseur. Perhaps they had fallen in love on one of their antique-foraging excursions — in any case that pursuit had provided a wonderful alibi for their disappearing together for hours on end. What a set! I thought to myself, shaking my head over the steering wheel.

What a world, I think now, more sombrely, as I read this through again. What a world of secret infidelities. Martin with Sandra Pickering, Carrie with Nicholas, Ralph with Marianne — and with me if he'd had his way. Even little Annabelle Riverdale is deceiving her husband with a packet of pills (not that I blame her). How many more deceptions shall I uncover? Is everybody I know cheating? Am I the only one with scruples and principles, as outmoded and inconvenient as Victorian crinolines? Am I missing something? I'm determined, anyway, not to let this episode make *me* feel guilty, make *me* feel uncomfortable. I thought about inventing another cold or other excuse for not going to Horseshoes on Sunday, but have decided to carry on as arranged.

25

'Everybody who lives around here sneers at Bourton-on-the Water,' Emily says to Helen. 'But I kinda like it.' Helen is at the wheel of her car, following Ralph Messenger's big Mercedes estate which has Carrie and the other children on board. Emily is riding with Helen in case she should get separated and lost in the narrow high-banked country lanes between Horseshoes and Bourton.

'Why do they sneer?' Helen asks.

'Oh, 'cos it's a touristy kinda place. It has like lots of tea-gardens and souvenir shops and stuff. A model village. Birds in cages. You get busloads of Americans and Japanese there in the summer. But it's real pretty. The river goes right through the middle.'

'What's the name of the river?' says Helen.

'Uh . . . I forget,' says Emily.

'The Windrush,' says Carrie.

'What a wonderful name for a river!' Helen exclaims. She and the Messengers have parked their cars and joined a little cluster of people gathered beside the river in the centre of the village. The Windrush flows, clear and sparkling, between brick-trimmed banks, with lawns and gardens on one side and the main street on the other, tumbling over a series of shallow waterfalls and passing under a number of ornamental footbridges, until it broadens out and slows down in the meadows outside the village. 'It's charming,' says Helen. 'And perfect for the Duck Race, I should say.'

'Marianne was lucky to get permission to do it here,' says Jasper. 'But she knows a few people on the parish council.'

'Why would they turn her down?' says Laetitia Glover. 'It's just Bourton's kind of thing.'

'Where does the race start from?' asks Reginald Glover, perhaps to divert attention from this somewhat ungracious remark.

'At the far end of the village,' says Jasper, pointing upstream. 'Marianne is up there. There are hordes of day-trippers clamouring to buy tickets. Unfortunately it's illegal to sell them in a public place.'

'Come along,' says Colin Riverdale to his wife and infant children. 'We don't want to miss the start.' He puts one child on his shoulders, seizes another by the hand, and sets off, followed by Annabelle pushing a baby buggy. Helen and the Messengers and the Glovers follow at a more leisurely pace.

The friends and acquaintances of the Richmonds, especially from the Faculty of Humanities, have turned out loyally to support Marianne's enterprise, and, as Jasper reported, there is also quite a crowd of casual Sunday afternoon visitors at the starting line, grateful for the unexpected diversion. Some of them, disappointed in the quest to buy tickets, make a donation to Marianne's charity anyway. She is glowing with self-satisfaction – it is clear the event is already a success. Oliver is beside himself with excitement. 'Hallo, Helen Reed,' he says. 'What number have you got?'

Helen looks at her ticket. 'Forty-eight.'

'I've got fourteen,' says Oliver. He goes round asking everybody he knows what numbers they have.

About a hundred ducks – identical yellow plastic bathtoys with numbers painted on them – are contained in a large net held over the parapet of a bridge by a team of Boy Scouts. At a signal from Marianne, they release the ducks into the water with a splash, and a cheer goes up from the spectators, most of whom walk along the footpath beside the river, keeping pace with the progress of the ducks. Some of the children run ahead, and line the parapet of the next bridge to watch the ducks pass underneath. At first these move in a congealed yellow mass, but they quickly separate and become strung out in separate clusters, small groups, pairs and solitary individuals. By the halfway mark one duck is twenty yards clear of all the rest.

'It's surprising,' Helen comments, walking beside Ralph, 'considering they're all identical, and they all started at more or less the same time.'

'Yes, it would make a good illustration of chaos theory,' says Ralph.

'Ah, I know about that,' says Helen. 'Professor Douglass told me.'

'Did he?' Ralph sounds surprised. 'When?'

'At your birthday party. It's the butterfly effect. So many variables.'

'Very good,' says Ralph. 'Especially at the beginning, with all the ducks knocking into each other at random. And then the river is full of currents, eddies, variations of windspeed across the water. That little duck,' he says, pointing to the leader, 'has had all the lucky breaks.'

'So far,' says Helen.

'True,' says Ralph. 'He could get caught in a whirlpool further along, or some obstruction under a bridge. But that's the only thing that will stop him winning now: a catastrophe.'

'Just like the great duck race of life,' Helen says.

Oliver Richmond is racing up and down the footpath in a state of high excitement. Helen calls to him, 'What's the number of the leader, Oliver?'

'Seventy-three,' says Oliver, slowing his pace to walk beside them.

'Not mine, alas,' says Helen.

'Nor mine,' says Ralph, looking at his bunch of five tickets.

'And forty-two is second and nine is third and eighty-two is fourth and twenty-four is fifth,' says Oliver, without faltering. 'My duck is fourteen, it's twenty-seventh.'

'You should be a horse race commentator, Oliver,' Ralph says jocularly.

Oliver looks at Ralph. 'You're Ralph Messenger,' he says.

'Yes,' says Ralph.

'Have you got a Sainsbury's Reward card?'

Ralph looks disconcerted. 'I think perhaps my wife has.'

'What number is it?'

'I've no idea,' says Ralph.

'My Mum has a Sainsbury's Reward card. It's number six three four one seven four double oh one eight six five one two three nine double seven oh.'

'Very good,' Ralph says.

Oliver runs off. Ralph stares thoughtfully after him.

'How does he do it?' Helen wonders.

'Autistic people often have these unusual specialized abilities,' says Ralph. 'Idiots savants, they used to be called before the days of political correctness.'

'Computers are a bit like that, aren't they?' says Helen.

Many ducks come to grief in various ways – getting trapped under the waterfalls, bumping against the piers of the bridges, or snagging in the reeds where the river broadens out. They are fished out of the water by the Boy Scouts wielding nets on long bamboo poles, and eliminated from the race. The majority, however, float on, bobbing and spinning in the water, past the real ducks paddling in the stream, who turn their backs on the interlopers and disdain to notice them. The eldest Riverdale child, trying to free a yellow duck caught in an overhanging branch, falls into the river and has to be rescued by his father, who gets his shoes and trouser bottoms soaked in the process and takes the whole family home in high dudgeon. Duck number seventy-three steadily increases its lead and sails serenely past the winning post at the village limits, a whole minute ahead of its closest competitor. The owner of the lucky number turns out to be Professor Douglass, whom Jasper Richmond trapped in Staff House one day and persuaded to buy a ticket.

'What a shame that he isn't here,' Helen says.

'Oh it's not Duggers' sort of thing,' says Ralph. 'He's a reclusive bugger. I don't know why he came to my party. He doesn't approve of me.'

'Yes, I rather gathered that,' says Helen.

'How?'

'Oh, just something he said.'

'What?'

'Something quite trivial.'

'Tell me,' he says, with some insistence.

'Something about your being the master of the scientific sound-bite.'

Ralph gives a short, mirthless laugh. 'I can't help it if the media ring me up, and not him, every time they want a comment on artificial intelligence.' When Helen does not comment, he goes on. 'They tell a story about Duggers, before I came here. He was always sneering about media dons then, as now, but one day he came into the coffee room looking pleased as punch and let drop the information that he'd been invited to appear on a radio discussion programme for a fee of fifty pounds. "What are you going to do about it, Duggers?" somebody asked him. "Oh, I thought I might as well accept," he said. "So I've sent off my fifty pounds." '

Helen laughs. 'I don't believe it,' she says.

'Neither do I, unfortunately,' Ralph says, grinning, his poise restored.

The rest of the ducks arrive and are collected in a net by the Boy Scouts, pulled out of the water and borne away in a great dripping bundle. The crowd at the finishing line begins to disperse. Carrie comes up and asks Ralph to go with the children to buy ice-creams, and he moves off obediently. 'And bring us one each,' she calls after him.

He turns. 'What flavour?'

'You choose,' Carrie says. 'Surprise and delight us.'

'This is Bourton-on-the-Water, Blondie,' he says. 'We're talking village shop here, with a fridge full of paper-wrapped cones and choc-ices on sticks, not Howard Johnson's.'

'I know,' Carrie says. 'Whatever.' To Helen she says, 'You know, that's what I miss more than anything about home, the ice-cream.'

On his way to the ice-cream shop, Ralph meets Stuart Phillips and

Marianne supervising the Boy Scouts as they pack the plastic ducks into cardboard boxes.

'Hallo Stuart, I didn't know you were a scoutmaster, on top of all your other skills,' Ralph says.

'Yes. You'll be glad to know I'm introducing a computing badge,' Stuart says, with a grin.

With a movement of his head Ralph draws Marianne aside for a private word. 'Oliver just asked me if I've got a Sainsbury's Reward card. What was that about?'

'Did he recite the number of my card?' Marianne asks.

'Yes, he did,' says Ralph.

'It's a favourite party trick of his.'

'Oh. It wasn't a hint about seeing us in the car-park that day?'

'Oliver doesn't know how to hint,' Marianne says.

'Has he said anything to Jasper?'

'Not as far as I know,' says Marianne.

'Thank Christ for that,' Ralph says. 'How are you anyway, Marianne?'

'I'm all right, thanks.' She looks away from him towards the Boy Scouts.

'Well, I'd better be going. I've got to get some ice-cream.'

'Mitchell's is best. Halfway up the street on the right.'

'Thanks,' says Ralph. 'Can I get some for the Scouts?'

'No, I promised them a cream tea.'

'Right,' says Ralph, and moves off.

Helen and Carrie sit down on a rustic bench in the shade of a large oak tree, facing the river. The spectators have all drifted away, back to the village.

'About last Friday,' Carrie says.

'You don't have to explain anything to me, Carrie,' Helen says quickly.

'You must have wondered what was going on.'

'It's none of my business.'

'Well, maybe it isn't,' says Carrie. 'But I'd like you to know a few things anyway.'

'I haven't told anyone else, and I don't intend to.'

'I know you won't, Helen. You're not a gossip, you're a writer. You store up all the dirt and recycle it in your novels.'

Helen glances at Carrie as if to gauge the feeling behind this remark. 'If that's what you're worried about, I can assure you —'

'You don't need to, Helen,' Carrie says, smiling. 'You told me the other day, at the Brine Baths, you wouldn't write anything that would embarrass anyone.'

'Oh. Well, good.'

'But I was less than honest with you,' Carrie says. 'I said I trusted Messenger not to play around with his female post-docs and graduate students. And that's true. He's far too smart to get trapped that way. But that's exactly how far I trust him — not an inch further. I know he has other women when he's away from home.'

'How do you know?' Helen says.

'I've developed an instinct. When he wants to have sex as soon as he gets back from a trip, for instance, that's a sure sign. He's trying to demonstrate that he missed me while he was away.'

Helen smiled. 'You must have more to go on than that.'

'Sure. Sometimes faculty who go to the same conferences as Messenger tell their colleagues or their wives what he's been up to, and eventually it gets back to me. Sometimes I get anonymous letters. Those are probably from guys in Messenger's field who hate him, or maybe they're from women who hate me, or people who hate both of us. There's a lot of envy and malice out there. When *Private Eye* ran a paragraph about Messenger being a woman-chaser, three anonymous informants sent me the clipping, just in case I hadn't seen it. As it happens I had — some thoughtful friend slipped it into my Fanny Farmer cookbook at one of our parties.'

'How horrible,' Helen murmurs.

'The main thing is not to betray for a moment to anybody that you've been upset, or even that you got the message. You just ignore it. Deny them any satisfaction.'

'That must be difficult sometimes,' Helen says.

'Once a woman he'd had a fling with in Australia wrote to me herself. Signed the letter. She felt she'd been used. She wanted revenge.'

'What did you do?'

'I tore it up.'

'You didn't confront Ralph with it?'

'What would be the point? He's not going to change, and I don't want to divorce him. We make a good team. He's a good father. The kids would be devastated if we split up.'

'I don't think I could be so tolerant. I *know* I couldn't,' Helen says.

'Well, I made it clear to Messenger that I wouldn't stand for anything in my own back yard, meaning the University, Chelten- ham, anywhere round here. I never spelled it out, but it was understood between us. Then it began to dawn on me that this was a very one-sided arrangement. I mean, there was no way *I* could have an occasional adventure, because I don't get to swan off on trips abroad on my own or pop up and down to London to meet publishers or make TV programmes requiring location shoots and stopovers. Then Nick came on the scene. We had a lot in common – history of art, interior decoration, period furniture. He's good company. And he's very kind, very considerate. He thinks ahead, about little things that might please you, and he does them. We became close friends. Then Nick wanted more than friendship, and I thought, why shouldn't I? It's been going for over a year now, and you're the first person who's caught us off guard. Lucky it was you. I guess we've been getting a little careless.'

'Did you know,' says Helen, 'that some people think he's a celibate gay?'

Carrie laughed merrily. 'Yeah. Nick and I have had a few laughs over that. He doesn't know who started it – *he* certainly didn't. But he hasn't bothered to deny it, either. Messenger believes it, which is kinda convenient . . . No, Nick isn't gay, though he was confused sexually as a young man. Those English public schools, you know. He likes to be spanked. Otherwise, he's completely straight.'

'He likes to be spanked?' Helen says, wide-eyed.

'Yeah, and you know what? I get quite a buzz out of it too. It's fun to be the dominant partner in the bedroom for a change.'

'I see,' says Helen.

Carrie laughs. 'Don't look so shocked, it's only playacting.'

'I'm not shocked – really. It's just . . . surprise.'

'What about that scene in *The Eye of the Storm*, with the rope and the masks?'

'That was fiction,' Helen says, with a touch of embarrassment.

'You never did that type of thing yourself?' Helen shakes her head. 'You should try it some time,' says Carrie. 'Here's Messenger coming back, we'd better change the subject.'

Helen looks about her, as if in search of one. A wink of yellow on the river catches her eye. 'Oh look,' she says, pointing. 'The last duck.'

Ralph joins them and distributes ice-cream cones.

'I take it all back,' he says. 'I found a little place that makes home-made ice-cream.'

'Mmm, delicious!' says Carrie, tasting hers.

'What were you pointing at?' Ralph asks Helen.

'A duck,' Helen says. 'A straggler.'

They go to the edge of the river bank and watch the little toy bobbing along in a sluggish current. Who knows why it is such a long way behind all the others? Perhaps it got caught in some obstruction further upstream, and was overlooked by the Boy Scouts, but then freed itself. Anyway, here it comes, towards the finishing line, the last to cross it.

'Shouldn't we try and fish it out?' Helen says.

Ralph looks around, sees a broken branch lying on the ground, and, leaning out perilously from the bank, with Helen clinging to his belt, drags the duck to the side of the river and pulls it out.

'What number is it?' says Carrie.

'Forty-eight,' says Ralph.

'My number,' says Helen.

When the Messengers get back to their house in Pittville Lawn, the little red light on the answerphone in the kitchen is flashing to indicate that several messages have been received while they were out. Ralph presses the playback button, and Carrie fills the electric kettle to make a cup of tea.

'*Carrie, this is Mom,*' says the voice of Carrie's mother, as clear as if she is speaking from the other side of Cheltenham rather than from California. '*Bad news, I'm afraid, honey. Your father's sick. They think he's had a heart attack.*'

'Oh my God,' says Carrie, dropping the kettle with a clatter. She goes across to stand beside Ralph, listening intently to the messages, recorded at intervals during the day, from Carrie's mother, sister and brother-in-law. The children who come into the room whistling, or with questions and demands, are shushed and made to wait, silent and motionless, until the messages have finished. They become grave and subdued, as they absorb the information that their grandfather has had a serious heart attack and is in hospital, in intensive care.

'I'll have to fly out tomorrow,' says Carrie, dialling. She calls her mother and her sister. Both of them are at the hospital, but she talks to her brother-in-law, Gary, who tells her that her father has had a second heart attack and his condition is critical. 'I'll get there as soon as I can,' Carrie says, and puts down the phone. She turns to Ralph. 'Can you book flights on a Sunday evening?' she says.

'Sure, if you go direct to the airlines. You don't want to wait till tomorrow morning? See how things are?'

'No, do it for me now, will you?'

'I can't go with you. We're interviewing for the new post all this week.'

'I know. Anyway, you'll have to look after the kids.'

Ralph calls British Airways and books Carrie a business class seat on a plane from Heathrow to Los Angeles at noon the following day. Carrie and Emily prepare a scratch meal of scrambled eggs and ham.

They eat the meal at the kitchen table. Hope breaks a silence.

'Is Grandpa going to die?'

'No, honey,' says Carrie.

'It's possible,' Ralph says at the same moment.

Carrie flashes Ralph an angry look.

'There's no point pretending,' he says defensively.

'And there's no point assuming the worst.'

'I wasn't assuming the worst. But we might as well be prepared for the possibility.'

'What happens to people when they die?' Hope asks.

'They get buried,' says Simon. 'Or they get burned.'

'Simon!' Carrie says, frowning.

'Try not be an asshole, Simon,' says Emily.

'And enough of that language,' Carrie says to Emily.

'Sock is, however, perfectly correct,' says Ralph.

'Not necessarily,' says Mark. 'In India they put corpses on the tops of buildings for vultures to pick their bones clean.'

'That's so gross,' says Emily.

'Is that true, Daddy?' Hope says.

'Could we change the subject, please,' says Carrie.

'I believe so,' Ralph says to Hope. 'But only one particular religion does it, and it's not allowed here, or in California, so you needn't worry about it, Kitten.'

'Shirley Blake's grandpa died last term and Miss Hackett said he's gone to heaven,' Hope says.

'That's right,' says Carrie.

'No it's not,' says Ralph. 'Some people believe that, Kitten, but they're wrong. There's no such place as heaven. It's a nice idea, but it's made up. It's like a fairy story.'

'Messenger, I really object to this very strongly,' Carrie says, in a level but steely voice.

'So where will Grandpa go when he dies?' Hope says.

'He won't go anywhere, sweetheart,' says Ralph. 'His body will be buried in the ground, or cremated, as Sock says, but it won't really be Grandpa anymore. Grandpa won't exist, except in our minds. We'll think of him and remember all the nice things he did for us and the presents he gave us and the stories he told us.'

Carrie gets to her feet and walks out of the kitchen, leaving her meal unfinished. Ralph carries on talking as if nothing untoward has

247

happened, but the children are silent and ill-at-ease. He leaves them to clear the dishes and goes out of the room. He finds Carrie in their bedroom, on the phone, talking to British Airways, with the flight details which Ralph wrote down, and her own credit card, in front of her. There is a half-filled suitcase open on the bed.

'What are you doing?' he asks.

Carrie concludes her conversation and puts down the phone. 'I've booked a ticket on that flight for Hope. I'm taking her with me.' Carrie resumes packing her suitcase, walking backwards and forwards between the bed and the fitted wardrobes and chests of drawers.

'Why?'

'I couldn't believe what you were saying just now. You were talking like Daddy was already dead.'

'It seemed to me a good opportunity to get Hope used to the idea of what death means. When kids ask these questions, it means they want to know the truth.'

'The truth! Who knows the truth? Who really knows what happens to us when we die? You don't know, Messenger, not for sure.'

'I know there's no such place as heaven.'

'If a kid wants to believe in it, why not let her? Until it drops away naturally, like a milk tooth coming out. Why use force?'

'I'm not going to have an argument with you, Carrie —'

'I thought we were already having one.'

'You're upset, understandably. Just tell me why you're dragging Hope all the way to California.'

'She always had a soft spot for Daddy, and he for her. It may do him good to see her.'

'You're going to take a young kid into an intensive care ward, to see an old man with drips and tubes coming out of him? You must be crazy!'

'Who's trying to protect her from the truth now? Your trouble is, Messenger, you're very hot on facing facts in the abstract, but not when they're physical, in your face.'

'She'll miss at least a week's school.'

'Too bad . . . And if the worst should happen, well, I'd rather she was with me than with you. I don't rate you very highly as a grief counsellor, Messenger.'

Ralph is silent for a moment, ruminating with pursed lips.

'OK, have it your own way,' he says. 'I'll drive you to Heathrow in the morning.'

'You needn't bother,' Carrie says.

'I don't have anything important till the afternoon.'

'I'll book a car with a driver. I'd prefer it that way. It's less stressful.'

'As you like,' says Ralph, with a shrug, and leaves the room.

26

It's Wednesday, 16th April, 9.05 p.m. A day to remember. A day to record–though not on the Pearlcorder. I'm at home in my study, writing this straight on to the computer. The kids are all in their rooms doing their homework or watching TV, or possibly both simultaneously (teenage behaviour is the best evidence I know for consciousness as parallel processing. I once found Mark in his bedroom watching a football match with the sound off, listening to Oasis on his personal CD player, *and* writing an essay on the Corn Laws, all at the same time, without apparent difficulty), but even so I don't feel like dictating this, just in case one of them should come quietly up the stairs with some question or request and overhear me saying that this afternoon I fucked one of England's finest contemporary novelists. That's how she's described on the back of Carrie's paperback edition of *The Eye of the Storm*, which lies on my desk at this moment. 'A novel of exquisite sensibility and artful restraint,' the *Spectator* said. Well, she wasn't at all restrained this afternoon, and I have lovebites on my left shoulder to prove it. She damn nearly drew blood. I hope to hell the marks fade before Carrie gets back.

Fortunately it seems likely that she will be away for at least another week. Daddy Thurlow's condition has stabilized, and it looks as if he's going to pull through, though whether this will be a cause for rejoicing remains to be seen. He may be seriously disabled. Carrie is staying on for a while, anyway, to see how things develop and give her mother support. Which is fine by me. I'm glad the old man didn't die, because if he had I think Carrie in some irrational way would have blamed me for it, or at least associated it with my allegedly cruel and heartless handling of Hope's questions over supper on Sunday. Needless to say I made no apology for that. Carrie went off to Heathrow the next morning in a huge hired Daimler with a dark-suited driver, as if to a funeral, wearing a black topcoat and a grim expression. She spoke only of practical arrangements over breakfast, and offered me her cheek, not her mouth, to kiss when we parted. Hope looked on anxiously, picking up the bad vibrations, so I gave her an extra big hug and cracked a joke to make her smile. She waved to me through the back window as the car turned out of the drive, but Carrie kept her head turned sternly to the front.

I remember thinking to myself, as I drove into the University later, that with Carrie away, on the other side of the world, conditions would have been ideal for a dalliance with Helen Reed, thinking what a pity it was that she had turned me down so unequivocally a few weeks ago, kicking myself for having made my pitch too soon, too early in our acquaintance, or perhaps just too crudely. She looked so attractive at Bourton-on-the-Water, in a close-fitting pair of white jeans that showed her shapely bum to advantage, and her breasts moving about interestingly under her sweater. And she was teasing me a little, with her quips about 'the great duck race of life' and computers being autistic (though that's a shrewd comment, actually, typical of her to just throw it off, maybe I'll use it; computers for instance have fantastic memories but no common sense, they have a deficit of affect, they can't tell the difference between a true story and a fiction, they don't know how to lie . . .) yes, she was definitely winding me up a bit with these *bons mots* and then quoting Duggers' snide comment, *'the master of the scientific sound-bite'*, glancing at me to see how I took it, but not at all nervously, still less flirtatiously. She obviously felt at ease with me, whereas I like any woman I'm with to feel, if only very faintly, in danger.

That was how it looked on Monday morning: the cat was away, but the mouse I was interested in wouldn't play. When I got to my office, I thought I would call her anyway, on the thoroughly plausible pretext of telling her about Carrie's father. Naturally she was very sympathetic, and asked how I was going to manage house and family while Carrie was away. I told her that Edna was going to do extra hours and there was a stack of prepared meals in the freezer. She offered to come over and cook dinner for us one evening and I booked her at once, for Friday. Then I asked diffidently if she would care to have lunch in Staff House on Wednesday, expecting to be turned down, but to my surprise she said yes. *'And why don't we go to a pub this time, the food in Staff House is so ghastly.'* Of course I agreed, trying hard not to give the impression that I was wagging my tail and licking my chops in delight.

My first thought was to take her to the King's Head, a nice little pub near Horseshoes, where we often go for Sunday lunch when Carrie doesn't feel like cooking; but on reflection I didn't want to entertain Helen at a place where I was well known, and from which mischievous gossip might get back to Carrie. So I rang up a country pub called the Anvil near Burford which I'd been to only once before, without Carrie, and reserved a table in their bar-restaurant. I remembered it as somewhat over-endowed with antique agricultural implements hanging on the walls, but the grub was good and it was pleasantly uncrowded. It's in *The Good Pub Guide* but it's so hard to find that I'm sure lots of potential customers give up in despair and go home to their locals instead.

I cancelled a couple of supervisions I had in my diary for this afternoon – not because I had any inkling of how it would turn out, but because I didn't want to rush the lunch, and the Anvil is a good forty minutes' drive from the campus. Helen commented on the distance we seemed to be covering on the way there, and I said I hoped she wasn't bothered about getting back promptly. 'No, not at all,' she said. I said I had a free afternoon. 'So have I,' she said, and this banal little statement suddenly became charged with significance. It was like the moment in Prague when I said, *'I can think of several things,'* and Ludmila blushed. Helen didn't blush, and neither did I, but we fell silent for a minute or two. The thinks bubbles over our heads filled up. I was wondering, 'Is it possible that I'm going to get lucky this afternoon? Has she changed her mind about me for some reason?' I had no idea what was in her bubble, however, and resolved to proceed with extreme caution. If this was a second chance, I didn't want to bungle it. I let her break the silence. 'What a lovely day!' she said, turning her head to look out of the car window. 'I do love the spring.' Which was a conversational filler if ever I heard one.

I glanced quickly across at her. She was wearing a red shirt with a silk scarf loosely knotted round her neck, a fawn cardigan round her shoulders and a pair of matching tailored trousers. Gold earrings and a classy-looking brooch. She looked good. She's always well turned-out, but it seemed to me that she had taken particular care with her appearance today. A good sign.

The Anvil was as I remembered it, whitewashed brick and thatch on the outside, exposed beams and rafters and agricultural ironmongery on the inside. We sat down at a snug corner table. 'Watch that scythe on the wall,' I said, 'and don't wave your arms about when you talk, or they might have to re-name this pub the Amputee.' She laughed more heartily than the joke was worth. Another good sign. Ditto that we spontaneously chose the same dishes from the lunch menu, *moules marinières* to start, followed by pan-fried duck breast. I suggested a glass of white wine to go with the mussels and a bottle of Pomerol for the duck. The *moules* were excellent. 'This is what I call a gourmet pub-lunch,' she said, spooning up the liquor with relish.

I gave her an update about Carrie's father. She talked a bit about her own parents, who sound like a right pair of old fogies, and she asked me about mine. I told her they were both dead. She said, 'Oh, I'm sorry.' I didn't go into details. I wanted to steer the conversation away from this gloomy topic as soon as possible, and fortunately I had another one up my sleeve.

I'd taken the trouble to speed-read *The Eye of the Storm* the night before. It's a rather tedious story of a woman going into and coming out of a depressive illness, and the effect this has on the people around her, her husband, children, parents and friends. Her depression lifts suddenly in the course of a trip she makes with her husband to Paris, where they spent their honeymoon years before. Most of this episode is a typical Francophile rhapsody about recovering the forgotten charms of Paris – the boulevard cafés, the aromas of garlic and freshly baked bread, the patter of tyres on the cobbled squares, the bookstalls along the Left Bank, *etc. etc.*, the usual Frogbollocks, but there was one interesting bit, about the reawakening of the heroine's interest in sex, which has been at a very low ebb during her illness. The couple are staying at a five-star hotel, somewhere like the Ritz, because the husband's on a journalistic freebie, and one day, while he's out, the heroine, her name's Anna, finds in a drawer in their white and gold Second Empire bedroom some intriguing objects evidently left behind by the previous occupants: two black velvet facemasks and some lengths of thick silky cord. She takes them out and handles them with a thudding heart, wondering what to do with them – hand them in at the desk? throw them in the waste basket? In the end she puts them back in the drawer and shows them to her husband when he comes in. At first he laughs and makes a few ribald jokes, but Anna can see that he's quite excited by the discovery. When they're going to bed, he takes the masks out of the drawer and hands one to her. 'Put it on,' he says, and goes into the bathroom taking the other one with him. Anna puts on the mask, which covers the top half of her face, and looks at herself in the mirror. 'A depraved stranger stared back at her through the eyeholes of the mask,' the text says. Anna takes off her nightdress, and poses in the room's long mirrors, naked but for the mask. Her husband comes in, also masked, naked – and erect. They look at each other 'with smiles of licentious complicity'. Anna takes the heavy coils of silken cord out of the drawer and holds them out to him. 'Tie me up,' she says. Annoyingly, the chapter ends there, but we're given to understand from Anna's retrospective thoughts that they enjoy a night of unprecedented orgiastic sex, from which Anna emerges a new woman, finally purged of her angst.

When I said that I had been reading one of her novels, Helen tossed her head nervously and pulled a face. 'I wish you hadn't,' she said. 'But on the other hand, I'm surprised it's taken you so long. Most of the people I meet rush off immediately to borrow my books from the library. Then they make a point of telling me and seem to think I should be grateful.'

'I put off reading your books in case I didn't like them,' I said. 'I'm not very good at disguising my opinions.'

'So why did you change your mind?'

'I feel we know each other well enough now for it not to matter.'

'Which one did you read?' she said. I told her. 'And did you like it?'

' "Like" wouldn't be the right word,' I said. 'To be honest, it's

not my kind of thing. It's what used to be called "a woman's book",
though you're not allowed to say that any more. But I admired it. I
could appreciate the skill that had gone into it.'

' "Thank you, sir, she said." ' This with a little ironic bow.

'No, really, it's beautifully written,' I said. 'And there was one
scene that really made me sit up. Towards the end, when they're in
Paris.'

She laughed a little self-consciously. 'You mean the bedroom
scene? With the masks? I'm afraid that's everybody's favourite
chapter,' she said, 'except for my parents.'

I asked if it had any basis in fact.

'Oh, Messenger!' she said, 'I'm disappointed in you. Everybody
asks me that.'

I said I was sorry, and I did feel a bit of a prat; but what impressed
me more was that she had called me 'Messenger'. I couldn't recall her
having done that before. Only the family, and very formal colleagues
like Duggers, call me 'Messenger'. It seemed to move us on to a new
level of intimacy. I don't know whether she was aware of it herself.
Since I would have to drive later, I had replenished her glass rather
more often than my own, and she was a little flushed and inebriated.

'The long weekend in Paris is based on experience,' she said, 'and
the luxury hotel, but not finding the masks and the silk cord in the
chest of drawers. I made that up.'

'You've never experimented with that sort of thing yourself?'
She shook her head. 'You should try it one day,' I said.

'Someone else said that to me recently,' she said, with a rather
strange smile.

'There you are, then.'

She shook her head again. 'I'm too old for such antics.'

'Nonsense,' I said. 'It's the only way to resist ageing. Feed the
flame of sex. Keep it burning at all costs.'

The girl who had been serving us our lunch came up with the
bill.

'Can I share this?' Helen said, reaching for her handbag.

'No, it's my treat,' I said. I paid with cash and tipped the girl
generously.

'Well, thank you very much,' Helen said. 'It was delightful.'

It was the first time she had allowed me to pay for her meal. Another good sign. I decided to take the plunge – literally and metaphorically.

'It's far too nice an afternoon to go back to work,' I said. 'Why don't we drive over to Horseshoes and have a hot tub?'

'I don't have a swimming costume with me,' she said.

'You won't need one,' I said. 'There's nobody there. The deck isn't overlooked.'

Our conversation had reached the point where she usually says that she isn't going to have an affair with me, but this time she didn't. 'Perhaps you could find the things I wore last time,' she said.

'All right,' I said. 'But it's actually much nicer without anything on.'

'Yes, I can believe that,' she said.

It isn't easy to drive with an erection. You have to lean forward over the wheel with your chin practically on the dashboard, as if you're short-sighted. I don't know whether Helen closed her eyes to spare my embarrassment, but after a while I realized she had fallen asleep, and I was able to relax. She didn't wake until I drew up outside Horseshoes. 'Goodness, I nodded off,' she said. 'It must be the wine and the food.'

'Actually,' I said, 'perhaps we should rest for a while before we go in the tub. Digest the lunch.'

'You mean, "have a nice lie-down"?' she said, echoing a line of my own from that lunch in her house.

'Exactly,' I said.

Horseshoes, as usual, was quiet and deserted. Only the drone of a distant tractor disturbed the deep rustic peace, and the shriek of the burglar alarm in the hall when I opened the front door. I silenced the alarm and closed the door behind us. Then I kissed Helen long and hard. She did not resist. Indeed, I was the one to break off. 'Let's make love,' I said.

'I've forgotten how to do it,' she said. 'It's been such a long time.'

'I'll remind you,' I said, taking her hand. I led her up the stairs and into the master bedroom. 'First you have to take all your clothes off,' I said.

'You must draw the curtains, then,' she said. 'I feel shy.'

I drew the curtains, thinking of that afternoon in the Yorkshire Dales many years ago when Martha drew the thin cotton curtains across the window of my room in the farmhouse, filling it with soft pink light. These were thicker, but there was enough light for me to see Helen's naked body, and not be disappointed. I took a condom from the bedside cabinet and made sure she saw me place it ready to hand.

The sex was short but sweet. I didn't want to give her any time for second thoughts, and I soon discovered that there was no need for any elaborate foreplay. In fact she came with astonishing rapidity, almost as soon as I entered her. I suppose it's the same for women as for men, abstinence makes the sensations of intercourse more intense, and in her case the dry season had been a very long one. She came like a flash flood, and I saw no reason to hold back myself. I fell almost immediately asleep. When I woke, I found she had covered us with a sheet. She was lying on her back, with her head on the pillow, and her face had the soft blurred look of a satisfied woman. She gave me a strange little smile, both shy and wry. 'So, how was it for me?' she said.

I had envisaged the hot tub as a prelude to sex, but in the event we had it afterwards — much the best order, lolling satisfied and languorous in the bubbling water. After a while, though, I started fooling about and got aroused again. I wanted to have sex out there in the tub, under the open sky, but she wouldn't. I offered to take her into the house and tie her up. That was when she bit me.

Emily is calling up the stairs about something the boys have, or haven't, done, asking me to intervene. Time to save this.

27

WEDNESDAY 14TH MAY. It's some time since I made the last
entry in this journal. I haven't felt like writing anything down, even
for my own eyes only, about the events of the last three weeks. I've
been too preoccupied with living them. No, that's not the real
reason. A journal is a kind of mirror in which you look at yourself
every day, candidly, unflinchingly – without the protective disguise
of a mask, without even the flattery of makeup – and tell yourself the
truth. I haven't felt like doing that since Messenger and I became
lovers. I didn't want to record my behaviour because I was afraid that
scrutinizing it and analysing it might awaken scruples of conscience
and inhibit my pleasure. (In fact I still shrink from examining this
experience with the straight unflinching gaze of the first person. Let
me try it another way . . .)

For that was what she had become, a woman of pleasure, a scarlet
woman, a woman of easy virtue, a woman no better than she should
be – or so she would have been described in the pages of an old
novel. Not in a modern one, of course. She was only doing what
everybody else was doing, evidently: fulfilling her desires, making hay
while the sun shone, squeezing every drop of joy from her ageing
body before it was too late, because *'This is the only life you will have,'*
etc., etc. And whatever happened she would never regret it, it had
been so exciting.

Nerve-racking, too, at times, because they had taken tremendous
risks. Twice she had gone to the house on Pittville Lawn to cook
dinner for the family, and stayed overnight on the pretext that she'd
drunk too much wine to drive home, and on both occasions he crept
into her room and her bed in the middle of the night, just as she had

fantasized on the night of his birthday party, and they made love that was somehow all the more sensuous and passionate because they dared not make a sound, in case one of the children should wake and hear them. They had to mime their ecstasy to each other like a pair of dancers, in the movements of their limbs and the expressions on their faces. They lay on a sheepskin rug on the floor because the bed creaked, and he held his hand over her mouth as she reached her climax. She bit on the cushion of flesh at the base of his thumb as if it were a bridle or a gag, to stop herself from crying out, and heard a sharp intake of breath as he stood the pain. (He called her 'Biter' in pillow-talk. He seemed to like it, but she had stopped doing it, because Carrie was coming home soon, and mustn't find her husband visibly nibbled and gnawed, like a joint attacked by mice.) After the silent, balletic sex, she had to unlock the door and peer out on to the landing to make sure that it was safe for him to slink back to his own bedroom, for it was always possible that one of the children would get up to go to the toilet and see him coming out of the guest room.

One afternoon they were in bed at Horseshoes, and a car drew up outside and someone rang the doorbell. Messenger crept, naked, to the window, and peeped out through a gap in the curtains. 'It's the VC!' he whispered. 'It's Sir Stan and Lady Viv. What the fuck are they doing here?' Helen found this untimely visitation terribly funny, and got the giggles, but Messenger was afraid of discovery and hissed at her to keep quiet. His car was parked in the drive, so the visitors knew he was in the house or not far away. Helen and Messenger lay low in the curtained bedroom until they got tired of ringing the doorbell and calling over the garden wall, and drove off. Messenger went downstairs and came back with a scribbled note he'd found on the doormat: *'We happened to be passing and saw your car parked, but obviously you're out. Another time, I hope. Stan.'* He vaguely recalled that Carrie had invited them to drop in at the cottage at any convenient opportunity. 'They were very interested in seeing the hot tub,' he said. 'They'd have been even more interested if they'd found the two of us in it, stark naked,' Helen said. 'And having sex,' he added with a grin, for she had indulged him in that ambition one day. It wasn't particularly successful, for herself anyway, but he was delighted. He liked to have sex in unusual places, even public places. The risk of discovery seemed to sharpen his pleasure.

One Sunday Helen joined him and the children at Horseshoes, and they managed to take a walk together on their own in the afternoon. The boys wanted to watch a rugby match on television, and Emily was too idle to join in the expedition Messenger proposed: to show Helen a prehistoric barrow called Belas Knapp. Emily had seen it already and knew what a stiff climb it was. Messenger, needless to say, made no great effort to persuade her.

It was indeed a strenuous walk, especially the last part, up a steep grassy hill, a mile or more from the nearest road. The sheep stopped cropping the grass to stare at them, as if they had never seen human beings so high up. Messenger said they were the Cotswold long-haired breed, whose wool was favoured for making rugs and hard-wearing cloth. He seemed surprisingly knowledgeable on the subject of sheep. When she commented on this, he explained that he had worked with a shepherd in Yorkshire for several months as a teenager. At the top of the hill there was a copse and a narrow footpath between the trees which became a little avenue, and at the end of the avenue was the barrow, a whale-shaped mound about forty yards long, covered with turf. It had been partially excavated to expose some of the dry stone walling and a kind of porch blocked by a great slab of stone. An English Heritage information board erected nearby explained that the bones of about thirty people belonging to the Late Stone Age had been found on the site, together with animal remains and shards of pottery. They had been buried there about four thousand years ago.

Helen was impressed that people so primitive should have taken the trouble to bury their dead at this inconvenient site. Was it because it was at the top of a hill, where the earth was nearest to the sky? Did they have an idea of heaven, a place up above, where the individual's spirit would go after death, she wondered. Messenger kissed these questions from her lips. The isolation of the place, no sign of human civilization visible except for the relics of these remote ancestors, seemed to excite him sexually. Nothing would satisfy him but to spread his cagoule on the sloping side of the barrow and copulate with her, like a Stone Age man taking his mate, short and sharp. 'No, no,' she protested, half amused and half annoyed, as he fumbled with her clothing. 'No, don't, Messenger, I am not Lady Chatterley nor was meant to be.' But her literary wit was lost on him. She beat at his head and shoulders with her fists as he pushed her down. 'Stop it, Messenger, someone may come.' But he was indifferent to her protests and her puny blows, so in the end she let herself become slack and shameless, opened her legs and let him take his pleasure, patient and open-eyed as a ewe being tupped by a ram (though there were no sheep similarly occupied on the hillside, it was the wrong time of year apparently, the end of the lambing season) looking up at the fleecy clouds passing slowly across the blue sky as he thrust and grunted, feeling totally detached from reality and curiously happy. No doubt we are not the first couple to have made love here, she thought afterwards, as she pulled up her knickers and brushed down her skirt – it must have been a favourite spot for lovers through the ages, so remote, so sheltered, so secret. On their way back through the copse they met a group of middle-aged ramblers with maps and walking sticks who smiled and said 'Good afternoon.' 'Good job they didn't get here five minutes ago,' Helen muttered to Messenger. 'We would've heard them coming,' he said with a grin, but she wasn't at all sure about that.

For herself, she much preferred to make love indoors, on a bed, behind drawn curtains, and to sleep for hours afterwards – though that last luxury was one they had been able to enjoy only once, when Messenger had to stay in London overnight in order to be on a television breakfast show the next morning. He was commenting on the defeat of the world chess champion, Gary Kasparov, by a computer. Helen went up to London by an earlier train on the same day, casually informing anyone who might be interested that she had to meet her tenants to discuss whether a faulty dishwasher should be repaired or replaced. This was a genuine reason up to a point, though the business could probably have been sorted out by telephone.

It was in fact the first time she had been back to London since she started her job at the University. In the early weeks of depression and alienation she had been afraid to go back, even for a day, in case she couldn't bear to return to the campus, and was tempted to desert. Then, as her life in Gloucestershire became more interesting and involving, she thought less and less of London. It was quite a shock to step down from the train at Paddington into the clamour and bustle of the great station, and then to descend into the infernal labyrinth of the Tube and squeeze into the press of bodies inside the carriages. She felt deafened by the mechanical noise, suffocated by the stale air, and tense at the close proximity of so many silent impassive strangers. It had never struck her so forcibly before how people on the Tube avoided eye contact, how determinedly they tried to withdraw from this hideously uncomfortable form of travel by reading a book – one-handedly if necessary, hanging from a strap with the other – or listening to a personal stereo, or just staring at the diagram of the Tube line above the faces opposite. Only the tourists chattered to each other. The seasoned travellers, like the unfortunate rape victim she had read about, tried as far as possible to separate their minds from their bodies and to retreat into the former.

It was a strange sensation, also, to revisit her own house after an interval of nearly three months. Her first impression was how shabby the outside looked, how badly the woodwork needed a coat of paint. Inside, it was both familiar and slightly, disturbingly, altered. The furniture had been rearranged; strange coats hung on the hallstand; other people's books and magazines were displayed on the shelves and coffee tables in the living-room; smells of a different kind of cooking from her own lingered on the air of the kitchen. The Weismullers had been responsible tenants, but they made the most of her visit, taking her on a tour of the house and pointing out various flaws and faults in politely reproachful counterpoint. Helen placated them by agreeing to replace the ailing dishwasher, and went

262

immediately to her local discount store to purchase a new one and arrange for it to be delivered and installed.

Then she went to the hotel the BBC had booked Messenger into, and took a room for herself. He had proposed that she pretend to be Mrs Messenger and share his room, but Helen thought this would be going too far. So they dined in the hotel's restaurant like a couple of old friends who had met by chance, said goodnight in the bar, and went separately to their rooms, meeting later in Messenger's (in case one of the children tried to call him) where they had an orgiastic night. The BBC sent a car to the hotel at 6.30 the next morning. Watching him later on the TV in her own room, explaining lucidly how Deep Blue's program worked – scanning the consequences of millions of possible moves in a matter of seconds – and how different this was to the intuitive methods of a human player, she was amazed how fresh and collected he seemed, showing no trace of the excesses of the night before.

His style as a lover was very different from Martin's. With Martin foreplay tended to be very elaborate and extended, and the act itself over rather quickly. With Messenger it was the other way round. He liked to get inside her quickly and copulate in various positions before he achieved his orgasm, bringing Helen to several in the meantime. He was immensely strong in the arms and shoulders, and flipped her effortlessly this way and that, over and under him, like a wrestler practising 'holds'. Sometimes it seemed to her that he was straining too hard, that he wanted to reduce her to a helpless quivering bundle of sensation, to force the astonished, languageless sounds of pleasure from her throat, to make her beg for mercy, slapping the mattress like a beaten wrestler.

Yesterday, though, he was the one who had had to admit defeat. He called in at the maisonette on his way home, bringing with him some literature about the consciousness conference just in case he ran into somebody and needed an alibi. He wasn't able to stay long because Emily was cooking the evening meal and he dared not be late for it, so he began to undress Helen as soon as the front door was shut behind him. They went upstairs to the bedroom and lay down on the bed, but for once he was impotent. He was a picture of despondency. 'Don't worry about it,' she said. 'It's psychological. It was a bad idea trying to make love against the clock.' 'We've had to be quick before,' he said. 'Well, perhaps you've been overdoing it, lately,' she said jokingly. 'For a man of fifty.' He bridled at this. 'Rubbish,' he said. 'It's most likely the Staff House curried chicken I had for lunch. I've had indigestion all afternoon.' 'You're always complaining of indigestion,' she said. 'You should do something about it.' She suddenly heard herself sounding just like a wife, and the shock of this realization abruptly silenced her. But he didn't seem to notice. 'All I need is a couple of Rennies,' he said. He dressed quickly, kissed her, and left.

Helen took a bath. Was she falling in love with Messenger, she wondered, as she lolled in the water, topping it up occasionally from the hot tap with her toe. She had been attracted to him from the first moment they met, in the Richmonds' living-room, but she wouldn't have described it, to herself or anyone else, as 'love' in the traditional, romantic I-can't-live-without-you-and-only-you sense. And she hadn't supposed for a moment that he was expressing such an emotion when he described himself as 'falling in love' with her, that day when he brought her the modem and she gave him lunch. The first time she went to bed with him had been entirely opportunistic and experimental. She was still reeling from the encounter with Carrie and Nicholas Beck in Ledbury, and Carrie's revelations beside the river at Bourton. In this new light, her principled rejection of Messenger's advances in the preceding weeks looked suddenly redundant. If Carrie was having an affair with Nicholas Beck, there seemed no good reason why she herself shouldn't have a fling with Messenger. The circumstance that Carrie flew off to California at that precise moment made it easier to act on this conclusion. And the gradual extension of Carrie's absence from days to weeks (as her father's condition very slowly improved) had allowed the 'fling' to develop into a fully-fledged and very carnal affair. For three weeks they had thought of little else – at least, *she* had thought of little else – except finding opportunities to make love. It was surprising to Helen that nobody in their circle of acquaintance seemed to have any suspicion of what they were up to. Hadn't her students discerned the lineaments of gratified desire in her countenance? Didn't Messenger's colleagues smell the scent of sex on him when he hurried back to a meeting from a lunchtime assignation? Didn't anybody notice that they were frequently absent from view at exactly the same time? Apparently not. Only Sandra Pickering, she thought, might have sensed a subtle alteration in her demeanour. Sometimes Helen would come back from some erotic reverie in the middle of a class and find the young woman regarding her quizzically, as if trying to work out how she had changed. Otherwise, everybody seemed to be too preoccupied with their own affairs, private and professional, to take any notice of Helen's and Messenger's behaviour, or draw any inferences from it.

It had helped, no doubt, that the General Election was the object of so much excitement and attention at this time. She and Messenger attended the Glovers' party on Election Night, but hardly spoke to each other. They slipped away, separately and inconspicuously, soon after the first results indicated the scale of Labour's victory, and rendezvoused at Helen's house. When people asked her in the days following, 'Were you up for Portillo?' referring to the most sensational Tory defeat of the night, she had to reply rather sheepishly, 'No, I was in bed,' and hope that she didn't blush.

After Messenger had left her to return home in the early hours of that morning, Helen put on her dressing gown and made a pot of tea and sat in front of her TV for an hour or so. She watched the delirious celebrations of Labour supporters on the South Bank, and the triumphal appearance of the new Prime Minister and his wife, and felt a twinge of regret that she hadn't participated in this great historic event. She hadn't canvassed, she hadn't voted, she hadn't even watched television much, because of her absorption in her own erotic adventure. Her guilt was perhaps exacerbated by the aura of virtuous connubial love radiated by the handholding Blairs. Messenger had at least taken the trouble to vote (a tactical one, for the Lib Dem candidate in Cheltenham) but to him the result was merely the least of the available evils. He had a deep contempt for politics and politicians. Politics, he maintained, was the curse of the modern age, as religion was of ages past. Just think of the sheer quantity of human misery caused by politics in this century – in Central Europe, Russia, China, Africa – he would urge rhetorically. Are you an anarchist, then, she asked. But of course he wasn't. He seemed to have a rather old-fashioned Enlightenment faith in the perfectibility of society through the application of science. He made a stark opposition between the pursuit of knowledge, which was science, and the pursuit of power, which was politics. All forms of pseudo-knowledge, from divinity to deconstruction, he maintained, had to impose their false world pictures on others by becoming political. It sounded quite plausible in the glow of post-coital well-being (for such was the usual context of their conversations).

But now Carrie was coming back (her father was going to be discharged from hospital, though he would require round-the-clock nursing care at home) Helen could no longer go about in an erotic trance, thinking only of their next assignation. Quite apart from the practical difficulties of continuing to meet clandestinely under Carrie's nose, as it were, the latter's presence would give the affair an entirely new moral and psychological context. As long as Carrie had been away it had been possible for Helen not to think of her as a rival, or even an obstacle. But with Carrie back in the frame, as wife, mother, manager, housekeeper, Helen's position immediately became marginal and problematic. That Carrie herself had a lover made no difference. Hence the force of the question that Helen asked herself in the bath: was she falling in love with Messenger? And if so, what did that portend for the future, not only in the short term, but in the longer term? Would she be content to let the affair end when her job at Gloucester finished, at the end of the semester, and she returned to London? Her heart answered immediately, no. Would she be content to be an occasional mistress, meeting Messenger for short snatched hours of passion in London between his meetings and media appearances, or plotting to join him on one of his trips abroad somewhere? She had a mental image of herself sitting in a luxurious hotel room, with a basket of fruit on the dressing table and a bottle of champagne in a bucket of melting ice, waiting impatiently for Messenger to extricate himself from some conference seminar or official reception, and she did not relish the picture. Then she thought — she couldn't help herself — suppose Messenger and Carrie divorced, and he married me? The idea was enticing, but she only had to imagine little Hope's dismay to reject it. Gloom enveloped her for the first time in weeks. She wondered if it wasn't the shadow of Carrie's impending return that had suddenly cooled Messenger's ardour and made him impotent.

28

W HEN Ralph gets home, Emily is in the kitchen with her boyfriend, Greg, a tall, gawky eighteen-year-old who is in some awe of Ralph and says as little as possible in his presence. They are squatting on their haunches, peering into the oven through its glass door, at the meatloaf which Emily has prepared for supper.

'I think it's ready,' Emily says. 'Only I forgot to set the timer. I don't want to burn it.'

'It looks done to me,' Ralph says, squatting beside them. 'But isn't meatloaf made with beef?'

'I used lamb mince,' Emily says.

'A luxury meatloaf. Good. Let's eat.'

The meatloaf is excellent. Ralph takes a second helping, and congratulates Emily. While the others are clearing up after the meal she draws on the credit of her cooking to ask a favour.

'Can Greg sleep over tonight, Messenger?'

Ralph suppresses a belch. 'You mean in your room? I think not, Flipper.'

Emily frowns. 'Why not? Mom lets us.'

'I can't take the responsibility.' Emily rolls her eyes in exasperation. 'As it happens, I don't approve, but that's not the point. It's up to Carrie, and she isn't here.'

'You don't approve?' Emily says in tones of incredulity.

'No, I think it's disturbing for the boys. They're at a sensitive age.'

'You don't think it's disturbing when you have Helen sleeping over?' Emily says.

Ralph stiffens. 'That's entirely different. She was a guest, sleeping in the guest room.'

'Yeah,' says Emily, in a slightly insolent drawl. She looks at Ralph as if she might say more if challenged.

The telephone rings. It is Carrie, confirming that she and Hope are leaving LA tomorrow night and will arrive at Heathrow early on Friday morning. Ralph offers to meet them at the airport. Carrie says, no, not to bother. She has already booked the chauffeur-driven car from Cheltenham. She expects to be home by the late morning.

'Wonderful,' Ralph says. 'We've missed you.'

'Missed me or missed my cooking?' Carrie says.

'Well both,' says Ralph. 'Though Emily made us a terrific meatloaf tonight . . .' Ralph catches Emily's eye as he says this. 'By the way, Greg is here, he helped her with the meal. Is it all right if he sleeps over?'

'If it's all right by you, fine,' says Carrie.

'OK, then. See you tomorrow. Love from everybody.' Ralph puts down the phone and says to Emily. 'Your mother says it's all right.'

'Thanks, Messenger,' says Emily. She goes smiling out of the room.

Ralph puts a hand to his side, and belches again. He goes to his bathroom and finds a packet of Rennies in the medicine chest. He swallows two of the tablets.

On Friday morning, before Carrie and Hope have got back home, Ralph goes to see his GP, an Irishman called O'Keefe, whose surgery is on the ground floor of a tall narrow house in a Georgian terrace not far from the Messengers'. 'I live above the shop,' he likes to say. He is about Ralph's age, a little stouter, with a red leathery complexion and big hands. In the hairy tweed sports jackets he favours he looks more like a farmer than a doctor, but he has been a good GP to the family. Ralph has very rarely had occasion to consult him.

'What can I do for you, Professor?' he says, when the brief formalities of greeting are over. It seems to please O'Keefe to address Ralph in this way.

'It's only indigestion,' Ralph says. 'Intermittent, but I can't seem to get rid of it. Rennies don't seem to work any more.'

'Any other symptoms?'

'A sort of sensation of fullness just here.' Ralph places a hand just below the right side of his rib cage.

'Let's have a look at you, then. Take off your clothes. You can leave your underpants on.' O'Keefe gestures to a couch behind a screen in one corner of the room. While Ralph is undressing he washes his hands carefully in a sink, and chats about the weather.

O'Keefe makes a very thorough examination of Ralph's abdomen, whistling faintly through his teeth as he palpates the flesh.

'A little bit of middle-aged spread, I'm afraid,' Ralph says lightly.

O'Keefe nods. 'That's to be expected.' He pushes, presses, probes with his big spatulate fingers. 'All right,' he says. 'You can put your togs back on.' He goes back to his desk to write some notes in Ralph's file, using a gold-nibbed fountain pen.

'Well?' Ralph says, sitting down in the patient's chair.

'You've got a lump on your liver,' O'Keefe says, continuing to write.

'What kind of lump?'

'I don't know. You'll need to see a specialist.' O'Keefe looks up at Ralph. 'Are you covered by private medical insurance, Professor?'

'Yes.'

'There's a good gastrointestinal man in Bath, Dick Henderson. I've played golf with him. I could give him a call, if you like. He might be able to fit you in on Monday.'

'Is there any urgency, then?' says Ralph.

'There's no point in wasting time,' O'Keefe says.

'Are you saying it might be serious?'

O'Keefe gives Ralph a level look. 'The liver is a vital organ, Professor.'

'Yes, of course, silly question. Could it be cancer?'

O'Keefe pauses for a moment before replying. 'I'd be a liar if I said no,' he says finally.

'What else might it be?'

'I've no idea,' says O'Keefe. 'That's why the sooner we get you to a specialist, the better. He'll take the weight off your mind.'

'Or not, as the case may be,' says Ralph. To which O'Keefe makes no reply.

Shortly after Ralph gets home, O'Keefe's receptionist rings to say that Mr Henderson can see him at the Abbey Hospital in Bath at eleven-thirty on Monday morning. Ralph accepts the appointment.

The house is silent, Emily and the two boys being at school. Ralph makes himself a mug of coffee in the kitchen and sits at the table, sipping his drink, and gazing out of the window at the empty yard. Then he goes upstairs to his study and does some work on his computer. Sometimes his fingers stop moving and he stares at the screen for a minute or two, but his eyes are not focused on the text. He clears his workspace, and logs on to the Internet. He goes to a search engine, and enters '+liver+cancer' in the search box. About half an hour later he hears through the open window the sound of a vehicle drawing up on the drive below, a car door opening and shutting, and the sound of Hope's excited voice. He disconnects from the Internet and hurries downstairs.

Ralph gives Hope a hug in the hall, sweeping her off her feet and whirling her round on the black-and-white-chequered floor. The child laughs with glee. Then he kisses Carrie and looks at her.

'What's the matter?' she says.

Ralph waits until Hope has scampered off to her room to be reunited with her favourite dolls and toys. Then he tells her about his visit to O'Keefe.

'Who is this guy Henderson?' is Carrie's first question.

'I don't know. O'Keefe thinks very highly of him.'

'I think you should go to a Harley Street specialist. The best.'

'I haven't got time to be running up and down to London just now,' Ralph says. 'There are bound to be tests and so on. Con-Con is only three weeks off. There's a hell of a lot of work to do.'

'Delegate it.'

'That's easily said. My deputy is Duggers. Social organization is not his forte. Anyway, let's not get over-dramatic. It's probably nothing.'

'Jesus,' says Carrie. 'I thought I was through with hospitals and doctors for a spell.'

'Don't let this spoil your home-coming,' Ralph says. 'We'll just forget about it till Monday. OK?'

'If you say so, Messenger,' Carrie says, with a tight smile.

Later, when they are planning the weekend over lunch, Carrie asks if she should invite Helen over to Horseshoes on Sunday.

'No I think not,' Ralph says.

'It's just that you said she helped out while I was away –'

'Let's keep this weekend to ourselves. Just the family,' Ralph says.

'Fine,' Carrie says.

In the afternoon Carrie takes a nap and Ralph goes into the University to catch up on some admin. He phones Helen from his office, and tells her about the lump.

'Oh dear,' she says. 'That's worrying.'

'Well, it was a bit of a shock, I have to admit,' he says. 'I went to the doctor's with indigestion and came out with possible cancer.'

'I'm sure it can't be anything like that,' says Helen. 'You've not been behaving like a sick man these last few weeks.'

'Except last Wednesday.'

'That was nothing,' she says. 'It can't be serious.'

'Well, I shall soon find out,' he says. 'I have you to thank for making me go to the doctor's. Something you said, that I should get my indigestion sorted – remember?'

'Yes,' she says.

'Did you have any suspicion . . .'

'None at all. It was just a casual remark. In a silly irrational way, I wish I hadn't said it now.'

'No, I'm very grateful. Really.'

'I know.'

'I would've had to see a doctor eventually, and the sooner the better.'

'Yes.'

There is a pause in the conversation, as if neither of them is sure what to say next.

'When shall I see you again?' Helen says at last.

'I don't know,' he says. 'Not this weekend, if you don't mind.'

'Of course not,' she says quickly.

'I'd like to ask you over to Horseshoes, but Carrie's a bit upset. I think she'd prefer it if we were on our own.'

'Of course, I understand completely.'

'What will you do with yourself?'

'I have lots of work to do. Student assessments. The end of the semester suddenly seems very near.'

'I know. This thing couldn't have happened at a worse time for me, with Con-Con coming up.'

'Tell me how it goes on Monday.'

'I will. I might not be able to call till Tuesday.'

'All right.'

'Bye then.'

'Goodbye Messenger.'

In spite of her nap, Carrie is still tired from her journey. She and Ralph are alone in the living-room after supper, reading newspapers and drinking herbal tea, when she tells him she is going to bed.

'I'll come too,' Ralph says, tossing aside his newspaper. Carrie looks surprised. 'I've missed you,' he says.

'Have you?'

'Of course.'

Carrie gets heavily to her feet. 'I'm exhausted, Messenger. Better leave it till tomorrow night.'

'OK,' he says. 'I'll do some work instead.'

Outside their bedroom door he kisses her goodnight and proceeds up the extra flight of stairs to his study. He logs on to the Internet again.

The following Monday, Ralph drives himself to Bath to see the specialist, Mr Henderson. The Abbey private hospital is a new building of sleek glazed brick and brown-tinted windows on a greenfield site on the outskirts of the city. Its reception area and waiting rooms are hushed and comfortable, with fitted carpets and upholstered couches, like a business-class lounge in an airport. After a short wait, Ralph is admitted to a consulting room where Henderson greets him with a smile and shakes his hand. He remarks that he has seen Ralph on television. The consultant appears younger than O'Keefe. He wears a dark blue pinstripe suit with a row of pens and pencils in the breast pocket, and what looks like a golf club tie. His gleaming white teeth protrude slightly, especially when he smiles, which he does rather frequently.

Once again Ralph strips to his underpants for an examination. Once again his abdomen is pressed and squeezed and probed by knowing professional fingers. Henderson confirms the presence of a lump.

'Could it be cancer?' Ralph asks.

'Can't rule it out,' Henderson says, smiling as if this is good news. 'I need to find out a bit more about it. I'd like to book you in for an ultrasound scan as soon as possible, and do an endoscopy at the same time. That's a visual examination of the stomach and small intestine, using fibre optics.'

'Keyhole surgery?' Ralph asks.

Henderson laughs heartily. 'Oh no, it's done via the mouth and throat. Sounds uncomfortable, but you won't feel a thing. We'll give you a local anaesthetic. But you'd better not drive yourself home afterwards.'

'I can go home the same day, then?'

'Absolutely. You'll need to fast overnight beforehand and take a laxative, to make sure that bowel shadows don't interfere with the ultrasound.'

'I'll ask my wife to come with me.'

'Excellent,' says Henderson. 'Are you free on Wednesday?'

'I can arrange to be,' says Ralph. 'When will you get the results?'

'The same day,' says Henderson.

Late on Tuesday morning Helen calls Ralph at his office.

'Helen! Sorry – I was going to call you, but I just haven't had a moment –'

'It's all right. I don't want to be a nuisance, but –'

'Of course you're not a –'

'It's just that I won't be available for the rest of the day,' Helen says. 'I'm teaching. I wanted to know how the consultation went.'

'Well, he confirmed there was a lump.'

'Oh.' Helen sounds despondent.

'Hardly a surprise.'

'No. I suppose not. I couldn't help hoping your GP might have been mistaken.'

'He'd be a pretty lousy GP in that case,' says Ralph. 'There's not much else to report. I've got to go back for some tests on Wednesday.'

'I see. Is there anything I can do?'

'Not really. Carrie is going with me to the hospital.'

'Oh, right.'

'I'll call you later in the week.'

'Right. I'll be thinking of you.'

'Thanks. Bye, then, Helen.'

'Goodbye Messenger.'

He adds, 'Thanks for calling,' but she rings off at the same moment.

Early on Wednesday morning, Ralph drives himself and Carrie to the hospital. He leaves their departure rather late and the rush-hour traffic in Cheltenham is heavy, so he drives fast on the rolling two-lane road to Bath to make up time. 'Don't let's get killed on the way to the hospital,' Carrie says, as he passes a long Continental trailer-lorry just before a sports car comes over the brow of a hill towards them.

'Well, it would be one way of ending the suspense,' Ralph says.

'Don't joke about it, Messenger,' says Carrie.

Ralph is given a mild tranquillizer by intravenous injection before the endoscopy, as well as a local anaesthetic mouth spray, and is still slightly woozy when he and Carrie go to Henderson's consulting room to learn the results of the tests. The consultant reads aloud from the report: ' *"An unusual cystic lesion is seen in the right lobe of the liver with low echogenicity in the centre. Appearance could indicate a necrotic secondary. A CT scan is recommended for evaluation . . ."* ' Henderson looks up from the document. 'I think that's a good idea. You know what a CT scan is of course?'

'Yes,' says Ralph.

'I don't,' says Carrie.

Henderson smilingly explains. 'Oh you mean those things that were in Messenger's TV programme,' she says. 'Showing you cross-sections of people's brains.'

'Exactly,' says Henderson. 'Only in this case it's the abdomen.'

'What was that about a secondary?' Ralph asks.

'Your lump could be a secondary cancer metastasized from the bowel. I had a patient like that not long ago. A CT scan may not give us enough information to eliminate that possibility, so if you agree, I'd like to arrange for you to have a colonoscopy at the same time.'

'How long will that take?'

'With preparation, three or four days.'

'In hospital?'

'Well, you could do the preparatory diet at home . . . but it would be easier in hospital. Unless you're good at fasting.'

'He's not,' says Carrie.

'I haven't got three or four days spare in the next three weeks,' says Ralph.

'Yes you have,' says Carrie. 'How soon can you do it?' she asks Henderson.

'I could set it up for early next week,' he says. He looks enquiringly at Ralph. 'If you come in on Saturday, we could do the preparation over the weekend.'

'All right, set it up,' says Ralph.

Carrie takes the wheel for the drive back to Cheltenham. 'What d'you think of this guy Henderson?' she says after a while.

'He seems very professional,' Ralph says. 'Covering all the bases. Leaving no stone unturned.'

'Why does he smile so much?'

'I think it's an unconscious habit. A kind of nervous tic. Probably comes from having to give bad news to people so often.'

'I don't trust him.'

'Why not?'

'I don't know. I've seen so many doctors in the last few weeks . . . You develop a nose for the really smart ones and the so-so ones. Henderson is one hundred per cent so-so.'

'Henderson's all right. After all, it's the tests that matter.'

'I think you should go to Harley Street.'

'I'll stick with Henderson for the time being. Hopefully the tests will be positive. I mean negative. If not, we can always get a second opinion.'

Carrie puts her left hand on Ralph's thigh. 'I don't want to lose you, Messenger,' she says, without taking her eyes off the road.

Ralph shoots her a quick glance. 'Hey! Don't talk about losing already.'

'I'm sorry. It's just . . .'

'I know.' Ralph covers her hand with his and squeezes it. Carrie puts it back on the wheel, and drives in silence for a while.

'We'll spend whatever it takes to get you the very best treatment,' Carrie says. 'Whatever it takes.'

When they get home there is a message on the answerphone for Ralph from his secretary, saying that the VC's office has been trying to contact him all day. *I think it's something about the student newspaper,'* the message ends cryptically.

Ralph goes to his study to phone the VC's office and is put through immediately to Sir Stan.

'Oh, 'allo Ralph, they tell me you've been in hospital all day. Nothing serious I hope?'

'No. Just a few tests.'

'Good. I don't suppose you saw today's *On Campus?*'

'No.'

'Well they've run a story about Donaldson's honorary degree.'

'What on earth for?'

'There's some sort of peace group in the Students' Union stirring up trouble. Let me read you a few bits. *"University to honour Ministry of Defence mandarin . . . Links with Holt Belling Centre . . . Government funding for Gloucester research into brainwashing techniques and guided weapons . . ."* Is there any truth in it?'

'Well, you know that the MoD is funding some of our work, Stan.'

'On brainwashing?'

'I suppose they're referring to an interactive virtual reality program –'

'Hold on, Ralph, not so much of the jargon.'

'Sorry, Stan,' Ralph says. 'For instance, there's a well-known program called "Eliza" that acts like a psychiatric counsellor. You log on and it asks, *How are you today?* and you type in *I feel like shit* and Eliza asks, *Why do you feel like shit?* and so on and before you know where you are you've told her the story of your life and you feel much better.' On the other end of the line Sir Stan chuckles. 'The MoD want us to develop a program that acts like an interrogator, for training servicemen how to respond when they're captured and questioned. I suppose that's what they mean by "brainwashing techniques".'

'And the guided weapons?'

'The Ministry is supporting our robotics research for possible application to mine-laying and mine-clearing operations,' Ralph says.

'Mine-*laying*? Pity about that, Ralph. Mine-*clearing* is all right.'

'All right?'

'Politically correct. This peace group is threatening to demonstrate. Picket next week's meeting of Council.'

'*What?* I thought that sort of thing went out of fashion with flared jeans and Jesus beards.'

'Apparently not. It's only a small minority, but they could cause us some embarrassment. If Donaldson gets wind of it, he could pull out. That might jeopardize your future funding.'

'I'll speak to the editor of the rag,' says Ralph.

'Well, tread carefully. If you could write something for them that gives a more favourable spin to the facts . . .'

'I'll see what I can do,' Ralph says.

'Good man,' says Sir Stan. 'By the way, Viv and I were sorry to miss you the other day at your rural retreat.'

'Yes, pity about that, I'd just gone for a walk. Found your note when I got back.'

'Taking the afternoon off from work, eh? We should all do it more often.'

'I find I can think more clearly in the country.'

'I'm sure. How's Carrie?'

'Fine. She's just come back from the States. Her father's been ill.'

'Sorry to hear that . . . You were on your own, then?'

'What?'

'At the cottage.'

'Oh yes. On my own.'

'I've got to go, Ralph. Inaugural lecture by the new chair of Metallurgy.'

Ralph puts down the phone and says, 'Fuck!' aloud. He goes downstairs to tell Carrie the gist of the VC's call.

'Troubles never come singly,' she says.

'I wonder who leaked the story to the student rag,' Ralph says.

On Thursday morning Helen phones Ralph at his office.

'Helen! I was going to call you –'

'Were you?'

'It's just that things have been getting a little fraught around here.'

'How did the tests go?'

'Inconclusive. I've got to have more tests on Monday.'

'That's a bind.'

'It really is. What with the conference, and now this stupid storm in a teacup about Donaldson's honorary degree. Did you see *On Campus* this week? The student rag?'

'No. What's in it?'

'Too complicated to explain now. I've got a meeting with the editor in a few minutes.'

'When will I see you?'

'Come to Horseshoes on Sunday. No, shit, I'm going into hospital on Saturday –'

'I mean when can I see you *alone*, Messenger.'

'Oh.' Ralph pauses for a moment. 'Ah . . . I don't think I'm in the mood right now, Helen.'

'I don't mean for sex, Messenger,' Helen says. 'I just want to talk to you.'

'Sorry . . . Well, let's see, I told Carrie I'd be working late this evening. I'll look in on the way home. About seven. OK?'

Helen's next-door neighbours are just leaving their house, dressed for tennis and swinging their racquets, as Ralph draws up in the service road alongside the terrace. He stays in the car, pretending to be studying a document, until they are out of sight. Then he rings her bell. She admits him instantly and shuts the door quickly. They embrace, leaning up against the door.

'Oh Messenger,' she says. 'I've had such a miserable week.'

'It hasn't been too wonderful for me either,' he says.

'No, poor you. Tell me about the tests.' She leads him into the living-room. 'Would you like a drink?'

'Some juice if you've got it. Henderson said no alcohol.'

'Henderson?'

'My consultant.'

'Oh, I was mixing him up with the other man, the one in the newspaper. I picked up a copy this afternoon.'

'That's Donaldson,' Ralph says, following Helen into the little living-room. He sprawls in an armchair as she fetches a carton of orange juice from the fridge, opens it, and pours two glasses. 'I saw the editor this morning,' Ralph says. 'Little smartarse from Cultural Studies, with his sights set on a career in the tabloids. I asked him where he got the story from. He had the cheek to say it was public knowledge.'

'Isn't it, then?'

'Well it's public knowledge that Donaldson is a big wheel in the MoD of course. And there are references to their funding some of our research in Senate papers if you know where to look — though they're supposed to have limited circulation . . . But who drew the connections? Who pointed the rag in the right direction? Smartarse wouldn't say. Perhaps he doesn't know — it could have been an anonymous tipoff from somebody who doesn't like the Centre. Or doesn't like me. Thanks.' Ralph takes a glass of juice from Helen. She sits down on the couch.

'Tell me more about what happened at the hospital,' she says.

Ralph describes the tests he had the day before, and the consultation afterwards with Henderson.

'What's a colonoscopy?' she asks.

'They stick a little TV camera up your rectum and look at the inside of your intestine,' he says. 'It's the medical equivalent of Channel Five.'

Helen grimaces. 'Poor you.'

'Yes, I can't say I'm looking forward to it.' He looks at his watch and puts down his glass. 'I'd better be going.'

'Already?'

'Afraid so. Carrie may've phoned the office and be wondering where I am.'

'Messenger . . .'

'What?' Helen does not answer, but goes red and looks as if she might be going to cry. 'What's the matter?' he says, more tenderly, getting up and going over to the couch. He puts an arm round her shoulder.

'I'm confused,' she says. 'I don't know what you want of me.'

'Want of you?' he repeats, frowning.

'For three weeks we have a mad passionate affair. We meet nearly every day. We make love practically every day. Then suddenly, bang, the shutters come down. I don't see you for days on end. I sit around waiting for telephone calls that never come, I —'

'Darling, I'm sorry. I've had this damn thing on my mind —'

'I know, I know.'

'I love you, Helen, and those three weeks were wonderful, truly, but . . . I just don't feel like sex at the moment.'

'Neither do I, Messenger, neither do I.' He looks at her blankly. 'Is that all you wanted me for, then?' she says. 'Would you prefer if I just dropped out of your life now that you're ill? Got out of the way?'

'Of course not.'

'Then don't freeze me out. Let me into your thoughts. Tell me what you're feeling. Let me help.'

Ralph looks at her in silence for a few moments. 'You really want to help me?'

'Of course. If there's anything I can do . . .'

'Anything? You really mean that?' He looks at her intently.

'Why do you say it like that?' Helen says, a little fearfully.

'I'll tell you something I wouldn't tell anyone else,' he says. 'You must promise to keep it to yourself.'

'All right,' she says.

'If this lump turns out to be malignant, I'm not going to hang around while it does its thing. I know what you're going to say. I know what the medics will say. There are all kinds of treatments available nowadays, improving all the time, blah blah blah. But cancer of the liver is bad news. I looked it up on the Internet. You might get some remission with chemotherapy, but there's no cure. Transplants are dicey, and likely to be attacked by the same cancer. I don't want to put up a brave fight. I don't want to be ill for a year or two and then die, helpless, wasted, incontinent, bald. No thanks. I saw my father die of cancer, and I don't want to go through that. As soon as I'm quite sure I have an irreversible terminal condition I shall make for the Exit while I'm still able to walk out unassisted. Well, perhaps not entirely unassisted.' He pauses and glances meaningfully at Helen.

'You want me to . . . ?' Helen looks shocked. She shakes her head. 'No.'

'Carrie won't help me, I know that,' Ralph says. 'When misfortune strikes, her response is to throw money at it. I can already see the plans forming behind her eyes. To call in the whole of Harley Street. Fly me to the Mayo Clinic. Buy me a liver transplant on the black market ... Anything to keep me alive, in a wheelchair if necessary.'

'Messenger, this is horrible. I don't want to listen any more.'

'I thought you wanted to help me.'

'What do you want me to do then?' she says, her voice rising. 'Hold a plastic bag over your head? Kick the stool away from under your feet?'

'Calm down, Helen. I haven't thought about ways and means yet. It may never come to that. I desperately hope it doesn't. I've had a good life. I should be sorry to finish it, very sorry. But I will if I have to. And obviously I'd want to manage things so that it caused the least possible distress to the family. That's where it might be useful to have someone else's help.'

'I know,' says Helen brightly. 'I could arrange to run you over in University Avenue. Make it look like an accident. You could step out from behind a tree at an agreed moment. We would have to synchronize our watches.'

'I'm not joking, Helen,' Ralph says.

'No, I wish you were,' she says. 'What about the distress to me?'

'I know I'm asking a lot. But it would be an act of . . . of love.'

'*Love?*' Helen laughs, a little hysterically.

'Suppose someone you love – your mother or your father, even one of your children, was dying in unendurable pain. Wouldn't you help them to die if you had the means?'

'Possibly. But that's different.'

'I don't see the logic. Why make people go through hell before you help them out of it? Why not help them to simply avoid it, if that's what they want?'

'I feel sick,' Helen says. 'I don't want to talk about it any more.'

'You won't help me?'

'No.'

'But you won't hinder? You won't say anything to anyone about this?'

'I said I wouldn't.'

'Good.' He looks at his watch again. 'I must go.'

'Messenger,' Helen says. 'It's *because* I love you.'

'I know,' he says, and kisses her lightly on the cheek. 'I'll see myself out.'

'You're late,' Carrie says when Messenger comes into the kitchen. 'You said seven-thirty. The dinner's overcooked.'

'Sorry,' Ralph says. He kisses her on the cheek. 'I called on Helen Reed on the way home.'

'Oh?' Carrie looks mildly surprised.

'I had to give her some stuff about the conference. You know she's agreed to do the Last Word?'

'That's nice of her.'

'I took the opportunity to explain why we hadn't been in touch this past week.'

'Good,' Carrie says. 'Maybe I'll call her, invite her over to Horseshoes on Sunday. Or do you want me to visit you in hospital?'

'No please don't. Visit me, I mean. Did you do anything interesting today?'

'I did a little shopping. I ran into Nicholas in Montpellier Street, so we had lunch together at Petit Blanc.'

'Lucky man to have so much leisure,' Ralph says. 'I hope you didn't discuss my medical condition.'

'I mentioned you were having some tests. You can't keep it a secret, Messenger.'

'I know. I just hate being the object of people's sympathy and morbid curiosity. The less our friends know about this, the better.'

'How much did you tell Helen Reed?'

'Not much. And it was in confidence, anyway.'

From: ludmila.lisk@carolinum.psy.cz
To: R.H.Messenger@glosu.ac.uk
Subject: Conference
Date: Thursday 22 May 1997 20:35:28

Hi Professor Messenger,
This is your Czech friend Ludmila. Do you remember me? I hope so.

I was sending you a letter three weeks before but I think you do not recive it because I get no reply. So I looked up Gloucester University on the Internet and find your Email address. I am wishing I thought of that before.

My letter was aksing you for confirmation that I am invited to present a poster at your conference this end of May. The British Council will give me travel scholarship but they need your confirmation. As time is short I would like it if you are quick. Please excuse my bad English.

Yours sincerely,
Ludmila Lisk.

PS: My poster is called 'Modelling Learning Behaviours in Autonomous Agents' You remember I tell you all about it that nice evening in Prague.

From: R.H.Messenger@glosu.ac.uk
To: ludmila.lisk@carolinum.psy.cz
Subject: Consciousness Conference VI
Date: Friday 23 May 1997 9:25:15
----
dear ludmila,
thanks for your email. Of course I rmemeber you, how could I not? I'm terribly sorry but the conference is absolutely full. There's a strict limit on the number of people we can accommodate. Perhaps you could attend next year's conference. I believe it's going to be held in Florida – might be fun. I'll email you information when I get it so you can apply in good time.

best wishes,
Ralph Messenger

○ ○

From: ludmila.lisk@carolinum.psy.cz
To: R.H.Messenger@glosu.ac.uk
Subject: Conference
Date: Friday 23 May 1997 11:14:02

Dear Ralph,

I hope you are not thinking I am rude to begin this way but you telled
me to call you Ralph that nice time in Prague. I am very sad that the
conference is full. In fact I weep when I am reading your email. It is
not easy to get travel grants in Czech Republic. I do not think the
Britsih Council will pay for me to go to Floirida. Please let me come to
your conference at Gloucester. I do not mind to sleep on the floor. I
bring sleeping bag. I do not expect such a nice comfortable bed that
we had in Prague.

Your friend, Ludmila

From: R.H.Messenger@glosu.ac.uk
To: ludmila.lisk@carolinum.psy.cz
Subject: Consciousness Conference VI
Date: Friday 23 May 1997 12:15:10

----

dear ludmila,

alas, its not the sleeping accommodation that's the problem. our
biggest lecture room only takes 200 people and there are all kinds of
rules and regulations that forbid us to enrol more people on the
conference than that. Im so sorry to disappoint you but theres nothing I
can do about it this time unfortunately.

Best wishes, Ralph Messenger

PS: I'm on the advisory board of AI Newsletter, published at Winnipeg.
If you'd like to write a paragraph about your research project, I'll see if
they will include it in their Noticeboard column.

From: ludmila.lisk@carolinum.psy.cz
To: R.H.Messenger@glosu.ac.uk
Subject: Conference
Date: Friday 23 May 1997 13:14:02

Dear Ralph,

thankyou for your email. It is kind of you to suggest the paragraph in AI Newsletter but it is more important to me to attend your conference and explain my research to all the top people in the field. I think you can find me place in your conference if you really wish it. I think perhaps you do not wish me coming to Gloucester. Are you afraid that I will tell your colleagues and maybe your wife what a nice time we had together in Prague? I promise you I will not say nothing. But if I cannot come to the conference and I lose my travel scholarship I will be very sad and angry. Perhaps I will write all about what we did in Prague together and post it on the Internet.

Your fiend,
Ludmila

From: R.H.Messenger@glosu.ac.uk
To: ludmila.lisk@carolinum.psy.cz
Subject: Consciousness Conference VI
Date: Friday 23 May 1997 15:35:18
cc: scirep@britcoun.cz

Dear Miss Lisk,
Thank you for your Email. I'm sorry your original letter went astray.

Happily I can confirm that we are able to accept you as a delegate at the conference, to present a poster on 'Modelling Learning Behaviours in Autonomous Agents'. A conference information pack will be airmailed to you as soon as possible. I am copying this letter to the

British Council in Prague.

I look forward to seeing you here at the end of the month.
Yours sincerely,
R.H.Messenger
Conference Convenor

'Bitch,' Ralph murmurs under his breath, as he clicks on the 'Send' key to dispatch this message. The telephone on his desk rings. It is the VC.

'Oh, hallo Stan,' Ralph says. 'I saw the editor of *On Campus* yesterday. He's promised to print a letter from me in next week's issue. That should settle the dust.'

'Glad to hear it, Ralph,' Sir Stan says, 'but that's not what I'm calling you about.'

'Oh.'

'I've got Detective Sergeant Brian Agnew with me, from the Gloucestershire Police. The what unit?' This last question is not addressed to Ralph, who hears a muffled exchange between Sir Stan and his visitor before the former comes back on the phone. 'From the Paedophile and Pornography unit. He wants to talk to you.'

'What about?'

'I think he'd better explain that himself,' says Sir Stan. 'Can you see him this afternoon? Now, for instance?'

'Well, I suppose so, if it's urgent.'

'Good man. I'll send him over. Hang on.' There is another muffled exchange between the VC and Detective Sergeant Agnew. 'Yes – are you still there, Ralph? The point is, for security reasons he won't identify himself as a policeman when he arrives. He'll just say he's Brian Agnew and you're expecting him. All right?'

'All right,' says Ralph. He puts down the phone. 'Jesus Christ,' he says under his breath. 'What now?'

'We have reason to think,' Detective Sergeant Agnew says, 'that someone in your Department is downloading child pornography from the Internet, via the University computer network.'

'Who?' Ralph says.

288

'We don't know as yet, sir.'

'What's the evidence then?'

'I'm not at liberty to say, sir,' says Detective Sergeant Agnew. He is a tall, big-boned man in his thirties, with a moustache that curves down at the ends to give him a permanently lugubrious expression, wearing a navy-blue blazer and a blue shirt with a plain tie. He speaks with a local accent. 'This is part of a wider investigation into a ring of people exchanging and distributing illegal material,' he says. 'We believe one of them works here. Would you have any idea who it might be?'

'No. None at all.'

'No member of your staff who has shown any interest in such material at any time?'

'Not that I can think of. Of course I don't suppose there's a single person in the country with access to the Internet who hasn't had a look at a porn site at one time or another. It's natural human curiosity.'

'There's nothing natural about the stuff we're concerned with, sir,' says Detective Sergeant Agnew.

'That's my point. One of the postgraduates organized a sort of competition last year, to see who could find the rudest picture on the Internet that you didn't have to pay for . . .' Ralph laughs at the recollection, but Detective Sergeant Agnew doesn't crack a smile. 'It was just a laddish prank. But some of the women in the Centre complained to me about it, so of course I put a stop to it.'

'Who was that, sir?'

'Jim Bellows, but I'm sure he's not involved in child pornography. The pictures I saw were of adults. Very well developed adults, one might say.' Again Ralph tries and fails to raise a smile from the policeman.

Detective Sergeant Agnew writes the name in his notebook. 'We'll check him out,' he says.

'I'm sure he's not the man you're looking for.'

'Probably not, but we have to follow any lead. We can't check every hard disk in the building.'

'God, no. It would bring the Centre to a grinding halt.'

'Though you could, if you wish, eliminate yourself from our enquiry, sir,' Detective Sergeant Agnew says.

'What d'you mean?'

'If you would allow me to check your own hard disk.'

'Well, I don't know . . . Have you got a warrant or something?'

'What I'm suggesting would be entirely voluntary, sir.'

'I see . . .' Ralph frowns and thinks for a moment. 'Seems to me I'm in a double bind here. I don't see why I should, on the other hand if I don't, you'll think I've got something to hide.'

'It's up to you, sir.'

'There's a lot of confidential information on my computer.'

'Naturally confidentiality would be respected.'

Ralph thinks for a moment. 'Well, all right. Go ahead.'

'Thank you, sir. But I won't bother you just now.'

'Oh. I thought . . .'

'Who's your chief administrator of systems, sir?'

'Stuart Phillips.'

'Is he trustworthy?'

'Completely, I would say.'

'Of good character?'

'Absolutely. Married to a teacher, they have two children. He's a bell-ringer for his church, I believe. Runs marathons for charity. Leads a scout troop.' DS Agnew, who has been nodding approvingly, suddenly stops nodding. 'Perhaps I shouldn't have mentioned that,' says Ralph.

'Why not, sir?'

'Well, I suppose it makes him a suspect, doesn't it? Frankly I wonder they can get anybody to be a scoutmaster these days. Actually Stuart's the salt of the earth.'

'You were right to mention it, sir. You can't have too much information in this game. I'd like to meet Mr Phillips. D'you think you could get hold of him now?'

Ralph gets through to Stuart Phillips' extension and is told he just left for home. Detective Sergeant Agnew says he will come back next week to examine the Centre's systems and will need Stuart Phillips' assistance.

'Are you going to take him into your confidence?' Ralph asks.

'That depends,' says Agnew. 'I have to meet him first.'

A provisional meeting is arranged for the following Wednesday, since Ralph will be in hospital on Monday and Tuesday.

'If you discover anything, you will tell me immediately won't you?'

'Certainly, sir,' says Agnew.

'Only it could be very damaging to us in PR terms.'

'Of course, if an offence has been committed, and an arrest is made, it will become public knowledge.'

'Well the longer that's deferred the better,' says Ralph. 'We're mounting a big international conference here next weekend.'

'I doubt whether there will be any major developments before then, sir,' says Detective Sergeant Agnew.

'How was your day?' Carrie asks, when Ralph gets home.

'Don't ask,' he says. 'Whatever Henderson says, I need a drink.'

'Better not, Messenger,' says Carrie anxiously.

'One drink is not going to kill me,' he says.

'Well, all right, just one,' she says doubtfully. 'I'll fix it for you. What would you like?'

Ralph considers. 'You used to make a mean dry martini,' he says.

'You know, I haven't had a dry martini in years,' Carrie says. 'I'll join you.'

29

EENIE, meenie, mynie, mo . . . testing, testing . . . It's Sunday afternoon the ah, 25th of May, and I'm in the Abbey Hospital in Bath. I was almost glad to be admitted here yesterday, to get away from the Centre, from home, from Email, faxes, telephones . . . there's a phone beside my bed, but not many people know about it . . . to get away before I received any more unpleasant surprises. The Abbey seemed like a port in a storm, a haven of tranquillity . . . an ideal place to hole up in for a few days, to get my breath back and get on with some work. I brought a lot of books with me and my IBM Thinkpad. Good name, that . . . Unfortunately the reason I'm here was the most unpleasant surprise of all, and it's been difficult to concentrate on anything else.

I can't complain about the accommodation. I've got a room to myself, air-conditioned, with a big picture window overlooking the landscaped car-park . . . fitted carpet on the floor . . . Impressionist reproductions on the walls . . . a high-backed armchair, in which I'm sitting at this moment . . . two upright stacking chairs for visitors, and a coffee table. A TV mounted on a wall bracket. A state-of-the-art hospital bed that goes up and down and tilts and jack-knifes in the middle if required. An en-suite bathroom with shower and loo . . . It's as good as a four-star hotel room, except that you can't hang a *Do Not Disturb* sign on the doorknob. Nurses and ancillary staff are popping in and out all the time to take down details or check your pulse or your temperature or your blood pressure or bring you food or just to ask you if everything is all right. Everything always *is* all right. Except you.

Just now, there's a pause in the activity. It's visiting hours . . . So I got out the old Pearlcorder. I don't know why exactly . . . but since I'm not going to have any visitors I thought I might as well talk to myself, and I can be reasonably confident that I won't be interrupted by some nurse barging in for an hour or so . . . They're remarkably good-looking nurses, mind you, and kitted out like a wet dream, in tight-fitting short-sleeved uniforms of blue and white poplin . . . with broad black belts and sheer black stockings. Somehow you know they're stockings and not tights. It's all part of the four-star service . . . Nurse Pomeroy is particularly fetching. Blonde tresses, peaches-and-cream complexion, a perfect smile, great tits I bet under the starched uniform bib . . . and if what's underneath her skirt is as shapely as what you can see below the hemline, well . . . Nurse Pomeroy has been very friendly and attentive. She's seen me on television and regards me as something of a star . . . In another mood I might fancy my chances with Nurse Pomeroy, there's a saucy gleam of invitation in her eye sometimes . . . but the fact is that my libido is on hold at the moment. Ever since O'Keefe uttered those seven little words, *'You've got a lump on your liver,'* I've lost interest in sex . . . In having it, that is, I doubt if you ever stop thinking about it . . . *I think about sex, therefore I am* . . . I tried to force myself to make love to Carrie the second night after her return from California, but it didn't work. She was very understanding . . . I haven't even tried anything with Helen since my medical saga began. If the lump turns out to be malignant I may never have sex again. A depressing thought . . . But at least I can say I went down with guns blazing, in our remarkable three-week affair . . . Except for the very last time, when I was impotent. Pity about that.

It's not sexual appetite which is bugging me at the moment, it's ordinary appetite . . . I'm on a special low-residue diet of tasteless pap. They're gradually emptying my intestines so they can have a good look round on Tuesday, and I feel hungry all the time. At lunchtime I could smell the roast beef on the food trolley being wheeled along the corridor to other patients in this wing, a mouthwatering aroma . . . it seeped under the door and my starved senses picked it up. How I craved for a generous helping, with golden brown roast potatoes and lashings of gravy poured over the Yorkshire pud. Of course in principle I don't eat beef now, but when you've got a potentially malignant lump on your liver, the million-to-one chance of catching

CJD doesn't seem a very pressing concern . . . if I'd been allowed to eat a normal lunch I wouldn't have gone for the poached salmon or the vegetarian lasagne but straight for the beef. I happen to know the full menu because it was thoughtlessly given to me by an orderly this morning. Must stop thinking about food.

I've tried to feel the lump myself, but without success . . . I have to restrain myself from poking really hard, in case I do some damage. It doesn't hurt . . . which isn't necessarily a good sign . . . Cancer of the liver is often painless in the early stages. But it's strange to be possibly in mortal danger, and not to feel anything except a little indigestion . . . Even that's gone away with the low-residue diet. 'A vital organ,' O'Keefe said . . . I read somewhere that the ancient Assyrians thought the liver was the seat of the soul. Interesting. The Egyptians thought it was the heart and the ancient Greeks the lungs, I think . . . and Descartes thought his soul was in his pineal gland . . . but the Assyrians plumped for the liver, though they can't have had a clue what it was for, metabolically speaking.

The sun is shining brightly outside, bouncing off the windscreens of the visitors' cars . . . the women look as if they've arrived for a wedding, getting out of the cars in summer dresses, grasping bouquets of flowers . . . I wish now I hadn't discouraged Carrie from coming today. I feel somewhat orphaned without visitors. She and the kids will be at Horseshoes, sunning themselves in the garden after lunch. Don't let's think about lunch. Not Helen though, she told Carrie she had too much marking to do. Not the real reason, of course . . . She's edgy about meeting Carrie again, a mixture of guilt and rivalry I suppose. I can't say I'm sorry. Who knows what might have happened if they'd been alone together this weekend, talking about me? Suppose Helen had a sudden impulse to confess all? Jesus.

The past week, unpleasant as it's been, has made one thing clear to me – I want to stay married to Carrie, whatever the result of the tests . . . The old cliché that these things bring a couple closer together turns out to be true . . . Looking back, I've been very stupid, fooling around with Marianne, then getting seriously involved with Helen . . . I broke my unspoken contract with Carrie, no affairs on her home ground. If she found out, God knows what she might do

. . . Fortunately Helen will be leaving Gloucester soon. But in the meantime I must take great care to keep things on an even keel.

Trouble is, I'm afraid she may be falling seriously in love with me . . . She was in a highly emotional state the other evening. In hindsight it was a mistake to ask her to help me top myself if the worst comes to the worst. It was something I'd been thinking about, and it just came out, without premeditation. I was almost thinking aloud. It's important to me to consider all possible eventualities and to have plans ready to meet them as they arise, it gives me a sense of being in control of my life . . . But it's all hypothetical . . . abstract . . . Being a writer, she has a vivid imagination, she immediately sees herself in some lurid scenario, and gets upset . . .

On the other hand if things turn out well, I'm afraid she'll want to go on with the affair . . . Well maybe, when she's moved back to London, we might see each other occasionally, but it would be better to let it die a natural death . . . not the happiest of metaphors . . . It was great while it lasted, it was some of the most exciting sex I've ever had . . . but I don't want to give Carrie any reason to suspect what went on between us while she was away . . . There's enough risk she'll find out from other sources. I think Emily has her suspicions . . . the way she looked at me that evening when I said Greg couldn't sleep over . . . maybe she heard something, quiet as we were, on the nights when Helen stayed . . . or maybe it's just female intuition . . . And then Sir Stan and Viv calling at Horseshoes when we were upstairs in the bedroom . . . something in the tone of his voice on the phone the other day suggested he didn't believe my story about having gone for a walk. I wonder if there were any clues that Helen was with me . . . Something belonging to her left on the passenger seat in my car . . . a jacket, a scarf? I can't remember what she was wearing that day, dammit . . . Of course if Stan has any suspicions, he wouldn't pass them on to Carrie . . . but Viv might, out of female solidarity, or just mischief-making . . . One way or another I fear I'm no longer the VC's blue-eyed boy, what with the Horseshoes episode, and the row over Donaldson's honorary degree . . . and now this pornography business on top of everything else.

That was a tense moment, on Friday afternoon, when Agnew

asked if he could check my hard disk . . . It was a difficult one, and I had to make my mind up quickly . . . there's no child pornography on my disk, no porn of any kind . . . I've surfed the porn sites on the Web occasionally, but only at home . . . so I had nothing to fear on that score . . . But what I *do* have on my office computer are the transcripts of all my experimental monologues and journal entries . . . with lurid details of my relationships with Helen and Marianne and lots of other compromising personal material . . . seeing Emily in the bath, for instance . . . I didn't relish the idea of Detective Sergeant Agnew fishing around in those files . . . But then I thought to myself, he'll be looking for images, not text . . . and if I refuse to cooperate, he might get suspicious . . . and if he has to get a warrant to examine my disk he's going to look at it much more thoroughly than if I agree to let him check it out now . . . So I agreed – and he let me off the hook . . . Perhaps it was just bluff, perhaps he had no intention of checking the disk there and then . . . perhaps the fact that I agreed was enough to eliminate me from the enquiry . . . crafty bastard . . . After he'd gone, I thought about deleting the sensitive files, but what would be the point? You can never completely remove data from a hard disk, short of destroying it . . .

As to the fuss about Donaldson's honorary degree . . . who fed the student rag with the information about our links with the MoD? It must be somebody with access to Senate papers . . . and a motive . . . Jasper Richmond, for instance . . . If Oliver has been talking about what he saw in the car-park at Sainsbury's, Jasper might be trying to get his revenge . . . Or could it be somebody in the Centre itself? Could it conceivably be Duggers? He was never keen on our contracts with the MoD – muttering about the Official Secrets Act undermining academic freedom *etc., etc.*, though really he was just jealous of the amount of dosh I'd managed to raise, none of which would be going to *his* team of postdocs . . . But would he sabotage his own institution? I wouldn't put it past him . . . if there were such a fuss that I was forced out, say . . . or, more likely, resigned in disgust . . . then he would step into my shoes, or so he might think . . . he would rather be head of an impoverished Centre than number two in a thriving one . . . I hope he doesn't find out why I'm having these tests . . . I can just imagine the little thrill of expectation it would give him . . .

I'm getting a little paranoid . . . but it's been a trying week, one damn crisis after another . . . just when I could have done with some peace and quiet to get ready for the conference . . . which reminds me of another little potential problem stacked up in the sky, waiting to land . . . Ludmila Lisk . . . All I need now is a Czech groupie following me around at the conference . . . cosying up at every opportunity to reminisce about our romantic night in Prague . . . getting up Carrie's nose . . . and conceivably Helen's too . . . If everything goes wrong that could go wrong in the coming week I may find myself diagnosed with terminal cancer . . . fought over publicly by three women . . . threatened with divorce by one of them . . . the Centre exposed in a porn scandal . . . its research funding cut . . . my status damaged . . . my enemies triumphant . . . Of course if the first of these possibilities turns out to be the case, none of the others will matter very much . . . or for very long. Which is perhaps why I feel surprisingly calm . . . The thing to do is to take defensive action where one can, and stoically await the outcome where one can't.

30

TUESDAY 27TH MAY. Messenger is having his tests today. I called him yesterday evening to wish him good luck. I'd spoken to Carrie earlier, so knew she wouldn't be with him. Apparently he told her he didn't want any visitors at the hospital during the preparation days. I suppose it makes him feel less like someone who is ill. Carrie is going over to Bath today to be with him when they get the results of the tests, and to drive him home afterwards. The wife's part. He said he would try and phone me this evening to tell me what happened, but it would more likely be tomorrow, from his office. He doesn't like to call me from home in case Carrie should pick up the phone on another extension and hear us talking. He doesn't have a mobile – says he would never have a moment's peace if he did – so we can only speak when he's in his office.

He sounded a little tetchy yesterday evening, not surprisingly. He's bored, hungry, worried. And all I could do was wish him good luck. Because that's all we believe in now: luck. Chance. Randomness. Chaos. And we know we can't control it, so 'wishing good luck' to someone is a peculiarly empty gesture. Once I would have said, 'I'll say a prayer for you.' Once – quite a long time ago – I would have gone into a church and lit a candle in the Lady Chapel and prayed to the Virgin Mary to intercede with her Divine Son to make Messenger's lump go away. How bizarre that idea seems to me now – partly because of Messenger himself. He has made it impossible for me to pray for him. How he would mock me if I suggested it. I can just imagine him saying, '*Tell me, exactly how is this prayer business supposed to work? Supposing, for the sake of argument, that there is a God, how does he decide which prayers to answer? Why would he cure my cancer, and let other poor buggers with the same condition die, not to*

*mention the kids with leukaemia in the children's ward? Once he starts
intervening in the course of nature, how does he decide when to stop?'*

I had some difficulties myself, even when I was a pious convent
schoolgirl, with the notion of petitionary prayer. I used to pester the
old nun, Sister Rita, who took us for Religious Instruction in the
Fifth Form, with casuistical questions, like 'What does God do if a
farmer is praying for rain for his crops at the same time we're praying
for fine weather for the School Sports Day?' Or more boldly, 'Were
German Catholics wasting their time praying for victory in the
Second World War?' 'These things are mysteries, Helen Driscoll,'
Sister Rita would say, going a little red, 'and will be revealed to us in
the life to come.' That kind of prayer now seems to me the purest
superstition, and yet I miss it. It gave one something positive to do in
threatening situations, it gave relief. I hate this state of just waiting
helplessly to see how the dice will fall.

And the fact is that I can't entirely suppress a feeling of guilt, a
feeling that we brought calamity down upon ourselves by our
conduct. By giving in to lust. Betraying Carrie (never mind that she's
been betraying Messenger in her turn). At bottom, let's face it, I feel
as if we have sinned, and deserve to be punished. The moment
Messenger said, 'I've got a lump on my liver,' I felt a cold qualm of
fear, and yet no surprise – it was as if I had been unconsciously
expecting some such blow, and now it had fallen. There's superstition
for you. Messenger's lump was probably there before we even met,
but telling myself that makes no difference. The sin brought it out,
nourished it, made it grow faster. That's what my superstitious self
says. I can't stop her silly, hysterical voice, even though I try to stop
my ears. I don't like it. I'm in the worst possible plight, to still believe
in sin but no longer in the possibility of absolution.

Calm down, Helen Reed. Take a grip on yourself. Examine the
facts clearly. Messenger has a lump. It's probably benign. No, cancel
that, be exact, it *may* be benign. Nobody knows yet. If it's benign, it
can be treated, cured. Life will go on as before. The same moral
problems of love and lust, fidelity and betrayal, will remain, waiting
to be resolved, needing to be worked through, but having nothing to

299

do with the state of Messenger's liver. How silly you will feel, then, about this panic attack. If, on the other hand, the lump is a tumour . . . Yes? What then? Well that has nothing to do with love, lust, fidelity *etc.*, either. It's a physical condition with physical causes, which could happen to anybody – which could have happened to you, but which happened to happen to him. There is no reason to read any moral message into it.

Well, that's all very well, but if he's got incurable cancer he intends to take his own life before it kills him, and he wants me to be ready to help. He asked me, and I refused. Because I was shocked, frightened, horrified at the idea. Basically, I'm a coward. I lack the courage of my unbelief. So there's nothing I can do for Messenger, except wish him luck and watch as events take their course. Watch but not pray.

When I was fifteen I read Graham Greene's *The End of the Affair*, surreptitiously because I was fairly sure Daddy wouldn't think it was suitable. In fact of course it was the perfect book for a devout Catholic adolescent girl just beginning to be aware of her own sexuality. The allusions to the adulterous couple's passionate love-making, specially Sarah's capacity for orgasm, her 'strange cries of abandonment', intrigued and excited me, while her subsequent journey of spiritual discovery inspired me. For months I fantasized myself as Sarah, enjoying ecstatic carnal intercourse (rather vague in detail) with Bendrix, then promising to God to give him up if he wasn't killed in the bomb blast, and then keeping my promise at the cost of my own earthly happiness, dying of a bad cold and ascending to eternal bliss at the end, leaving behind a little trail of miracles to trouble my lover's unbelief. Goodness how I cried over that book! How I yearned to be like Sarah when I grew up, to experience everything, and atone for my sins in a grand heroic gesture of self-sacrifice. Now I find myself in much her situation, but without her faith.

It's 11 p.m. Messenger hasn't called. I'm going to bed.

WEDNESDAY 28TH MAY. Messenger phoned me this morning as soon as he got to his office. I was waiting for the call, but the ring still made me jump, and I dropped the receiver in my nervousness as I picked it up. The results of the tests turned out to be inconclusive. The colonoscopy showed nothing abnormal, which is good, but the scan showed a 'cyst-like mass' about ten centimetres in diameter in the right lobe of the liver. I got out my tape measure just now, and ten centimetres seems frighteningly big. It's not causing any obstruction, which apparently explains why he's not feeling any pain, but Messenger said Henderson appeared to be a bit puzzled by it. 'He almost seemed disappointed that it wasn't a secondary from colonic cancer, which is what he'd suspected.' Henderson wants him to have a liver biopsy, to establish for sure whether it's a primary cancer or something else. He proposed referring him to a liver surgeon in Bristol, but apparently Carrie has taken the matter in hand. It seems she doesn't have any faith in Henderson, so she's at this very moment on the phone to anybody and everybody she can think of to try and find out who is the top liver man in the country. Messenger seems content to leave it to her.

I'm left with a feeling of anticlimax. I'd assumed that the results of yesterday's tests would be clear-cut, and lying awake in the early hours of this morning, turning it all over in my mind, I decided that if the news was bad I would tell Messenger that after all he could count on my help, whatever it was he wanted me to do. It seemed to me that if that undertaking was what he wanted of me, then I should give it; and the fact that I dreaded the possible consequences would make it, in a peculiar and perverse way, an act of generosity, of love, a Sarah-like gesture. I tried to put myself in his place, to imagine myself as him, learning that he had terminal cancer, and I thought I understood why he would want to anticipate the inevitable. For Christians suffering has some point and purpose – it can be 'offered up', it can be a way of 'making a good death', as the nuns used to say. And there are people who cling on to life even in the direst straits just because they *don't* believe there is another one, for whom every sunrise and sunset, every moment spent with their loved ones, is precious, whatever state they are in. But not Messenger. I couldn't picture him slowly declining, withering, wasting away, first on sticks, then in a wheelchair, then finally in a bed, with tubes and catheters and God knows what attached to him. There's something Roman about Messenger's character, as well as his profile: he's a fighter, but if defeat is inevitable, he would rather fall on his sword than be paraded in chains. I could see that, and so I decided, whatever it cost me, I would do whatever he wanted me to do.

Having screwed my resolution up to this point, I awaited his call with dread. When he told me the results were ambiguous I felt some relief that the news wasn't worse, but also disappointment that it wasn't better. The suspense continues. Of course I said nothing about my private agonizing, and the conclusion I had come to. I just commiserated with him for the continuing uncertainty. He said that fortunately he had plenty of other things on his plate to occupy him. He asked if I had seen today's issue of *On Campus*. Apparently he has a letter in the paper. It didn't seem to have occurred to him that I wouldn't have gone out of the house until getting his call. He also told me that the BBC are sending a TV crew to film the conference, for use in a documentary about Artificial Intelligence. He's delighted by this development, because of the publicity for the Centre, but it only increases my misgivings about speaking at the end of the conference. I wish I'd never agreed to it, now.

7.30 P.M. I tried to distract myself with work this afternoon, writing up the assessments of the students in the MA course for next week's Examiners' Meeting. It seems incredible that we are already in the last teaching week of the semester. I received the External Examiner's report today. He's Austin Osgood, a poet and short story writer who runs a similar course at Lincoln University. I met him once at Hay-on-Wye, and didn't take to him greatly. He has a loud, boisterous laugh which seems at odds with his rather calculating too-close-together eyes. But he was very complimentary about the students' work, giving them all good marks, nothing under B+. When I sent him the manuscripts I asked him to look particularly carefully at Sandra Pickering's, without explaining why of course. Rather to my surprise he gave her A(−), one of the highest marks. Well, at least she won't have any grounds to complain of personal bias. To give her her due, I think she's made an effort to make *Burnt* less embarrassing to me. In the two chapters she's written over the last few weeks the story has taken a fresh turn and the Alastair character has been replaced by a new love interest for the heroine. Tomorrow is my last meeting with the group. I can't tell them their results, but I shall intimate that everybody has passed creditably, and I'm giving a little party for them afterwards. I wish I felt more in the mood for it.

I bought a copy of *On Campus* this afternoon and read Messenger's letter about his Centre's links with the MoD. It's a clever letter, as one would expect, though not very prominently printed. The front-page story was all about a threatened rise in student rents. It seems that the University was going to announce the increases in the vacation, when nobody is around, but the paper got hold of the plan. The Union is up in arms, and calling for a demonstration before the end of the semester. Quite like the old days.

FRIDAY 30TH MAY. Messenger is on his way to London to see the best liver man in the country, and my own liver can't be in brilliant shape this morning. I have a bad hangover.

Yesterday was a very full day. I spent the morning preparing food for the party, then had lunch with Messenger. I phoned him up and complained that I hadn't seen him for nearly a week. He hesitated, said he was terribly busy, but agreed in the end. We acted out a little charade of meeting by chance in Staff House, and ate in the waitress service canteen. As it happened we had the same table by the window as at our first lunch, months ago. I told him how I had seen him approaching that day, and loitered in the lobby beside the awful landscape paintings, hoping he would notice me, and pretended to be surprised when he accosted me. He smiled at this confession, but he seemed a bit put out. I think he assumes he always takes the initiative in affairs of this kind, and it disconcerted him to discover that a woman was working her wiles on him without his being aware of it. He looked a little thinner than usual, I thought, no doubt because of his diet in hospital. He had fried fish for lunch, carefully removing the batter and leaving it on the side of his plate, with broccoli and no chips.

He told me Carrie had been on the phone for hours, being passed from one medical friend's friend to another, in a chain that stretched all the way to California and back, and finally established that the best liver surgeon in England was a man called Halib. Somehow Carrie bullied or bribed or charmed Mr Halib into seeing Messenger in his Harley Street rooms tomorrow morning. They're going up on the early train, and will get back just about in time for the opening of the Conference. I said it sounded like a gruelling schedule and he said he much preferred it to sitting around in hospital. 'Though I daresay I shall have more of that in due course,' he added with a grimace.

The lunch was a short one because both of us had things to do in the afternoon, and frustrating, because it was all so public. We had to make it look like a casual social encounter, talk lightly about matters of life and death, or find other topics to talk about. Messenger enquired about Lucy, and I told him I had just had an Email from her saying she was flying home at the end of June. Paul is going to Mexico before he comes home. He's also discovered that I'm wired, and has actually started writing letters to me. Messenger asked me if I ever used the Internet, and I said not much, I could never seem to find anything I wanted. I told him one of my students – it was Gil Baverstock – had informed me there was a website at a liberal arts college in Wyoming dedicated to my work, but when I entered 'Helen Reed' in the Alta Vista Search box it came up with one million three hundred thousand pages. I tried one at random and it turned out to be a young lady offering 'up-skirt' photos of herself with no panties on. Messenger laughed and said there were ways of limiting the search which he would show me. He asked me if I had downloaded any of the pictures, and I said no. He asked me if had ever looked at porn on the Internet and I said certainly not. He said not many people knew that everything you downloaded from the Internet was stored on your hard disk for ever. I said, 'Like the recording angel writing down your sins?' and he said, 'Exactly. The recording angel is a hard disk.'

While we were having coffee, we heard a hubbub outside, faint at first and then growing louder, and finally a long procession of students appeared, chanting and wielding banners. They marched round and round Staff House. On the top floor members of the University Court – a body composed of the great and the good of the county, local businessmen, *etc.*, which has a largely symbolic role in the structure of the University's government – were being entertained to lunch by the VC, and the students had seized the opportunity to protest against the threatened rent increases. I remarked that this issue seemed to have arisen rather luckily for Messenger, since it had clearly distracted attention from the matter of the honorary degree for the Ministry of Defence man. 'Luck has nothing to do with it,' he said. 'I leaked the new rent tariffs to the student rag.' I gawped at him. 'How did you know about them?' I said. 'Keep your voice down,' he said. 'I'm on the Senate Ways and Means committee.' I suppose I must have looked a little shocked, because he added, 'Somebody leaked the Centre's links with the MoD. When your enemies play dirty you have to do the same.' 'Who are they?' I said. 'I don't know,' he said, 'but they're out of touch. Students these days are more concerned about what hurts their pockets than about principles.'

We parted on the steps of Staff House – without a kiss, of course, without even touching. I thought he might have murmured, 'I love you,' or something of the sort, since no one was within earshot, but he didn't, so I didn't either. Though I fear I do love this man – fear, because I don't see much prospect of happiness in it. I walked to the Humanities Tower to take my last workshop with the MA group, and made an effort to put Messenger out of my mind for the rest of the day.

To celebrate the end of the course, I had asked each student to read from their work for not more than ten minutes, and there was to be no discussion after the readings, only applause. This went off very well. Sandra Pickering read a passage diplomatically chosen from her first chapter. Then we adjourned to Maisonette Row, where I had prepared dips and salads and quiches and a good supply of wine and beer. It was a fine evening and I opened the sliding window of the living-room which gives on to a little paved patio, jollied up for the occasion by a garden table and chairs and parasol borrowed from my next-door neighbours. I'd invited Ross and Jackie to join us for a drink, but was rather relieved when they excused themselves because they were going kayaking on the lake. The party was very much a rite of passage for the students. They had very sweetly clubbed together to buy me a present, a first edition of Virginia Woolf's *The Common Reader*, 2nd Series, Hogarth Press 1932, with Vanessa Bell's jacket, only slightly torn, which was not only very generous of them but very thoughtfully chosen. I must have mentioned to one of them that I own a Vanessa Bell lithograph. Simon Bellamy presented the gift with a very witty speech in which he complimented me as a teacher in the styles of ten different writers from Alexander Pope to J.D. Salinger, sending up my penchant for setting fiendishly difficult imitation exercises. I made a rather tearful speech in reply and told them what a wonderful and talented group of people they were and how I was looking forward to reading the reviews of their first books and following their glittering careers. We had all had rather a lot to drink by then, and after the speeches we had more. It was one of those balmy summer nights, so rare in England, when you can sit outside after nightfall without feeling damp or chilly. The students carried out extra chairs and cushions and sat round in a circle. Bob Drayton had brought along his acoustic guitar and plucked away quietly in the darkness, occasionally breaking into folksong in a very pleasant tenor voice. Somebody circulated a joint or two. It was a highly successful party, but I despaired of ever getting them to leave, so began clearing up the soiled plates and stacking them in the kitchenette by way of a hint. Sandra Pickering lent me a hand, slightly to my surprise, and then said she was going. 'Thanks for the party,' she said. 'And thanks for the course.' 'Do you think you learned anything from it?' I said. 'Oh yes,' she said, without elaborating. 'I'm sorry you had to find out about Martin from me,' she added, 'but it was fate.' 'Yes, I suppose it was,' I said. We shook hands rather formally. 'Good luck with *Burnt*,' I said hypocritically. 'Thanks,' she said. 'What about you? Are you writing anything?' 'No, not really,' I said. 'I've been too busy with you lot.' 'Don't leave it too long,' she said. I thought this was a bit presumptuous of her and I suppose my expression showed it. She said, 'That's the most important thing I learned from the course. You have to go on writing, no matter what.' And with that, she left.

I went back into the garden and told the rest that I was sorry but I had to go to bed before I fell asleep on my feet, and would they let themselves out of the house quietly when they were as tired as I was. Upon which they all bade me cheerfully goodnight, and settled down for a few more hours. But they had all gone this morning, and the dishes and glasses were stacked up by the sink, washed and dried, as if by fairies.

I I . 2 5 P . M . Some good news at last! Well, encouraging, anyway. I feel I must restrain my joy, in case it turns out to be a false hope. (Superstition again.) Messenger was in sparkling form tonight, presiding over the opening of the conference – a mainly social occasion: reception with drinks followed by dinner followed by a cash bar. The conference is being held in Avon House, a facility rather like an airport hotel on the north side of the campus, purpose-built to accommodate events of this kind and money-making 'post-experience' courses. As soon as I came into the big lounge where the reception was being held, and caught sight of Messenger moving among the delegates, smiling, shaking hands, slapping shoulders, laughing and joking, I knew things must have gone well in Harley Street. Carrie was there too, in one of her billowing silk kaftans, looking tired and less elated, but smiling calmly. As I moved through the throng towards them I saw Professor Douglass – it was hard to miss him in his dark suit and polished black shoes. Most of the delegates – the male ones anyway, and there weren't many women – were casually, not to say sloppily, dressed in open-necked sports shirts or tee-shirts and baggy cotton trousers. Some even wore trainers. I had got accustomed to the grunge style of dressing favoured by Messenger's students and most of his colleagues, but it seems to be the international style in cognitive science and associated disciplines.

'Congratulations,' I said to Douglass. He looked startled, and blushed. 'On what?' he said. 'On winning the Duck Race, of course.' 'Oh *that*,' he said dismissively. 'The prize was a case of champagne, and I don't drink.' 'The conference seems to have got off to a good start,' I said, looking round. 'Have you had much to do with the planning?' 'More than I would have wished,' he said. 'Our leader has been away most of the week. I'm told he was in hospital for tests. Is he ill?' There was an eager inquisitiveness in his tone that I didn't like. 'I really couldn't say,' I said, and moved on through the babbling mêlée towards Messenger.

He managed to murmur in my ear, 'Good news, Halib thinks it's probably a hydatid cyst.' But as I said, 'What's that?' he was accosted by a bearded American in a lime-green sports jacket and red polo shirt. 'I'll explain later,' Messenger said, before introducing me to Steve Rosenbaum, of the University of Colorado, who is giving a paper on 'Building a Functioning Mind'. 'And are you really building one?' I asked. 'Sure,' he said confidently. 'And what does it think about?' I asked. 'Only about automobile parts, at the present time,' he said. 'We're building it for General Motors.' 'Helen has a different interest in the mind,' Messenger said. 'She's a novelist.' 'That right? Crime fiction?' said Professor Rosenbaum. I said no, I was afraid I didn't even read it. 'Elmore Leonard's my favourite,' he said. 'You should check him out.' I promised to do so, and moved on to greet Carrie.

We kissed on both cheeks. It was the first time we had met face to face since she flew off to California, and in a way it was a relief to me to do so on a big social occasion. So much had happened since then of which she was unaware, of which she must remain unaware, and I was not altogether confident that I would still be able to perform the role of friend and confidante convincingly. It was easier to practise first in public. 'I gather from Ralph that the consultation in London went well,' I said. (I stopped myself just in time from referring to him too familiarly as 'Messenger'.) 'Yes,' she said. 'We mustn't count our chickens, but it's looking hopeful. This guy inspires confidence.' She wouldn't volunteer any more information and I could hardly ply her with further questions, so I was left in a state of frustration and suspense. I was seated at dinner at the same table as Messenger and Carrie, but not near them. I was between two neurobiologists who gave up the attempt to make conversation with me about halfway through the soup and then talked across me about their respective experiments on monkeys. This evidently entailed slicing off bits of their brains and seeing what difference it made to their behaviour. When I remarked that it sounded horribly cruel they assured me that the brain feels no pain. A curious paradox, that the organ that tells us we are in pain feels no pain itself.

Messenger made a speech full of in-jokes that went over my head but seemed to amuse most of the other people present. Soon after dinner Carrie went home. As we parted I said I would stay on for a little while to get my conference legs. She looked puzzled, as well she might, by this ponderous trope. 'As in sea-legs,' I explained. 'Oh, yeah. Right. Well, I'm bushed. It's been a long day. Do me a favour, Helen, would you? Make sure Messenger doesn't stay long.' I agreed readily – it was the perfect excuse for me to seek him out in the bar.

He was at a table with a group of delegates, and he waved me over to join them. They were all men except for a slim dark girl sitting next to him, whose conference lapel badge identified her as Ludmila Lisk, from the Carolinian University, Prague. She said nothing, but followed the conversation avidly, her dark alert eyes flicking from speaker to speaker. The group around the table changed as people came and went, but she sat on, frugally sipping her glass of lager. Messenger introduced her jocularly as someone who had given him a guided tour of Prague. I asked her if she was giving a paper at the conference. She shook her head and said, 'No, a poster.' I gathered that at a certain time in the programme the more junior or less distinguished conferees display illustrated accounts of their research called 'posters'. After a while Messenger, who was drinking straight tonic water himself, asked if anyone wanted another drink. I said, 'I'm going, Ralph, and I promised Carrie that I would send you home first.' 'Yes, maybe I should call it a night,' he said. Ludmila looked at me with frank hostility as we said goodnight and left the bar.

'Did you sleep with that girl in Prague?' I said, as we left the building. 'No, of course not,' he said. 'What makes you ask?' 'She seemed to attach herself to you like a leech,' I said. 'She's hoping I'll give her a post-doc job here,' he said. 'And will you?' I said. 'I might,' he said, 'if I'm still around.' Immediately I felt ashamed that my first question when we were alone at last had not been the one I had been waiting to ask all evening, but a petty discharge of jealousy. 'You said the consultation was good news,' I said. 'Well, it was encouraging,' he said, 'but I won't know how encouraging till next week.' 'Tell me all about it,' I said. 'I'll walk with you to your car.'

We walked across the campus to the Centre, where his car was parked. It was a fine, dry night, with a moon. The thud of bass-notes came from the Student Union where an end-of-session ball was in progress, and down by the lake young people in long strapless frocks and dinner-jackets canoodled and cavorted. A man in shirtsleeves tipped back his head to drink wine from a bottle, and then hurled the bottle into the lake, shattering the reflection of the moon. 'Halib is a little round bald-headed Asian guy,' Messenger said. 'He doesn't look too impressive at first sight. He's so short I should think he has to stand on a stool to operate. But as soon as he gets into gear, you trust him. He took the X-rays and scans and ultrasound data I'd brought with me from Bath, and pored over them for a long while, then he examined me. It was the most searching physical examination I've had. His fingers seemed to get deep into my abdominal cavity, it was as if I could feel them moving about inside me. When I was dressed Carrie and I – she was with me all this time – waited for him to speak. You can imagine the tension. His first question was, 'Have you ever been in close contact with dogs or sheep, Professor Messenger?' Carrie said afterwards it was about the last thing in the world she expected him to say. But of course the answer was yes – I told you the other day, I worked on a sheep farm in Yorkshire when I was a sixthformer. He looked pleased when I told him. 'I think this may be a hydatid cyst,' he said. 'It's caused by ingesting the eggs of the dog parasite *Echinococcus granulosus* – tapeworm, as it's commonly known. If you happened to swallow any infected water . . .' 'I used to swim with the dogs,' I said. 'Excellent,' he said. 'That increases the probability. There's a simple blood test which should tell us.' He took a sample off me before we left. We should get the result early next week,' Messenger concluded.

'And if it *is* a whatsitsname cyst?' I said. 'What then?'

'It can be surgically removed. But first they shrink it with drugs, and Halib says they've had good results with a new one lately. Sometimes the cyst disappears entirely.'

'And is it really possible that you've had it all these years?' I said.

'Apparently,' he said.

'Well, that's marvellous news,' I said.

'It is if it's true,' he said.

'Shouldn't the other man, Henderson, have thought of it?'

'Yes, he should,' Messenger said. 'Carrie was absolutely right about him.'

We approached the Centre's car-park. On the second floor, under the grooved dome, a solitary window was illuminated through a half-closed venetian blind. 'Duggers at work on his algorithms,' Messenger said.

'Kiss me, Messenger,' I said. He didn't reply, staring up at the window. In the moonlight his face seemed carved of marble. 'Messenger,' I said. 'What?' he said absently. 'Kiss me.' He looked around to check that we were unobserved, then drew me into the shadow of a wall, and we kissed. But his mind seemed to be on something else. His cyst, probably.

SUNDAY 1ST JUNE. It's late – 10.30 p.m. I've just come in, feeling exhausted and panicky. Exhausted by two days' non-stop discussion of consciousness, and panicky at the thought of having to say something about it at the last session tomorrow afternoon.

The conference programme goes on all day from 9.30 in the morning to 6 o'clock in the evening, alternating big plenary lectures held in the main auditorium with smaller seminars running simultaneously in thematic streams, when you have to choose between papers on artificial intelligence or cognitive psychology or neurobiology or a catchall category called Alternative Approaches. Choosing is difficult, especially when you know little or nothing about the speakers or their topics, and I've found myself trapped in some impenetrably boring sessions in consequence. I don't think I'm the only one to suffer in this way, though, because occasionally some bold spirit will get up in the middle of a talk and leave the room, presumably hoping to find a more interesting seminar elsewhere in the building, but I lack the nerve to follow their example.

There are breaks for morning coffee and lunch and afternoon tea, but the talk goes on unremittingly in these intervals too. The presence of the TV crew has contributed to the atmosphere of feverish debate. They cruise the anterooms and corridors between lectures and seminars, interviewing speakers and eavesdropping on conversations. You can see people becoming aware that they are being filmed, as the long sound-boom, with its muffled mike dangling from the end like a dead animal, hovers over their heads, and they start to perform for the benefit of the camera. The filming of the plenary sessions has required extra lighting which makes the auditorium hot and stuffy, adding to one's fatigue. Sometimes I longed to go and lie down somewhere in a cool dark place, but I slogged dutifully up and down the corridors and staircases of Avon House (unfortunately two of the lifts are out of order) to be enlightened on 'The Prefrontal Cortex as a Basic Constituent of the Self'. 'The Unification of Cognitive and Phenomenological Approaches to Consciousness', 'Emergence of Emotional Expression in Robots', 'The Theory of Relativity and the Cognitive Binding Problem', *etc., etc.* There was a paper, which I missed but wish I had heard, entitled 'Is the Brain like a Bucket of Shot or More like a Bowl of Jelly?' By the end of the first day mine was definitely more like jelly. I took notes, but when I looked at them afterwards I could barely understand them or remember what they referred to. '*Afference, Efference, Ex-afference, Re-afference . . . Schema=reproducible co-activation of neurones . . . Synergetic view of brain opposed to Cartesian . . . Dynamical process, interactions, self-drive . . . Buddhist meditation neural firing measured at 40hz . . .*' What could these jottings mean? There were occasional lucid sentences, generally of an anecdotal kind. '*Pain in phantom limbs surgically amputated under anaesthetic less acute than in limbs lost in accidental injury . . . Speaker from the floor claimed she developed a different concept of her "self" when she moved from America to Norway and learned Norwegian . . .'* And best of all, *'Correspondent to Lewis Carroll on reading Jabberwocky: "It seems to fill my head with ideas, but I don't know what they are." '* My sentiments exactly, at the end of the first day.

Today there were more lectures and seminars and this evening the poster session, at which about thirty or forty additional explorations of consciousness were summarized and illustrated on freestanding noticeboards, with their authors standing beside them ready to answer questions, like stall holders eager to sell their wares to passing customers in some informational bazaar. *'A phase-state approach to quantum neurodynamics and its relation to the space-time domain of neural coding mechanisms.' 'Subjective time-flow: effects of pre-operative medication and general anaesthesia.' 'From quanta to qualia.' 'The effects of Kriya Yoga on the brain's electrical activity.' 'Modelling learning behaviour in autonomous agents.'* That one belonged to Ludmila Lisk, thin and sharp as a knife in a tight black dress and high-heeled shoes. It seemed to have something to do with simulated children's games. She was explaining it animatedly to Professor Rosenbaum, and flashed me a perfunctory social smile over his shoulder as I passed. Rosenbaum gave his paper today on 'Building a Functioning Mind'. It seems to be a computer program that will take over some of the functions of human managers, and eventually all of them. He admitted under questioning that it would never be able to see or hear or move about, and could only communicate by Email. 'But, hey, lots of my friends are like that,' he quipped. The more I hear at this conference, the more convinced I become that cognitive science is light years away from replicating the real nature of thought, but I simply don't have the competence or the confidence to say so in public.

I sought out Messenger and tried to get out of speaking at the last session. 'Let me off,' I pleaded. 'I don't know what to say. I haven't understood half of what I've heard. I shall make a fool of myself, and it'll all be recorded by the TV people.' 'Don't worry,' he said. 'Just say what you think about the problem of consciousness.' 'Is that all?' I said ironically. 'Tell us how it looks from a literary perspective,' he said. 'People will be interested. They've never had that before. They

313

won't throw brickbats.' 'They'll ask me questions, though,' I said, 'and I won't be able to answer them.' 'No they won't,' he said. 'There won't be any time for questions.' Well, it was a relief to know that, anyway. And I've only got to speak for fifteen minutes.

What I need is a text, something to anchor my thoughts, to stop me waffling. Say I took a bit of Henry James, and analysed that, as an example of the literary representation of consciousness. Strether by the river . . . ? No, it's been done. Kate Croy at the beginning of *Wings*, then. No, it's too easy, too limited an exercise. What an anticlimax at the end of three days' high-level scientific discussion, a piece of routine practical criticism. The text ought to be *about* consciousness, not just a representation of consciousness.

Funny how one cares about these things, how desperately one wishes to make a good impression, how frightened one is of failure. It's pure vanity of course. Or perhaps, to be kinder on oneself, professional pride. There are so many other more important things in my life to worry about, and yet what matters most to me at the moment is thinking of something clever to say at the last session tomorrow. Messenger's the same – totally wrapped up in the conference, paying attention to every speaker, making sure everything is going smoothly, schmoozing his star speakers, keeping the TV people happy. Nobody would guess that he's waiting for the result of a blood test that could mean the difference between life and death. I suppose it's a blessing really, that we both have something to distract us.

I've decided to come home at lunchtime tomorrow, skip the early afternoon seminars and use the time to prepare my talk. But if I'm going to weave it around a text I shall have to get it duplicated tomorrow morning. Or better still, transferred on to transparencies. Every speaker at the conference has used an overhead projector. This, apparently, is standard practice among scientists, but it's a novelty to me. In all my years at Oxford I don't think I ever attended a lecture on English literature where the lecturer used an overhead projector to show an illustrative diagram, or a list of dates, or quotations from the work under discussion, or any other visual aid. If you were lucky, you got a smudgy stencilled handout. The speakers at this conference

○ ○

however all have a summary version of their talk prepared on transparencies, which they peel off from their backing sheets with practised ease and lay on the OHP, page by page, as they proceed, speaking in a semi-improvised, informal way to the visual display. The appearance of the transparencies varies. Sometimes they are immaculately printed and beautifully laid out, like the pages of a book, and sometimes they are scribbled by hand in feltpens of different colours, scarcely legible, but giving an exciting impression of having been produced in a burst of creativity the night before. I have no intention of speaking without a carefully prepared script, especially in the presence of television cameras, but it would be nice to have slides as well, if only to distract attention from myself from time to time.

31

'SOME of you may be wondering what I am doing on this platform, presuming to address you on the subject of this conference. I assure you that no one is more surprised by the presumption than I am. But please don't blame me, blame Professor Messenger, whose idea it was.

'Before I came to Gloucester University, and met him, and was shown round his Centre, I wasn't even aware that scientists were concerned with consciousness. Now at least I understand their interest in the subject. In a way it's the most fascinating subject of all, because the investigation of consciousness is an investigation into what makes us human, and how it is that we know what we know. Or think we know. Are we animals or machines, or a combination of both, or something different from either? Understanding consciousness, it occurred to me this weekend, is to modern science what the Philosopher's Stone was to alchemy: the ultimate prize in the quest for knowledge.

'The search for a substance that would turn base metal into gold was of course vain, because no such compound exists or could be manufactured; but in the experimental process many genuine discoveries were made – from porcelain to gunpowder. Perhaps we shall never fully understand consciousness – I understand there are experts who take that view, and I must say I find it intuitively appealing – but the effort to do so has already yielded many fascinating discoveries about the brain and the mind, some of which have been described to us over the past three days.

'There has however been very little reference made to literature in the proceedings. This I find surprising, because literature is a written record of human consciousness, arguably the richest we have. I'm going to hang my observations on a short literary text, a poem – or to be precise, three stanzas from the middle of a poem. The poem is called 'The Garden', by the seventeenth-century English poet Andrew Marvell, and it is a kind of rapturous ode to the joy of experiencing nature in a state of cultivation. The first of the three stanzas describes the sensuous pleasures of an ideal garden. If all goes well it should now appear on the screen . . . Oh. Sorry. I'm not used to these gadgets. There.

> *What wond'rous Life in this I lead!*
> *Ripe Apples drop about my head;*
> *The Luscious Clusters of the Vine*
> *Upon my Mouth do crush their Wine;*
> *The Nectaren, and curious Peach,*
> *Into my hands themselves do reach;*
> *Stumbling on Melons, as I pass,*
> *Insnar'd with Flow'rs, I fall on Grass.*

We have heard a lot about qualia in the last three days. There is division of opinion, I understand, about whether they are mind events or brain events, whether they are first-person phenomena forever inaccessible to the third-person discourse of science, or whether they are regular patterns of neurological activity which only become problematic when we translate them into verbal language. I am not competent to adjudicate on this issue. But let me point to a paradox about Marvell's verse, which applies to lyric poetry in general. Although he speaks in the first person, Marvell does not speak for himself alone. In reading this stanza we enhance our own experience of the qualia of fruit and fruitfulness. We see the fruit, we taste it and smell it and savour it with what has been called 'the thrill of recognition' and yet it is not there, it is the virtual reality of fruit, conjured up by the qualia of the poem itself, its subtle and unique combination of sounds and rhythms and meanings which I could try to analyse if there were world enough and time, to quote another poem of Marvell's – but there is not.

'In the next stanza Marvell turns to the private, subjective nature of consciousness. I hope I can get it the right way up this time. Oh dear. There.

> *Mean while the Mind, from pleasure less,*
> *Withdraws into its happiness:*
> *The Mind, that Ocean where each kind*
> *Does streight its own resemblance find;*
> *Yet it creates, transcending these,*
> *Far other Worlds, and other Seas;*
> *Annihilating all that's made*
> *To a green Thought in a green Shade.*

There is an allusion in the fourth line to a quaint but widely held belief of the time, that all land creatures had their counterparts in the sea, which places the poem in a pre-scientific age. But this is only a trope, which doesn't affect, it seems to me, the validity of the stanza's basic assertion: that human consciousness is uniquely capable of imagining that which is not physically present to the senses, capable of imagining things which do not exist, capable of creating imaginary worlds (like novels) and capable of abstract thought – of distinguishing for instance between the concept of colour ('a green thought') and the sensation of colour ('in a green shade').

'Is this dualism? Well, if making any distinction between mind and body is dualism, then I suppose it is, though it seems to me hard to avoid, so deeply is it engrained in our language and habits of thought. Even the fiercest opponents of the ghost in the machine would I think grudgingly allow us to use the terms, *mind* and *body*, as long as it was understood that the former is a function of the latter and inseparable from it.

'Marvell however, like all men of his age, was a dualist in a much stronger sense than that, which becomes evident in the next stanza. Success at last.

> *Here at the Fountains sliding foot,*
> *Or at some Fruit-trees mossy root,*
> *Casting the Bodies Vest aside*
> *My Soul into the boughs does glide:*
> *There like a Bird it sits, and sings,*
> *Then whets, and combs its silver Wings;*
> *And, till prepar'd for longer flight,*
> *Waves in its Plumes the various Light.*

Descartes, I have been told, believed in the immortality of the soul because he could imagine his mind existing apart from his body. Marvell expresses that idea in the very beautiful image of the bird. He imagines his soul leaving his body temporarily to perch on the branch of a tree, where it preens and grooms itself in anticipation of its final flight to heaven. I don't expect to carry you with him there. Such an idea of the soul would seem fanciful today even to believing Christians. But the Christian idea of the soul is continuous with the humanist idea of the self, that is to say, the sense of personal identity, the sense of one's mental and emotional life having a unity and an extension in time and an ethical responsibility, sometimes called conscience.

'This idea of the self is under attack today, not only in much scientific discussion of consciousness, but in the humanities too. We are told that it is a fiction, a construction, an illusion, a myth. That each of us is 'just a pack of neurons', or just a junction for converging discourses, or just a parallel processing computer running by itself without an operator. As a human being and as a writer, I find that view of consciousness abhorrent – and intuitively unconvincing. I want to hold on to the traditional idea of the autonomous individual self. A lot that we value in civilization seems to depend on it – law, for instance, and human rights – including copyright. Marvell wrote 'The Garden' before the concept of copyright existed, but the fact remains that nobody else could have written it, and nobody else will ever write it again – except in the trivial sense of copying it out word for word.

'The poem is a celebratory one, so it focuses on consciousness as a state of happiness. It is about bliss. But there is a tragic dimension to consciousness, which has also been hardly touched on in this conference. There is madness, depression, guilt, and dread. There is the fear of death – and strangest of all, the fear of life. If human beings are the only living creatures that really know they are going to die, they are also the only ones who knowingly take their own lives. For some people, in some circumstances, consciousness becomes so unbearable that they commit suicide to bring it to an end. 'To be or

319

not to be?' is a peculiarly human question. Literature can help us to understand the dark side of consciousness too. Thank you.'

There is applause, appreciative if not rapturous, at the end of Helen's talk. Ralph joins in, clapping his hands as he steps on to the stage. 'Thank you very much, Helen,' he says, as the applause dies down. 'That was really interesting and thought-provoking.' He turns to the audience. 'As I said earlier, there won't be any questions. The idea of this Last Word session is to pull down the curtain on this year's conference, and perhaps leave some threads loose to be taken up at next year's. And I think Helen has done that admirably. So, in the immortal words of Bugs Bunny, that's all folks! Except for tonight's Gala Dinner, which is seven-thirty for eight, remember. I'll be saying a few words then to thank all the people who've made this conference such a success, but I'll promise to keep it short.'

Another, fainter round of applause is followed by a buzz of conversation, as the delegates get to their feet, stretch, yawn, gather up their belongings, and file out of the auditorium. The TV crew turn off their lights, and the sound man plays back his tapes through headphones to check the sound quality. Helen, stepping off the stage, is accosted by some members of the audience who thank her for her talk. A woman in a headscarf and long cotton skirt asks if she is going to publish it.

'Oh, I very much doubt it,' Helen says.

'Only if you do I'd be so grateful if you would send me a copy,' says the woman. 'I thought it was such an inspiring talk.' She gives Helen her card, which says 'Zara Mankevitz, holistic therapist', with an address in Sausalito, California.

Helen and Ralph are the last to leave the auditorium. 'Thanks,' he says, 'that was great.'

'Was it really all right?'

'It was exactly what I'd hoped you would do.'

'But you don't agree with a word of it,' says Helen.

'No, I don't,' he says, smiling. 'But you did it so beautifully, it was a pleasure to listen to you.'

'I didn't dare to look at the audience's faces,' says Helen, 'in case they looked outraged or bored or asleep.'

'They were spellbound,' he says.

'Liar.'

'Well, intrigued. You could tell from the people who came up to talk afterwards.'

'I doubt if I converted any scientists, though. My biggest fan is a New Age therapist from California,' says Helen, showing him the card.

'Yes, well, this conference attracts all kinds. As you said, it's the subject of subjects. Can I buy you a drink?'

'No, I'm going home to shower and change for the Gala Dinner.'

'Don't raise your expectations too high. It's the same food, with an extra course and free wine.'

In the lobby of Avon House a tall man waits with his feet apart and his hands clasped behind his back. In his navy-blue blazer and perma-creased grey trousers, he stands out from the delegates in their coloured sweatshirts and tee-shirts and jeans. He has a neatly trimmed moustache which turns down at the ends. He seems to recognize Ralph, and sends a wordless message to him across the floor of the lobby.

'There's someone over there I've got to talk to,' Ralph says to Helen. 'I'll see you later.' He goes across to the man, and after a brief exchange they go out of the building together.

Ralph and Detective Sergeant Agnew walk side by side across the campus to the Holt Belling building. It is a warm and sunny evening. Students are disporting themselves on the grass, reading, talking, drinking from cans, playing with balls and frisbees. Some are canoeing on the lake, or windsurfing very slowly in the faint breeze.

'It looks more like a holiday camp than a university, doesn't it?' DS Agnew remarks.

'It's the last week of the semester,' Ralph says. 'Classes and exams are over. The students are just waiting for their results.'

'It reminds me of Gladeworld, where we went for our holiday last summer,' says DS Agnew. 'Ever been there, sir?'

'No,' says Ralph. He looks round to make sure that they are not within anyone's earshot. 'So what have you got to tell me?'

'I've got a name for you.'

'Who is it?'

'Professor Douglass.'

'Are you sure?'

'About seventy per cent sure.'

'I see,' says Ralph.

'You don't seem very surprised,' says DS Agnew.

'No, well, it's strange, but the other day it suddenly occurred to me that it might be him. It was after we spoke, and anyway I had no evidence . . . It was just a hunch. He's a strange man. What are you going to do now?'

'Well, I'd like to examine his hard disk.'

'There'll be more than one,' says Ralph. 'He has a lot of equipment in his office. Have you got a warrant?'

'No. I could probably get one, but I'd rather not at this stage.'

'How are you going to proceed, then?'

'I'd like to ask him to cooperate. I think his reaction will tell me what I want to know. When could you arrange for me to meet him?'

'He may be in his office now,' says Ralph. 'I didn't see him at the last session of the conference.'

The Centre is closed and largely deserted, and Ralph has to use his swipe card to open the sliding glass doors. The secretaries have all gone home and the staff and postgraduates have been attending the conference. When Ralph calls Douglass's extension, however, it is answered. 'I wonder if you'd mind coming to my office, Duggers,' he says. A minute later there is a knock on the door and Douglass enters the room without waiting for an invitation. 'I hope this won't take long, Messenger?' he says, irritably. 'I'm very busy.' He shoots an enquiring glance at DS Agnew, sitting in an armchair at an angle to Ralph's desk.

'This is Detective Sergeant Agnew, of the Gloucestershire Police,' Ralph says, 'from the Paedophile and Pornography Unit.'

Douglass goes very white. 'Yes?' he says, after a moment.

'The police think that somebody in this building is downloading child pornography from the Internet,' Ralph says.

'What has that got to do with me?' Douglass says.

'I thought that, as Deputy Director of the Centre, you would wish to be informed.'

'Yes, of course,' says Douglass, flushing. He turns to DS Agnew. 'Whom do you suspect?'

'We don't have a name yet, sir,' says DS Agnew.

'It's a delicate operation, Duggers,' says Ralph, 'and Detective Sergeant Agnew is going to need our cooperation. So first he needs to eliminate the two of us from his enquiry. He's checked my hard disk and now he needs to check yours.'

'If you don't mind, sir,' says DS Agnew.

'I certainly do mind,' says Douglass. 'The suggestion is outrageous.'

'Oh, come on, Duggers,' Ralph says. 'It's only a formality. He's done mine.'

'You can please yourself, Messenger. There's a lot of confidential data on my hard disk.'

'What kind of data, sir? If I might ask,' says DS Agnew.

'Research data.'

'I don't think DS Agnew would steal your research, Duggers,' says Ralph, with a faint smile.

'*Stop calling me Duggers!*' Douglass screams. His body is rigid, his face flushed, his eyes bulging behind the thick lenses of his spectacles.

There is a charged silence in the room broken by the ringing of the telephone on Ralph's desk. He picks it up.

'Professor Messenger?' says a female voice.

'Yes. Could you call back later?'

'This is Mr Halib's secretary, Professor. He's very anxious to speak to you before he goes home.'

'Oh. All right.' Ralph covers the phone. 'Sorry, I'd better take this,' he says to the two men. Douglass is looking at his feet. Agnew is looking at Douglass. Ralph swivels his chair so that his back is turned on them. He hears Halib's smooth, slightly sibilant voice.

'Professor Messenger? Halib here. How are you?'

'Very busy at the moment Mr Halib, but if you've got any news —'

'I have indeed. Good news. The blood test is positive.'

'It *is* a hydatid cyst?'

'It is.'

'Thank God for that. What now?'

'I've put a prescription in the post for you. Take as directed. It's a twenty-eight-day course. Make an appointment to see me towards the end of next week, and we'll see how much the cyst has shrunk. As I told you, there's a good chance that we won't have to operate. But if we do, there's nothing to worry about.'

'Well, that's wonderful. I can't thank you enough.'

'You're very welcome. Ring me if you have any questions about the prescription.'

Ralph puts down the phone and swivels round to face the two men, who have not moved.

'Would you like to take me to your office, Professor Douglass?' DS Agnew says gently.

Without a word, Douglass turns on his heel and walks out of the office, followed by Agnew. The policeman turns at the door. 'Will you be around for a while, sir?' he says.

'I can stay till half-past seven,' says Ralph.

Agnew nods, and leaves the room. Ralph turns back to the telephone and dials a number. 'Carrie?' he says. 'Halib just called. The test was positive. No, no, that's *good!* Yes!' They talk jubilantly for a few minutes. Then Ralph says, ''Bye then. See you at the dinner. I love you too.' He puts down the phone, gets up and walks restlessly up and down the room. He smacks a fist into the palm of the other hand. He looks out of the window, but doesn't seem to be focusing on anything in particular. He goes back to his desk, and picks up the phone again. He dials a number, drumming his fingers on the desk as he waits for a reply. 'Helen? Good news.'

Ralph has been speaking to Helen for some minutes, when

◦ ◦

Detective Sergeant Agnew bursts abruptly into the room. He stands at the threshold, opens his mouth to speak and then closes it as he sees that Ralph is on the phone. Ralph covers the mouthpiece. 'What is it?'

'You'd better come, sir,' says Detective Sergeant Agnew. 'It's Professor Douglass.'

'What about him?'

'I'm afraid he's dead, sir.'

Ralph says into the phone, 'I have to go,' and replaces the receiver.

32

ONE, two, three, testing . . . It's Tuesday, the 3rd of June, 5.35 p.m. I'm alone for the first time today. It's been one meeting after another . . . the VC, the police, the Head of Public Relations, the staff of the Centre . . . Everybody's in a state of shock . . . except me. I wonder why. It's not because I disliked him. . . . I'm not *glad* that he's dead. In fact I feel sorry for him, probably for the first time in my life. But I'm not in a state of shock, though of course I say I am, like everyone else . . . 'It's a shock', I say. People would think I was a monster of callousness if I didn't.

Poor Agnew really is in shock. He blames himself, though I don't see why he should. Who could have anticipated that Duggers would top himself like that — so quickly, so unhesitatingly, the moment he saw he'd been found out? He seemed to recover his self-control after the outburst in my room. He led Agnew to his office and unlocked the door and pointed out the various bits of computing equipment, answered a few questions about his software with frigid politeness, and then excused himself to go to the toilet. Agnew saw nothing unusual in that . . . the people he questions often get the squitters, as he put it. He sat himself down at the PC on the desk and began to trawl through the Internet files, and it was only after ten or fifteen minutes that he got alarmed at Duggers' absence, and went looking for the Men's room on the second floor. He looked under the doors of the stalls, saw a pair of feet in black shoes hanging a foot above the ground, kicked in the door and found Douglass, dead. He'd hanged himself from a ventilator grille, with a computer lead. Tied it round his neck, stood on the lavatory seat, and stepped off into thin air. Into oblivion.

He must have had a plan. He must have thought about contingencies in advance . . . like me, with my lump . . . He must

326

have said to himself, *if they ever find out, if they come for me, I'm not going to wait to be exposed, arrested, put on trial* . . . Perhaps he'd actually worked out how he would do it . . . identified the ventilator grille, tested its strength . . . perhaps he even calculated the drop, and kept a lead ready in a drawer . . . I can't help admiring his decisiveness. It gives me a new respect for him. In theory I was prepared to do it myself, but fortunately I wasn't put to the test. In a way I almost feel as if he died instead of me . . . No, that's silly, delete that . . . And yet, if I were superstitious . . . if I believed in fate, providence, the stars . . . There was a strange symmetry about yesterday evening, the way my reprieve arrived from Halib at the very same moment that catastrophe stared Duggers in the face. It was as if we were balanced on a pair of scales, and Halib's call was the thumb in the pan that brought me safely down to earth and sent Duggers flying up into the air, hanging by his neck . . .

I was shown some of the stuff they found in his filing cabinets. Hundreds of photographs. Nothing really nasty, Agnew said, and he should know . . . Mostly pictures of pre-pubescent girls, naked, or nearly naked, sometimes with boys of the same age, but no boys on their own. Peeing, exposing their bottoms, exposing their genitals . . . childish stuff . . . some arty ones like Lewis Carroll used to take . . . You'd say it was almost harmless, until you wonder how the photographs were obtained . . . There's no evidence that Duggers took any of them himself, or that he had any physical contact at all with children . . . He belonged to a ring of people who passed the pictures around between them on the Internet, using some encryption software, it was a kind of circulating library or co-op . . . Presumably he did it all from his office rather than home to prevent his mother or his sister accidentally discovering anything . . . I've sent them a letter of condolence. Not an easy one to write . . . There'll be an inquest of course . . . and a funeral I suppose, a private one presumably. There won't be a memorial service, that's for sure . . .

When I looked up at the window of his office from the car-park, last Friday evening, the only room in the building with a light still burning behind the blind, it suddenly came into my head that he was the man Agnew was looking for. I don't know why I hadn't thought

327

of him before. I suppose I had him down as a kind of ascetic, exclusively interested in his subject, sexually neuter . . . Always a mistake, to suppose that you know what's going on inside anyone else's head. But looking up at the window, joking to Helen about Duggers working late at his algorithms, I remembered meeting him coming into the Centre on a Sunday morning as I was leaving it, and the glare of surprise and fury he gave me through the glass doors, and the penny dropped . . . He had a similar look on his face as he lay on the floor in the Men's toilet yesterday evening, similar but more exaggerated . . . the eyes bulging, the face suffused with blood, lips curled in a kind of snarl . . . and he had a deep red weal round his neck, where Agnew had removed the plastic flex . . .

I left Agnew to call a doctor, ambulance, inform the local police, and campus security. I was late for the reception, but not for the dinner. I'd already informed Carrie quickly by phone, and sworn her to secrecy. I didn't want the news circulating at the dinner. It would have soured the atmosphere, and I knew that if the TV people got hold of it they would feature it in their coverage of the conference. It's just the sort of thing they love. But nobody knew, and nobody guessed, that anything untoward had happened. Duggers' unoccupied seat at the dinner didn't attract much attention – his dislike of social occasions was well-known. The trickiest moment came when I had to make my speech thanking everybody who'd helped with the organization of the conference. What could I say? 'And my thanks to Professor Douglass, who unfortunately couldn't be with us tonight . . . for personal reasons . . . due to unforeseen circumstances . . .' I couldn't think of any form of words that wouldn't sound like a sick joke to myself, to Carrie, and eventually, when the truth came out, to everybody else. So I simply made no reference to him in my speech. Helen came up to me afterwards and said in a slightly accusatory tone, 'Shouldn't you have thanked Professor Douglass? He was complaining to me at the reception about all the extra work he'd had to do.' 'I forgot,' I said. Later I took her aside and told her what had happened . . . She was, of course, shocked.

Helen, yes . . . What am I going to do about Helen? I'm standing at the window of my office now, looking out over the Science end of the campus and speaking into the Pearlcorder, just as I did that rainy Sunday morning in . . . when was it? February . . . when I saw her come round the corner of Biology, a solitary figure in calf-length boots and a smart raincoat, whose face I couldn't see at first because of her umbrella . . . A lot has happened since then.

I feel pretty good at this moment. I feel physically well, for one thing, though I haven't even started Halib's course of drugs yet. It may be the effect of psychological relief, or it may, as Carrie half-jokingly said, be the result of knocking off booze and red meat for the last two weeks. We made love last night, the first time for weeks. I didn't initiate it, neither did she, it wasn't necessary, it was an unspoken agreement between us in the car coming home, it was implied in the way I softly locked the bedroom door and the way she looked at me as she lifted and bent back her arms to undo her necklace . . . perhaps neither of us wished to speak of it in case the other thought there would be something unseemly about having sex with Duggers' body hardly cold. But that was why we needed to fuck . . . to put it out of our minds . . . to celebrate my reprieve . . . to affirm life over death. Afterwards we slept like babies.

I feel a sense of achievement this evening, satisfaction and serenity. I feel that my life is back under my control. I don't have a life-threatening illness. The conference was a success, a feather in my cap, and I managed to stop Duggers' suicide from overshadowing the last evening. Even this morning most of the delegates left without knowing what had happened. There's going to be a certain amount of fuss in the media, inevitably . . . but with the long vac starting next week, there'll be fewer people around to keep the pot boiling . . . The protest over Donaldson's degree has fizzled out . . . and it wasn't Duggers after all who leaked the Senate papers to *On Campus* – it was almost certainly Reginald Glover . . . the editor of the rag as good as told me. He was over here this afternoon to get a statement about Douglass and I winkled it out of him. Whether Glover did it out of principle or nostalgia for the sixties or to punish me for humiliating his wife at the Richmonds' dinner party, I don't know, or care . . . Donaldson will get his D.Phil, and the Centre will get its fat research contracts from the MoD . . . Oh yes, and I fixed up Ludmila Lisk with a post-doc job at Boulder . . . I told Steve Rosenbaum to be sure to look at her poster and she did the business on him. So she won't be getting in my hair any more . . . though you have to admire that babe's determination . . .

Which leaves Helen as the only outstanding problem. She's going back to London on Friday, and she'll expect me to say something about the future before we say goodbye . . . What shall I say? I could say I'm too shocked by Duggers' death to think straight at the moment . . . but she wouldn't believe me . . . I know she was amazed at my self-possession last night, the way I went through the whole dinner as if nothing had happened . . . I could say, *I don't feel I'm out of the wood yet as regards my health, I still might have to have an operation . . . let's leave our thing on hold until I'm really well again . . . then we'll sort something out* . . . Yes, more plausible . . . I must find the right moment, though. Not over the phone, or sitting in the Staff House restaurant . . . some time when we can be alone together . . . a last loving kiss . . . Perhaps more than a kiss, who knows? It bothers me still, the memory of our last time in bed, when I was impotent . . . I don't want that to be the way she'll remember me. *[recording ends]*

33

WEDNESDAY 4TH JUNE. Messenger just phoned to ask if he could come round tomorrow afternoon, 'to say goodbye'. He added quickly, 'I mean you're leaving on Friday, aren't you, and we may not be able to meet for some time.' I told him I had to attend an Examiners' Meeting in the School of English tomorrow afternoon and didn't know how long it would last, so he said I should leave my key under the loose brick by the front door, and he would come round at about four and let himself in if I wasn't back. We did this once or twice before, in our mad time. He said he had meetings himself all tomorrow morning, and Carrie would be coming back in the evening. I said, 'Coming back from where?' and he said she was taking Emily to a matinée at Stratford, to see *As You Like It*, one of her set texts for 'A' level. So then I knew why he was so keen to see me tomorrow afternoon, when Carrie would be out of the way. He wants to go on with the affair. Which is ironic, because I thought he wanted to end it, and after much heart-searching I had come to the conclusion that it would be better if we did.

I spent the whole of yesterday indoors, cleaning the house in preparation for my departure. It's part of the agreement you sign when you move in, to leave the place clean and tidy when you go, but I went far beyond my contractual obligations, scrubbing and hoovering and washing down and polishing in a frenzy of activity, occupying my body while I turned it all over in my mind. It seemed to me that we'd taken incredible risks, and survived incredible dangers, and that we shouldn't push our luck any more. Douglass's suicide, though it had nothing to do with our relationship, had everything to do with my decision. It put me into a state of fear and trembling. It opened up such an abyss of unhappiness and wrong-doing and pain, into which it is so easy to fall once you stop listening to your conscience. James has a fine sentence about illicit love somewhere, one of the Prefaces I think, comparing it to a medal made of some hard bright alloy, one face of which is somebody's bliss and right, and the other somebody's bale and wrong. Something like that. I can't deny that our affair was blissful for a while, but the longer it goes on the more likely it is to do harm. Now is the time to end it. And if Carrie has any sense she will come to the same conclusion, after all the alarms and crises of the last few weeks.

I know what he will do tomorrow afternoon. He'll try and get me into bed and persuade me to change my mind. I hope I have the strength of mind to resist. I have to admit that my first reaction to his call was a visceral thrill of pleasure, knowing that he still desires me.

34

IN the event, Helen was not required to struggle against temptation – which in any case would have been much less consequential than she imagined, since Ralph had no intention of continuing the affair, merely of having sex with her one last time.

At about twenty minutes to four on the Thursday afternoon, Ralph left his office and walked across the campus to the terrace of little houses that Helen called Maisonette Row, reflecting not for the first time that it was fortunate it was tucked away in such an obscure corner of the campus, where there was little chance that he would be observed by anyone who knew him. The service road was, as usual, deserted. He rang the doorbell once, and receiving no response, removed the spare key from under the loose brick where Helen had left it and let himself into the house. The little hallway smelled pleasantly of polish and disinfectant, and the living-room looked exceptionally clean and tidy, which he took as a good omen, assuming it had been spruced up in his honour. He caught sight of himself in a gleaming wall mirror, and stepped up to look closer at his reflection, turning his head from side to side, checking for grey hairs. It seemed to him that he had acquired some new ones – not surprisingly, he reflected, considering what he had been through lately.

It was warm in the room from the afternoon sun flooding through the patio window. Ralph slid open the window a foot or so and drew the curtain a little. He took off his jacket and draped it over an upright chair. He sat down on the sofa, crossed his legs, and idly surveyed the room. His eyes came to rest on Helen's desk, and the objects on its surface: a few books, a magazine, some letters and bills stuffed into a wire rack, a china mug holding pencils and ballpoint pens, a compact inkjet printer, and Helen's Toshiba laptop. Ralph recalled how he had installed the software for Helen's Email on the computer. It was closed now, and switched off, though connected to an electric wall socket by a lead.

It occurred to Ralph that this flat, drab, grey plastic box, the size and shape of a hard-back book, must contain Helen's journal, the detailed record of her private thoughts, and therefore a kind of tracing or imprint of what she liked to call her self or soul. He had tried once to persuade her to let him read it, offering to barter the transcripts of his confessional tapes in return, and she had refused. But since then they had become lovers, and the contents of her journal would now be of immeasurably greater interest to him. If he were to do the unthinkable . . . if he were to cross the room and sit down at the desk and lift the cover of the computer and switch it on and access the files of Helen's journal, he would discover why, after stating repeatedly that she wasn't going to have an affair with him, she changed her mind; he would learn what triggered this *volte-face*, how she felt when they made love for the first time, how she felt on subsequent occasions, what she really felt about him and their relationship and what future she saw in it.

His heart beat faster with the excitement of these thoughts. Did he dare? How much time did he have? He glanced at his watch. It was 4.15. There was no way of knowing when she might return. These meetings could go on for hours, but she might leave before the end. She might return at any moment. He would hear the sound of her key in the door, though. He rose from the sofa and approached the desk like a thief, slowly, softly, and sat down on the typist's chair, taking care not to disturb anything on the desktop, or alter the position of the computer. He undid the catch and levered the top open to expose the screen inside. He pressed the power button on the side of the machine. He heard the faint whirr of the hard disk as Windows 95 was loaded, and then a sweep of tinkling electronic harp strings from the speakers as the Microsoft desktop appeared on the screen, the program icons floating like kites against the background of blue and white sky. He clicked on the Word 95 icon and almost instantly a blank document page appeared, with the Word toolbars across the top.

Now he hesitated. It was wrong, what he was doing, very wrong. He ought to stop now, shut down the computer, close the top, go back to the sofa on the other side of the room, and wait for Helen. But he couldn't resist the temptation. It wasn't just personal curiosity, he told himself, it was scientific curiosity too. It was a unique opportunity to break the seal on another person's consciousness. It was, you might say, research. For a moment he actually entertained the idea of copying the entire contents of Helen's hard disk onto floppies and carrying them away with him to analyse; but the enormity of such a violation of privacy was too much even for Ralph to contemplate for long, and anyway there were practical obstacles – she didn't seem to have a zip drive, nor could he find any formatted blank diskettes in the desk drawers . . . time was running out . . . she would be back soon . . . He glanced at his watch: 4.17. There would only be time for a quick look at the journal, a random dip into its contents. It was now or never.

Ralph pulled down the File menu and looked at the filenames of the nine documents most recently saved. At the top of the list was 'C:\My Documents\JOURNAL\4th June'. He clicked on it. Instantly a text appeared. It began: '**WEDNESDAY 4TH JUNE. Messenger just phoned to ask if he could come round tomorrow afternoon, "to say goodbye".**' Ralph read rapidly through the journal entry, smiling faintly to himself, until he came to: '**Now is the time to end it. And if Carrie has any sense she will come to the same conclusion, after all the alarms and crises of the last few weeks.**' *Carrie?* His smile vanished. A fight-or-flight reaction kicked in with a rush of adrenaline. For a panic-stricken moment or two Ralph thought this reference must mean that Carrie knew about his affair with Helen, that Helen had told her about it. If so, when? How long had she known, and what did her silence imply? But hang on, he told himself, drawing his forearm across his brow (he was sweating in spite of being in shirtsleeves, he could feel the perspiration trickling down the sides of his torso), hang on, that doesn't add up. '**If Carrie has any sense she will come to the same conclusion . . .**' But logically Carrie couldn't come to a conclusion about ending *Helen's* affair. Only about ending an affair of her own.

Ralph closed the document and looked at Helen's subdirectories. He opened the one called 'Journal', and scrolled through a long list of filenames with dates stretching back to the 17th February. He opened that one, clicked on Find in the Edit Menu and entered 'Carrie' in the dialogue box. He clicked his way rapidly through the document, speed-reading the passages in which her name occurred. Then he closed the file, opened the next journal document in chronological sequence, and repeated the procedure.

Helen meanwhile was walking across the campus from the Humanities Tower to Maisonette Row. Her Examiners' Meeting had gone on longer than she had anticipated, but she did not hurry. She didn't know what would happen when she met Ralph, and what was more disturbing, she didn't know what she wanted to happen. She had made up her mind yesterday to tell him that the affair must end. But in that case, why had she washed her hair that morning, and put on her most becoming underwear, and a dress Ralph had particularly admired? It was as if her body had done these things of its own accord while her mind watched, disapproving but powerless to intervene. So she took her time, walking at a leisurely pace in the late afternoon sunshine, almost hoping that time would run out for Ralph, that he would have to return to wife and family before he had an opportunity to try and coax her into bed.

When Helen let herself into the house, Ralph had just finished reading her journal entry for Friday 11th April. Hearing her key in the lock, he hastily switched off the computer without bothering to save the file, and closed the cover. 'Messenger?' Helen called, as she shut the front door behind her. 'Are you still here?' Ralph moved swiftly away from the desk. When Helen came into the living-room from the cramped little hallway, he was standing by the sofa as if he had just got to his feet. But Helen saw immediately that he was in a strangely perturbed state. 'What's the matter?' she said.

He stared at her for several moments before speaking, divided between an instinct to conceal what he had done and a need to answer the question that was burning in his brain. In the end his jealousy was stronger than his sense of self-preservation. 'Why didn't you tell me about Carrie and Nicholas Beck?' he said.

The question was totally unexpected to Helen, and she took her time answering it. She felt both relief that she was no longer burdened with this secret, and apprehension about all the complications that might now ensue.

'Because I thought it was none of my business,' she said at length. 'And then I gave Carrie my word.'

'She talked to you about it then?' Ralph said with eager intensity.

'Once, yes.'

'So it wasn't just some suspicion of yours – some fantasy, some scenario for one of your novels?'

Helen frowned, puzzled by this question, and his inquisitorial tone. 'I don't know what you mean,' she said. 'How did you find out, anyway?'

He did not answer her, but his eyes flicked to the laptop and away again. Helen followed the direction of his glance. 'You've been reading my journal!' she said incredulously.

'Yes,' he said.

'I can't believe it. It's despicable.'

'I know,' he said. 'It's despicable and inexcusable and unforgivable.'

'Why did you?'

He shrugged. 'I couldn't stop myself.'

'How much of it have you read?'

'I got as far as your trip to Ledbury,' he said. 'Is she really fucking that effete wanker? What does she see in him?'

'You'd better ask her that yourself,' Helen said. 'Now I'd be grateful if you'd go away and leave me alone.'

Ralph picked his jacket off the back of the chair and folded it over his arm. 'I'm sorry, Helen . . .'

'Just go,' she said.

'Goodbye, then,' he said, and left the house.

Driving back to Cheltenham, Ralph at first had every intention of doing what Helen had recommended – confronting Carrie, forcing the truth out of her, and then going round to Nicholas Beck's exquisite house in Lansdown Crescent and beating the shit out of him. But after a while he began to be aware of the weakness of his position. If he accused Carrie of infidelity, he would invite a counter-attack, and even if she didn't know about his involvement with Helen, there was always a risk that she might find out, possibly from Helen herself, who was now thoroughly disaffected. He was also fairly sure that Carrie had many good reasons to suspect his unfaithfulness to her in the past, reasons which she had chosen to keep to herself in the interests of marital harmony, but which she wouldn't hesitate to use in self-defence if challenged. It was, she would say, with some justification, tit for tat. She had defected knowing he had defected. And what would be the point or profit of dragging all this dirt into the light, and provoking a major row which might easily destroy the entire marriage? He didn't want a divorce. He didn't want either the emotional attrition or the material damage that would entail. Carrie's personal wealth was still ring-fenced, thanks to Daddy Thurlow's shrewd stewardship, and Ralph was well aware that he would come out of a divorce settlement with little more than a half share of the house and limited access to his children.

Ralph did not formulate these arguments in quite such explicit terms, but they were, as we say, at the back of his mind, as he raged inwardly at Carrie's treachery, her appalling choice of a lover, and the insult to his pride and self-esteem. Gradually they exerted a cooling influence on his thoughts of retribution and revenge. He grew calmer and more contemplative; his driving, dangerously fast at the beginning of his journey, had become more controlled by the time he reached the outskirts of Cheltenham; his mood, when he entered the house on Pittville Lawn, was surly rather than angry. Carrie and Emily had just got back from their expedition to Stratford. Ralph was unable to respond to their animated chatter about the production they had seen, but Carrie attributed his taciturnity to delayed shock at the death of Douglass and was not discomposed by it. After supper he went up to his study, booted up his computer, and worked late into the night on his Work in Progress.

Helen meanwhile packed up all her belongings ready for her departure from Gloucester University. She could hardly wait to get away from the place. She slept badly and woke before daybreak. Instead of waiting for her alarm to ring, she got up, showered, dressed, drank a cup of coffee, and loaded her car. She did this quietly, almost stealthily, to avoid disturbing her neighbours, whose bedroom curtains were still drawn. It struck her that she was enacting the fantasy she had entertained in her first depressed weeks on the campus, of running away in the early hours of the morning. Then she had imagined escaping under cover of the darkness of winter; now it was broad daylight by the time she drove away from the house, but the campus was quiet and the only human figures she encountered were a lone jogger and the security guard at the exit barrier to whom she gave the keys of her house in a brown envelope. Then it was down the avenue, on to the main road, on to the M5, the M42, the M40, London . . . There she got caught up in the tail end of the rush hour, but she was home by a quarter to ten.

She let herself into the house and walked from room to room, renewing her acquaintance with it as with an old friend. The Weismullers had gone back to America, taking all their possessions with them. Vera, Helen's regular cleaner, who knew the house well, had tidied up after their departure by arrangement, and on her own initiative replaced most of the furniture and much of the bric-a-brac in their accustomed places. Helen put a Vivaldi concerto in the CD player, and a sweet cascade of strings filled the high-ceilinged room with such clarity and resonance that she almost gasped. She realized how much she had missed this pleasure. The strains of the music followed her faintly as she moved through the house and up the stairs. The music system had been assembled with loving care and immense technical expertise by Martin. Indeed almost everything in the house was a reminder of him. Together they had bought it, restored it and decorated it, tearing out the horrible modern picture windows and replacing them with sash windows, sanding and polishing the wooden floorboards, stripping the brown paint of ages from the banisters, buying curtain material from Liberty's and rugs from Heal's. She came at last to the master bedroom. On the dressing table was a

339

framed photograph of Martin which she had taken herself when they were on holiday in Greece. She had put it away when she let the house, but Vera had found it in a drawer and put it back. Helen picked up the photograph. Martin looked young and healthy and happy, sitting at a café table in an open-necked shirt, smiling and squinting in the sun. The picture brought back a flood of memories, of the happy times they had had together. She began quietly to weep. She forgave Martin, and she wept for him.

Ralph Messenger needed after all to have an operation to remove the cyst. It was a complete success, but people who knew him commented that it seemed to knock him back a bit, and that afterwards he was perceptibly less assertive, more subdued, more middle-aged. He lost his reputation for chasing women at conferences and on similar excursions. He never confronted Carrie over Nicholas Beck, but she picked up vibrations of his suspicions and prudently terminated the affair, which had never deeply engaged her emotions. Carrie did not finish her novel about the San Francisco earthquake, but she took up sculpture, mostly modelling in clay, and opened a small art gallery in Montpellier Street to exhibit her work and that of her friends. Ralph published his book *Machine Living* to wide media coverage, and achieved gratifying sales. In 1999 Sir Stanley Hibberd put him at the top of the University's recommendations for Honours, and he was awarded a CBE for services to science and education in the Millennium Honours List.

A year after she returned to London, Helen Reed met a literary biographer in the café of the new British Library and they started going out together. He is divorced, with three teenage children. They see each other frequently and go on holidays together, but retain their respective houses. In the first year of the new millennium Helen published a novel which one reviewer described as 'so old-fashioned in form as to be almost experimental'. It was written in the third person, past tense, with an omniscient and sometimes intrusive narrator. It was set in a not-so-new greenfields university, and entitled *Crying is a Puzzler*.

Acknowledgements

I was first alerted, somewhat belatedly, to the current scientific and philosophical debate about consciousness by an article, entitled 'From Soul to Software', by John Cornwell, published in *The Tablet* in June 1994, which discussed two key books: Daniel Dennett's *Consciousness Explained* (1991) and Francis Crick's *The Astonishing Hypothesis* (1994). I am grateful for that initial stimulus, and I profited from John Cornwell's subsequent writings in the same subject area, and from attending the interdisciplinary conference he organized on 'Consciousness and Human Identity' at Jesus College Cambridge in September 1995. (Its proceedings, edited by John Cornwell, were published under the same title by OUP in 1998.)

Among the books and articles I read in preparation for writing this novel, in addition to the titles cited above, I found the following particularly illuminating or thought-provoking: David Chalmers, *The Conscious Mind* (1996); Rodney Cotterill, *No Ghost in the Machine* (1989); Richard Dawkins, *The Selfish Gene* (rev. edn 1989) and *The Blind Watchmaker* (1986); Antonio Damasio, *The Feeling of What Happens: Body, Emotion and the Making of Consciousness* (2000); Daniel Dennett, *Darwin's Dangerous Idea* (1995) and *Kinds of Minds* (1996); Adrian Desmond and James Moore, *Darwin* (1991); Robin Dunbar, *The Trouble with Science* (1995) and *Grooming, Gossip and the Evolution of Language* (1997); Gerald Edelman, *Bright Air, Brilliant Fire* (1992); Susan Greenfield, *The Human Brain* (1997); John Horgan, *The End of Science* (1996); Stephen Pinker, *How the Mind Works* (1997); Matt Ridley, *The Origins of Virtue* (1996); V.S. Ramachandran and Sandra Blakeslee, *The Brain and its Phantoms* (1998); John Searle, *The Rediscovery of the Mind* (1996); Galen Strawson, 'The Sense of the Self', *London Review of Books* 18 April 1996; Tom Wolfe, 'Sorry, But

○ ○

Your Soul Just Died', *Sunday Independent*, 2 February 1997; Lewis Wolpert and Alison Richards, *Passionate Minds: the inner world of scientists* (1997). Ken Campbell's lively and informative TV series for Channel 4, *Brainspotting*, shown in 1996, also deserves mention.

My biggest single debt is to Aaron Sloman, Professor of Artificial Intelligence and Cognitive Science in the School of Computer Science at the University of Birmingham. Aaron patiently answered my elementary questions, gave me copies of his publications, introduced me to his colleagues, welcomed me to his departmental seminars, escorted me to an eye-opening international conference on consciousness (held appropriately enough at Elsinore) and generally acted as an indispensable guide to consciousness studies in general and artificial intelligence in particular. Though he shares some of the views of my fictional character, Ralph Messenger, on these matters, anyone who knows him will testify that they have nothing else in common. I am grateful to his colleagues who allowed me to pick their brains, over coffee or by Email, and especially to Russell Beale for practical advice about speech recognition software. Vijay Raichura generously found time in his busy life to advise me on medical aspects of my story, for which I am deeply grateful. The novel is dedicated to my daughter and elder son, who also gave me some professional advice and assistance in the course of writing it.

D.L.

Birmingham, August 2000